THE SOUL'S DOMAIN

DOMAIN

Book 1 of the Dreambringer Trilogy

By

KATHRINE EATON

2nd Edition

CHAPTER 1

DAY 1 – IT BEGINS

It did not know Its name. It thought It had one once, but it had been so long since the name had been uttered it had been forgotten.

It moved slowly, Its gait halting and ungainly. It did not travel aimlessly, It had a place to go, by instinct It was heading home. It was beginning to tire and underneath the tiredness It felt anger, an ever-present tight ache at Its core, waiting there for an outlet, for a way to ease its pain by inflicting it upon others.

Then It sensed a man moving through the trees and It knew 'what' that man was, and old feelings of jealousy and hate came back to Its ancient, warped mind. Old feelings that were the source of Its anger.

That mans 'kind' were the reason for Its loneliness. That man and all his 'kind' needed to be punished. And so, It shadowed the man through the trees hatching Its plan.

It loathed that man, but It needed him.

When It first touched the man's mind It was welcomed, after all the man was used to such things. But he soon realised that something was wrong, that this shouldn't be happening out in the woods, and that It didn't feel quite right. And so, the man started to fight It. But it was a battle the man could not win. Within minutes It had him under Its control. And It knew everything It needed to know. It knew the man's name and where he lived. It knew who he lived there with and what their purpose was, and in return the man knew the hatred It felt, and for who, and that he was trapped, helpless inside his own body, an unwilling witness to the evil his own body was about to perform.

CHAPTER 2

DAY 1 - CLAUDE

Mahesh Choudhary stood from his stool and stepped away from his easel to view his finished painting. He was pleased with what he saw. This was definitely his best yet. It was a simple landscape, but his use of colour and light was exceptional creating a mesmerising and beautiful scene of heather covered hills and cloud swept blue sky.

Yawning and rubbing at his tired eyes Mahesh shuffled across his room and lowered his small, aching body into the comfy armchair by the window. He closed his eyes for a few minutes enjoying the feeling of achievement and satisfaction that the finishing of a painting always gave him. When he opened them again he glanced out the window and caught sight of a familiar bulky figure making its way up the hill from the woods to the house.

It was his friend Claude Grey. He was glad to see him. He wanted to take his painting downstairs to the work room so he could show it to his friends and leave it safely to dry, but it was too big and heavy for him to manage on the stairs. He knew that Gina and Blake were in the house but neither of them had Claude's size and strength.

He watched from the window until Claude reached the patio leading to the open French doors at the back of the house then levered himself from the armchair and shuffled out to the top of the stairs.

When he heard Claude's footsteps in the hallway he called down to him.

'Hello Claude, would you mind coming up and helping me with something please.'

There was no answer but then Claude appeared at the bottom of the stairs and began to make his way up.

'I finished my painting and was hoping you could take it down to the work room for me.'

Claude still didn't say anything which seemed a little strange but Mahesh thought he'd given a little nod in answer to his request so he turned and went back into his room as Claude followed behind.

'There, what do you think?' said Mahesh indicating his painting. Claude stood in front of the painting as if taking it all in but again he said nothing. He stepped forward, lifted the painting from the easel, turned and strode from the room with it.

'Claude is everything okay, why aren't you speaking to me?' asked Mahesh as he trailed behind him.

He caught up with him at the top of the stairs where he stood side onwards to the staircase facing Mahesh, the painting in his arms, waiting.

He had a strange look on his face that Mahesh found a little disconcerting. It was like he was fighting several emotions at once, and his eyes looked somehow intense and yet blank at the same time.

As Mahesh approached him Claude made a sudden sideways movement with his arms releasing the painting from his grasp and sending it clattering down the stairs.

Letting out a strangled cry of distress Mahesh ran to Claude's side and looked down. The white painted wooden stairs were smeared here and there with wet oil paint and the canvas lay paint side downwards at the bottom.

'What have you done Claude, and why?' he asked in a shaky voice turning to his friend.

In reply Claude grabbed him by the front of his shirt with one hand and the waistband of his trousers with the other and with a terrible roar of anger lifted and threw the man after his painting.

As he fell Mahesh did not feel fear or anger; he did not even feel physical pain as his frail body made bone crunching contact with the wooden stairs. What he did feel was sorrow. Sorrow because harm had come to him at the hands of a man he thought his friend, and because his 'gift', a 'gift' that had served him well all his life, had failed to warn him of the impending danger, had failed to save himself and his friend from this terrible act.

The painter landed in a mangled heap besides his damaged painting, and slipped into darkness, his left hand draped across his final work in a strangely protective manner.

Gina and Blake were in the art room/lounge. Gina was struggling with a particularly tricky piece of the circular stained-glass windowpane she was working on and they did not hear the initial sounds of Claude arriving or the clatter of the painting coming down the stairs as Blake was playing his new song through on his acoustic guitar and singing gustily. But the sound of Claude's terrible roar of anger penetrated causing them to freeze and sending a chill down their spines.

The couple looked at each other in shock, unable to move for a few seconds as the initial sound was followed by ominous sounding thuds.

After a few seconds of silence the pair stood up and walked towards the door to the hallway a feeling of dread coming over them both.

The sight that greeted them at the foot of the stairs was shocking and upsetting. It was clear from the angle of his neck and the glassy look to his open eyes that Mahesh was dead. Gina let out a squeal of shock and pain and Blake pulled her to him and turned so they could no longer see the haunting sight. He wanted to comfort her with words but none would come.

Then they heard the sound of footsteps and both turned and looked up to see Claude descending the stairs.

'What happened?' asked Blake 'Did he fall?'

At this Claude smiled, or at least tried to but it turned into more of a grimace.

'What's the matter with you, why are you smiling?' Blake's voice waivered his mind trying to make sense of what was happening. Gina whimpered and shook in his arms. They were both very afraid. This thing coming down the stairs was Claude, but not Claude, something was very wrong. Blake could think of only one thing to do, there was only one word in his head and that word was 'RUN!'

Dropping his arms from around Gina he grabbed her by the hand. Instinctively she knew his plan and together they ran for the front door. Throwing it open they ran out onto the gravel driveway and headed for the trees off to the left.

The blonde couple were younger and much fitter than Claude and this and the fact that Claude had to manoeuvre around Mahesh's body gave them a small head start, but Claude wasn't too far behind as he followed at an ungainly yet fast pace.

As they entered the woodland they failed to see the pale shadow lurking amongst the trees too intent on their flight from the strange menace their friend posed.

After a while they took shelter behind a large, fallen tree, crouching to catch their breath and hoping they'd lost their pursuer. They daren't speak and tried to keep their breathing as quiet as possible. After a minute Blake gestured that it was time to move, and they headed away from their shelter.

They did not hear Claude approach until it was too late. He came from the right just behind them and the first blow from his makeshift weapon connected with the back of Blake's head with a sickening thud. Gina screamed as Blake fell releasing her hand and she stopped in her tracks. She threw her arms up to protect her head from Claude's second blow and screamed again as the piece of tree branch he wielded connected with her right forearm breaking the bone with a stomach-churning crack.

Gina started to fall clutching her wounded arm and leaving herself open to a third blow that glanced across the side of her head as she fell. She lay barely conscious waiting for another blow, helpless to stop it, but it didn't come. Instead, just before she lost consciousness she heard a groan and then a thump, then it all went quiet.

It viewed the scene from a few feet away. A scene of carnage which It had caused and It was pleased. It had wanted to do more but had lost its 'grip' on the man Claude. Controlling him had been such hard work, but such fun. There was more It wanted to do but it would have to wait. For now it needed to rest.

Eddie Oakley leaned out of the van window and keyed his code into the keypad in the entry box for the gate. After a couple of seconds the large, ornate, black Iron Gate began to swing open before him. As he drove forwards through the gate he heaved a large sigh just as he always did when he returned home. The van was full of art supplies, and his friend Mason Winchester sat beside him in the passenger seat. Eddie was a happy man. The day he'd been appointed Warden of 'The Gateway Art Commune' had been the proudest and happiest day of his life. He'd had what people referred to as a misspent youth, full of unruliness and the odd petty crime.

At twenty-two he'd joined a motorcycle gang. The gang hadn't exactly been the nasty, criminal bunch of Hells Angels often depicted in the media, but they hadn't exactly been a bunch of decent, upstanding citizens either. He had enjoyed the life for several years but by his early thirties the allure had faded and he quit the gang.

After leaving the gang he'd had trouble finding a decent job and somewhere to live. This was mainly due to the fact that although he was no longer a gang member he still rode a motorbike and refused to alter his appearance. He was 6' 4' with broad shoulders and a heavy muscular build. His hair was long and strawberry blonde (a term that seemed at odds with his looks) and a handlebar moustache and sideburns that were oddly a shade redder than his hair. His arms were covered in tattoos (as were other unseen parts of his body) and his wardrobe consisted solely of jeans and t-shirts emblazoned with rock band logos.

However, he also had warm, grey-green eyes and a friendly smile that was at odds with the rest of his scary biker look. Against people's advice he resolutely refused to change his image, it was who he was and if an employer didn't like it then that wasn't the job for him.

He had eventually found a job as a bike courier for a company called 'The Somnium Foundation'. He had come across the job in rather an odd way. He had awoken one morning convinced that he would find a job that day. The conviction had somehow come from a dream. He did not remember the dream; he just knew it was the reason he felt so confident about finding work. After going out to buy the local paper he had turned to the job vacancies pages and there it was, an ad for his ideal job. He'd phoned the number in the ad and had got an interview for that afternoon. The interview had gone well with him feeling no nerves at all and he'd been offered the job there and then.

He'd felt at home within 'The Somnium Foundation' immediately and had found out that his employers were a Global Foundation set up and run by a powerful, rich family named Vecchini who amongst other things funded several art communes around the world. Being a gifted comic book style artist himself he felt even more strongly that this was an ideal company to work for.

Over time Eddie's job had diversified as his employers discovered that he could turn his hand to pretty much any manual type of job. He fixed things around the office, helped with any heavy lifting, did the odd stint as night-time security and even learned the basics in IT. He was paid well, was happy in his work and his employers were happy with him. So happy in fact that he had eventually been promoted to what had unexpectedly proved to be his actual dream job.

As Warden at 'The Gateway', one of the Foundations art communes he was in charge of the maintenance of the house and more importantly the security and wellbeing of the five artists in residence. Part of the job had also entailed being made privy to the more 'secret' aspect of 'The Somnium Foundations' true purpose. He had felt honoured and strangely unburdened by the fact that the Foundation had trusted him with their 'secret' although he was aware that there was more to this 'secret' than he was told. Still his was a demanding and important job and he loved it. He loved the house, and he loved the people in it especially the man sitting next to him.

Mason Winchester was a talented and respected Luthier who's beautifully crafted guitars and mandolins were always in demand. He was also an all-round decent guy and the best friend that Eddie had ever had.

The two men had hit it off immediately upon meeting and had become good friends very quickly. Physically however they made an odd duo with Eddie's pale skin and hard man exterior contrasting strongly with Mason's dark skin and Caribbean good looks. Both men were tall but where Eddie's six-foot four frame was bulky and muscular Mason at six foot had a slim, athletic build. Where Eddie's fair hair was straight and a little unkempt Mason's was meticulously styled in short, neat dreadlocks, and his small goatee style beard was neatly trimmed compared to Eddie's thick sideburns and handlebar moustache. Also, despite the fact that Eddie at forty-one was five years younger than Mason it was Mason who appeared five years junior to his friend.

As diverse as they were physically however the two men shared a lot in common, not least their love of their home and their jobs. As Eddie drove the van along the tree lined driveway he knew that sitting beside him Mason was just as glad to be home as he was.

Unfortunately the happiness of both men was about to be shattered.

As they neared the end of the driveway a figure suddenly burst from the trees to their right and ran into the path of the van. Mason shouted a warning at the same time as Eddie reacted by breaking hard and swerving to the left. Although he managed to avoid a head on collision the two men felt and heard the slight thump as the van clipped the moving figure.

For a few seconds after the van came to a shuddering halt both men sat frozen in shock. Then, almost in tandem they opened their doors and stepped out of the van. The person they had hit lay on the driveway several feet behind the van with their back towards them. As they drew near however the person rolled onto their back and turned their head towards the two men. Mason gasped in shock as they recognised the blood-spattered face of their friend Claude Grey.

Sofia Vecchini had been driving for about an hour, her brand new, white fiat 500 eating up the miles at a steady pace. Luckily the road was fairly straight and almost empty because Sofia's mind was not fully focused on driving. Her mind was still full of the weak, but haunting images and sounds from the dream she'd had only a couple of hours ago.

She had slept in late after a long night driving and as she had dreamt happily of a hill walking trip she had recently taken things had suddenly got strange. As her dreaming eyes gazed upon the beautiful, green landscape another image had appeared superimposed over the rolling hills. It was the ghostly image of a large, beautiful, red brick house surrounded by woodland. And then on top of this image the dreaming Sofia had seen an even fainter image of another building. This one was an unusual, low, castle like structure in grey stone. The images lasted only for a few seconds and as they disappeared Sofia had heard the haunting sound of words without a voice. Those words had been 'Help us'.

She had awoken from the dream with those words still echoing through her mind and the faint images still visible in her mind's eye. Sofia had known immediately that this dream was a real cry for help and not just a dream. She had even known who had sent it though not in an exact sense. She had not known which individual had sent her the dream but she had known which 'kind' of individual had sent it. This dream was a strange, and as far as she knew, unheard of event and even now, two hours later, she was having trouble processing it.

At first Sofia had not known what to do. How do you deal with a situation that you, and probably no one else, had ever dealt with before? After thinking things through for several minutes she had sat up in bed and reached for her mobile phone. She needed information and someone at the Foundation must be able to help her.

Although she had been part of the family business all her working life and had been 'trained' for her role in it since childhood her current position within 'The Somnium Foundation' was still relatively new to her. She had spent the last two months settling into her new role as Marshal and what with all that entailed she had so far only managed to visit two of the five 'art communes' designated to her. She somehow knew that the red brick house in her dream was one of her 'art communes' but as neither of the two she had visited matched the images from her dreams she had needed help. Over the phone she had given a description of the red brick house from her dream (leaving out the other building and the dreams message) to a woman called Barbara who was General Secretary at Head Office and had asked her to find out which of her 'art communes' matched the description. She was sure that Barbara must think it a strange query, but she was also sure that she would carry out her instructions to the best of her ability and without question.

Whilst she waited for Barbara to call back, she had taken a shower and got dressed. She'd put on her usual 'uniform' of black pencil skirt, white blouse, tights and black high heeled shoes. She had just finished tying her long, straight, black hair back into its usual ponytail when her phone rang.

Barbara gave her the name of the art commune in question and Sofia felt a wave of unease flow through her. She had her files out ready to look up the details of her destination once she got its name, but now she knew which one she didn't have to look it up, she knew where it was even though she had never been there, she knew all about it. This particular commune was unique, it had a history unlike any of the other communes and the fact that there was a problem there was alarming her. But for now she just needed to focus on getting herself there ASAP. Luckily it was not too far away from where Sofia was, and she'd estimated it would take her approximately two hours to drive there.

She'd tried phoning the house before she left to let them know she was coming and to check if there were any problems but had got the answer machine. She'd decided not to leave a message, after all what could she say?

Therefore, Sofia had set off in a state of unease not knowing what she would find at her destination.

Eddie and Mason reached Claude at the same time and sank to their knees beside him. Their friend was in a terrible state; his face was streaked with what looked like tears mixed with what was obviously blood. But worst of all was his expression. His pudgy features were contorted into what could only be described as agony. The two men mistakenly interpreted this as physical agony but this was not the case. Physically Claude was feeling nothing, his body numb with shock. The agony was in his mind. His eyes were glassy and unseeing and the low grunting and moaning noises he was making were disturbing to hear.

'Claude, where does it hurt?' asked Mason his voice shaky.

But there was no answer from Claude, just more unsettling noises.

'Please Claude tell us where it hurts' pleaded Mason.

In seeming answer Claude suddenly raised his arms and clutched his hands to his head.

'Is it your head, did you hit your head?' asked Mason

'No!' cried Claude, and then louder 'No, no, no, no, no, no!' Then suddenly he began to roll his body until he was several feet away from Eddie and Mason. He then began to clumsily struggle to his feet. Surprised the two men stood up and began to approach the now standing Claude whose hands were again clutching the sides of his head in what appeared to be pain. As they drew alongside him however he backed away saying 'Leave me alone'.

'We can't leave you, you're hurt' stated Mason.

'I'm not, I'm not, it's them, I hurt them' replied Claude and then covering his face with his hands he began to mutter unintelligibly to himself. Mason glanced questioningly at Eddie hoping his friend would know what to do next.

'Let's try and get him in the van and back to the house' suggested Eddie 'he can't be too badly hurt if he got up by himself, he may just be in shock. We can call a doctor from the house'.

Mason nodded his agreement and they moved to stand one each side of the still muttering Claude. Gingerly Mason put his arm around Claude's shoulders in what he hoped was a reassuring manner. Claude dropped his hands from his face and folded them tightly across his chest. With his head bowed he was still muttering to himself but he let Mason slowly guide him forwards to the van where the two men managed to manoeuvre him into the seat between them, all the while Claude continued to mutter unintelligibly under his breath.

It was only a short drive to the front of the house and so they were soon guiding Claude through the open front door where their next terrible shock awaited.

The sight of Mahesh's body at the bottom of the staircase stopped them in their tracks. What on earth was happening? Mason stood with a suddenly silent Claude in the doorway whilst Eddie approached Mahesh's crumpled form. There was no real need to check the man's pulse, it was clear he was dead, but Eddie did it anyway. He then straightened and turning to Mason shook his head. Both men were then startled as Claude found his voice again.

'I told you' he said, 'I hurt them.'

'What happened here Claude, what do you mean you hurt them?' asked Eddie.

'I hurt them' repeated Claude 'Mahesh, Blake and Gina, I hurt them. I didn't want to, but I couldn't help it, It made me do it'. Claude's voice sounded frighteningly robotic and his words were confusing.

'We don't understand Claude' said Mason 'Where are Blake and Gina, what happened to them. What happened to Mahesh?'

In the same robotic tone as before Claude answered him.

'We killed him, and we killed them, out in the woods, they're dead, they're all dead.'

For long seconds no one moved or spoke. Claude stood silent his arms crossed tightly across his chest rocking slightly on the balls of his feet. Mason stood beside him, Eddie beside Mahesh's body, both men trying to make sense of what was happening. Did Claude really mean what he said? Were three of their friends dead at the hands of another friend? And if so why?

Eddie recovered from his stupor first. He was The Warden after all; it was his job to look after these people, to deal with problems, to 'take care' of things. He needed to sort this mess out.

'Okay Mason' he said, 'you go out to the woods to see if you can find Blake and Gina, you have your mobile right?' Mason nodded 'Okay, then call me on my mobile when you find them, I'm going to use the land line to phone for an ambulance in case it's needed.'

'What about Claude?'

'Don't worry I'll keep an eye on him.'

'Okay.'

Having received his instructions Mason took a deep breath and tried to clear his head as best he could before heading back out towards the woods at a run. Meanwhile Eddie all but frogmarched Claude through the door to the right of the hallway into the room known as the Office.

It was a very spacious room with two large, nine pane sash windows affording a view of the circular driveway in front of the house and the woodland beyond. Two large, comfortable, cream coloured leather armchairs and a small, wooden table sat between the windows. Towards the back of the room in the centre stood a large, antique wooden desk, behind which was a black leather swivel chair. On the desk there were two telephones and two computer screens, one a normal PC with keyboard, the other was linked to the control box for the gate intercom and security system. Along the wall to the right of the desk were three five-foot-tall metal filing cabinets and along the wall to the left was a large wooden cupboard next to which there was a door which lead to two guest bedrooms. The walls of the office were painted a delicate dove grey; however, little of the paint was visible as the walls were liberally covered with a collection of impressive drawings, photographs and paintings of all ages and styles as well as shelves containing small sculptures and ceramics. The floor was original, polished wooden floorboards.

Eddie sat the unresponsive yet pliable Claude in one of the armchairs and then all but ran to the desk. He picked up a phone and started to dial. The number he dialled was one he had been instructed to memorise when he first started work as The Warden at The Gateway. It had been drummed into his head that this number must be used only in an emergency and that it should be dialled before any others, even before 999. This number was 'The Somnium Foundations' own version of 999 and he had been assured that their emergency services had a far quicker response time than the national one. He had never doubted this fact.

After he had dialled the number he heard a few clicking and buzzing sounds and then it began to ring. After only three rings the call was answered with a simple 'Yes?' As quickly, yet clearly as he could Eddie explained who and where he was and what the nature of the emergency was. He explained that one resident was dead, two others were missing, possibly also dead and that another resident was claiming responsibility for their deaths and was currently in what appeared to be a state of extreme shock. There was no immediate response from the person on the other end of the phone, just the occasional whoosh of background noise. Finally they spoke.

'Leave it to me. I'll organise ambulances and a doctor you just sit tight and I'll call you back shortly with details. In the meantime give me a call if you hear anything about the missing residents'.

'Okay, I will, thanks.'

Eddie put the phone down and let out a long sigh of relief. Things were bad, really bad but he trusted that the Foundation would handle things with their usual efficiency.

After searching the woods that bordered the driveway to the house for what seemed like an age but was in fact only about ten minutes Mason came across what looked like the opening scene from an episode of CSI.

Blake and Gina lay side by side, Blake on his front, Gina on her back. As he approached he saw that the back of Blake's short, blonde hair was matted with blood and a small red pool had gathered beneath his head. There was some blood in Gina's blonde hair too and her left arm lay at an awkward angle. Mason's heart was racing, and he felt close to being sick but he needed to check their vital signs.

As he crouched down next to Blake, he was startled by a sudden movement caught out of the corner of his eye. The fingers on Gina's right hand had moved he was sure of it. Hope flared within him. Leaning over Blake he put two fingers on Gina's neck feeling for a pulse. To his immense relief he felt one and as he withdrew his hand he heard her make a quiet moaning sound. Thank goodness, she was still alive. Now what about Blake? Blake's neck was slick with blood but Mason tried to ignore the fact so as not to become queasy as he checked for a pulse. He thought he could feel a faint beat but was worried his own loudly beating heart and racing pulse were affecting his judgement. Best to leave it for the professionals he thought withdrawing his hand and wiping the blood off on his white t shirt. Taking his mobile from a pocket in his tan cargo pants he called Eddie who answered on the first ring.

'I've found them. They both have head wounds and it looks like Gina's arm is broken. Gina is still alive, but I'm not sure about Blake, I think I felt a weak pulse. There's a lot of blood Eddie, is the ambulance on its way?'

'Yes, it's coming Mason, you should try and stem the bleeding if you can and I'll call when the ambulance arrives at the gate so you can go out onto the driveway and lead them to Gina and Blake.'

'Okay, I'll do my best.'

As Eddie ended the call with Mason the land line rang. It was the person who had answered his emergency call.

'Hello, the ambulances will be with you in approximately twenty minutes, I've arranged for two in case they're needed. Have you found your missing residents yet?'

'Yes, they've been found in the woods. One of them is alive; the other is touch and go.'

'Okay, that's encouraging news. Now I've also arranged for a doctor to come and attend the resident you say is in severe shock. Is he causing you a problem at the moment?'

Eddied glanced across the room to where Claude was sat hunched in the armchair where he had left him silently staring into space.

'No at the moment he's very subdued, almost catatonic I'd say.'

'Well the doctor should be with you in about forty minutes and I should be there myself before then. The doctor is employed by the Foundation and is totally trustworthy and reliable. The same goes for the paramedics as the ambulances are private and will take your residents to a private Foundation run hospital. You may want to move the deceased out of respect, please feel free to do so. As you know the Foundation likes to keep the police out of things. We'll deal with this ourselves. Anyway, as I said I'll be there shortly myself, but if you need me beforehand don't hesitate to call.'

'I won't, and thanks again.'

'Okay, see you soon.'

'Okay, bye.'

After putting down the phone Eddie realised that he didn't know the name of this woman who would be with them soon.

Out in the woods Mason had taken off his t-shirt, torn it up and used part of it to bandage Gina's head as best he could. Her head wound appeared a lot less severe than Blake's and her pulse was weak but steady. Although she had not moved again she had moaned a little when he had gently lifted her head to bandage it. He had talked to her whilst he did it trying his best to reassure her (and himself) that she would be alright not knowing if she could hear him or not. When it came to Blake however he was less sure of what to do. With all the blood it was hard to tell where the wound or wounds were and he was afraid to move Blake's head. In the end he decided to wad up the rest of his torn t-shirt and press it against the back of Blake's head in an effort to stem the blood flow. All the while he muttered reassurances to both of them whether they could hear or not.

When his mobile phone started to ring it startled him. It was Eddie of course. The ambulances had just been let in the gate and he needed to run out to the driveway to wave them down and direct the paramedics to his wounded friends. Luckily it wasn't far and he was a fast runner. When he cleared the trees he saw that the ambulances were only feet away along the driveway moving slowly obviously on the lookout for him. They spotted him immediately and came to a halt. He was half naked and smeared with blood, but it didn't seem to faze them, but then he was sure they'd seen worse.

They unloaded their stretchers and medical kits from the vehicles and followed him back into the woods. Luckily the ground was pretty even and the trees quite widely spaced in this part of the woods so they got to the injured couple reasonably quickly and effortlessly. The paramedics immediately set to work, one team of two on Gina the other on Blake as Mason collapsed onto the ground exhausted. He tried to keep up with what the paramedics were saying to each other but there were a lot of medical terms and they spoke quietly. He didn't want to get too near for fear of getting in their way but he heard and saw enough to know that Blake was still clinging to life, if barely.

After assessing their patients and carrying out what emergency treatment they could the paramedics set about loading them onto the stretchers. They then set about transferring them to the ambulances. Even though the ground was reasonably even it was still not suitable for any sort of wheels to navigate very well, therefore, they had to carry the stretchers themselves. Mason offered his assistance but they declined and so he simply began to lead them back to the driveway. As they negotiated the trees he asked them how his friends were doing. They told him that Gina was stable and Blake was critical but that head wounds were tricky so they couldn't tell him anything more.

Once the stretchers had been loaded he told them they would be best to drive on and turn around in the circular driveway in front of the house. They took his advice and drove away leaving him to walk to the house alone. As they passed him heading out he sent a heartfelt wish to his friends, 'Please be well'.

From his vantage point at the office window Eddie watched as the ambulances turned in the driveway and then sped off. After remotely opening the gate to let the ambulances out he returned to the window in time to see his friend emerge from the trees. As he drew near he saw that Mason's bare chest and trousers were smeared in blood and it was obvious from the look on his face that the scene at the clearing had been a traumatic one.

As Mason entered the house he caught sight of Mahesh's body at the foot of the stairs. It was a jarring sight even the second time around and he had to look away, he had seen too much horror today. Turning to his right he entered the large office.

'How are they?' enquired Eddie as his friend entered the room.

'All I can tell you is that they were both still alive when they went in the ambulances. The paramedics say that head injuries are tricky so they couldn't give me a detailed prognosis. All I know is that Gina is stable and Blake is critical.'

'I'm sure they're in good hands, all we can do now is hope for the best.'

'What are we going to do about Mahesh? I can't bear to see him lying there like that.'

'Me neither, but now you're back I can sort it. You stay and keep an eye on Claude; I'm going to move Mahesh.'

'Should you do that? I mean it's a crime scene right?'

'It's okay, the Foundation basically gave me the go ahead, the police won't be involved and there's a Foundation doctor coming to see Claude, who hasn't moved or spoken since you left by the way. Also, someone from the Foundation is on their way too to help sort things out.'

'I can't get my head around all this, it's crazy.'

'I know. Look, you just wait here whilst I move Mahesh, then I suggest you go clean yourself up, by then the Foundation people will be here and we can all sort this out between us, okay?'

'Okay.'

Eddie lifted Mahesh with ease and as he held his friends small, frail body he felt a lump form in his throat and for the first time in his adult life found himself fighting back tears. Mahesh had been a great friend, a great painter and a great man. He didn't deserve to die this way.

Eddie turned to the left and entered the room opposite the office. This was the lounge / art room. It was decorated in the same colour scheme and décor as the office, its walls also covered with yet more artwork. The right hand side of the room contained a spacious seating area consisting of two large, black leather sofas and two matching armchairs all arranged around a big screen TV system. The left hand side of the room, nearest the two windows, was the more incongruous art room section contained a number of benches and work surfaces of different types, and against the back wall two large, wooden cupboards and a stainless steel sink. In between the two cupboards there was a door which led to a guest double bedroom with en suite shower room. In the right hand corner behind the door there was an upright piano. Eddie laid Mahesh gently on the largest of the wooden work surfaces. He then opened one of the cupboards and found a clean sheet used to protect surfaces from paint etc. and covered his friend with it. Returning to the foot of the stairs he picked up Mahesh's painting.

Even though the paint was smudged quite badly in places he could see that it was a beautiful painting, and this deepened his feeling of sorrow. Glancing up the staircase he noticed several smears of paint on the white wood. 'I'll have to clean that up later' he thought as he returned to the lounge with the painting and propped it up against the legs of the bench that held the artists body. He then returned to the office to relieve his friend of guard duty so he could get himself cleaned up.

Sofia reached the gates to 'The Gateway Art Commune' after a fraught hour and fifty-minute drive. The house was very secluded and hard to find for those not in the know, but luckily Sofia was one of those who was in the know so it was not the difficulty in finding the house that had made the journey an anxious one. She had spent the first hour and a half of the journey in a bit of a daze not knowing exactly why she was making the journey or what she would find when she got there. Then she had received the call from The Warden Eddie Oakley. Whatever she had expected it had not been the terrible story he had related to her. The call however, had sharpened her focus and set her into efficiency mode. Although, as far as she was aware nothing like this had ever happened before she was fully trained in dealing with emergencies and so had dealt with the initial call calmly and efficiently. A feat made all the more impressive by the fact that she had dealt with it whilst driving, her state-of-the-art hands free mobile having proven itself to be an essential piece of equipment. Deep inside however she was shocked to the core that something like this had happened. She had always thought that the artists who lived and 'worked' at the communes were good people, people of peace. Surely the way they were chosen would guarantee this. How could one of them have turned on their fellow artists this way?

Sofia had been aware of the 'secret task' carried out by the inhabitants of the many 'art communes' scattered all around the world since she was a child, she was a Vecchini after all, and it had been the Vecchini family's job to look after these special, talented people for centuries.

She had worked within the Foundation all her adult life in various administration roles until at the age of twenty-nine her inherited 'talent' was fully recognised, and she had been chosen to take on a more important role within the Foundation.

As part of her training to become a Marshal she had learnt of the deeper secret that the Foundation had been set up to protect. Not all family members were given this extra knowledge, only those, who like her were chosen to become a 'Marshal' or one of the other important roles within the Foundation could know the full truth about the inhabitants of the art communes. Other family members and the most trusted employees of 'The Somnium Foundation' including the Wardens at each commune knew the true function of the artists, but this deeper secret was kept even from them.

The rest of the employees of the Somnium Foundation knew only that they worked for a Global Foundation set up by the Vecchini family to fund and run art communes around the world using money made through various investments. These employees were kept loyal with good pay and working conditions. They included lawyers, accountants, doctors and various other professionals as well as office and maintenance staff. All in all 'The Somnium Foundation' was a well-run and respected company. It was also the keeper of a very special secret.

Despite all her knowledge and training Sofia had yet to come across any major problems in her new role and so had experienced moments of doubt during her journey but had ignored them as best she could. Mentally she was a very strong person but not having ever come across such a serious situation as this either in her personal or professional life she could not know how she would cope. This personal strength however, meant that as she arrived at the house she was able to convince herself that she could manage the situation. Still, she took a minute to take in a deep, calming breath letting it out slowly before pushing the call button on the gate intercom.

As she drove through the gate Sofia found that despite all that was going on she was still able to appreciate her surroundings. The large, ornate, black Iron Gate was impressive, its design unusual and hard to describe in words. It looked almost organic like it had been grown rather than made, the patterns reminiscent of vines with flowers/leaves sprouting from it, but that was not quite it. It had its own unique style and Sofia had never seen anything like it. Once passed the gate she found herself on a wide driveway enclosed on either side by beautiful, lush, green woodland. She navigated the driveways gentle curves and corners for a little under a quarter of a mile, then it opened out into a large, circular driveway on the opposite side of which there was a triple garage, and suddenly the house from her dreams was before her. It was a large, red brick, Georgian style house with sash windows spaced symmetrically around the central doorway. Five wide, shallow stone steps led up to the front door which was panelled and painted white (as were the window frames). The door itself was topped by a fan light and framed by an elaborate crown supported by decorative pilasters.

She pulled up near the front door next to a blue Fiat Doblo van and climbed out of the car. As she approached the door it was opened by a tall, well-built man with long, strawberry blonde hair wearing jeans and a faded Led Zeppelin t-shirt. As she reached him he held out his hand and said 'Hi, I'm Eddie Oakley, the Warden.'

'Sofia Vecchini, good to meet you' she replied as her small hand was dwarfed by his in a firm handshake.

'Come in, we're in the office through here' said Eddie as he tried to process the fact that an actual member of the Vecchini family had come to help them.

She closed the large front door behind them and followed him across the light, spacious hallway to the right. She was a little surprised by his appearance but had never been one to judge a person on looks alone. Her next surprise was the so-called office. It was a large, airy, beautifully decorated room that despite being a strange mixture of office and stately home, what with all the artwork upon its walls, still managed to look very stylish and welcoming. Fleetingly she wished she had the time to inspect the beautiful artwork more closely but now was not the time.

Standing to her right next to an armchair with his back to a large, sash window with a view of the driveway was a tall, slim black man dressed in neat beige combat trousers and a crisp white t-shirt.

'Hello, I'm Mason Winchester' he said extending his hand.

'Sofia Vecchini' she repeated as her hand was again dwarfed in a firm handshake.

There was another man sat in the armchair by Mason. The angle of the chair meant that Sofia could only see him in profile. He was a large man with thinning brown hair and was slumped in the chair with his arms crossed tight across his chest, his head bowed slightly. He had not turned his head or indeed moved at all at her entrance. She also noticed with a slight shudder that there were smears of what looked like blood on the side of his face that was visible to her. Stood next to her Eddie gestured towards the man in the chair.

'This is Claude Grey' he informed her, his voice tight with emotion.

'Has he said or done anything since we last talked?' she asked.

'No, he's barely moved and apart from a few low, unintelligible mutterings he's been quiet' Eddie replied.

'So you still have no details as to why he attacked your friends?'

'No he hasn't said much and what he has said doesn't tell us much. We don't even know if he's injured from where I hit him with the van. After I hit him he seemed to be in pain but he doesn't appear to be in any pain now.'

'Well, the doctor should be here soon so he can check him over. How long ago did the ambulances leave?'

'About fifteen minutes.'

'And what about the deceased, I'm sorry I don't know his name, where have you put him?'

'His name is Mahesh Choudhary and I've put him in the lounge opposite.'

'Okay, good. Now I've told the doctor who's coming that Mahesh fell down the stairs and that Claude here witnessed the fall; he was then hit by your van when rushing for help and is now severely traumatised by the events. He does not know about your other two friends. The doctor is a trusted Foundation employee so if Claude does tell him what really happened we would be okay but I think it better to keep things simple'.'

'That's fine, but what's the story we're giving about Gina and Blake to those who do know about them?'

'At the moment that's not a problem. The hospital is a private one owned by the Foundation and the doctors will be too busy treating your friends to ask many questions. When and if it comes to it the Foundation will give them a believable story so don't worry on that score.'

'Is it really necessary or even possible to keep the police out of this though?' Mason interjected.

'Its Foundation policy in a situation like this to keep the police out of it. Do you really want Claude in the hands of the police in his condition? With all he knows do you want to risk him telling all to the authorities?'

'No, you're right, I get it, but what do we do with him?'

'I'm working on that. Let's just see what the doctor says about his condition first' and then to Eddie 'Do you mind if I use your desk, I need to make a few phone calls.'

'No, go ahead' said Eddie, and then remembering his Warden role 'Would you like a drink or anything?'

'A cup of coffee would be great, white, no sugar, thanks.'

'No problem, anything for you Mason?'

'No thanks Ed.'

'Okay.'

Eddie left the room and Sofia went to sit behind the desk. Once seated she looked up at Mason who had followed her and now stood on the other side of the desk.

'We need to have a long chat soon, alone' she said, 'Eddie's done great so far but we both know there are things he is unaware of, problems only the two of us can deal with.'

She was looking Mason directly in the eyes as she said this and in that moment Mason knew for sure that he could trust her completely, her tone of voice and the look in her eyes told him more than words could convey. They told him that she knew all that he knew, and possibly more and that she was there to share his burden.

He knew that as a member of the Vecchini family she would have the special innate talent that a number of Vecchini's were blessed with and he was reassured. With his four fellow artists gone or indisposed and having been unable to confide in his friend Eddie, Mason had started to feel panicked at the thought of dealing with certain things alone, but now he realised that wasn't the case he felt relieved and even a little hopeful. Sofia saw the relief in Mason's eyes and was glad; she really needed to talk to him properly, but now was not the time. For a moment they were both lost in thoughts of the magnitude and seriousness of the task before them until the sound of a car pulling up outside brought them back to the present. The doctor had arrived.

Mason opened the front door and welcomed the doctor inside. The doctor was a small man with thin arms and legs and a little pot belly. He had a halo of salt and pepper hair around a shiny bald spot and wore large, round glasses that seemed a little too big for his thin face and which magnified his brown eyes a little. He was carrying an old fashioned looking black bag that Mason had only ever seen doctors on TV carry. After their initial greeting the two men did not speak as Mason led the doctor to the office. Sofia had moved from behind the desk and stood near the doorway. She held out her hand to the newcomer as he entered. This time the hand she shook was almost as small and delicate as her own. She smiled.

'Hello Dr Gordon, thank you for coming at such short notice.'

'Oh it's no bother Miss Vecchini, I'm glad to be of help' he replied, then, after glancing around him he exclaimed 'What a beautiful room this is.'

'Yes it is lovely' replied Sofia.

There was a slightly awkward pause before the doctor went on to ask, 'So where's the patient then?'

'It's the gentleman in the armchair, his name is Claude' Sofia replied, 'As I explained on the telephone he was hit by a vehicle, only a glancing blow we think but I'm afraid he's still unresponsive so we don't really know the extent of his injuries.'

'Okay, well let's have a look at him then, see what I can do.'

The three of them moved towards Claude, Sofia and Mason stopping to stand behind the armchair whilst Dr Gordon moved round to stand in front of Claude. He studied his patient for a minute, his magnified brown eyes making a brief visual appraisal. He noticed that there were splatters of dried blood both on the man's face and on his clothes but saw no sign of an injury from which the blood could have come. He deduced therefore, that the blood was not his patients. He was of course curious about whose blood it might be but he knew his place. He was employed by the Foundation to treat people when and how asked without asking any unnecessary questions. He was paid well for his work and was treated with respect; he also trusted the Foundation implicitly. If Miss Vecchini felt he needed to know whose blood it was she would tell him, if not then it was none of his business.

Having finished his initial appraisal he moved on. Speaking in a friendly, soothing tone he addressed Claude.

'Hello Claude, my name is Dr Gordon. I understand you have had a bit of a traumatic day today and that you may be hurt. Can you tell me, are you in any pain?'

There was no reply; in fact although the doctor stood directly in his eye line Claude appeared to not even see him standing there. So the doctor tried again.

'I'm here to help you Claude.' He said in the same soothing voice. 'But first I need you to help me. I need to know where you are injured. If you don't feel like talking to me maybe you could just point to where it hurts. Could you do that for me?'

Still there was no movement or reply from Claude. It was then that Eddie returned with Sofia's coffee. Sofia took the steaming mug from him, thanked him and then introduced him to the doctor. The two men shook hands.

'I'm afraid I'm not having any luck getting through to your friend' explained the doctor to Eddie, and then addressing them all he continued 'I would like to try to examine him now but I'm not sure how he will react if I touch him, plus it would be easier to examine him if he was laying down.'

'We could try and get him into one of the guest rooms' suggested Eddie. 'He was compliant before when we walked him in from the van so we could give it a try.'

'Where are the guest rooms?' enquired the doctor.

'Just there' replied Eddie pointing to the door across the room next to the cupboard 'there's a small room with a single bed and a larger one with twin beds, they've both got a small shower room attached.'

'That would be perfect especially as I may have to sedate him. I suggest we attempt this together as he knows and trusts you and I need to gain his trust.'

Eddie agreed, though without any enthusiasm. The 'Warden' part of him wanted to help his friend in any way he could, however, the knowledge of what Claude had done to his other friends meant he had little sympathy for the man's condition. He was aware that if he didn't keep his feelings in check he could well end up grabbing Claude and shaking him until he explained himself, until he justified his actions, if, that is, there was any justification for what he had done.

Eddie suddenly realised that Mason, Sofia and Dr Gordon were all staring at him expectantly. And so giving his mind a mental shake he set about the task whilst doing his best to keep his feelings under control.

'Okay doc,' he said, 'If you stand one side of him and I'll stand the other side.' They got into position. 'Right, now I'll try talking to him first.'

'Claude, this is Doctor Gordon' he began 'He's here to help you. We need to find out if you are injured. So, if it's okay with you we need to get you to a bed in the guest room so the Doctor can examine you. Is that okay Claude?'

There was no verbal answer but Eddie thought that maybe Claude had given a little nod.

'Can you get up by yourself or do you need our help?' he asked.

Claude did not answer but he moved slightly in the chair leaning forward a little and shifting his bottom forward slightly on the seat.

'How about we help you a little?' he enquired as he tentatively reached out and placed one hand on Claude's shoulder and the other under his elbow.

When Claude made no move to shrug him off or push him away the doctor mirrored Eddie's position on Claude's other side saying, 'Okay Claude let's get you up slowly.'

Gradually, with a little help from Eddie and the doctor Claude got to his feet. At one point the doctor and Eddie both noticed a distinct grimace of pain on Claude's face. The pain must have brought Claude out of his stupor slightly as once on his feet his eyes seemed to focus a little and turning to Eddie he muttered very softly 'It hurts.'

Eddie wasn't sure if he felt relief or distaste at the pathetic tone of Claude's voice, but he managed to hold himself in check and calmly say 'It's okay the doctor will help you, let's just get you into the guest room and you can have a lie down.' Claude gave a little nod and with assistance from Eddie and Doctor Gordon he shuffled his way slowly across the room.

Mason strode ahead and opened the doors for them and with a little effort they managed to get Claude into the first, smaller bedroom and lain down on the bed. The room was a lot smaller than the one they had just left but it was light and airy due a large window matching the two in the room next door. The room was painted in an off-white colour with matching, plush carpet. It was sparsely, but elegantly furnished with a neatly made single bed, bedside table, small chests of draws and a small wardrobe all in antique pine. There was art upon the walls of this room too only in this case only three subtle and exceptionally well painted watercolours. Opposite the window at the back of the room was a door which led to a small, white tiled shower room. The room next door was pretty much the same but larger and with two beds, bedside tables, and a larger wardrobe.

Mason stood in the doorway watching as Claude was settled. Then Sofia entered the room and handed the doctor his black bag which she had carried through for him after putting down her un-drunk cup of coffee. He thanked her, placed it on the small table by the bed, opened it and began to rummage inside. Sofia turned to Eddie.

'Could you stay with the doctor whilst he does his examination please Eddie whilst Mason and I get a few other things sorted.'

Eddie nodded his agreement though in some ways the last thing he wanted to do was stay in that room. On the other hand though he felt a need to stay for the doctor's sake rather than Claude's as the doctor would be no match for Claude if he got difficult, or god help them, violent.

'We'll be fine.' He said in an effort to reassure himself as much as Sofia.

'Good, thank you Eddie.'

Eddie glanced at Mason then and could see all that he was feeling reflected in his friends dark eyes. They silently acknowledged these shared feelings before Mason turned and left the room with Sofia gently closing the door behind them.

Once back in the office Mason collapsed into the armchair next to the one Claude had been sat in and rubbed at his tired eyes. Sofia went to the left-hand window and stood looking out onto the driveway.

'We need to have that chat as soon as possible' she said softly and turned a little to face Mason. 'When the doctor has gone we need time alone to discuss 'things'.'

Mason nodded. 'Yes, we do, but I feel bad that Eddie can't be included. I couldn't have coped today without him; the guy has been amazing.'

'I know, and I agree he's done a great job, but he can't be involved in this part, you know that. Even if we did take him into our confidence, which as you know is totally against Foundation policy, it would take too long to explain, not to mention how long it would take him to digest the information, and that's time we don't have Mason.'

'I understand' replied Mason quietly.

'We cannot discuss things properly yet' continued Sofia 'Eddie or the doctor could walk back in at any moment, but there is one thing you can tell me now.'

'What's that?'

'Which one are you Mason?'

He smiled and answered her.

'I thought so' she said, 'Now quickly, tell me about the others.'

By the time Eddie and Doctor Gordon emerged from the guest room twenty minutes later Mason had given Sofia the relevant information on each of his friends and they had talked briefly about the important task they had ahead of them. Once the doctor left they would tell Eddie as much of the plan as Foundation rules would allow. Then after he did a few chores they would insist he got some rest whilst they proceeded with their task.

Mason had never seen his friend stressed before, but he knew from the look on Eddie's face as he came back into the room that that was what he was feeling. He also knew that Eddie would read the same in his own expression and demeanour. If Sofia was stressed she was hiding it well, and as for the doctor he was the lucky one, he didn't know enough to be stressed. In fact, he seemed almost cheerful as he related the status of his patient to Sofia.

'You'll be happy to know that your friend has sustained no life-threatening injuries, however, he does have a badly bruised left hip and knee from where he was struck by the vehicle. He also has a few other bruises and scrapes, probably from landing and rolling across your driveway. Strangely, I also found several splinters of wood in both his hands.'

As he was focused mainly on Sofia as he talked the doctor did not see Mason flinch at the mention of the splinters, nor the sick look that passed across his face as his mind flashed back to the blood-stained tree branch lying next to the battered bodies of his friends. Therefore, unaware of the impact his words were having the doctor continued.

'I have cleaned and disinfected the scrapes and removed the splinters. The bruising is quite severe but there isn't much I can do about that. I'm afraid the poor man began to get a little agitated as I examined him. The shock had obviously started to wear off which meant that the pain was starting to register. He was moaning and muttering about hurting and getting a little distressed so I thought it best in light of the physical pain and the emotional distress to sedate him. I've given him a pretty strong dose; he should sleep for a good six to eight hours.'

'Thank you Doctor Gordon' said Sofia sounding relieved 'we really appreciate your help.'

'You are most welcome Miss Vecchini, most welcome. I am going to leave you some strong pain killers for him plus a few more sedatives in case they are needed. He needs to stay in bed for a day or two. As to his mental state when he wakes up I'm afraid that's not my field. If it's just shock I'm sure he'll be fine in no time, but I have a feeling it's more than that. I assume the Foundation employs other doctors who can help him in that respect?'

'Yes, we do doctor, don't worry I'll make sure he gets all the care he needs.'

'Good, good. Well then I believe there is another sad matter you need my help with before I go.'

'Yes, as discussed briefly on the telephone earlier the unfortunate incident that started off today's terrible events resulted in the death of one of the other residents. He fell down the stairs whilst trying to carry a large canvas down. We put him in the room across the hall so if you would follow me.'

Sofia led the doctor from the room leaving Eddie and Mason in the office. She returned almost immediately leaving the doctor to his examination and paperwork.

They waited in silence, each lost in their own thoughts, each fighting their rising fears and worries. Could Claude's crimes really be hidden? Should they be? They all knew they had to be, especially Sofia and Mason as they knew exactly what was at stake here, they also knew that there was only one way to deal with it, and that was to let 'The Somnium Foundation' do what they had done for centuries, keep their secrets and keep them safe.

They needn't have worried in regard to the doctor. He believed their story about Mahesh's death, and his brief examination of the body corroborated their story as far as he could tell and so he did not hesitate to list the death as accidental.

The doctor returned to the office and went over the formalities with Sofia. Then, after assuring Sofia that he would return anytime if needed to help with Claude he left. Sofia then made one quick call to arrange for Mahesh's body to be collected and taken to a Foundation funeral home nearby as soon as possible. Once that was done the three of them moved to the kitchen for some much-needed sustenance.

The kitchen was at the back of the house directly behind the lounge / art room. It ran the same length as the lounge with, again, two sash windows, but it was smaller in width. Still, it was a large room, with fitted cupboards, granite worktops, a six-burner oven, a large, American style fridge, and all the other mod cons. There was also a utility room attached containing two top of the range washing machines, a tumble dryer and a chest freezer, and adjoining that a small downstairs toilet. To the right-hand side there was a large, round, wooden table and six chairs, which was where the residents sat to eat most of their meals together. The floor was covered with grey slate paving slabs and the walls were painted white.

Sofia and Mason sat down at the table whilst Eddie rummaged in the cupboards and fridge and then began to make them all sandwiches. None of them had eaten since breakfast their appetites having been dimmed by the day's traumatic events, but now they found it returning with a vengeance. Plus, appetite or not the three of them knew they needed to keep their strength up in order to cope with the trials of the coming days.

As they ate Sofia explained their plan of action (as far as she could) to Eddie. As expected he was not happy about being told to rest whilst they worked on. However, once it was explained to him what would be expected of him over the next few days he saw the wisdom of the plan and agreed to it. He couldn't help but feel afraid for his friend, however. Mason looked just as tired as he felt yet rest was apparently out of the question for him and Sofia, for several hours at least. Even with his limited knowledge of what exactly Mason needed to accomplish over the next few hours he knew his friend faced a difficult task. He also knew it was a task he regrettably did not have the 'skills' to help him with. A lot was riding on his friends shoulders and although he had every confidence in Mason's 'abilities' he knew that Mason was about to attempt something alone that was usually taken on by a group of equally talented people and Eddie feared it would be too much for him. Although Sofia would be there to help he had no idea what 'talent' if any she would bring to the situation.

After their meal was over, Eddie left them to their 'work' and set off to get on with his own chores. He had a van to unload, check for damages and put in the garage. He would also put Sofia's car in the garage for her, then prepare the double guest room adjoining the lounge for her stay. He also needed to clean the paint off the stairs. Then before retiring to his room to rest he would make a brief visit to the guest room to check that Claude was still sleeping soundly.

Once Eddie had left the room Sofia and Eddie were free to talk. Sofia told him of the dream that had set her on her journey to them confirming his faith in her inbred 'talent' and proving she had a good connection to their group and that her talent was strong. He needed as much help as possible and was now reassured that Sofia was the best person to give him that help.

They talked a while longer and then with their plans fully made Sofia stood at the kitchen window watching as Mason walked down the sloping lawn at the back of the house towards the darkening woodland below. He was headed to a place the inhabitants of The Gateway called the Factory, a place that only he and his friends could go. A Place that held a secret.

Once he was out of sight she headed for the guest room from where she would do what she could to help Mason before getting some sleep in preparation for the days ahead.

It is resting and making plans. It is pleased with what It has achieved so far but the effort needed has taken Its toll. It is tired, so tired. It has found a place to hide and is again dwelling on the fact that It cannot remember Its name. It feels that It deserves to have a name and therefore decides to give itself one.

And the name It gives Itself is Talionis.

CHAPTER 3

DAY 2 - MORE HELP

Wings flutter gently against his skin, many, many wings brush against his body, and there, that face. The deep brown eyes, the dark, dark skin and that dazzling smile.
'What do you want?' he cries

Max Millig cried out in his sleep waking himself up in the process. He was lying on his back, his arms flung above his head and the sheets twisted around the bottom half of his body.

Wow, that had been one hell of a dream. So vivid, and yet what the hell was it about? He lay blinking at the ceiling for a minute or two recalling the dream and waiting.

He knew what was coming next and he both craved and dreaded it.

The feeling started in the pit of his stomach, reached out tendrils to make his fingers twitch and then fizzed upward to explode inside his head. He squeezed his eyes shut in an attempt to stop the flow of images. He needed sleep. But it was no use, sleep would not come now. Reluctantly he gave in to the feeling.

By the time he'd untangled himself from the sheets however fanaticism had overtaken him and he found himself bounding across the hallway and flinging open the door to his workroom.

As soon as he had the equipment and materials ready he ploughed into the wet clay using skilled hands to mould a face that was him, but not his.

Several hours later Max was sat on his sofa with a cup of tea and a cigarette. He wasn't a big smoker but enjoyed a roll up every now and then and was puffing on one now as he took a well-earned rest and reflected on his days' work. His white t-shirt was covered with dried smears of clay, as were his pyjama trousers. There were also bits of clay dispersed throughout his mess of long, light brown hair, the odd small piece stuck to his short beard, and a spatter or two on his glasses but Max was unconcerned, the mess never bothered him.

There were three busts of clay sitting in his workroom, and none of them were right. But then what did he mean by that anyway? Why did he feel that somehow it was his face that he was trying to create when clearly it was not for the most part? The dominant face in the clay was the face from his dream. Yes, he knew that and yet he could barely remember what that face had looked like now. Yet he had busts of it upstairs.

Max reluctantly, and painfully got up from the sofa. He ached all over and he was very tired, but he just had to go and look at his work again.

Fighting the urge to close his eyes Max made himself study the three faces. He found them somewhat disturbing. It was like looking at special effect models from a movie of Jekyll and Hyde or something. The busts seemed to be a strange mix of two faces, Max's own face and that of the man in his dream.

The first bust mostly resembled the man in the dream. Or at least that's what he assumed as his dream had faded almost completely now. The third bust mostly resembled Max and the bust in between seemed to be a strange mix of the two. It was kind of creepy.

Max let out a breath he hadn't realised he was holding. This was beginning to really freak him out. But that was enough for one day; it was time for bed and hopefully no more strange dreams.

It was early morning and Mason was headed for his bed or at least a different bed to the one he'd spent the night in. The first stage had been thankfully easy and although he knew things would get much harder Mason was relived. He had help, not as much as he would normally have had but help just the same. And he had belief, in himself and in those who were helping him. Things had started well and now he could rest a while. The next few nights would be tough, but he had hope how, and a determination to succeed. He would succeed. He had to.

As Mason was laying down to rest Eddie was headed to the guest room to check on Claude. The sedatives the doctor had given him would have worn off by now and Claude would surely be thirsty if not hungry and so Eddie had prepared him a mug of tea and some toast, he was also taking some water and the pills the doctor had given them. After eating and drinking it was thought best that Claude should be sedated again. Sofia was in the office on the phone as usual and he gave her a little smile and nod hello as he passed. She gave him a returning smile as she continued to talk.

When Eddie entered the room he was relieved to see that Claude was still in bed. As he approached though he realised that the man was not asleep. He lay on his back and was staring up at the celling, his eyes glassy and his body rigid with tension. Eddie placed the tray on the bedside table and stood looking down at Claude. The man didn't seem to register that he was there and he didn't react when Eddie said hello and asked how he was feeling so he tried wafting his hand in his eye line. At first he didn't even blink but then he suddenly snapped out of the seeming trance and turning his head he focused his still glassy eyes on Eddie.

'Hey there, I brought you some tea and toast if you're up to it. Do you think you can sit up?'

Again Claude was slow to react but he did in the end start to try to sit up. Eddie helped him a little, placing the pillows behind his head to make him comfortable. Once he seemed settled he carefully handed him the mug of tea and it was taken from him by slightly unsteady hands. Claude took a tentative few sips and then drained most of the mug before handing it back to Eddie who then tried him with the toast. Claude managed to finish the one slice but didn't appear interested in another so Eddie handed back the mug of tea for him to finish. Eddie asked him again how he was feeling but again he received no answer.

When he had finished his tea Eddie asked him if he needed the toilet and although he still did not speak he did appear to give a little nod and so with Eddie's help he got up from the bed and walked slowly to the bathroom. He thankfully managed to go in by himself whilst Eddie stood outside the open door with his back turned and when he heard the toilet flush he helped the man back to bed.

'I have some more tablets for you,' he said once he had him settled back in the bed 'they'll help with any pain you may be having and you can go back to sleep, would you like them?'

This time the reaction was quicker as his hand came up to accept the tablets followed by the glass of water.

'You should drink all the water too, if you can't manage to eat much you should at least keep hydrated.'

The patient did as he was told much to Eddie's relief, but then as Eddie tried to get him to lay back down to sleep Claude began to resist him and then he spoke.

'It wasn't me'

The words were faint, but Eddie heard them. And for the first time since Claude had been locked in that room he was looking straight at Eddie. It was kind or eerie.

'Did you say something Claude?' he asked

'I didn't do it'

This time the words were louder and unmistakeable. Eddie moved nearer and before he could say anything his friend repeated the phrase only even louder this time and now he appeared to be getting a little agitated.

'It's ok Claude, stay calm, I'm listening. You didn't do what?'

'I didn't hurt my friends, it wasn't me.'

'No? Then who was it? Who hurt them?'

'The thing, the thing in my mind.'

Okay, this was getting a little weird now, Eddie was not cut out for this sort of thing, what should he say? What should he do?

'The thing, the thing, the thing, the thing!' as he spoke Claude began to hit himself in the side of the head with the palm of his hand as if trying to dislodge something.

Eddie slowly reached for his friends hand and gently pulled it away from his head. Claude let him do it, then looking straight into his eyes he said 'Help me Eddie' then he went limp, his eyes closed, his chin on his chest. Eddie was more than a little disconcerted by this and could not think what to do. Claude's breathing had been heavy and quick but appeared to be slowing now as the pills began to take effect. With a little difficulty he managed to lay Claude down and get him into what looked like a comfortable position and then, when he was sure the man was definitely asleep he picked up his tray and left the room making sure to lock the door.

'How's Claude?' asked Sofia as Eddie came into the office.

He told her what had happened hating the pained expression his news caused.

'What happened to that man, and what on earth does he mean by 'the thing' in his head? His mind appears to be very damaged.'

'I know, it's not good, the sooner they find him professional help the better if you ask me.'

'I'll phone the Foundation and update them and see where they are with their plans, we really do need them to take him off our hands, it's not helping anyone having him here' she said already reaching for the phone.

Whilst she made her call Eddie took the tray back to the kitchen and made them both a cup of coffee.

When Eddie entered the office with her coffee Sofia was just finishing her call.

'I made you a coffee, thought you might need it.'

'That's very thoughtful of you, thanks.'

'No problem. What did they say?'

'They are going to send an ambulance to pick up Claude as soon as they can but they need to make a few arrangements first. As I'm sure you understand it's a tricky situation with the things that Claude knows they can't just send him anywhere as in his state who knows what he might say.

Although the Foundation run a lot of Medical facilities, they don't have much in the way of psychiatric care, to be honest I think it's not really something that's been much needed in the past. Anyway, they have decided on a suitable facility but they just have to make sure that they have trusted staff in place to look after him twenty four hours, but basically Claude will be off our hands by this evening which I'm sure you'll agree is a relief.'

'Yeah, I really don't feel equipped to look after him, I don't have the skills needed plus I have conflicting feelings whenever I'm with the man, he's a friend and I want to help him but then I remember what he did and it makes me sick to my stomach and I just want to shake him until he tells me why he did it.'

'I totally understand and so this is best all around. I have other news too. The Foundation are sending us a couple of people to help out, they're kind of temporary replacements for Gina and Blake and although they can't help Mason directly they will lighten his load which will help a lot. They should be here mid-afternoon.'

'Okay great, I'm sure Mason will appreciate any help they can give him.'

After a brief discussion they decided that the new arrivals could put their things in the twin guest room to start with and then once Claude was gone if they'd rather have separate rooms then Eddie could clean the single room up so one of them could use that.

So with the brief discussion over Eddie headed upstairs to continue his work. It was now his sad duty to clear Mahesh's room and also Claude's room plus the room that Gina and Blake shared. Mahesh could never return and even though it was hoped Gina and Blake would recover they would never return here either. And as for Claude who knew what would happen to him. Others would arrive soon to take their place and so the rooms needed to be prepared for them. It was something that would have happened someday in the not too distant future anyway but the circumstance of their early departure made it a depressing task.

As Eddie made a start on Mahesh's room Sofia was answering the phone. She'd expected it to be Barbara again with more news / instructions and so was a little shocked to hear a male voice instead.

'Hello Sofia, this is Cedric Neale, how are things going your end?'

'Its errr it's going as well as can be expected' she stuttered as little taken aback by the identity of the caller.

Cedric Neale was the Head of the British division of The Somnium Foundation and therefore her boss. She had of course met the man but hadn't really had many dealings with him during her time at the Foundation. He was a very important man and she wondered what warranted a call from the big boss now when up to that point things had been left to her and Barbara.

'Good, good, it's a terrible business but I'm sure that you and Barbara are managing things well.'

'Thank you Sir.'

'Now then, I'm calling to tell you about another problem we are having to deal with. It's pretty serious I'm afraid, but don't worry I'm not expecting you to do anything, you have enough on your plate as it is, I just wanted you to be aware of what's happening.'

'Thank you Sir' she was repeating herself but couldn't think what else to say. Her heart was beating fast at the thought of another 'serious' problem and it only got worse as Cedric Neale continued.

'Unfortunately there has been another death. Rita Deacon died on Saturday afternoon. It was natural causes; the poor woman had a massive stroke. As you would expect William took his wife's death very badly, in fact the poor man was so bereft that he did nothing for over twenty-four hours. We assume he spent that time just sitting with his wife's body in a state of shock and severe grief until he finally called us on Sunday evening.'

'That's terrible, the poor man.' Sofia felt she should say something however inadequate.

'Yes, quite. Tragic as the poor woman's death is the consequences of her passing and her husband's severe reaction make it all the more devastating.'

'Oh my god' gasped Sofia as she realised the implications of what her boss was telling her.

'We do not know the full details but we believe that before the stroke that killed her Rita may have suffered a mini stroke and that this may have rendered her unfit to carry out her duties to the full extent' he continued 'in her weakened state she was vulnerable to suggestion, and then with Rita gone and William for all intents and purposes shut down their guard was completely down and well the inevitable happened.'

'It got out?'

'Yes I'm afraid so, their 'charge' escaped sometime on Saturday we think. William is so devastated it was a little hard to get any sense out of him. We are of course doing all we can to locate the escapee but as you can appreciate it is a very difficult task.'

'Do you need me for anything?'

'No, no, as I said you have enough to do, I just felt you needed to be aware of the situation as unfortunately we need to concentrate all the resources we can on containing this situation, therefore, we may not be able to help with yours as much as we would have liked.'

'It's okay, I understand.'

'Barbara will still be available to help you and I'm not saying we can't help you in other ways, I'm just warning you how things are here at the moment.'

'I appreciate that Sir, thank you.'

'I have every faith in you Sofia, and I know you will do a good job even under these difficult circumstances. I wish you good luck and I will make sure you are advised of any progress we make.'

'Thank you Sir.'

'Well, I will say goodbye then, and hopefully next time we speak I will have better news.'

'Goodbye Sir and good luck to you too.'

'Thank you, goodbye.'

Sofia replaced the receiver and slumped back in the chair. The implications of what she had just been told were staggering. But as her boss had said she had enough to deal with herself, there were plenty of other capable people dealing with the bigger problem; her job was to deal with The Gateway problem as best she could.

She decided she wouldn't tell Mason about this, he didn't need to know, he needed to concentrate on his own task and she couldn't tell Eddie. She would just put it to the back of her mind and get on with things. She had a job to do and it was time she got back to it.

Phoebe Wray stood on the gravel driveway staring up at the house as the Foundation driver retrieved her and her companion's bags from the car boot.

'It's so beautiful' she said

'Hmmm' said her companion unimpressed.

Phoebe had to laugh; Mark Lau never seemed impressed by anything. Or if he did he didn't show it. They had spent most of the journey in silence; but with neither of them being much of a talker this was not unusual. Phoebe had spent most of the time reading and Mark playing a game on his tablet. What little conversation that had passed between them had obviously been about where they were headed and to what.

The pair had been to The Gateway before but under slightly different circumstances. They had of course been briefed and knew that one person had died and three were incapacitated but they had not been given details. As far as their 'job' was concerned they knew more, how could they not. Their role within the Somnium Foundation was a transient one. They were basically what in other lines of work would be called a temp. When anyone at one of the art communes was long term sick or needed to leave the commune for more than a day they were sent in as 'cover'. Between these spells of 'cover' they travelled round the different communes staying in each one for a week or two to help out, lightening the 'workload' of the other inhabitants for a short time. Or maybe heightening it was more accurate.

The pair had been in the 'job' for just over a year and in that time they had been to The Gateway three times. They were of course aware of its special circumstance and so they were both feeling a little apprehensive about what to expect, but at the same time were a little excited. Their job would basically be the same as usual but they felt things would be a little more intense on this one.

The new arrivals were not a couple in the romantic sense but were very close, more like brother and sister. Not that they looked like brother and sister as although they were both tall and slim their colouring differed dramatically. Phoebe had very long, almost white blonde hair whereas Marks was jet black although he did also wear it long. Phoebe's eyes were large and pale blue and Marks were smaller and black/brown. Their demeanour was very similar though. Both were quiet and a little shy though always pleasant and friendly.

Like the commune occupants they visited they both had considerable artistic talents. Phoebe was a gifted classical pianist with a beautiful soprano voice, and Mark painted amazing, and usually very large, abstract works and was also a talented cartoonist. Along with their other talent this made them an important part of the Somnium Foundation.

Thanking the Foundation driver they picked up their bags and headed towards the house. As they approached the front door was opened by an attractive woman with dark hair.

'Hello, my names Sofia Vecchini' she said, 'I'm the Marshal for this site.'

They introduced themselves and then followed her inside. Sofia took them into the Office.

'Take a seat' she said indicating two comfy looking armchairs 'I'm going to go and find Eddie who I believe you know from your previous visits. He can give you a hand with your luggage and then once you're settled in we can have a chat.'

When Eddie arrived he greeted the new arrivals and then carried their bags to their room apologising about them having to share but assuring them it was temporary and that the reason would be explained to them shortly. They told him they were fine sharing for now and so he left them to settle in telling them to come to the kitchen when they were ready and he would make them all some lunch.

Over lunch Sofia explained about the occupant of the other guest room. She decided to tell them the truth, it was only fair. As expected they were very shocked and upset about what Claude had done and she quickly assured them he was no threat now as he was sedated and locked in the room and that it was temporary as the Foundation were sending an ambulance later that day to transport Claude to a place more suited to his needs.

As they were finishing their food Mason entered the kitchen. He had rested as best he could but was aware the new arrivals were due so had come downstairs to say hello to the newcomers. The others stayed around whilst Eddie made Mason something to eat and then Eddie headed upstairs to continue his work whilst the other four stayed sat at the table for more talk.

'We're so happy and grateful to have you here' said Mason 'I know you can't help me directly with what I need to do but your help is very much needed elsewhere and what you do will ease my load'

'That's what we're here for' said Phoebe 'and we are more than happy to help.'

'We'll let you settle in a little longer, you can go to the lounge and relax whilst I get an update from Sofia and then I can take you to the Factory and we can get to work.'

'Oh yeah that's right you guys call it the Factory, very tongue in cheek' commented Mark as he and Phoebe got up. Once the young couple had left Sofia updated Mason on what was happening regarding Claude and he was understandably relieved having had similar mixed feeling for the man as Eddie had. As planned Sofia did not tell him about the call from Cedric Neale. Then with their little update over Mason headed out to the Factory with Mark and Phoebe. After making a brief call to Barbara to confirm the new arrivals were settling in okay Sofia headed upstairs to see if Eddie needed her help for a bit.

A few hours later when the ambulance arrived for Claude Sofia called Eddie and he took a break from his work to come and unlock the door then stood with Sofia in the office as the paramedics wheeled the still sedated man through the office and out to the ambulance. The pair followed them out, said their thanks and they were off, thankfully taking one of their burdens with them. Hopefully Claude would get the help he needed and they would have answers to the reasons for his actions.

Whilst Claude was being taken away Mason was hard at work along with his two new 'helpers'. Thankfully the newcomers connected to their 'task' quickly and easily and so Mason was able to concentrate all his energies on his own task. Things should get easier now with any luck.

CHAPTER 4

DAY 3 - MAX

He hears a sound like the beating of wings. He feels weightless. He feels the wind against his skin. He sees nothing but whiteness. He is flying. He feels a jolt. And then he is falling. Tumbling through the air, plummeting. Suddenly his fall is broken. Many arms hold him. He looks to his left into the beautiful, cloudy green eyes of a young, dark haired woman. She smiles. Next to her stands a dark-haired young man with eyes that seem to change from brown to green and back again. The young man also smiles. Their smiles radiate warmth and love. He looks to his right into the friendly face of a woman with fiery red hair, her knowing smile soothes him. Beside her stands an intimidating looking man with dark eyes and a probing gaze. He radiates strength so he feels safe. He looks to the front. And finds himself staring into the dark eyes of the one who is him, but not him.

'Join them' the man says.

This time Max Millig awoke more slowly. No shouting himself awake. It was another strange dream but this time he felt calmer. He lay staring at the ceiling, his mind wandering. He should be used to strange dreams by now, he'd had enough of them over the years, but then these dreams were strange in a different way, more real, more meaningful somehow. And also he was sure that these two dreams had been the only ones he'd had over the last two nights. Usually he woke up with the vague memoires of a whole nights worth of dreams spinning through his head with the dream he woke from being the clearest.

He had developed a bit of a love hate relationship with his dream 'habits' over the years. On the one hand he enjoyed his dreams, they were crazily entertaining to look back on most of the time, and some even inspired his work as a sculptor. On the other hand he never woke up totally refreshed, all that dreaming wore him out, he was sure of it.

Well, the dream he'd dreamt the morning before had definitely inspired his work only this time it had been extra intense, it was on a new level and he couldn't understand why. There were three slightly disturbing busts sitting in his workroom right now to prove it.

Max had spent all of the day before in his workroom working on those three busts, or the 'Jekyll and Hyde Trio' as he now thought of them. Unlike his first dream however this one didn't seem to be fading. The face of the man at the end of the dream was still crystal clear in his mind, and he was now convinced that this man was the same one from the other dream, the same man whose image he had created in clay. The same man whose image he had then merged with his own to make the second sculpture before finally sculpting an idealised yet recognisable representation of himself. This was all a little too weird even for him. And now he felt it happening again. The faces of the young man and woman from his latest dream were beginning to crystallise in his mind and as they did the old familiar feeling in the pit of his stomach began to make itself known.

Max had never understood why his need to sculpt had always manifested itself in such a physical way. He'd tried to explain the feeling to his parents once. They'd just looked at him strangely and then changed the subject. He'd never tried to explain himself to anyone again after that.

Fighting the impulse to rush Max made himself get up slowly and get changed into his 'working' clothes before entering his workroom. He considered trying to pop downstairs for a bit of breakfast before starting work, but the pull was too strong.

His workroom was a mess as usual, but he didn't care. The three finished busts sat on his 'drying bench' on the left had side of the room next to his small kiln. On the right-hand side was his work bench underneath which he kept his packs of clay, spare armatures and other tools. Luckily, he made sure he was always well stocked as he never knew when the urge to sculpt would take hold and it would be a nightmare if a two-hour round trip to the supply shop was needed before he could start work. He did, however, make a mental note to visit the shop as soon as possible as after five busts his clay supply would be getting low.

He decided to start with the young woman. Her beautiful, long hair would be a challenge, but then he liked a challenge. He also found himself extra excited by this project. He still found the 'Jekyll and Hyde Trio' a little disturbing, but this young couple were much more fun, and they were definitely a couple, he was sure of that. Within minutes Max was happily lost in his work.

CHAPTER 5

DAY 3 - MARY

Suddenly they were just there.

There were four of them, one woman and three men. All four of them gave off a great sense of power. She felt drawn to them, connected. They form a circle around her. They are silent. She turns from one to the other, trying to see their faces. She cannot make them out clearly, they are in shadow. 'What do I do?' she asks them. The figures shimmer. One moves. And suddenly he is in front of her. He is tall and slim with broad shoulders. His hair is dark, his face unclear, shadowed. Except for his eyes, which gaze into hers. They are brown, no green, now brown again. 'Let me help you'' he says.

Then he moves to stand behind her. A shiver of pleasure passes through her as he places his hands upon her shoulders. 'This way' he says, as he guides her forward towards one of the surrounding figures. The figure is clearer now as she gets nearer. It is a man. She looks up to meet his dark gaze. She reaches up her hand to gently touch the curved scar upon his face. 'Who are you?' she asks him.

'I am the Gatekeeper' he replies.

The hands upon her shoulders guide her on to the next person. She faces a slim man with long, light brown hair, and a neat beard. She reaches up and places a hand upon his shoulder. 'Who are you?' she asks

'I am the Dreamcatcher' he replies.

Again she is guided by the strong hands upon her shoulders. The next shadowy figure awaits. The figure becomes clear and she stands face to face with a full-figured woman who has pale, freckled skin and beautiful red hair. She holds out her arms and embraces the woman. 'Who are you?'' she asks.

'I am the Seer of Dreams' the woman replies.

This is our beginning she thinks.

Mary Temple woke from her dream feeling relaxed but puzzled. What an unusual dream. The focus of the dream had undoubtedly been the strangers. They had seemed so real, so recognised yet at the same time unknown. She had no clear picture of their faces now, even his, yet she'd touched him, connected with him on some deep, unconscious level. She had stared into his eyes, and yet now she could not remember what colour they were. Had they continually changed colour? No, that was absurd.

She had dreamt about people she didn't know plenty of times before, had felt a connection with them for a brief period after the dream even, but never like this. This went deeper. She had the feeling this dream was telling her something important. There was a truth to this dream, to the feelings it had evoked in her. But somehow this truth, whatever it was, eluded her. How could she analyse a feeling that was rapidly fading, a feeling that she couldn't accurately identify? It was so frustrating.

'The strangers are real'

The phrase suddenly popped into her head and stuck, echoing in her mind over and over.

Mary groaned and pressed the heels of her hands to her eyes. This was just too strange. But there was no time to dwell on it now, here alarm was due to go off any minute then it was a quick shower and off to work.

'Had any good dreams lately?' Stella asked.

Mary continued shelving the thriller paperbacks her colleague handed her as she considered her answer. Should she tell Stella about the strange dream she'd had that morning? The dream that had been playing on her mind ever since she'd had it. No, it didn't feel right somehow. This particular dream was not for sharing. At least not with Stella anyway.

'No, not really' she found herself saying.

'Oh that's a shame, I like to hear your dreams, you always remember them so well. I don't have many dreams at all myself.'

'Yes you do, you just don't remember them that's all.'

How many times had she said that to people? Was she the only person who ever remembered her dreams these days? Was she some kind of freak, or were they the ones with the problem?

A Dreamfreak, that's what she was, it was a name that she'd given herself a while ago, but she hadn't told anyone that, they'd just think she was weird. She'd always had vivid and plentiful dreams; no-one she knew dreamt like she did and she'd always wondered why. She also wondered what her dreams meant.

In her early teens she'd read a load of books on the meaning of dreams. Then she'd written a dream diary and tried to translate them using the book definitions, but dreams were too complex to be defined by the simple little explanations in the books, at least her dreams were. So she'd given up and just enjoyed them for a while.

As she grew older and her love of writing really kicked in she realised that a lot of the imagery in the poetry she wrote came from her dreams. She began to write a dream diary again which she studied and tried to make sense of. She realised that some of the things she dreamt were just interpretations of things she was going through; things that had happened or she knew were going to happen that were troubling. She decided that she had these dreams as a way of processing these troubling things, of helping her through them. So – to her – this meant that her dreams gave her inspiration and they helped her get through her waking life. She had a feeling there was more to it than that but couldn't work out what so she decided not to worry about it. She'd enjoy her dreams, take what she wanted from them and be happy with that.

Stella sighed bringing Mary back to their conversation.

'I wish I did remember my dreams like you Mary, then maybe I could write poetry too.'

Mary smiled at her colleague.

'I wouldn't worry Stella, you have other talents, you don't need poetry.'

Stella giggled. Mary raised her eyebrows comically and giggled too. She had to laugh at Stella's apparent jealousy of her poetry writing as although Stella knew she wrote she had never once expressed an interest in reading any of Mary's poems. She told people that Mary was a great poet but showed no interest in finding out if this was actually true.

Mary had worked at the book shop for a little over five years now, Stella for nearly three. They were almost the same age, Mary at 26 being the slightly older of the two. The two women did the same job but each approached their work in very different ways. Mary's approach was based on a love of books, Stella's on a love of flirting and socialising. Stella could chat to anyone and flirted outrageously with any attractive male customers, she even managed to get the odd date from it. Mary was good with the customers in a more professional way. She could talk to anyone but only if it was about books. She felt confident helping people find what they wanted, giving advice and making recommendations but she found it difficult to make small talk especially with the attractive male customers. She envied Stella's confidence and relaxed, friendly manner.

Stella loved it when the shop was full of people, when it was loud and chaotic, but Mary preferred the quieter times when she could take time to help a customer. The chain store mentality suited Stella but Mary would have preferred to work in a dusty old-fashioned bookstore where she could read a book herself when it was quiet. It wasn't that she was lazy, in fact it was Stella who would duck out of her share of the scut work whenever she could get away with it, Mary would just prefer the less sterile, bookish atmosphere of the standalone bookstore.

The two young women couldn't have been more unalike in looks either. Mary was 5' 2' with a petite but curvy figure, long, wavy dark auburn hair and pale grey/green eyes. Stella on the other hand was 5' 8' with long perfectly styled blonde hair, sparkling blue eyes and a perfect, slim figure. They both wore the bookstore uniform of logoed black polo shirt and black jeans but whilst Mary paired hers with doctor martin boots Stella alternated through several pairs of high fashion shoes all with high heels. Stella also had an extensive collection of fashion jewellery and spent a lot of time each morning on her perfect make up whereas Mary wore only a watch and a little mascara and eye liner.

Despite their differences however, the two women got on well, although they didn't socialise outside the workplace.

'Oooh, talking of talent' said Stella 'that guy over by the sports section looks like he needs some help' and with that she set off to offer the lucky guy her help leaving Mary to finish rearranging the paperback bestseller section. Another talent of Stella's, leaving Mary to do the work whilst she had the fun.

For the next couple of hours Mary was kept pretty busy by customers and scut work but when she finally had a quieter moment her mind returned to her dream that morning and in particular the guy in her dream and a shiver of pleasure coursed through her. Who was he? Was he real? Would she dream of him again? And what about the others, and those strange words/names – The Gatekeeper, The Seer of Dreams, The Dreamcatcher, what the hell was that about?

Suddenly she felt a familiar urge. She started to get 'words in her head'. This was a fairly normal event, after all she was a poet and the 'muse' could hit at any time, but today it felt different. As the words began to form sentences in her mind Mary began to get agitated. She was desperate for a pen and paper, afraid that if she didn't get the words written down she would lose them. This had happened to her many times before, but not with this intensity. She checked her watch, ten minutes until lunchtime, she could cope with that, just.

The ten minutes had felt more like thirty but finally Mary was headed to the door behind the counter that led to the staff room. Pulling her bag out from under the staff room coffee table she collapsed into one of the worn armchairs set around it. Placing the bag on her lap she rummaged around inside for her notebook and pen. Once she had them she tossed the bag carelessly to the floor and opened the notebook in her lap. Her hand shook a little as she put pen to paper.

The words flowed easier than they had ever done, and their subject was unlike anything else she'd ever written. They meant something these words; they were important somehow. Was that big headed of her? To be honest she didn't really care. She was pleased with the three poems she had written and it felt good right then and that was important. Whatever the dream was about it was having a positive effect on her and that could only be a good thing.

This is what she had written.

He is the Gatekeeper of Dreams,
He has power,
And lets only the brave in.
You have to be strong,
To face the dreams that he brings,
Only souls that can learn,
May know the secrets he keeps.
If your spirit is weak,
He must stand guard,
And not let you in.

He is the Dreamcatcher,
Angel of daring and fear,
Who can teach you to fly,
Help your soul grow its wings.
He'll show you places to hide,
And keep you safe from your Demons.
If you fall he wakes you,
And he wakes you to scream.
If he fails in his duty,
You will never wake again.

She is the Seer of Dreams,
Premonition she brings.
Giving warnings of danger,
Showing you future things.
She'll lead you along paths,
To places and people of dreams,
Places you may soon visit,
People you are destined to meet.
And she'll help fill your mind,
With creative things.

After reading back the poems Mary realised that there wasn't a poem that related to the guy that had been the main focus of her dreams which seemed a little strange, but then it was all strange so why worry about it.

CHAPTER 6

DAY 3 – AARON

He stands in the middle as they circle around him. 'Who are you?' he asks but they just smile at him. There are three of them, three strangers, circling. Their mouths move, but he hears nothing. The circle breaks and another stranger walks toward him. She stops in front of him. He meets her gaze and is lost, falling as he sinks deep into large, cloudy, green eyes. His focus gradually returns and his gaze moves to take her all in. She has a petite, curvy figure and long auburn hair. Her face is shadowed, but her beautiful eyes are clear. For long seconds they stare at each other. He knows that he must guide her. 'Let me help you' he says. Then he reluctantly breaks her gaze and moves to stand behind her. He places his hands upon her shoulders and their first touch sends shivers of pleasure all through his body. 'This way' he says and he guides her towards the first of the circle of figures. They stand before a man. He has short, dark hair with a smattering of grey, and intense, dark eyes. Next to his left eye he has a small, curved scar. He takes in every detail of the man's face then he moves her towards the next figure in the circle. A slim built man with long, thin, brown hair and a neat, trimmed beard. He has lively blue eyes and a kind face. He takes in every detail of the man's face before guiding her to the last figure. A woman this time, with a Rubenesque figure. She has long, fiery red hair and a beautiful welcoming smile. As he takes in every detail of the woman's face he finally hears the chant. 'Join us, Join us!'

The sound of a door slamming brought Aaron Sinclair back to reality. He lay still, his heart thumping. As he lay there his dream came back to him. It had sure been a weird one, but then weren't they all. No, but this one was different somehow. Those eyes. He'd never seen such eyes, such an unusual colour. What else had he dreamt? He tried to recall, but his dream was already fading, except for those eyes.

There was the sound of footsteps passing his door, he heard a smattering of conversation and someone laughed. He pulled the covers up over his head and groaned. This place was so noisy. What were the walls made of cardboard? Slowly he drifted back off to sleep hoping to dream again of cloudy green eyes. But it wasn't to be as the shrill sound of his alarm woke him what seemed like only seconds later. It was time to get up for work, the dream was over.

'What the hell do you think you're doing? Stop daydreaming and get on with your work you lazy git!'

Mick's podgy face was bright red with anger as he berated his employee.

'I don't pay you to stare into space all day Aaron' he continued.

'Sorry boss' replied Aaron not sounding sorry at all.

'You are seriously trying my patience' said Mick through gritted teeth whilst jabbing a stubby finger at Aaron's chest.

Aaron had to fight the urge to laugh in his boss' face. The two of them must look comical standing face to face like this. Mick was 5' 7' with a large beer gut and short, stumpy legs. He was doing his best to intimidate Aaron who was 6' 2' with a slim, muscled build and broad shoulders. It wasn't working. Aaron wasn't intimidated at all and this is what was making Mick even angrier. Aaron held up his hands in mock surrender.

'Okay, Okay, I'll behave myself I promise' he said.

'I don't want any of your lip, you just shut up and get to work. I'll be back in half an hour and that wall had better be finished or there'll be trouble!' threatened Mick and with that he stomped out of the room.

What a dickhead thought Aaron. He hated his boss and he hated his job. He was so bored. He was also very distracted. The dream he'd had that morning was still playing on his mind. Although he dreamt a lot and at times his dreams had affected his mood for the rest of the day, none had this kind of effect on him. It was like the dream was important somehow but its message was just out of his grasp. The people in the dream were strangers, yet so real. Aaron let out a deep sigh and picked up his brush. He'd better get some work done or Mick would have a fit. He figured that the only reason he still had a job was because he was so good at it, but there was only so much that Mick would put up with. He may hate his job, but he needed it. A guy had to eat after all.

Aaron had left home when he was seventeen and now, after twelve years he still didn't have a permanent home. He'd travelled around quite a lot picking up odd jobs when he could. He'd stayed in a vast number of hostels and cheap hotels as well as spending an occasional night or two on a friend's sofa.

He'd had all sorts of jobs. He'd worked in shops and warehouses but had mostly worked in the building trade. He had no real qualifications but was good with his hands and so could do almost any sort of basic manual work with no problem. His ability to capture a person's likeness in pencil or oil paint had also earned him some cash here and there. When people learned of his talent most were more than willing to let him sketch them and they were invariably pleased with the results. Some were just willing to be his model for pleasure, but most bought the sketches from him and some even asked him to sketch their loved ones too. He made a little money this way and sometimes the sketches were exchanged for a few beers or a good meal. He had also managed, on occasion, to make a little cash as a 'pavement artist' but it wasn't his favourite way to work.

Occasionally, to his delight some people would then ask him to do a proper portrait in oils. He offered two types of portrait. For a quicker and cheaper option, he could paint in a more modern, freer style where the painting would take him a few hours and although the likeness would be spot on the painting would have a rougher feel to it with no background detail and unfinished edges. But for those with more time and money he could do the kind of portrait he enjoyed the most, a proper, classic portrait in oils. For this he would spend three to four hours with the subject making sketches and taking photographs on his phone. He would then work on the painting from the sketches and photos to produce the finished painting over the course of several days.

The time he spent working on these portraits were the happiest times in his life, but they were unfortunately few and far between. He'd struggled a bit on a few occasions when work and therefore money was scarce. He had even spent a few weeks here and there living on the streets, but for the most part he'd been happy with his way of life. That was until recently. For about a year now he had been enjoying the constant moving around less and less until about four months ago he had finally decided that he wanted something more stable, more permanent.

After a couple of weeks scouring newspapers and job centres he had struck lucky with a painting and decorating firm. It was a permanent position, yet still involved moving to different sites within a fixed area to do different jobs. He's felt it was the ideal job for him. He'd thought he would enjoy the painting because of his artistic flair and that it would be the perfect transition from the constant moving around. He would be able to establish a home base, to finally have a 'home' and yet still be able to travel around a bit and not be stuck in a single place of work.

It wasn't quite working out to plan though. He had found that his 'artistic' talent wasn't put to use as much as he'd expected. The customer's he'd worked for so far had shown a distinct lack of style and imagination. He desperately hoped that the next customer would want something a little more original. He loved colour and felt that he would enjoy the work more if the colour scheme excited him.

His other problem was his boss. They just didn't get on. Sometimes he wondered how he still had a job, how he hadn't been fired or walked out after a row. He was beginning to think that

31

maybe his boss was just cantankerous all the time with everyone and it wasn't just him. Only time would tell. At least this was the last day of this particular job, then he had a day off before the new job started, and hopefully this next job would be more artistically fulfilling. But he doubted it.

At 4.30 he was finally finished for the day. His dream had played on his mind the whole time he worked and the faces of the strangers in the dream remained vivid in his mind. Now he was free and there was only one way he wanted to spend the rest of his day. He needed to get back to his boarding house asap, get his pencils and sketch pad out and get those faces down on paper.

Aaron spent the evening sketching the four faces from his dream, taking particular pleasure in drawing the girl with the green eyes. The fact that his dream memory of her face wasn't crystal clear meant the sketch had a very other worldly feel to it which he decided he kind of liked.

When he'd finished it was late and he was very tired but he felt really good. He laid the four A3 sheets of paper out on his bed to get a good look at them. He was very pleased with his work and decided that there was no way he could leave that one of the girl at just the sketch, he needed to portray that beautiful, shadowed face in oils.

Although he was a talented portrait artist, he had never attempted to capture the likeness of a face from a dream. That just wasn't normal. But it would be a challenge, and a challenge he would relish. He hadn't painted a portrait for quite a while now, his nomadic lifestyle made it impractical to do much work as there was no way he could carry all his work around with him. The two A3 size portfolios full of pencil drawings and paintings on textured paper and a few small canvases were pretty bulky and then there was his easel and toolbox of paints etc. The fact that he had few clothes and other possessions were the only reason he could manage even that amount.

This portrait needed to be painted though; he felt it just had to be done. He decided that the next day he would go out and buy a canvas and some new oil paints, this face required the best, and he would spend a blissful day painting it.

CHAPTER 7

DAY 3 - CLEA

There is a strange, circular, castle like building surrounded by trees, and it is calling her to it. Now she stands at its enormous ornate wooden door.

'Is this my true home?' she murmurs.

Five circles appear spaced around the wooden door, they start to glow and then a face appears in each circle. One of the faces is hers.

In the circle nearest the one with her face is a man's face. He has long hair, a beard, and a kind smile. Then he fades. And a carved symbol replaces his face.

In the next circle is the face of a man with an intense gaze and a scar beside his left eye. She holds his fierce gaze. Until his image fades and a carved symbol replaces his face.

A young woman stares out from the next circle. She has beautiful long hair and large eyes. The young woman's gaze shifts to the next circle on from which a young man stares with a brooding gaze. His image turns to return the young woman's gaze as their silhouettes fade. And two symbols replace their faces.

In the last circle her own face stares back at her, she returns her own smile as the image fades and a symbol replaces her face.

When Clea Monroe woke from her dream she was disorientated. For a moment she forgot where she was and almost flew into a panic. Then she grew calm as her familiar room came into focus around her. Slowly she sat up, drew a deep, calming breath and then let it out slowly.

'Now that's what I call a vivid dream' she said to herself as she got out of bed.

The strange building had seemed so real, she could still see the detail of the stonework and the enormous, beautifully ornate wooden door. And the symbols, what had they been, what did they mean? They had appeared to her clearly, but only for an instant as had the faces. One of the faces she'd recognised as her own, but the other faces from what little she had seen of them were not the faces of people she knew. How Strange. And the building, she had never seen such a place with her waking eyes.

Clea made her way slowly downstairs and began to make herself some breakfast the dream still on her mind. She had been known to see people and places in her dreams that she had not encountered in reality before, but none of the other dreams had been so vivid or so haunting. Yet this one seemed to be fading more quickly. Clea smiled to herself. Never mind she thought, with any luck she would dream of the strange building again. In the meantime she'd try to get what she'd seen down on paper, any excuse or inspiration to draw was always welcome.

Clea stared at the drawings laid out in front of her amazed. She'd been sat in her comfy chair for a couple of hours now with her feet tucked up underneath her ample bottom, her long red hair tied up out of the way, and her sketch pad and pencil in her hands. Her coloured pencils lay in her lap their colours mixing nicely with the bright splashes of colour in her favourite dress. The one she called her inspiration dress. Well it had worked this time.

After having filled several pages with vague doodles and a few failed attempts she'd finally got the symbols down on paper, the symbols from her dream. Or to be more exact stylised and coloured versions of the symbols she had seen in the circles on the door in her dream.

33

Firstly, there was her symbol. The one that had replaced her face in the circle. What she had drawn was a human eye but where the iris and pupil would be she had drawn a swirled, brightly coloured spiral pattern. The next drawing represented the symbol she'd seen replace the face of the man with the beard. It was basically a feather which she had drawn in shades of brown and gold. The third drawing belonged to the man with the scar. This drawing was of a gate like the ones you find on old castles, a big black iron metal studded affair she believed was called a portcullis. The black and silver colouring on this drawing was a departure from her usual colourful work but you couldn't have a rainbow coloured fortress gate could you. And now for the couple. The man's symbol had been a bare branched, twisted tree and that was easy to translate into a drawing although again she had to resist her usual use of bright colours. The woman's symbol had been hard to figure to start with, just a circle within a circle, but then on reflection she had realised there had been markings within the inner circle that had seemed familiar, then it came to her, the symbol represented the moon. Again there was no use for her usual riot of colour but she found a silver pencil and paired with a grey one she made it look pretty enough.

She realised that simplified versions of the designs would look great embroidered onto fabric and so she made a start on converting them.

Once they were all finished she leafed through them and gave herself a mental pat on the back. They had worked out great, definitely some of her best work, and where had the inspiration come from, her dream, perfect. They were unlike any of her other embroidery designs, she felt they had more meaning, they were much more personal and therefore special. And how she had a record of her amazing dream she could never forget it, or the strangers who had inspired them. Their faces had faded in her memory a little but now she had their 'symbols' down on paper they would never be truly forgotten.

In the past she had dreamt of people and places she didn't know only to then come across them in her waking life. It was rare, but it did happen. She had a gift; one she didn't share with many people. She only told those she felt would believe her, those who wouldn't ridicule her.

Did this mean that the building she'd dreamt of was real? That one day she would actually visit it? And the faces, were they people she would meet one day too? Only time would tell. Not every strange person or place she dreamt of turned out to be real. This dream hadn't felt the same as the other dreams though. In fact this dream had felt unlike any other dream she'd ever had.

Okay, that's enough now she thought. It was no good dwelling on it. She would find out soon enough if this dream was some kind of premonition. In the meantime she had things to do. Polly Jenkins was coming to collect her dress shortly and now she had five new designs to make garments for so she could embroider them on. She put her pad and pencils on the table beside her and hefted herself out of the chair. Time to get to work.

First she needed to iron the dress she'd made for Polly Jenkins before Polly arrived at to pick it up. She liked the clothes she made to look their best and a good iron always helped. She was particularly proud of this dress. Polly wanted it to wear to her twenty first birthday party. Like Clea Polly was on the large side and so found it difficult to find the right dress in the shops. Clea was pleased to help her out. The main reason she had started to make her own clothes years ago was because she'd had similar problems to Polly.

The dress she'd made for Polly was a beautiful deep blue colour with a low, square cut neckline (to show off Polly's amble bosom). The dress then flared out under the bust in an empire line. Clea had embroidered a lovely ivy leaf design onto the fitted top part of the dress in a slightly lighter blue than the material and she was very pleased with it. She just hoped Polly felt the same.

When Polly arrived she was eager to try her dress on. Clea had already hung the dress behind the screen she kept in her large but cosy front room. Polly slipped behind the screen and emerged minutes later ready to check her new look in the full length, freestanding mirror beside the screen.

'Oh my god!' she exclaimed 'It's beautiful.'

'No, you're beautiful' said Clea 'the dress just brings your beauty out.'

Polly was looking at her now, a big, beaming smile on her face.

'Thank you Clea, thank you so much.'

'My pleasure lovey, I'm glad you're pleased with it.'

Polly spun back around to admire herself in the mirror, her hand gently tracing the intricately embroidered design on the dress.

'I can't wait until tomorrow night' she said striking a pose 'Everyone will be so surprised and no one will have a dress anything like this one.'

'Okay Cinderella' said Clea with a smile 'Why don't you change back into your other clothes and I'll go make us some tea and you can tell me all your party plans.'

Polly gave her a playful pout but then disappeared behind the screen to change.

Twenty minutes later the tea was all drunk and Clea knew every detail of Polly's forthcoming party. Polly was very excited and Clea was pleased for her. They were sitting in a sudden lull in the conversation when Clea noticed that Polly kept glancing at the framed photo that sat in the middle of her bookshelf. She waited for the question she knew was coming.

'Who's that?' Polly asked.

Clea got up from her armchair, walked across to the bookshelf and picked the photo up. The familiar face stared back at her and she smiled. The photo was of a man in his early thirties. He had unruly, light brown hair, very blue eyes and a beautiful smile.

She turned and handed the photo to Polly so she could get a better look.

'That's my husband' she said.

'Oh, I errrrm...' stuttered Polly.

She knew what the girl was thinking. Despite the rings she wore on her left hand everyone who came to the house knew she lived alone and therefore assumed she was single and had always been so. She never put them straight unless they asked her outright. Polly hadn't exactly asked the 'are you married' question but the answer was the same.

'Yes, that's Andrew' she said, 'he died.'

Polly gave a little gasp.

'Oh Clea, I'm so sorry' she said.

'It was five years ago. He was thirty-six when he died, I was thirty-one. We'd been married for nearly seven years. It was a brain aneurysm.'

Clea recited the details hoping to cover all the questions that usually got asked.

'I'm so sorry' Polly said again, then 'he looks like a very nice man.'

'He was' replied Clea as she took the photo from Polly and put it back on the bookshelf.

It was clear that the girl didn't know what else to say, but who did. Clea found that a lot of people were surprised by the news that she was a widow because she seemed so happy all the time. But who said widows should be miserable all the time? She had been a very upbeat, happy person before Andrews's death and had gradually returned to that after he was gone. However, if anyone was to look closely into her eyes they would see her sadness. She'd been devastated by his death, had cried non-stop for days, but she was a strong woman and her gift had helped to give her that strength. Her thoughts were interrupted by a nervous little cough from Polly. She realised she'd been standing with her back to her lost in thought for a while. She composed herself and turned to face her with her usual big smile.

'Would you like another cup of tea?' she asked.

'Erm, no thanks, I'd better be going now, I'm going shopping with my mum to get some shoes for the party.' The girl was obviously feeling a little embarrassed and awkward now. Clea hoped it wouldn't stop her coming back again.

'Ok lovey' she said, 'I hope you find some fantastic shoes to go with your dress.'

'Thanks again Clea, I really do love the dress' said Polly getting up from the sofa 'and I'm sorry if I upset you about your husband' she added.

'It's okay' Clea reassured her 'I'm fine and I hope to see you again soon.'

'Oh yes, I'm sure I'll need your help again sometime' said Polly sounding relieved.

Clea saw the girl to the door, and then returned to her front room to collect the dirty teacups. She knew there was a danger that she would end up sat on her sofa dwelling on thoughts of Andrew so she bustled around in an effort to dispel the sad mood.

Suddenly she remembered her dream and the symbols.

'Thank god' she said to herself out loud.

Pushing all thoughts of her dead husband to the back of her mind she headed upstairs to her workshop. It was time to get started on the garments for her 'dream' symbols.

She always did the drawing of her embroidery designs sat in her comfy chair in the lounge but all the actual clothes making and embroidery itself was done in her workshop. Her workshop was actually the back bedroom but it did not resemble a bedroom at all.

She entered her workshop and stood in the centre of the room taking in its familiar atmosphere and aroma. To her left along almost the whole length of the wall was a wooden bench. Her sewing machine sat on the end nearest the window whilst the rest of the bench was a clear space used to lie out and cut fabric. A comfortable, expensive, office style chair sat in front of the sewing machine. To her right against that wall were two unusual pieces of furniture. The first was a large wooden box about five feet long by two-foot-wide and three foot high. In this box, stood on end were several bolts of fabric. Next to this box was a tall chest with three shallow draws at the top and four deeper draws at the bottom. The shallow draws were filled with Clea's needles, cottons, scissors and pins etc. The deeper draws held folders full of her patterns and embroidery designs.

Propped in the corner next to the chest was the folded ironing board she'd used earlier. The iron sat atop the chest. Opposite the door was a bay window. In the alcove of the window was an upright but comfortable padded chair; beside the chair was a small wooden table. This is where Clea spent many hours sat embroidering delicate and beautiful designs onto the clothes she made.

Also in the room behind the door in the left corner was a metal framed clothes rail on wheels hung with several clothes hangers. This was where she hung the clothes to be altered or that were part finished when she wasn't working on them.

Standing in the middle of the room she decided that her own symbol was to be embroidered onto a nice, simple peasant style blouse. Having made that decision she headed over to her box of fabric to make her choice. She chose a jade green, soft cotton and placed it on her workbench then went to fetch her much loved peasant blouse pattern. She decided that when the blouse was made she would embroider her symbol on in a nice yellow/gold thread that she had with touches of other bright colours for the swirling iris of the eye. And so humming contentedly to herself she set to work.

CHAPTER 8

DAY 3 – GETH

He stands guard. His arms crossed, his stance firm, as a sea of forms and faces move in the mist before him and the chant fills his ears. 'Let me in.' He fights the urge to cover his ears until the voices fade a little and then four figures break from the mist and move towards him. Three stop and one moves closer. A woman with a full figure and long red hair. She holds a needle and thread in her small hand. No need for her to speak the words. He knows what to do. He lets her in.

The next figure moves towards him. A slim man with long hair, a short beard and glasses. He holds up his hands, they are covered in clay. There is no need for the words to be spoken. He moves aside to let the slim man pass. He lets him in.

The final two figures approach him together. A tall, broad shouldered dark-haired young man, who holds a paintbrush in his hand and a pale, dark haired young woman who holds a pen and paper in hers, their free hands join them together. The words again remain unspoken. He lets them in.

The chorus of voices becomes louder again and he feels the urge to cover his ears once more. 'Please, no more' he begs as the chorus of voices raises in volume.

Geth Hudson awoke, his heart hammering in his chest and the sound of his own voice ringing in his ears. Had he actually shouted the words aloud? The fact that he may have shouted 'Please, no more' in a pathetic, pleading voice was embarrassing even though there was no one there to hear him. Geth was a man who was very rarely fazed by anything. He was also used to having weird dreams; he had loads of them after all. Yet, he felt very unnerved by this dream. It felt different, it felt important but he didn't know why. He hated not knowing why.

After a brisk shower and a large mug of strong, black coffee Geth Hudson was feeling much better. It was only a dream after all. Though of all the many dreams he'd had, good and bad, none had affected him like this one had. Although the images of the faces and the actual sounds of the voices had faded the words still stuck in his mind, 'Let me in'. Why those words? Despite being a prolific dreamer Geth had never really stopped to think about what his dreams meant, and he didn't intend to start now. Now wasn't the time for introspection, now was the time for work.

Geth placed his coffee mug in the sink and headed for the stairs. At the bottom of the stairs there were two doors, one straight ahead and one to his right. The one straight ahead led to a short corridor at the end of which was a door leading onto the street outside. But Geth's current destination was through the door on his right which he now unlocked to walk through and into his place of work.

Turning on the lights he stood surveying the room in which he spent most of his days. In doing so he caught his reflection in the full-length mirror put up so his customers could admire themselves and his work. He took a minute to study his reflection, not out of vanity, rather as an assessment as to whether his demeanour and expression were fit for company.

The mirror showed a man of average height, with broad shoulders and a stocky build, dressed in black jeans, grey t-shirt and black boots. His short hair was dark and receding slightly at the front, with a sprinkling of grey at the sides. He saw a face that showed its thirty-nine years through rough, weather beaten skin, a large, crooked nose, and two days' worth of dark stubble. The eyes staring back at him were dark brown, almost black, and intense. His intense stare and the fact that his lips rarely turned up into a smile made a lot of people wary of him. And the scar didn't help. It formed a semi-circle starting at the corner of his left eye and ending on his left cheekbone. He was aware that he could come across as intimidating, but there wasn't a lot he could do about that. He was who he was. Luckily it didn't seem to affect his business, but that could be due to the fact that some of his customers were even more intimidating than he was.

Geth had been the proud owner of 'Studio Ink' for almost seven years now. He had started his apprenticeship as a tattoo artist nineteen years ago and after twelve years or so practicing his art and building his reputation in various studio's he had finally taken the plunge and opened his own. It had been a risky venture, going it alone with a business loan, but he'd made it work.

It was only a small studio with room for three tattooists. At the moment, however, there were only two, himself and a guy named Chris James, but they also had an apprentice called Rick Davies. Rick was young and a little shy but he had a great artistic talent and they had high hopes for him. Chris had worked for Geth for nearly four years and he was the only other tattooist that Geth had ever really got along with. Even then it wasn't like they were best buddies or anything, Geth didn't do best buddies, he didn't let anyone that close, but they rarely argued and they respected each other which was good enough for him. He was even finding that he liked Rick too. Maybe he was getting soft if his old age?

Geth wandered over to the table set to the left of the front door. It was an enormous, solid, wooden table behind which Rick sat to greet customers and set up appointments. It was also used by Geth and Chris to consult with their customers and then draw out their tattoo designs. Rick would then make the designs into stencils using the special copy machine also placed on the table; the stencils would then transfer the design onto the customer's skin ready for tattooing.

Opposite the desk was a large, worn, brown leather sofa for the waiting customers to sit on. Next to the sofa was a five-foot-high wooden bookshelf holding several folders of tattoo 'flash art' designs, tattoo books and magazines.

Next to the desk, past the door to the upstairs flat and towards the back of the room was Geth's workstation. Opposite Geth's station was Chris' station next to which, on the wall was the full-length mirror, and on the other side of the mirror was the spare station (which would hopefully become Rick's soon).

Each station consisted of a chair for the tattooist and a cupboard (fixed to the wall) to put their equipment in with room on top to lay out their ink etc. when working. Scattered around and in between their stations were various chairs and 'beds' for the customers to sit/lay on whist being tattooed. In the middle of the back wall of the studio there was a door which led to the toilet and a small kitchen/staff area. The floor was lacquered oak wood flooring and the walls were painted white and decorated with photos of tattoos and artwork all done by Geth or Chris. Geth had spent many happy hours in this place. It was his place of work and it was his home.

Flipping open the appointment book that lay on the table Geth checked his bookings for the day and was pleased to find that as he thought he was booked up pretty much all morning which was good, it was good for business and it was good because he needed something to keep his mind off that damn weird dream.

Geth began to walk back towards his station to start setting things up for his first client when there was a suddenly loud banging noise, and then a voice shouted, 'Let me in!' For a minute he was disorientated as the sounds and images of his dream crashed through his mind and his heart thudded loudly in his chest. Then he heard a rattling noise and the voice said, 'Come on Geth open up' and relief flooded through him. It wasn't the people in his dream haunting him (what an absurd idea) it was Rick at the front door waiting to be let in to help him set up for the day.

Geth went to let him in vowing that that would be the last time he let that damn dream bother him.

Geth's first tattoo of the day was an intricate and interesting design and so it left him little time to reflect on that mornings dream, but the next two clients wanted smallish, pretty bog standard tattoos, the sort that he kind of hated but that made up a lot of his work and were the basic bread and butter of his business. And today he hated them more than usual as the lack of concentration needed to do them meant that his mind had time to wander and it inevitably wandered back to his dream.

He kept seeing the faces of the four strangers in his dream as they came towards him, arms outstretched, and of course the chorus of 'Let me in' kept echoing through his mind.

Then, about halfway through the second boring tattoo something weird began to happen. One of the stranger's faces would come into his mind and then fade away to be replaced by strange lines and colours that would swirl around and form into a picture, or to be more exact they would form into an idea, an idea for a tattoo design, or what in the tattoo trade was called 'flash art'. By the time he had finished the tattoo he had four designs swirling around in his mind. it was a little disconcerting, but at the same time exciting.

Whilst Rick took payment from his client and then began to tidy up Geth's station he walked over to Chris who was just finishing up with a client himself.

'I'm gonna go upstairs for a bit, I have something to do, my next client isn't due for a couple of hours but obviously if you get any drop in's and you're busy just give me a shout'.

'Okay, no problem' said Chris

Geth almost ran up the stairs to his flat. The designs were becoming clearer in his mind and he needed to get them down on paper as soon as possible. He was a little unsure why he felt the need to come upstairs to do them in private as he would usually just sit downstairs in the studio and work on his designs, but there was no time to ponder this. Grabbing a sketch pad, pencils and colouring pens Geth sat at his small kitchen table and began work.

By the time Chris shouted up to tell him his next client had arrived Geth had managed to get the four basic designs down on paper. He knew the designs were inspired by his dream but wasn't quite sure how as the images didn't really match what he'd seen in the dream. They still needed work, but he had done enough to relieve the urgency and was therefore quite happy to leave them and thoughts of where they'd come from for a bit and get back to work.

CHAPTER 9

DAY 3 – THE GATEWAY

It still rests, and It watches, but not with Its eyes. It watches with Its mind sensing those he was once so close to but that now reject him. It fears them and hates that they make him feel ashamed. It will find a way to make them pay.

It also senses those within the red building. He does not know them but they are still his enemy. They radiate strength and It is too weak now, but if It can surprise them It can control them and use them to have Its way. And so It seems It must wait, soon one must stray and then It would have them. Talionis would have Its day.

Eddie's arms and back were beginning to ache. After all the boxing up he'd done the day before his strong physique was starting to feel the strain. Still, at least he didn't look like he hadn't slept for a month like Mason did. Sofia looked pretty tired too. The last couple of days had been hard on all of them, and despite his aching body he knew he had the easiest job.

Although he didn't know exactly what Mason's 'job' involved he knew enough to know that it was an extremely difficult one and that there was a lot riding on the outcome. He didn't envy his friend one bit.

Sofia seemed to spend half her time on the phone, the rest of the time she was either gallantly trying to help Eddie with his removal duties or having 'intense' conversations with Mason. Eddie was sure she must be feeling the stress the same as himself and Mason but she was pretty good at hiding it. As for the two new arrivals he had seen little of them since lunchtime the day before but was sure they were working hard too.

In regard to his other friends there was good news and bad news. The doctors at the Foundation hospital had phoned early that morning with an update. They said that Gina was doing well and that physically they expected her to make a full recovery. She was, however, suffering from severe emotional trauma and so was being kept heavily sedated.

As for Blake, his head wound had been much more severe and so the doctors had put him into an induced coma in order to combat the swelling in his brain. Until the swelling was reduced and it was safe to bring Blake out of the coma there was no way of knowing if he had suffered any permanent brain damage. There was also the possibility that Blake would not come out of the coma at all.

Eddie was trying to remain optimistic about the future of his two friends but he knew whatever the outcome their lives would never be the same and as for Claude who knew what the future held for him

That morning Eddie had cleaned the guest room after Claude so that it was ready for Phoebe or Mark when and if they needed it and had then finished the last bit of packing up his friend's belongings and it was now time to start transporting all the boxes stacked in three of the four upstairs rooms up to the attic. He was not looking forward to it, but it had to be done.

Phoebe and Mark had spent the whole of their first night in the Factory some of it sleeping but most of it working. They were taking their new job very seriously and didn't want to let their new 'team' down. They felt they had settled in very well but as expected the work had been much more 'intense' than they were used to. Still they knew that Mason was grateful to them for their efforts.

They had provisions where they were and so hadn't had any real need to return to the house the evening before but they were planning a brief visit back in the late afternoon so they could have a relaxing lunch and a chat with their friends before stocking up and returning to carry on their work.

It was late afternoon and Sofia and Mason were in the office having a brain storming session. Well, at least that was how it had started out. After an hour of fruitless brain strain however, they had both fallen silent and were now each lost in their own unhelpful thoughts.

Mason was slumped in one of the armchairs staring blindly out at the driveway and the woodland beyond. He was tired and he was stressed but he was doing his best to stay strong. The last few days had been hard both mentally and physically and he could only hope he had the strength to finish what he had started; what needed to be done. A lot depended on him and his task was a colossal weight upon his shoulders. He was grateful for the help and support the others were giving him, and he knew they were tired and stressed too, but he also knew that the onus was on him to get the job done. He was trying his best to believe in his own ability and in the abilities of the others around him. The apparent success of the task so far was encouraging but it didn't diminish his fear of what lay ahead. Therefore, Mason decided he was feeling both scared and hopeful.

Sofia sat at the office desk fiddling with the cord of one of the telephones. The brain storming session was not going well and she was annoyed with herself. She was usually so good at this sort of thing. She was a problem solver, a fixer, which was after all one of the reasons she was a Marshal. The practical parts had been easy; Eddie was being a trooper and getting on with his work and she had liaised with The Foundation to make all the other arrangements. However, helping Mason with the main issue had been a lot more difficult. She realised that there was a limit to how much she could help him as she didn't share his 'talent' but it still frustrated her.

This session of brainstorming however should have been her 'thing', after all it was a practical issue they were trying to solve. On the one hand she knew she was being hard on herself, after all no-one could be expected to be operating at full capacity when they were as tired as she was; but on the other hand the plan they were trying to come up with right now should have been relatively easy to figure out.

Sofia glanced over at Mason. It was clear from his posture and the look on his face that he too was struggling with his emotions over their lack of success.

Sofia was frustrated and frustration always made her fidgety, therefore, during the last few minutes of thought her hands had been busy untangling the telephone cord and re-arranging the stationary in the top draw of the desk. She now opened the next draw down, after all if she couldn't bring order to this situation she could at least bring it to the desk.

She found that the draw was full of a random selection of letters, pamphlets and business cards. They had just been thrown into the draw in a big, messy pile. Well at least this is one mess I can easily clear up she thought as she began to empty the draws contents out onto the desktop.

The sound of a large pile of papers slapping onto the desk roused Mason from his reverie. When he saw what Sofia was doing he made no comment, as far as he was concerned if it helped her think she could tidy the whole house and he had no doubt that despite what it looked like she was still mulling over their problem.

As Sofia began to sort through the pile she discovered that it was mainly junk mail advertising products, events and services all of an artistic nature. There were art supply brochures, art course pamphlets, invites to art gallery openings and flyers advertising various art related events. She assumed that Eddie kept them all 'just in case' but noticed that a lot of the information was out of date, therefore she began to sort them into two piles, those to be thrown away and those to be kept 'just in case'. As she sorted one particular event flyer caught her eye; it was bigger, glossier and more professionally done than the others and where most were for small, localised events and businesses this one advertised something far bigger. As her eyes scanned the page a smile spread across her face and a tide of excitement and relief flooded through her body.

'I've got it' she shouted jumping to her feet.

Mason also 'jumped' his heart suddenly racing as he was ripped from his solemn thoughts by Sofia's sudden, loud words. He rose from his chair, his right hand unconsciously held over his pounding heart and stepped towards her as she all but ran towards him waving a piece of paper.

'Look, its perfect' she said thrusting the piece of paper into his hand.

As Mason read down the page his heart lifted. She was right, it was perfect. He smiled for what felt like the first time in ages; another hurdle had been overcome.

'This is great Sofia' he said, 'just what we need, well done.'

'Thanks, but it was just a fluke' she replied modestly.

'Well fluke or not we've got our meeting place so we should get to work as soon as possible.'

'I agree we need to get started soon but I think we should have something to eat and a little rest first. I really think we need to gather your strength a little before we attempt this next phase.'

'Okay' he agreed reluctantly 'we'll get something to eat and relax a little, and then I'll head out to the Factory and get started'.

CHAPTER 10

DAY 4 - SHARING

Floating high in a clear blue sky I look down upon a vast field scattered with numerous large, white marquees. Faint sounds reach my ears, music, voices, laughter and the general buzz of a large gathering of people.

Then I sense their presence. I am not alone, there are four others floating like me, hearing what I hear, seeing what I see. I cannot see them but I know they are there.

It is important that we meet here, in this place.

We begin to descend.

It is time for us to join together.

This is an unusual dream, and very rare, because five people share it. They dream it and inhabit it all at the same time. It is an amazing feat on the part of those who 'bring' the dream, and its success now depends upon its five dreamers. It is time for their 'task' to truly begin.

Clea awoke from her dream slowly. She was tired and her body fought to return to sleep. She wanted to return to the dream, she wanted to experience that floating, flying feeling and to feel the presence of the others around her, but it wasn't to be, the dream slipped away and reality crept in. She had another busy day ahead, so despite her tiredness she figured it was time to get up. After all busy was good, busy left no time for feeling bored or lonely.

After a quick, energising shower Clea put on her 'inspiration' dress. Its bright colours and soft, flowing fabric always made her feel better. She headed downstairs to the kitchen for a quick breakfast.

Clea had just finished her tea and toast when the telephone rang. It was a woman who needed some alterations done. She'd seen Clea's advert in the local paper and wanted to know how much Clea charged. Clea gave her a price but when the lady asked when she could do the work she hesitated. Despite the fact that she had no other 'work' on at the moment Clea was loathed to take any on. Her work on her symbols was taking up all her time and she felt disinclined to put it on hold for anything else. She had never turned a job down before, how could she when it was her livelihood, and yet she now found herself lying her way out of a job. She told the woman that she was sorry but she was up to her eyes in it at the moment, but if it wasn't urgent she could phone back in a week or so and Clea could see what she could do. The woman had seemed a little shocked and put out and had said she'd maybe call back if she didn't find someone else. Clea had a feeling she wouldn't be hearing from her again but felt surprisingly unworried about it.

She was headed towards the stairs when, as on many other occasions, she was side-tracked at the bookcase that held Andrew's photo. She picked up the photo and ran her finger across his cheek. She always got reflective like this when someone asked about her late husband. Polly's innocent enquiry yesterday has started it off and Clea knew it would last a few days.

Clea had met Andrew at a friend's party when she was twenty-four and he was twenty-nine. They had hit if off immediately. As they chatted for the first time she'd had a strange premonition that their relationship would be a short but happy one. At first she did not doubt her ability to 'see' how things would be and assumed that they would just have a fling, a brief, fun romance that would fizzle out. However, when after a couple of months they were both madly in love and their relationship only seemed to be getting stronger she began to wonder what her premonition meant. She couldn't imagine how the love she felt for Andrew would ever end and she knew he felt as strongly. When he asked her to marry him after only nine months she said yes without a second thought and decided to forget her silly premonition and get on with her life.

Then, after almost seven years of happy marriage she had a dream. In the dream Andrew was moving further and further away from her. She held out her arms trying to bring him back and shouted, 'Where are you going?' and as he faded from her sight she faintly heard him reply 'I have to go now'.

She woke up in tears and when Andrew woke up and saw the state she was in he was alarmed. He knew she was a prolific dreamer and was aware that on occasion her dreams did in some small way come true, but he'd never seen her so upset by a dream before. He asked her what she'd dreamt but she wouldn't tell him, instead she begged him not to go to work that day but to stay home with her. He agreed not wanting to upset her further.

Clea had asked him to stay home because she was convinced her dream meant that something bad would happen to him that day. She hoped that if he stayed home he would be okay. She was wrong. After lunch as they sat talking at the kitchen table Andrew had suddenly collapsed to the floor and seconds later had died in her arms.

Andrew had died of a brain aneurism and would have 'left' her that day no matter what she did. Her only comfort was that he'd died at home with her and not alone at work or amongst strangers in the street.

This was the first time that her 'gift' had given her anything negative and so for the first time she viewed it as a curse. For days after her husband died she hadn't slept properly for fear of anymore unwelcome premonitions, but in the end she could not help but fall into a deep sleep and when she did she dreamt not of the future, but the past. She dreamt of the happy times with Andrew and her dreams were filled with love and healing. She realised that she had been silly to fear her dreams. As with everything else in life you had to take the good with the bad. She began to see her 'gift' as a blessing again and found that her dreams were a major factor in helping her cope with her grief. Clea still missed her husband every day but she could still remember his touch, his smell, his voice, all because he was still alive in her dreams and always would be.

Clea wiped the tears from her eyes and returned Andrew's photo to the bookcase. It was time to get to work. Her new, exciting dreams had come at the right time. For a while at least her thoughts of Andrew would be pushed to the back of her mind as she worked.

Her workshop clothes rail now held two garments, her blouse and a t-shirt for the bearded man from her dream. Her blouse only needed a few finishing touches to the sleeves and the t-shirt needed a little more work on the embroidered symbol. She'd decided on a t-shirt rather than a fitted shirt mainly due to the size problem. For a proper, fitted shirt you needed much more exact measurements, whereas for a t-shirt you could go with more basic average measurements. It was all a little crazy really this size business, how could she know what size these people were, she'd only seen their faces and after all they were probably only figments of her 'dream' imagination. But she had decided to go on intuition and just make the garments as if they were for 'real' people, what else could she do?

She'd done a little research not having made any men's clothing from scratch before and had made notes on what chest sizes constituted small, medium and large etc. Having no patterns from men's clothes and being too impatient to go out and buy some before starting work she had used a women's pattern as a template to make her own, slightly altered men's version. For the bearded man's t-shirt she had gone for medium size and had chosen a soft cotton fabric in a light fawn colour. She had embroidered the feather symbol on the left breast of the shirt in a chocolate brown thread.

Strewn across her large workbench were the pieces of fabric she had cut out for the t-shirt for the man with the scar. She'd decided his t-shirt should be a large and had chosen thicker, black cotton. For the portcullis symbol, again to go on the left breast, she had chosen a grey thread. It seemed a strange choice, but the right one.

So, that meant she had a little stitching to do on her own blouse, a little embroidery to finish on one t-shirt, and pretty much the whole of the second t-shirt to finish, then she had two more garments to design and make. She decided to finish her own blouse and the bearded man's t-shirt first, then get the t-shirt for the man with the scar finished before starting the two new garments, besides, she needed time to think of styles and colours for them first and she could think about those whilst working on the garments she'd already started.

Clea took her blouse off its hanger and laid it over her arm. She then went to her set of drawers and took out the needles and thread she needed then took it all to the chair by the window, sat down and got to work.

Aaron opened his eyes, his dream images replaced by the sight of his sparse little room. His eyes focused on the small bedside table, then moved around the room taking in the scruffy chest of drawers, the tiny wardrobe and the single (semi) comfortable chair. It wasn't a great room but it was clean and he'd stayed in a lot worse.

He rolled onto his back and lay staring at the ceiling. His latest dream was still very clear in his mind. But what did it mean? It was definitely linked to the dream he'd had the morning before, he was sure of it. The strangers in his dream felt very real to him, he felt linked to them somehow. He smiled to himself as he remembered his plan to paint the green-eyed girl. He'd get up in a minute and head to the art shop for the canvas and oil paints, but for now he just wanted to lie there enjoying the content feeling his latest dream had left him with.

Aaron had always had an active dream life. He didn't talk to anyone about his feelings on his dreams, he was afraid they'd laugh. He didn't tell anyone that he thought his dreams gave him directions. They told him where to go and supplied him with answers to dilemmas. He couldn't really explain how they did this; he just knew it happened. He'd told a few people that his dreams gave him inspiration for his art though, that was much more palatable to them and didn't elicit too many weird looks.

Aarons mobile phone rang interrupting his reverie. It was his boss Mick. The new job was cancelled. Mick didn't explain why, but he didn't sound happy. All he told Aaron was that he didn't have any work for him now for at least three weeks. No explanations and no sorry. Mick told him he'd contact him if anything came up and hung up.

Aaron lay back in bed stunned his thoughts in turmoil. He didn't know whether to laugh or cry. On the one hand three weeks of no work was great, he could sleep in, he could paint, he could do whatever he liked. On the other hand three weeks without any money coming in was not good. He wouldn't starve or anything, but it would mean using some of the money he'd been putting aside since starting work for Mick, money he'd been saving towards a deposit and rent on a flat. A proper home at last. And what if it was longer than three weeks, what if Mick was pissed because this cancellation left his company in trouble? What if he got laid off?

This rising fear was new to Aaron, he'd had so many different jobs in the past which had all been temporary from choice, and he'd been worse off than this financially on many occasions. But that was all before he'd tired of the nomadic life and had decided to put down some roots. Was that sort of life just a dream for someone like him? Was he destined to be a homeless wanderer all his life? He hoped not. So this job hadn't turned out as ideal as he'd thought, but it was a start and he'd been determined to stick it out at least until something better came along, thought what that something could be he had no idea.

Taking a deep breath Aaron tried to calm himself. Panicking wouldn't help, and since when was he the type of guy to panic anyway? He was usually so laid back and calm, and on the few occasions when things did get a little difficult he'd always found solace in his painting. So that was what he would do now. Time to get up and head to the art store.

Mary didn't want to open her eyes. She was hoping she could return to the dream. It felt like the best dream she'd ever had, and yet at the same time the most frustrating. She needed to know more.

Damn it, she hated getting up in the mornings. The transition from the freedom of dreams to the routine and responsibilities of real life was always difficult for Mary. She didn't have to get up quite yet, her first alarm hadn't even gone off yet. She had the two alarms because she needed those ten minutes in-between to wake up properly, to shake off the dream world and enter the real one. She also used it to sometimes jot down quick notes about a particularly good dream she'd had. She'd then use the notes to either simply write up the dream in her dream diary and/or use them in a poem. Her poetry notebooks were almost as thick as her dream diary's. Whatever anyone said about the quality of her poetry one thing was sure she was a very prolific poet.

Suddenly she remembered her dream from the morning before. What she now realised was that the two dreams were somehow linked. It was just getting stranger.

Mary squinted through half open eyes at her digital alarm clock, she wanted to know how long she had to enjoy the strange, happy feelings her dream had left her with before its shrill ring intruded. She had less than six minutes. Not good. Still she would make the most of it.

All too soon the sound of her first alarm interrupted her sleepy thoughts, and then she groaned as she remembered that after work that day she was due to meet her Mum and Stepdad for their monthly dinner. Always at the same restaurant, always the same old boring conversation. From dreams to a nightmare that would be her day.

For the second morning running Geth woke with a jolt, although this time without the heart thumping fear and the girly shouting. What the hell was going on? This new dream seemed like a continuation of the one from the morning before and that was kind of weird. A dream sequel, huh, that was strange even for him and his amazing capacity for dreaming all night, every night.

He glanced at his bedside clock. Nearly time to get up. Good, he didn't really feel like going back to sleep, he might have another dream.

Once up Geth headed for the bathroom. Seeing as he was up a bit early and his stubble was well on its way to becoming a beard he decided to have a shave. After a shower and a shave he needed his morning fix of caffeine. As he drank his coffee he sat at the kitchen table and studied the four new designs he'd worked on the day before. They were good, maybe even great he decided and he was looking forward to working on them later. The dream from the day before had faded a little and therefore was bothering him less and he realised that the new dream that morning, although just as strange had left him with a much calmer feeling.

He knew these new designs were linked to these dreams but he didn't want to think about it too much. He would get his mornings work done and then work on them some more like he had done the day before.

When Max awoke this time he felt a strange mixture of contentment and dread. He was unsure where the contentment came from but was fully aware of the cause of the dread. His hands were still aching from the hours he'd already spent in his workroom over the last couple of days and his work was not yet done. And now he'd had another dream. As if it wasn't enough that he still had two faces from his dream the morning before swimming in his head begging to be moulded into clay, now there was yet another strange dream to think about.

He wondered how long it would be before the fanaticism would consume him again and both longed for and dreaded it at the same time. As he waited a sudden thought struck him sending him into a brief panic. He was supposed to help out at the youth centre today. He had volunteered to give the kids a clay sculpture lesson, but he was so tired, and he had so much work to do. Maybe the need to sculpt the last two faces from his dream wouldn't come he thought hopefully, not yet at least. But before the thought was even finished, he felt a slight fluttering in his stomach.

Okay he reasoned, the class wasn't until 4.30pm, maybe he could get this out of his system by 3.30pm and still make the class. Deep down he worried that this plan was unlikely to succeed; nevertheless, he felt he needed to try. Moving fast in order to get things done before the artistic urge took over Max threw on the clay stained clothes he'd worn the day before and then retrieved his mobile phone from its usual place on the old-fashioned chest of drawers on the left-hand side of his bed.

The phone was a pretty basic model that he'd had for almost three years. It was also under used, a bit temperamental and sported several clay stained fingerprints. One function it did have though was an alarm.

Until recently Max had worked as a part time Youth Councillor for the local government authority as well as doing the odd freelance job for other organisations. He had a knack for getting through to troubled youngsters having a natural rapport with them, and they tended to trust him more than other adults. Recent government cutbacks however had meant that the council had had to let him go. The freelance work had also been a little sparse recently too meaning that even his trusted phone alarm had seen little action in the last three weeks or so. The sudden abundance of free time had been one of the reasons Max had started volunteering at the youth centre. He had been enjoying it but right now he was regretting making such a firm commitment. He didn't want to let the kids down, and yet at the same time he felt aggrieved that he would have to interrupt his work to meet his commitment to them. Therefore, he begrudgingly set the phone alarm for 15.30 and took it with him to his workroom.

Talionis did not wander far, It did not want to miss a chance and travelling even small distances sapped Its strength, strength It would need when one came his way. The new ones had passed near him once or twice but they always travelled together and It was safer for It if they were alone, at least to start with. And so It continued to watch and wait.

Eddie was at the kitchen sink washing up his morning coffee mug when he caught movement out the corner of his eye. Looking up and out of the kitchen window directly in front of him he saw Mason walking up the gently sloping lawn towards the house. Only walking was maybe the wrong word to use, staggering was closer to the mark.

Eddie left the kitchen at a run, dashing out into the hallway and towards the open French doors at the back of the house. He moved fast for such a big man and in seconds he was running down the lawn towards the struggling man.

'What's wrong?' he asked as he drew near.

'Nothing, I'm fine, just a little tired' replied Mason.

'A little tired? You look dead on your feet' said Eddie as he took Mason's dangling left arm and placed it around his own neck and shoulders, then putting an arm around Mason's waist he supported his friend as they walked back to the house.

'I'll put you in my room, it's nearer and I don't think we'll manage the stairs' suggested Eddie as they entered the hallway and headed towards the door just inside to the left. Opening the door he all but carried Mason the rest of the way across the small 'living' area of the large open plan room and over to his large double bed at the back where he gently lay Mason down.

Masons eyes were now closed and for a second Eddie thought he had gone straight to sleep but then he realised that Mason was talking, or rather whispering to be more exact. Eddie bent closer to his friend in order to catch what he was saying.

'....dream, no just sleep, no dreaming, but I did it, I think I did it, need sleep now, but no dreams, dreams are gone, all gone, hope I did it, had to do it, they will come, sleep now, sleep, but no dreaming' and then he was silent having fallen into a deep sleep.

Leaving his friend to sleep Eddie went in search of Sofia. He found her in the Office as usual.

'Hi Sofia, Mason's back, I've left him in my room sleeping, he was dead on his feet and I didn't fancy carrying him up the stairs, I've had enough stuff to carry up and down those stairs as it is' he laughed trying to lighten the mood.

'Good idea' she said with a strained smile 'I hope he's okay.'

'I'm sure he'll be fine after a good sleep.'

'I hope so. Did the other two come back with him?'

'No, I'm pretty sure they're still out there.'

'Okay, good.'

'I'm gonna go do some more work, I still have boxes to move.'

'And I have some arrangements to make. We'll meet up for dinner later with Mason and we can all catch up.'

'Sounds good.'

So as Sofia picked up the phone Eddie headed off to finish transporting the boxes up to the attic.

By lunchtime Clea had finished her blouse and the first t-shirt completely and the second t-shirt was now ready to embroider.

Whilst eating a cheese and tomato omelette she decided that for the young couple she would use the same fabric for both pieces. She had a soft, cotton fabric in a deep blue colour which would be perfect, and a lighter grey/blue cotton that would look great for the embroidery. For the young man she would stick with the basic t-shirt pattern she'd used for the other two men from her dreams. For the young lady she'd make a simple vest style top with a v neck tapered to thin shoulder straps.

Lunch finished and decisions made it was time to get back to work.

Geth had started his day in a good mood, but after an uninteresting morning tattooing he found himself getting a little grumpy and fidgety. The need to finish his designs was taking a hold of him so that when Chris asked him if he was feeling okay he almost hit him. He'd just finished tattooing a small butterfly on the shoulder of a skinny young woman who had whimpered for the whole twenty-minute session and he was feeling grumpy. The fact that Chris had noticed something was bothering him had instantly made it worse. But he wasn't a thug, and it wasn't Chris' fault so he restrained himself.

'I'm fine' he snapped instead 'I just hate cry-babies.'

He felt that was a sufficient excuse to get Chris off his back, but he was wrong.

'I'm not talking about the grumpiness' said Chris 'that's normal, I'm talking about the fact that you seem a little distracted.'

Geth was shocked; he'd thought he had things under control and that no one would know that something was playing on his mind

'Come to think of it you were kind of distracted all day yesterday too' continued Chris.

Damn it, why did Chris have to be so perceptive, why couldn't he be as dumb as he looked? No, that was a little unfair, he didn't look dumb, it was just that if it wasn't for the arms covered in tattoos and the skull tattooed on the side of his neck Chris would have been classed as a bit of a pretty boy. He had perfectly styled light brown hair, twinkly blue eyes and a slim, but muscular physique. He looked like a strange cross between a male model and a heavy metal bands roadie. But that was being stereotypical, Chris was a decent guy and a damn good tattooist. He had to give him an answer though, one that would keep him off his back and the only thing he could come up with was.

'It's nothing, I've just not been sleeping well lately that's all'

Chris looked like he was going to say something more but seemed to change his mind and just shrugged instead saying simply 'OK dude.'

Geth was relieved but was now a little wary of Chris. He'd have to keep his feelings a bit more guarded. This usually wasn't a problem; he was all about guarded normally. This dream thing really was becoming a problem.

The studio door opened then and his next customer walked in, luckily this one was a more interesting design and would hopefully keep his mind off things and improve his mood, plus it would be his last of the day.

Just over two and a half hours later Geth was finally sat back at his kitchen table ready to work on his new designs. His back was paining him a bit, but he hoped that working on the designs would take his mine off it.

Over the last year or so Geth had started to suffer the occasional bout of back pain. He was yet to see a doctor about it as he felt it was pointless. The cause was obvious, nineteen years of bending over people as he tattooed them. When he'd opened 'Studio Ink' he'd made sure to buy the best chair's he could afford for himself and the other tattooists, but he figured the damage had already been done.

The bouts had increased in frequency lately and he had on occasion considered changing his mind about seeing a doctor but had never got around to it and he didn't think they could do much about it anyway. He had told no-one about the pain, not even Chris. He didn't want him to worry. It had always been Geth's natural instinct to hide bad news from people, to shield them from it, and that was exactly what he was doing now. If he told Chris about it he knew he'd insist that he slow down a little, that he let Chris do most of the long sessions, but that wouldn't work, at least not until Rick was up to a standard where he could take on more of the smaller jobs. If and when Geth 'slowed down' it would be when he decided and on his own terms.

If he was honest Geth did think that maybe he could do with a break. He still loved his work but not in the intense, 'can't go more than a day or two without it' way he used to. He must be getting old, old and past it at thirty-nine, how depressing was that?

Giving himself a mental shake he got back to his designs and as hoped his back pain was soon forgotten as he worked.

Mary's day at work passed quite quickly which was good in one way, no one liked a draggy workday, but bad in another, it meant the time for the dreaded family dinner was fast approaching.

All too soon it was upon her.

'So, how've you been kid?'

Mary did her best to supress a grimace. Why did her stepfather think it was okay to address a twenty-six-year-old woman as kid? It annoyed the hell out of her but what could she do? She'd asked him not to do it several times but it never stuck. She wanted to correct him again now but knew it would be pointless so just gave her stock answer to his stock question.

'I've been good thanks.'

Her answer was short because another thing she'd learnt over the years was he didn't want details, he wasn't really interested, it was just an automatic question, something he felt he should say rather that an actual enquiry.

Mary had found that the best way to get through these dinners was to let her mind drift, to calm herself by thinking of other more pleasant things. The conversation was always sparse and unchallenging so there was no real need to concentrate so her system worked.

This particular day as she ate her dinner, she found it even easier to drift off into her own world as she was a little preoccupied to start with. Her mind was still full of the two dreams she'd had. It was very unusual to dream of the same four strangers twice in a row surely. Although she hadn't seen them in the second dream she had felt their presence. Then suddenly a thought occurred to her, in the dream she had flown over fields with tents in right, well that did sort of make sense as in all this preoccupation with her dreams she had forgotten that in a couple of days' time, for the first time in her life something exciting was happening in her home town, she had tickets to 'Artfest'.

'Artfest' was a new event that was basically a local arts and crafts fair meets Glastonbury. It was to be a celebration of all the 'arts'. There was to be a big outdoor stage for music and other performance arts as well as tents for both of those plus visual arts, crafts, tattoo art and then the one Mary was looking forward to most, creative writing. The event was to run over two days with all sorts of workshops, exhibits, demonstrations and performances going on, plus stalls selling art supplies and artists selling their work. And it wasn't just a local event, there would be artists coming from all over the country to take part in one way or another. Therefore, around the main field there would be fields for people to camp in just like at all the big music festivals.

One of the best things about it being local to Mary was that she wouldn't need to camp. Camping was not her thing at all. She had a ticket for both days but thankfully would be able to go home and sleep in her own bed. She realised that she may miss out on the extra atmosphere and the parties that would surely take place during the late evenings, but then she would be going to the event alone and would probably have felt vulnerable and out of place in a tent alone anyway. However, she was excited about the possibility of meeting new people, and like-minded people at that. She hoped to be able to overcome her shyness enough to talk to people, after all at least she could be sure they had something in common, and therefore something to talk about.

So this meant in a couple of days she would be spending two days in a large field full of strange people some of whom she would hopefully chat too and possibly make friends with and that was basically what she was dreaming about. Still it didn't explain how the dreams had made her feel, how different they'd felt to anything she'd dreamt before. It was weird how.....

'Mary snap out of it kid!'

'Huh?'

'Your mother asked you a question, so snap out of that dream world of yours and have the decency to answer her.'

Mary came back to reality with a thump, she was in trouble now. She'd gotten a little too wrapped up in her mind drift.

'I'm sorry Mum, what did you ask?'

'I just wanted to know why you didn't wear something pretty today like you said you would.'
Oh no, not this again.

'Mum I never said I'd wear something 'pretty' as you put it, you said I should and I said I didn't want to.'

'If it's about money I could give you some to get a nice dress or something, I'll even come with you to get it if you like.'

Mary made herself pause and take a deep breath before answering.

'Thanks Mum, but it's okay, I have plenty of clothes and you know I don't 'do' dresses.'

'I know sweetheart but I thought maybe you could just make a little effort, for me, surely it wouldn't hurt to dress up a little once in a while.'

Mary was really struggling to keep her temper now. She'd had this type of conversation with her mother so many times before and yet she could never get it through to her that she was not a girly girl, that she had her own style. What made it even worse this particular day was that Mary had made a bit of an effort. Yes she was wearing her usual black trousers, well leggings to be exact, but she had put on her little, flat Sketchers shoes instead of her usual doc martin boots and the top she was wearing, although basically a purple t-shirt, did have a silver peacock feather design emblazoned across the front. The top was a little 'flashier' than she usually wore but she had bought it with her mother in mind, hoping it would appease her, but that obviously wasn't the case.

She was about to explain that for her this was dressed up when her stepfather butted in.

'Okay girls, that's enough, let's just try to have a happy family meal, it doesn't matter what we're wearing as long as we're together.'

Mary nearly laughed at the ridiculousness of her stepfathers little speech. He made it sound like they were close when they so obviously weren't.

Annabel had been eighteen when she'd had Mary, the product of a 'holiday romance', her father having been the one on holiday. Her parents had met at a party; Mary was conceived that night and her father had returned home to America the next day. It had been a one night stand with no intentions from either party of carrying on the relationship after he returned to America and so they hadn't even swapped phone numbers. Therefore, when Annabel found out she was pregnant she'd had no way of contacting the father. All her mother, and therefore Mary knew about him was that his name is Mitchell Kelly, he has red hair and green eyes and he comes from somewhere in America.

Mary had one treasured photo of him, a grainy group shot of her Mum and her friends at the party where her parents met, with her father in the background side view on.

Mary and her Mum, despite having only each other for years were never really close. To Mary her Mum always seemed to be 'searching' for something else, with Mary just along for the ride. She was never very maternal and most of the time acted more like an older sister, though not in a good way.

Annabel took great pride in her appearance and had always looked good for her age. She had long, straight dark brown hair and big blue eyes. She was 5' 4" tall with a perfect, slim figure and a disproportionately large bust. With looks like that she had had plenty of boyfriends over the years none of which had lasted long. That was until she'd met Phillip Rodgers when Mary was eighteen years old.

Phillip was almost ten years older than Annabel but acted younger. He had thinning, sandy coloured hair and watery blue eyes and was not exactly good looking but he was always very tanned and kept reasonably fit playing golf and squash. He was the archetypal flashy businessman, owing his own, small but successful clothes manufacturing business. Mary had often wondered what her mother saw in him and in her more ungenerous moments had thought it might be his money, but they always appeared to get along well and were embarrassingly inclined to public displays of affection.

After meeting Phillip her Mum had become even more distant, making her new boyfriend and later husband her 'world' leaving Mary as the outsider.

They had moved in with Phillip after the wedding but Mary had never felt at home there.

When Mary started work at the book shop and began to make a steady wage they had suggested she get a place of her own. Mary had been only too glad to do so. They had helped her out a lot financially but she felt it was more about getting rid of her than helping her. They had paid her deposit on the flat, had given her money to furnish it and paid the first six months' rent.

On her twenty first birthday they had also brought her a car, it was a dark blue Vauxhall Corsa that had been two years old when she got it. They also still paid her an 'allowance' as her wages only just covered her bills. It was only a small amount really and sometimes she felt guilty about taking it, but on the other hand she couldn't deny that she needed it. She longed to be free, to be her own woman and she knew that as long as she took their money, she couldn't be that, but she couldn't see how to make it happen.

She enjoyed working at the book shop but would never make her fortune there, and as for her poetry she knew there was no real money to be made there either. She was trapped and she knew it and unless some amazing opportunity came along she felt she would never be free.

When the alarm went off at 15.30 Max nearly fainted with fright. The ridiculous little tune had sounded extra loud in the silent workroom. He took a deep, calming breath and restrained himself from throwing the phone across the room.

Once calm enough he appraised his work and his mood. The frantic need to work had subsided long enough around lunch time for him to pause for a quick sandwich and a cigarette but had soon returned with a vengeance. And now the bust of the red-haired woman was only half finished and with one more bust to go after it he still had a lot of work to do.

He stared at the half-formed face of the woman from his dream. What should I do he thought, can I tear myself away from my sculpture? The answer was obviously no. But how could he let the kids down? He'd feel bad if he did but deep down he knew that when it came down to it the pull of his 'dream' sculptures was too strong. Someone would have to cover for him, he was sick, yes that was it, he was too ill to do it. It wasn't far off the truth, he was mentally and physically exhausted and a little crazy maybe, that counted as ill surely. He wouldn't tell them that though obviously. A bad case of diarrhoea would do. He should have phoned earlier really to give them more warning, but what can you do, diarrhoea can come on sudden right?

His mind made up Max made the call, felt a bit bad about dropping them in it for a bit but he was soon immersed in his art, all other thoughts forgotten.

As planned Sofia, Mason and Eddie were having dinner and a catch up. Eddie had been told about the flyer that Sofia had found for Artfest and how it helped them. Now Sofia explained the plans that had been made to Mason and Eddie.

Tickets had been purchased and transport and accommodation arranged if you could call a tent accommodation. Mason had insisted when the initial plans were made that he needed to stay on site for the duration of the event and said that he had no problem with camping in a tent. Sofia had however ensured that the tent purchased for him by the Foundation had been one that was easy to put up and as comfortable as possible, after all the man had worked so hard for the last few days he needed some sort of comfort. She wouldn't budge on transport though; there was no way she was letting him make the long drive to the event himself. Therefore the Foundation was providing a car and driver to pick him up early in the afternoon the day before the first day of 'Artfest'. They would then drive him to a hotel near to the event site so he could spend a relaxing night preparing. The tent and other suppliers would be in the car ready; Mason need only pack his clothes.

Mason said he was happy with the arrangements and the smile he gave her was supposed to be reassuring but she'd spied the uncertainty in his eyes. There was a heavy burden on the man's shoulders and it was beginning to show. Mason's handsome face was looking a little drawn and his body language gave away the fatigue he must be feeling. Eddie was faring a little better his strong physique having coped well with the manual labour he'd had to put in over the last few days getting the house ready (hopefully) for their new guests. His worry over his friends and their future showed in his eyes however and Sofia knew that the same could be said of her own.

None of them knew if their plan would work, all they had was hope. Had they done enough? Only time would tell.

Whilst wandering around the art supply shop Aaron had made a slightly different plan regarding his painting. His sudden lack of work was playing on his mind and so considering a possible future lack of funds meant his plan needed altering slightly. A proper oil painting of the girl from his dream would have to be put on hold. Therefore, instead of a large, quality canvas and several tubes of oils he had bought a small, square, budget canvas' and just a couple of tubes of oils to supplement what he had already. The smaller canvas' would need much less paint and he would paint in his freer style concentrating on the face close in with no background detail.

After returning home Aaron had starting work immediately and time had flown by. Painting had always absorbed him but this was on a new level. He'd worried that working from the memory of a shadowed face from a dream rather than from a flesh and blood person in front of him or from a photo would be difficult but this fear had proven to be unfounded. The image in his mind had been translated onto the canvas with ease and he'd been so wrapped up in it he'd not even paused to eat. Now as he was starting to lose the light he made the final touches to the painting. And there she was, the girl from his dream, her face shadowed except for those beautiful eyes staring at him from the canvas. He felt happy, fulfilled and utterly exhausted. Tomorrow he would go back to the art shop and get three more canvases and some more oils, sod the expense, sod the worry of no work, he was an artist, he was in his element, his art was all he needed.

When she got home Mary got out her notebook and turned to her latest poems, her 'dream life poems' and smiled to herself as she read them. She went to bed that night hoping for another strange and wonderful dream.

By the time it got dark Clea had all but finished the five garments. The last two just needed a bit more work on the embroidered symbols but that would have to wait until tomorrow when she could work by daylight.

Clea felt that she had never done such great work, and definitely not in such a short time. Whether they would ever be worn she didn't know, except for hers obviously, but she felt proud of her work and had enjoyed making them immensely.

Now it was time for dinner, a little tv and then bed and maybe she would dream of that strange building or those faces once again.

It was getting late and Geths four designs were finally finished. He had the designs laid out on the table in front of him and he liked what he saw. These were special, not like anything he'd ever done before. They were simple designs but he felt they had more 'meaning' than his other designs and he felt proud of what he had achieved. Usually these new designs went straight in one of the flash books downstairs, or in the case of really good ones like this on the wall of the studio, but he knew that wouldn't happen with these. He had a few empty folders around somewhere and he decided he would put them in one of those and keep them safe somewhere. Safe from what he did not know, but that was as far as his plan went right now.

Geth stood slowly aware once again of his back, but to his relief he found it wasn't too bad, just a little stiffness. Hopefully, a long, hot, power shower would ease it, then it was time for bed and a well-earned and hopefully peaceful sleep.

At 11.45pm Max was finally finished. The last bust had been particularly tricky. He had worked hard to get the intensity in the man's expression just right. He also had the added complication of the man's scar to deal with. The scar was a new challenge, but Max was up for it.

Max glanced around his workroom taking in the strange sight before him. On the smaller left-hand bench sat the 'Jekyll and Hyde Trio' which he still found a little disconcerting. His larger workbench on the right was now looking a little crowded as the four 'dream' busts were taking up almost the whole bench. The overall effect was a little eerie.

Now the busts were finished they needed to dry, then once they were 'leather' dry he would have to cut each bust into two sections in order to remove the armatures from inside. Max constructed his own armatures using a heavy piece of wood for a base with an inch thick, long piece of wood screwed upright into the middle of it. Onto the top of the long piece of wood he attached a piece of aluminium wire and shaped it into a rounded arch, he then covered and filled the arch with scrunched up newspaper making a vague human head shape and setting it in place with sticky tape and elastic bands.

Once the armatures were removed Max would then have to 'hollow out' each section using special tools before sticking the two halves back together again using a mixture of clay and water known as clay slip. The busts would then be ready for firing in a kiln.

Max had two kilns, a small one in his workroom that was only big enough for two of the busts, and then a much larger kiln in the utility room downstairs into which he would be able to fit the others. But for now he was done, or rather he was done in. It was then that Max realised that he hadn't had time in his busy day to contemplate the meaning of his latest dream, but he decided that was probably a good thing. He was too tired to even think now. It was time for a shower and then bed. What he needed now was a good night's sleep.

CHAPTER 11

DAY 5 - DISCOVERY

It was early morning when Mason returned to the house. He had done all he could do for now, whether it was enough only time would tell. He felt like he could sleep for a week but most of a day would have to do.

Before going to his room he popped his head around the door of the room next to his where Eddie was busy giving the now empty room a good clean. This room was Gina and Blakes, or maybe now he should think of it in past tense because as sad as it was he knew that whatever happened the couple would not be returning to this room. Noticing his friend stood in the doorway Eddie said hi.

'How's it going?' asked Mason

'Pretty good thanks' replied Eddie not wanting to burden his friend with his problems he didn't want to let on how monotonous and back breaking the job was, not to mention the sadness involving in packing up his friends belongings 'how are things with you?'

'Things are going as well as can be expected I guess thanks.'

'That's good.'

'I'm gonna go sleep now but can you wake me at dinner time, as tired as I am I think I also need to get some food inside me, I need the energy, plus it would be nice to just sit down together for a meal before I leave for this Artfest thing cos who knows when we'll get time to just sit and talk after that.'

'Sounds good, do you think that the kids will want dinner?' he asked referring to Phoebe and Mark.

'I really don't know; sorry I should have asked.'

'It's no problem, I'll make plenty in case.'

It felt weird to both of them to be having such a mundane conversation after all the other crazy goings on of late, but it was also comforting. So they spent a few more minutes on mundane chat before Mason retired to his room leaving Eddie to his work.

Aaron was feeling restless. He lay in bed staring at the ceiling his mind buzzing after a night of little sleep. Maybe his lack of sleep was the reason he'd had so few dreams this morning, most of which he barely remembered. Having not remembered dreams was a very rare occurrence for Aaron but he felt more relieved than anything, besides he had enough to deal with regarding the dream he'd had the morning before. He was pretty sure that dream was the reason he felt so restless and uneasy. The dream itself had been a vague repeat of the dream he'd had the night before. Somehow though he felt this vague dream was pushing him in some way, but towards what? Well a field of tents obviously he thought and then had to laugh. It sounded so ridiculous.

Flinging back the bed covers he sprang from the bed, no use just lying around thinking, it was getting him nowhere. He needed fresh air and physical activity to keep his mind off things and he needed to get the supplies needed for his other three portraits.

After a quick shower and before leaving he took a quick look at the portrait he'd worked on yesterday. It was amazing if he said so himself, those eyes, so real. But there was no time to waste staring at it now, his other sketches awaited the same treatment, he needed to get going.

On his way to the art shop Aaron passed the local library. Glancing at its windows as he strolled past he saw something that stopped him dead in his tracks. Pinned in the window was a large A3 size poster, and on that poster was a familiar image, an image imprinted on Aaron's mind, an image from his dream. Stepping closer on shaky legs Aaron took a better look at the poster. It showed an aerial view of a large, grassy field scattered with billowing white tents. Yes it was definitely the image from his dream. Super imposed over the picture at the top and bottom of the poster there were words, and now the initial shock was wearing off Aaron read them his mouth agape in amazement. The poster was advertising something called 'Artfest' which was to be held locally in a couple of days' time.

'I have to go to this' he said aloud and then clapped his hand over his mouth and glanced around him embarrassed, but luckily no one was near enough to have heard him talking to himself.

He turned back to the poster his mind racing. How could this be, surely he must have seen this poster before, yes, that must be it, he'd seen it before the last time he'd passed the library and it had stuck in his mind for some reason and now he'd dreamed of it. He didn't have a clear recollection of seeing it before however, but that must have been what happened. But then that didn't explain the people in the dream and this sudden desperate need he had to be there.

What should he do? He needed more information, yes, that was it, he needed to know how to get tickets. Scanning the text on the poster again he read that tickets were available online or via various outlets which were listed online via the event website. He took out his phone, walked a few steps to the bench outside the library entrance, sat down and was soon onto the site, tapping the tab for tickets and then onto the list of outlets selling tickets. Then his heart froze as the words 'Sold Out' flashed before his eyes repeatedly against all those outlets listed.

What about online tickets he thought, there must be some left there surely. He realised it would be a bit difficult getting online tickets due to the fact that he had no debit/credit card but he could find a way, he had to. He clicked onto the online tickets tab and held his breath, but again he was crushed by the words 'Sold Out.'

No, it can't be, he needed a ticket, he was meant to go to this event, he was sure of it.

Okay, calm down and think he told himself, there must be a way. Taking a few long, deep breaths he went back to the home page and stared at the screen trying to think clearly.

A few minutes later he had an idea, what about those websites that sold concert and theatre tickets, maybe they'd have some. He eagerly began to search for websites and on the third site he tried he found some tickets. For a second his heart leaped, until he saw the price, it was extortionate, it would wipe out his funds almost completely, besides it was pointless anyway as he couldn't pay online. He had a few old friends he could maybe call and persuade to get the tickets with their cards and he'd give them cash, but how long would that take to sort and would the tickets still be available by then? But it was worth a try surely.

Whilst trying to think who his best bet to call would be he clicked back onto the event site just to see how much of a mark-up the ticket tout site had put on the tickets. It was quite a lot and it made him mad. His hands were shaking with anger and frustration and this caused his finger to jerk tapping accidently on another tab. The new page appeared on his screen startling him a little and he was about to go back onto the home page when something caught his eye. It was the words 'Help Wanted'. He scanned the words of the page his heart lifting. The organisers of the event were looking for volunteers to help set up the pitch's for those exhibiting, performing and selling. It would involve a lot of lifting and carrying and basic manual skills. It would be unpaid but anyone volunteering would get a free pass to the whole event. At the bottom of the page was a number to call if you were interested. Well Aaron was definitely interested. Making a mental note of the number he came out of the site and began dialling with shaking hands praying he had enough credit on his phone to complete the call and that they still needed volunteers.

It turned out that they definitely still needed people; in fact they were desperate for them. The organisers office was only about three miles away from the library, not too far away from the shopping centre he was headed to anyway so when they asked if he could pop by for an informal chat and to pick up details he readily agreed. He felt so relieved and happy. He was going to 'Artfest' and he felt sure he would soon know what all this craziness was about.

When Aaron left his 'chat' with the Artfest organisers there was a wide grin on his face and a spring in his step. As he'd expected the organisers had thought his past work experience made him ideal for the job, what he hadn't expected however was how well the three of them had got along.

Both men had been older than Aaron, one by quite a few years, but their love of art had bonded them together in the way only a shared love of something can. The informal chat had therefore turned in to a rather long and spirited discussion on art; particularly painting as it turned out the two men were both painters too. Aaron rarely got to talk to fellow artists like this so had enjoyed himself immensely, but eventually the organisers had to reluctantly end the conversation as they had work to do.

Aaron was on a bit of a high after leaving the 'Artfest' office and as he headed to the shopping centre he decided to have a look around a few more shops before going to the art shop so he could burn off a little of the excited energy he was feeling.

Mary was feeling very distracted and strangely excited. After all the strange and vivid dreams she'd been having lately she'd been bemused that morning to wake from an almost dreamless sleep. The dream she'd had was very vague. It was the same dream about the field of tents, but fainter. Things were getting stranger. And why did she feel like this, why did she feel this strong sense of excitement and anticipation? She'd never felt quite like this before, it was very intense.

Taking a deep, steadying breath Mary decided she needed to stop dwelling on this and just get on with her day. Lifting the pile of new paperbacks off the counter she headed for the romance section of the bookstore, she had work to do.

After re-stocking the romance section Mary headed towards the arts & crafts section as she'd noticed earlier that it was looking a bit messy so thought she'd tidy it up a bit. As she approached, she noticed a tall, dark haired man standing in front of the section she was heading for.

He was bending down to replace a large, glossy, art history book back on the shelf so she could not see his face clearly. She slowed her pace a little as she realised that he was directly in front of the section she needed to tidy, and she was just starting to turn away from him thinking she'd come back when he was gone when he suddenly straightened up as if sensing her approach and she found herself staring him in the face.

She felt a jolt of recognition followed quickly by confusion. She knew that face didn't she? But form where? And judging by the mirrored expression on his face he recognised her too. Then just as her brain registered where she knew his face from...........

Mary felt like she was going to faint as her vision dimmed around the edges and a rushing, buzzing sound filled her ears. But this wasn't a faint; it was much stranger than that. The fading sights and sounds of the man before her and the bookstore around them shifted and then disappeared so that she was surrounded instead but what she could only describe as grey fog and she could hear nothing.

Something made her turn her head to the side and for a few seconds she saw only more greyness, then she spotted a haze of whiteness like someone had turned on a light.

The 'light' was then joined by another, the two lights now hovering side by side a distance away in the grey fog. The lights began to draw nearer and as they did they grew and started to take on a vague shape. By the time they came to a stop about five feet away from her their shape had become more refined until they resembled two blurred human forms.

Then these two human shaped blobs of light drew together and merged into one before losing form, growing smaller and then disappearing altogether.

For a few seconds Mary was once again surrounded by greyness before the sights and sounds of the bookstore returned with a jolt.

Mary felt disorientated, confused and yet calm and turning her head back to face the man she had been staring at moments before she saw those same emotions mirrored in his eyes. As they gazed at each other she knew that he had just experienced exactly what she had, however weird that seemed she knew it was true.

'I know you' she said

'Yes, I know you too' he replied, 'and it sounds crazy but I think we just shared a dream whilst we were awake.'

Mary smiled and said, 'I think you're right; we did and it was amazing'.

Neither of them felt the need to voice the fact that how they 'knew' each other was from a dream and although this had to be the strangest thing that had ever happened to Mary it somehow felt so natural and true. Her heart was hammering in her chest and her stomach was rolling with butterflies but she wasn't panicked of freaked out, she was exhilarated. She couldn't stop staring at the man who'd shared this amazing experience with her and he seemed equally unable to break eye contact with her. She felt that she could say anything to him, tell him anything that came into her head and he would 'get it', but for now all she could think to say was 'I'm Mary and I'm really pleased to meet you'.

It was a bit lame, but it was true, and he replied, 'I'm Aaron and I'm really pleased to meet you too'.

They both wore matching wide grins and Mary couldn't help but giggle which felt like the most girly thing she'd ever done but she didn't care, she felt light and happy and more alive than she'd ever felt.

'I feel we have a lot to talk about, I'd really like to get to know you better' said Aaron 'when do you finish work? Maybe we could meet up somewhere?

Mary glanced at her watch.

'I finish in about an hour and twenty minutes and I'd love to meet up'.

'That's great, I guess I'll take a stroll around the shops then come back and meet you here and we can go somewhere we can talk.'

'Sounds good, I can't wait.'

'Me neither.'

For a few seconds they stood seemingly unable to break eye contact before finally Aaron reluctantly turned and began to walk away, pausing after a few steps to turn and give Mary a beaming smile and a wave before walking out of the store.

Mary had a feeling that the next hour or so would drag by so she figured the best way to get through it was to keep busy. So with that in mind she set about tidying the art books as she'd intended whilst trying to think of other tasks to keep her busy.

Meanwhile Aaron was walking towards the art supply shop; his original destination before being side-tracked by the book shop, and boy was he glad that the art book display in the store window had drawn him in because now it meant that he had literally met the girl of his dreams.

Part of him felt like he should be freaked out by what had happened, but he felt strangely accepting of it, almost like he'd been expecting it, or at least that it was more 'normal' than it was. He knew that if someone had told him a story about something like this happening to them he would have laughed and dismissed it as fantasy, but this was 'real', amazing but definitely real. In fact these last few days had been the strangest and most amazing of his life and he had a feeling that this was just the beginning, but the beginning of what, that was the question.

Geth was in a strange mood. He was not often subject to 'strange' moods, bad moods yes, but strange ones no. Other people found him complicated and hard to fathom, but to himself Geth was a straightforward, no nonsense guy. But now he felt somehow changed. These weird dreams he'd been having were confusing his usual clear mind and turning him into some sort of new age enlightened soul and he wasn't sure he liked it.

And after being haunted by dreams of strangers who somehow weren't strangers - dreams that had somehow inspired him to create four great new tattoo designs - he'd now had yesterday's dream again. And this time without the strangers' faces and tattoo designs swimming around in his mind he had had a moment of clarity and realisation. The place he'd dreamt of was somehow familiar and then he'd remembered something, it looked like the venue for a major new arts festival he'd heard about recently called 'Artfest' the fields and the marquees had looked just like the computer simulation he'd seen on the website for the event several weeks ago. But why dream of it now? And what did the four strangers have to do with it? He felt that maybe they were actually real people though how and why he was dreaming of them he didn't understand, and that was what was making him nervous.

Few things made Geth nervous which he guessed was why this was bothering him so much. After thinking it all through he knew that there was only one course of action for him to take, and as much as it went against the grain he knew what he had to do. He had to go to 'Artfest'.

The main reason that he disliked this course of action so much was that it meant he'd have to publicly change his mind about something that he'd been adamant he wouldn't and he never went back on a decision.

A few months ago Geth had been contacted by the organisers of 'Artfest' asking him if he would like a pitch at their up and coming major event. They had bigged up their project and of course had flattered and praised him, and in some ways Geth had been impressed by such a big celebration of art and had been glad that they had thought to include tattoo art, but he had ultimately turned them down. Why? Because to Geth his art wasn't about the prestige and the fame, it was about doing what he loved for himself; at least it was now anyway, it had been different when he'd started out. He'd wanted all the praise and glory he could get then, had wanted to make a name for himself, and he had succeeded too.

After working hard to learn and perfect his trade for a number of years his hard work and talent had paid off and he had become a 'name' in the world of tattoo art. He had even tattooed a number of celebrities at the height of his 'fame' and his work had been regularly featured in all the main tattoo magazines.

After a while however Geth had found being in the 'limelight' wrong for him. He had always been a very guarded, private person and so when all the attention had led to people wanting to know more about the man himself and not just his art he'd backed off. He'd loved seeing photos of his best work in all the magazines, but when the magazines had started wanting to send someone to do in depth interviews with the artist he'd flat out refused. They had pestered him for a while but had eventually given up and gone on to find other, new talents who were more willing to open themselves up to public scrutiny.

Although he had quickly faded from the limelight Geth was still respected in his field. Some of his work still made it into the magazines and people were often willing to travel quite a way in order to get a Geth Hudson tattoo, so he was perfectly happy with his life.

But now he needed to do something that he really didn't want to do. He had to phone the 'Artfest' organisers and tell them he'd changed his mind. But first he had to tell Chris.

Chris had opened up the studio that morning as Geth had no clients until early afternoon and was just finishing a small rose tattoo on a woman's hip so Geth waited listening impatiently to the mild flirting going on between Chris and his attractive female client.

Finally the tattoo and the flirting were done. After Chris' (happy) client left Geth told him he had something to tell him. Chris raised an eyebrow.

'Sounds serious' he said but with a smile.

'Not serious, but important' Geth replied 'It's about Artfest; I've decided that I do want to go after all'.

There were a few seconds of stunned silence before Chris spoke.

'Wow, really? I have to say I'm shocked, but pleased, you know I always thought it would be good for the business, but why the sudden change of heart?'

Geth knew that question would come but unfortunately he still didn't have a sensible answer to give Chris so had to make do with a simple

'I don't know, I've just decided to go after all.'

'Okay, well that's great, so they still have a pitch for you then?'

'Of course' replied Geth though his heart did a sudden dip at the realisation that there was a big chance that the pitch was no longer available, in the heat of the moment he hadn't really thought of that scenario.

'Well in that case good luck mate, hope you have a great time.'

Geth detected a note of jealousy in Chris' voice and felt suddenly guilty. He knew that Chris would have loved to represent Studio Ink at the event and had offered to go in Geth's place the first time round, but the organisers had wanted Geth, so he'd been disappointed. Geth knew this must be hard on his friend and felt bad, but he also knew that he had to go, and had to go alone both because of the 'mystery' of why he was going and for practical reasons, after all someone had to look after the studio. But he needed to say something to Chris, to give him more, the guy deserved it.

'Thanks Chris, I appreciate that you would've loved to go so this is probably hard for you but I've decided I really need to do this, it's important somehow, I can't explain it, it's just how it is.'

Chris was a little taken back as this was really opening up by Geth's standards.

'It's okay mate there'll be other events, and who knows if this one goes well they may do it again every year right?'

'Right, and next time you can go.'

'Yeah, next time.'

The conversation petered out, both men feeling a little embarrassed. Chris wandered over to his workstation to clear up it being their assistant Rick's day off, and with a quick word to Chris Geth darted off upstairs to his flat. It was time to call the event organisers to see if he could really pull this off.

First Geth had to find the number to ring. He was sure he still had the leaflet they'd sent him somewhere. After a few minutes searching he found it amongst a pile of mail he'd kept on the little table next to his sofa. He then took his mobile from his pocket, sat down on the sofa and dialled the number.

The first person he spoke to was very unhelpful and (rather sarcastically) informed him that he'd left it far too late as all the pitches were long gone. But Geth was determined. He remembered that the man who had called him originally to offer him a pitch was called Darren and that he was in charge of the tattoo section of the event and so he insisted he was put through to him.

The unhelpful woman was reluctant to do so at first but Geth's rather intimidating and forceful manner got to her in the end and so she finally put him through to her much more sympathetic colleague.

As Geth had remembered Darren was a fan of his work, hence the initial offer, and therefore was much more inclined to help. Although he confirmed that the pitch's had all gone he told Geth that in his case he may be able to 'add' a pitch for such a well-respected artist, but that he would need to check a few things first and so would have to call Geth back.

The next hour and twenty minutes were excruciating as he waited for the return call. He felt bad about leaving Chris alone in the studio downstairs but there was no way he could concentrate on any work or sit there chatting to Chris, therefore he ran quickly down and checked with Chris that there were no customers due (there weren't) and then explained he was waiting for an important call and told Chris to give him a shout if he needed him. Then he waited.

When the phone finally rang he all but shouted 'Hello!' down the receiver, but Darren appeared unperturbed. He happily proceeded to explain that having finally managing to track down his very busy colleagues they had all agreed that it was possible to add a pitch especially for Geth. He then asked Geth for his e mail address so that he could send all the details regarding directions, time schedules, parking etc. Geth happily gave him his e mail address and thanked him profusely. He had never been so grateful to anyone in his life and so generously offered to tattoo Darren for free either at the event itself or at a date that suited him. Darren was ecstatic at the offer and said he'd find Geth on the first morning of the event and organise a time. They spoke a little longer about details and then both men ended the call feeling very happy indeed.

Geth had a lot of organising to do in a short time, but he didn't feel intimidated by it, he felt exhilarated. He had a feeling his life was about to take a major new turn. But for now it was back to 'normal', he had a client due, the rest of his preparations would have to wait.

Clea was in her workroom. She was finishing off the t-shirts for the young couple from her dreams and she felt happier than she had in a long time. She was beginning to feel that her life had purpose again, though what that purpose was she wasn't yet sure. All she knew was that her dreams were leading her somewhere, to someplace special and after the dream she'd had this morning she felt that her journey would be starting very soon.

It had been the same dream as the morning before, though a little fainter maybe, but having had it before it was easy to recall and the feeling the dream had given her was only stronger.

Unlike the strange building from her first dream the setting of this new dream seemed familiar, yet at the same time she knew it was a place she had never visited. She was desperate to know where this place was, and knew that the knowledge was there, in the back of her mind somewhere, but she also knew that it was best to let it come to her naturally, that trying to force it would only bury it deeper. Therefore, she concentrated on her work instead. She had always enjoyed needlework and felt that these latest pieces were far more exciting than anything she'd done before.

Her mother had taught her to sew at an early age and her fondest childhood memories were of those times spent with her mother sewing, chatting and laughing.

Her mother had died thirteen years ago, and she still missed her terribly at times. Her father was still alive, but they had never been close, and she rarely saw him now as he had moved away after he retired to live by the sea where he could paint endless seascapes to his heart's content, and she didn't blame him for that.

Her mother may have taught her the basics of her trade, but it was from her father that she had inherited her artistic talent. When she was young, he had spent time teaching her to draw but had soon grown impatient with her when he realised her talents lay in drawing patterns and designs rather than painting landscapes and still life.

Then when she'd begun to use her talent to draw fashion and embroidery designs, he'd given up totally in disgust. Clea wasn't bitter about it, she was a little sad that her father disapproved of her choice, but she knew it was the right one for her and so hadn't let his disapproval stop her. At least she'd managed to make a living out of her art.

Whilst still living at home she'd helped her mother with her alteration and clothes making business. Then at twenty-one she'd left home to live with a group of 'artist' friends and had set up her own small clothes making business supplementing it with regular trips to arts and crafts fairs with her friends where they would all try to sell their work and get more business. In Clea's case she would buy cheap, plain cushion covers and embroider her own designs onto them to sell. She would also take along a selection of clothes to show off her work and hopefully get orders. She always did pretty well and had made a reasonable living.

After she married Andrew things had changed a little. She had felt less inclined to leave him and travel to the fairs further from home and so had only gone to those held locally. She had also started taking on more alteration work.

Her friends had been a little disappointed, but they had understood. She was still on good terms with them all. Some of them still travelled to the fairs, and still occasionally asked her to come along, but even after Andrew died she had not gone back to it. That part of her life had been great, but it was the past and she knew it wouldn't be the same now. In fact only the other week her friend Simon had e mailed her about some art event that they were all rather excited about. It was some new event called Artfest that was supposedly the biggest of its kind ever and for a brief moment she'd been swept up in her friend's enthusiasm. That was until she saw where the event was to take place. It was a long way from where she lived and so not a journey you could do in a day and her camping days were well and truly behind her. She couldn't picture herself in a muddy field pitching a tent ready to spend the night and so she had regrettably e-mailed Simon to say she wouldn't be going.

Wait a minute she thought, muddy fields, tents, oh my god! Clea suddenly sat bolt upright, the needle dropping from her fingers. Her dream, the place in her dream, she had seen it before. When Simon had sent her the e mail he'd included a link to a site advertising the event. The site had included a computer designed image of how the organisers envisioned the event would look. It had been an aerial view of a huge field dotted with large, white marquees just like in her dream.

Clea sat for a minute not knowing what to do as she tried to process this information. The e mail had arrived weeks ago and she hadn't really thought about it again since deciding not to go, so surely the e mail itself hadn't prompted the dream. So why dream of it now? There was only one reason she could think of and that was that the dream was one of her 'premonitions', which meant that she was meant to go to this event. No, stronger than that, she was destined to go to this event. This realisation and the excitement it caused took her breath away and it was a few minutes before she could get herself together enough to act.

Once she had herself sufficiently calmed, she reached for her phone which was on the small table by her work chair and scrolled through her contacts list until she came to Simon. Taking a calming breath she tapped the little phone symbol and waited.

'Hello' he thankfully answered on the fourth ring.

'Hi Simon, its Clea, how are you?'

'Clea, hi, I'm good thanks, how are things with you?'

'I'm fine thanks, how are Jenny and little Peter?'

She was desperate to get the point of her call but didn't want to be rude so found herself going through the usual formalities.

'They're both good too thanks. So to what do I owe the pleasure of this call?'

Thank goodness he'd been brief and she could get to it.

'This Artfest you e-mailed me about a few weeks ago, I was wondering, do you know if there are still tickets available, and if so how I could get one, only I've changed my mind and I'd like to come if possible.'

She held her breath as she waited for his answer.

'Well, as far as I'm aware all the pitches have been sold in the crafts tent, I managed to get one but ....'

'No Simon, it's okay, I'm not necessarily after a pitch, I just need to come to the event' she interrupted.

'Oh, okay, in that case I might be able to help you.'

'You can?' Clea said, her voice rising in excitement.

'I said I might. Are you okay, you sound a little...?'

'I'm fine Simon, please can you help me?'

'Well I do have a couple of extra tickets as I got a few at discount because I bought a pitch.'

Clea's heart lifted only to plummet again at his next words.

'The thing is I have already offered them to a friend and his wife.'

'Oh' the disappointment in her voice was clear.

'But' continued Simon 'they haven't confirmed they want to go yet.'

'I see' Clea dare not let her hopes rise again and why panic anyway; maybe she could get tickets elsewhere. Still Simon was her best bet, after all the event was only a couple of days away; surely the tickets were all sold by now?

'I tell you what I'll do Clea, I'll give my friend a ring and tell him someone else is interested and see what he says. To be honest I'm a bit annoyed with him for dithering for this long, but I did offer them and I can't go back on it if he decides to come.'

'I understand.'

'The other problem is I have two tickets and you only want one, I'm not sure I'd be able to get rid of the other in time and they are quite pricy even with my discount as they're for both days.,

'Don't worry about that Simon, I'll buy both and it doesn't matter how much they are.'

'Are you planning on bringing someone then?'

'I don't know, maybe' she lied 'but either way I'll have both.'

'Wow you really are eager aren't you?'

'Yes Simon I am.'

'Okay, I'll ring my friend now and give you a call back.'

'Thanks Simon.'

'No problem, bye.'

'Goodbye.'

After putting down the phone Clea slumped in the chair, her hand across her heart, her fingers crossed. She had to be at this event, she just had to, it was important.

The fifteen-minute wait for Simon's return call was interminable and when the phone did finally ring it made her jump out of her skin.

'Hello' she said breathlessly.

'Hello Clea, the tickets are yours.'

She almost jumped for joy and for a minute was speechless.

'Hello Clea, are you still there?'

'Yes, yes I'm still here. Thank you Simon, thank you so much.'

'It's no problem. You sounded so keen so I convinced my friend he didn't really need to come, I think he was kind of relieved in the end actually, besides, he's not an artist like us, just an appreciator of art as he calls it, but I think you'll get much more out of it.'

'Yes, yes I will definitely.'

'Besides, it will be nice to see you, it's been a while.'

'Yes, I look forward to seeing you too.'

Their conversation continued for another ten minutes or so as they discussed money and decided he would send the tickets by recorded post as he would be at the site early to set up his pitch and so could not meet her beforehand. He insisted that she not send a cheque for the money but give it to him in person on the first day instead. They settled details and said their goodbyes.

Clea put down the phone and let out a huge sigh. She was about to embark on an exciting new part of her life and she couldn't wait. But there was no time to waste, she had garments to finish and a lot to organise so she better get a shift on.

The art supply store was busier than usual and so Max stood waiting impatiently behind two other customers. He was fidgety with nerves as he was worried that the store's stock of clay would be too low to fill his usual order. He was a regular customer at the store and so they always made sure they had stock in for him on his usual by-monthly visit. However, it was only three weeks since his last visit as he'd used his two months' supply up in the space of a few days and he was afraid the store had not had time to replenish their stock.

As he waited his mind drifted back to that morning. He had been so relieved when he had awoken without having had any dream of wings or the faces of strangers, and for the first time in days he hadn't felt the urge to jump from his bed and head to his workroom. In fact he had almost managed to drift back off to sleep. But only almost. As he had started to drift off again he had had a sudden 'dream flash image' and his eyes had shot open again. On first awaking he had thought that he didn't remember having any dreams at all, but he had dreamt, and it had come back to him in a flash.

He had dreamt again that he was looking down upon a huge field full of large marquees and there had been four people with him. His dream self had begun to descend towards the field, the others descending with him, the four people that he could not see but who's faces he knew and suddenly he knew he must meet. He'd felt that this should be freaking him out but he'd felt quite calm although still mystified by it.

Over a leisurely breakfast he had made his simple, everyday plans. First he needed to make a trip to the art supply store. On the way home from the art store he planned to stop at the local supermarket, then return home for a relaxing, long lunch after which he would go back into his workroom and prepare his busts for the kilns. He would just have enough room to get them all in. Then he would rest, he needed it after the craziness of the last two days.

His plans made he had headed out to the garage. He wasn't keen on driving, preferring his push bike but although he was a keen cyclist the art store was almost an hour cycle away and a two months' supply of clay was very heavy and too cumbersome for a bike. Therefore he always drove.

He'd pulled up the garage door and stood for a second looking at the car. It was a 1988 Jaguar Sovereign XJ40 in metallic grey, with a doe skin leather interior. The car had belonged to his father who had loved it and kept it in pristine condition. When his father died five years ago it had become part of Max's inheritance, along with the house and everything his parents had owned as his father's death had followed shortly after his mothers. An orphan at twenty-eight Max had been left well off but alone. His parents had him late in life both having put their careers first, his father a doctor, his mother a teacher, and although strict, old fashioned and a little distant they had been good parents and he still missed them.

He tried his best to keep the car in good condition, making sure it was serviced and cleaned regularly but he didn't have the love for it that his father had. It was not his type of car; it was flashy and expensive to run. The expense was not really a problem in practice, but he always felt uncomfortable in it as he would have preferred something smaller, less ostentatious and much more environmentally friendly.

He could of course have sold it, but for some reason had never been able to. He felt his father would have wanted him to keep it, but then again, he also knew that his father would have been horrified to see it used only for transporting bags of clay and the monthly big shop.

Neither of his parents had ever understood his passion for art and clay sculpture in particular. They had wanted him to be a doctor like his father but he'd always known he didn't have the stomach for it. He had done his best to please them by going to college and becoming a councillor and had tried to convince them that his chosen profession was like a cross between a doctor and a teacher, and that he helped people as much as they did. They had done their best to accept his choices in life but he knew he had been a disappointment to them, yet he also had no doubt that they had loved him.

'Hey there Max, what you doing here so soon, you've not used all that clay already surely?'

The sound of the store owners' voice brought Max back to the present. The other two customers were gone and Paul, the owner was looking at him expectantly from behind the counter.

'Actually I have used it all' Max replied sounding apologetic.

'Wow, you have been busy' said Paul impressed.

'Yeah, the last few days have been a bit crazy and I erm, well I kind of need some more, how much do you have in stock?'

'Well, we haven't had our usual big order in yet, but I should have something out back, I'll just go look for you.'

'Okay, thanks'

Paul disappeared through the door behind the counter leaving Max nervously drumming the counter with his fingers. Realising what he was doing he shoved his hands into his trouser pockets and tried to look relaxed by casually glancing around the store. There were two teenage girls sorting through a box of oil paints on sale over to his right and over to his left near the door a middle-aged man was browsing the small art book selection. On the end of the counter to his left Max saw the familiar small display rack filled with flyers and leaflets. He took a step towards it intending to have a quick look through for anything new and interesting when something caught his eye. It was a large, glossy flyer depicting a familiar scene, a scene from Max's dream.

After paying for the thankfully sufficient supply of clay the art store owner had found in his store Max had loaded it into his car in a daze, and then sat in the car for several minutes not knowing what to do. Clutched in his hand had been the now rather scrunched up leaflet depicting the field of marquees, the field from his dream.

He'd laid the leaflet on his right thigh and smoothed it out a little with his shaking hands so that he could read the printed words again. Then he had thrown the leaflet onto the passenger seat and started the car. Forgetting his plans to do a supermarket shop followed by a leisurely lunch he had instead driven straight to the Youth Centre. He needed a computer and not having one at home this was his only option.

The staff had been surprised and pleased to see him and he had therefore felt a little guilty about letting them down the day before, but he desperately needed to use one of the three computers they had there for the kids to use.

When he'd asked if this would be okay they were thankfully fine with it. The computers were a few years old and therefore a bit slow but he'd managed to get onto 'Artfest' website without any problems. By this time he'd been more than a little worked up. Going to this event had suddenly become desperately important to him for reasons he did not understand. He'd always had a bit of a manic personality but this mania only usually applied to his sculpting, he'd never felt so 'compelled' to do anything else in his life before.

Upon discovering that tickets were all sold out Max had groaned 'No!' rather loudly causing all the staff and children to turn and stare at him. Blushing he had apologised and buried his face in his hands.

Maddie, a fellow volunteer, had then approached him. Always helpful Maddie was the youngest and most popular of the youth centre staff. She was petite and blonde and was always smiling. The kids loved her. She'd tentatively asked Max if he was okay and if there was anything she could do. Still embarrassed he'd explained that he was unable to get tickets to an event he desperately needed to go to feeling that she probably thought his reaction had been rather over the top. But if she'd thought that Maddie hadn't let on, instead she'd offered up a few suggestions that Max would never have thought of himself. He wasn't very computer savvy, didn't have one at home but had learnt the basics at college. All the social networking sites and suchlike were a mystery to him, however. Maddie on the other hand had zipped from site to site (as quickly as the old computer would let her that is) and within twenty minutes had found various sites where people were selling off tickets for the event.

Max had been so grateful he'd almost hugged the girl but his natural shyness had won over and he'd just thanked her profusely instead. Then with Maddie's help he'd decided on which tickets to buy (it had to be a full two-day pass), had found the best deal and had paid using his debit card. The price had been hefty and Maddie had gasped at it but Max didn't care, he was lucky enough to be able to afford it and even if he couldn't he would have found a way to pay. The tickets were to be sent to him overnight by recorded delivery, he just hope they arrived in time. Now he had the tickets he'd felt a little more relaxed and so decided to stay and help out with the kids for a bit to make up for the day before, and besides the kid's chatter would help keep his mind from dwelling on what it all meant.

Then later when he got home the busts would be dry enough for him to prepare and then put into the kilns.

Aaron was waiting for Mary when she left the bookstore just as he said he would be, not that she'd ever doubted it, in fact she's never been so sure of something in her life. This new confidence in something, or rather someone was new to Mary and she liked it. There was no awkwardness between them at all, conversation was natural and easy, they just felt 'right' together from the start. Mary suggested they go to a little café she often went to and as they walked the short distance to it they chatted away like old friends.

When they got to the café Mary ordered tea and Aaron coffee and they sat at a corner table and continued to chat. Mary told him about her job at the bookstore and how much she liked it, and he told her of his most recent job and how much he hated it. They talked a little of their families but it wasn't a favourite subject for either of them so they moved on to more fun subjects.

They discussed music discovering they both had wide, varied tastes some of which they had in common. They talked a little about TV and movies, a favourite subject of Mary's but not so much of Aaron's.

By this time the tea and coffee were long drunk, and they were beginning to get looks from the staff, so they decided as it was close to 6.30 they'd stay and order some dinner. So, with the café staff happy and their food on the way they continued their conversation turning to a subject they both loved, art.

When Mary found out Aaron could paint she was thrilled and when he said he did portraits she was impressed. She told him she'd always been awed by his sort of talent, that how someone could capture a likeness on paper or canvas like that had always amazed her. Aaron pointed out that she hadn't seen his work yet and might find it lacking, but she said she was sure his portraits were fantastic and that she'd love to see his work some day and was jealous because she couldn't draw to save her life.

'And I guess that explains that' she said pointing to the large bag of art supplies that he had placed on the empty chair beside him.

'Yeah, I've been very inspired these last few days and needed more supplies.'

'I know exactly what you mean, me too.'

'I thought you said you couldn't draw to save your life?'

'Oh no I can't, I mean the being inspired lately bit, I write poetry and it's my ambition to write a novel sometime in the not too distant future.'

'Wow, really, that's impressive.'

Mary was surprised and happy with this positive reaction, he seemed genuinely impressed, most people just laughed and/or changed the subject pretty quickly. But Aaron asked her questions about her poetry and he even said he'd love to read some of her poems and she could tell he really meant it.

Then Aaron told her about his recently acquired job at Artfest and she nearly jumped out of her seat in excitement. She told him that she had a ticket to the whole event and how excited she was about going and he said he felt the same and now even more so as 'he hoped' she would attend the event with him. She said she'd love to.

It was now almost 8.00 and therefore almost time for the shopping centre to close so they decided they needed a change of venue as they still had plans to make for Artfest and neither of them wanted their evening together to end yet.

Mary explained that she needed to get her car from the shopping centre car park then having established that he didn't have a car that she would drive them the short distance to a quiet pub she knew about. She explained that she wasn't much of a pub goer and that a crowded, noisy pub was not ideal for their needs, but that she'd heard that this pub was a quiet, cosy drinking spot rather than a rowdy boozer. Truth was it was Stella who'd told her about the place and what she'd actually said was it was 'quaint and boring' but Mary figured that was the type of place you went to when you wanted a good chat with excellent company.

The drive was short and the talk light as they were waiting to get to the pub before continuing their Artfest plans.

When they arrived Mary was pleased to find that her choice was a good one. The pub was about half full but quite subdued with no loud music playing. They got their drinks at the bar, a beer for him and a coke for her and found a table set in a cosy nook at the back of the room. The setting was ideal and they were soon deep in discussion.

They decided that Mary would pick Aaron up very early and drive him to the special 'helpers' entrance he'd been told to go to. He was convinced that she would be allowed in with him to help as he knew they were short-handed and the fact that she already had tickets would help.

If they didn't let her in, she would have to leave him and go to park in the visitors parking area and wait until the event opened and then they could meet somewhere inside. The uncertainty worried Mary a little but she was feeling a lot braver than usual and was willing to take the risk.

All too soon the pub was closing and it was time for them to leave. Once outside the pub Mary offered to give Aaron a lift home and seeing as it was too late to catch a bus he took her up on her kind offer. However, as he didn't know the area they were in very well he said he wasn't sure how to get home from there, but maybe they could head back to the shopping centre as he thought he could remember the way from there.

They didn't talk much on the journey partly because Aaron was concentrating on giving Mary directions and Mary on following them, and partly because they were lost in their own thoughts regarding all that had happened that day. They hadn't really discussed their dreams much, they hadn't really wanted to dwell on how unusual the whole situation was, they'd just wanted to enjoy each other's company, and now it was nearly time to part for the night.

Even above all the strangeness Aaron was finding it odd how easily he'd opened up to Mary during the evening. He found her so easy to talk to and he somehow knew he could trust her completely. She was special, and not just because she was beautiful, they had developed such a strong connection over such as short time he was amazed, excited and more than a little confused.

Mary was also thinking along much the same lines. She'd never been able to chat so easily to a guy before, especially not one she was attracted to. And the way they'd met had just been mind-blowingly strange and yet wonderful, and the mystery of the dreams was making it all so much more exciting.

All too soon they reached their destination and Mary was parking the car outside the boarding house.

After a few seconds of silence Aaron said, 'Thanks so much for the lift, and thanks for a great evening, it's been crazy but amazing.'

'I had a great time too' replied Mary turning to face him with a smile 'and I'm even more excited about going to Artfest now I'm going with you,'

'Yeah, I think it's going to be a great couple of days' he agreed returning her smile. 'By the way what are you up to tomorrow?'

'I'm working until three o'clock but we can meet after if you want to do something.'

'That's great, I can work on my portraits and then we could meet up when you've finished work.'

'Sounds good. I'd love to see your sketches and portraits so how about I come here straight from work then I can take a look and we could go back to mine and I'll cook us dinner.' Mary was a little shocked at her own forwardness and felt a brief moment of panic thinking she may have pushed it too far, but Aaron soon put an end to her worries.

'I'd love that, I have to admit I'm a bit nervous about you seeing my work but at the same time really want to share it with you.'

Mary beamed 'Great, that's the plan then.'

As they chatted they had both turned their bodies a little in their seats and so they were pretty much facing each other now. The only lighting was a nearby streetlamp so their faces were half in shadow. For a few moments they sat in silence gazing at each other drinking in a last look before they had to part company. Instinctively they moved closer together at the same time, and them still closer until their lips met. The kiss started off slow and gentle but quickly grew more passionate until they finally had to break apart in order to catch their breaths.

Still breathing a little heavy Aaron was first to speak.

'Wow, that was one hell of a kiss but I must admit I kind of half expected things to all get a bit foggy and weird again' he said with a mischievous grin.

Mary's grin was just as wide.

'Me too' she said and they both laughed.

It was the perfect end to an amazing day.

CHAPTER 12

DAY 6 – MEETING OF MINDS

The new day started as normal at The Gateway. Mason was sleeping after another tiring night, Phoebe and Mark were as usual doing their 'thing' out in the Factory, Eddie was upstairs cleaning the now cleared rooms and Sofia was in the office making calls.

With most of the plans already made Sofia was soon finished and found herself alone and at a bit of a loose end. There would be more work ahead, but right now she'd hit a lull and she didn't know what to do with herself. She decided she would ask Eddie if he needed any help in a bit but before that she decided she needed a bit of air and so would go for a walk.

The grounds around The Gateway house were vast and beautiful from the sloping manicured lawn at the back of the house to the woods that surrounded the house on all sides, so she decided to take advantage of the lovely weather and take in some of its beauty.

Heading down the lawn to the edge of the woods she decided to walk the treeline to make the most of the dappled sunshine. Coming around towards the front of the house she noticed that the woods were prettier and less dense than those at the back of the property so she decided to go a little deeper into the trees. After walking a little way she came across a fallen tree. It must have been toppled quite a few years ago as the underside of the trunk was covered in moss, but the top side was pretty clear and made for a good place to sit, so she decided to take a seat and rest a little. It was peaceful here and she sat with her eyes closed drinking in the quiet atmosphere.

A sudden cracking noise gave her a jolt, her eyes snapping open as she jumped to her feet. Looking around her she could see nothing but trees but it had sounded like twigs snapping under foot. Was someone else in the woods? She strained her ears to listen for other noises but heard only her own, slightly heavy breathing and bird song, but she still couldn't see anything or anyone. Maybe it was Eddie looking for her? But then she had her mobile on her so he would have called if he needed her surely. Should she call out, ask who was there?

Before she could decide though things started to get stranger. She had the sudden feeling she was being watched, she could see no one around but felt a definite 'presence' nearby.

Then suddenly she felt a flash of pain shoot through her head. She cried out, her hands instinctively coming up to clutch her temples even as the pain faded. What the hell was that? The pain had been intense but brief and now her head felt foggy. Before she could make any sense of it the pain came again causing her to fall to her knees. Again the pain was brief but stronger and more debilitating. She felt weak and confused. She needed help.

Her mobile phone was in the back pocket of her jeans, so she reached around and managed to get hold of it and turn the screen on, but as she attempted to bring up Eddies number her hand jerked involuntarily sending the phone into the air. It landed a couple of feet away in some dead leaves. She scrambled forwards on her knees rooting around in the leaves for it. She was really scared now.

Just as her fingers found the phone the pain pierced her once again. This time her limbs went numb and she toppled onto her side and then over onto her back. Then her whole body started to convulse and a strange whispery voice echoed in her head. The voice was saying 'do it, do it, do it.'

Sofia screamed then, long and loud, she still had control of her voice at least. The voice still repeated in her head but fainter now.

'Nooooooo!' she shouted as forcefully as she could even though she had no idea what the strange voice was urging her to do and the voice thankfully ceased. Her relief was intense and a little sob escaped her lips. She then realised that she had control of her limbs again. Moving slowly and carefully she stood up. Then she hunted around for her phone.

Eddie was in the kitchen having a snack break when his phone rang. He was surprised to see Sofia pop up as the caller ID.

'Hi Sofia, what's up?'

'Eddie I need your help, please come. I'm in the woods out front making my way towards the house I think. Somethings happened I can't explain but I need you to come meet me, I'm scared. Please come.'

'It's okay, I'm coming' Eddie reassured her as he set off at a run through the house and out towards the woods.

'Call my name' he instructed as he ran 'stay on the phone but keep shouting so I can track you.'

Sofia did as he said and five minutes later he found her. Without hesitation or seeming effort he scooped the shaking woman up into his arms and carried her quickly back to the house. Taking her into the office room he sat her in one of the comfy chairs by the window and sat himself in the chair opposite.

'It's okay, you're safe now. Take a minute to calm yourself and then you can tell me what happened.

Once Sofia had calmed herself she told Eddie what had happened to her. Eddie was dumbfounded by Sofia's account of her experience.

'I really don't know what to make of that' he said when she'd finished talking.

'I have no idea what is going on either but I felt a definite presence out in the woods before the pain started, like there was something or someone out there watching me.'

'Something like what?'

'I don't know Eddie; I can't explain it. We really don't need this right now and I don't think we should tell Mason what happened to me, he needs to concentrate on his own task and he doesn't need any extra stress. I will tell the Foundation obviously but not quite yet; I need to get my head around it a little first'.

'I understand, and I agree, we keep what happened to you from Mason.'

'Thank you Eddie you really have done an amazing job over the last few days and I really appreciate your help' there was a little waver of emotion in her voice.

'It's no problem; I'm just doing my job.' Said Eddie a little embarrassed at the praise and suddenly very protective of Sofia. She still seemed understandably rattled by what had happened to her and he felt at a loss as to what to do to help her, except for one other little thing that is, one little human thing that almost never failed to sooth someone a little. And so that's why when Mason entered the room a few seconds later he discovered Sofia and Eddie in mid hug.

'Hello, what's going on her then' he said in mock sternness.

The two sprang apart like guilty lovers caught in the act which made Mason laugh.

'No need to panic' Mason reassured them 'I'm sure it was innocent and if it wasn't go for it, but maybe in a more private room.'

'Are you telling us to 'get a room'' said Eddie making them all laugh this time.

'All joking aside' said Sofia 'we could all do with a hug now and then and I think if anyone else does its you Mason so why don't you come over here and join us.'

Mason didn't need any persuading as he readily joined in with the mini group hug.

As agreed they did not tell Mason about what had happened to Sofia, instead they had a leisurely lunch together before Mason went to his room to get ready as the Foundation driver was due any minute to collect him.

Mary's workday was dragging big time, she felt like she'd been there for hours but it was still only 11.45am. On the plus side she was in a very good mood. Despite being disappointed at not dreaming of Aaron that morning she'd woken up feeling great, not to mention excited about the afternoon and evening ahead.

They had exchanged a few texts early that morning and she had set off to work happy but knowing the morning would seem a long one. More than once so far Stella or a customer had jolted her from daydreams and now her mind began to drift again, back to the night before and the wonderful goodnight kiss. Aaron's lips were so beautiful, so full and soft, her stomach did flips just thinking about it.

Aaron had shared Mary's disappointment upon waking after a dreamless sleep and had enjoyed their short text conversation but luckily for him the morning was passing much quicker as he was spending it doing what he loved, he had always found that time passed quickly when he painted, and he was certainly glad of that now.

After a quick breakfast he'd began work on the portrait of the intimidating looking man next as his facial scar would be a new challenge for him and he relished a challenge. After prepping the canvas he began to paint and was soon completely lost in his art.

The plan had been that Mary would text him when she was leaving work as even though he knew what time she was working until he knew he'd be involved in his work so would need a heads up so he could tidy up a bit before she arrived.

When the text came Aaron was scrutinising his almost finished painting. He was pleased with his work so far but it just needed a little touch here and there. He just had time to do a few before he needed to clear up didn't he?

But inevitably he was soon engrossed and unaware of time passing; therefore, it was a shock to him when there was a knock on his door.

Damn it she was here and he wasn't prepared at all.

'Just a minute' he called as he began to frantically try to tidy the room a bit. It was embarrassing enough to have her see his crummy little room let alone see it in this mess.

He quickly threw his oil paints into the box he kept them in, moved the easel so his painting was facing the corner, and picked up the sheet he used to protect the carpet, screwed it into a ball and then shoved it under the bed with the box of paints. That would have to do. Wiping his paint splattered hands on his paint splattered t shirt he went to open the door.

'Hi' said Mary

'Hi, I was just tidying up a bit, come in. It's still a bit messy I'm afraid, sorry.'

Mary entered looking around.

'And I'm pretty messy myself too' he said indicating his messy t shirt.

'It looks fine, and so do you' she said smiling at him.

'And you look great' he said before planting a gentle kiss on her lips 'how was work?'

'Boring and torturously slow.'

'Not good.'

'No. How's your morning been?'

'Better than yours by the sound of it. I've been busy with my second portrait so time has flown by, but I'm really glad to see you. Take a seat' he said indicating the small armchair opposite the foot of the bed. 'I just need to give my hands a wash.'

Mary sat where indicated as Aaron went to the small sink to the left of the bed. After washing his hands he came and sat on the end of the bed facing her.

'Do you want anything to drink? I have some cans of coke or I can make some tea.'

'No I'm fine thanks, besides I really want a look at your sketches and paintings I've been looking forward to it all day.'

'You're eager.' he laughed 'I'll show you the sketches first.'

Aarons A3 portfolio was propped up against the side of the bed so he reached for it and laid it across his lap. Rummaging around inside he found the four pieces of A4 paper with his 'dream' sketches on. He was feeling a little nervous now. He hoped she liked them, especially the one he'd done of her.

'Okay, I'm saving the one of you until last but here we go.'

He handed them to her one by one, except for hers which he held back for now. She studied each one not saying anything until she had seen them all and so he was on tender hooks until she finally spoke.

'Aaron these are so good, I love the shadowed yet strangely detailed style, how on earth can you do that from just a glimpse of a face in a dream, it's so impressive.'

'Thanks' he said with a sigh of relief 'they came so easy and natural it amazed me too, I usually have the person in front of me the whole time I sketch so these should have been more difficult but they weren't.'

'I think they're amazing and I can't wait to see mine.'

'Okay, here goes' he said as he handed her the sketch 'and please bear in mind that in the dream your face was partly in shadow..

After studying the sketch for what seemed to him like ages she looked up at him her eyes glistening with tears.

'Is this how you see me?'

For a second or two his heart sank as he thought she was upset but her next words changed that.

'I can see that it's me and the eyes are amazing, but it's like a better me, I can't really explain what I mean, it's very flattering and I love it' she wiped away the single tear that had rolled down her cheek and smiled at him.

'I'm so glad you like it, and yes that is how I see you, or rather how I saw you in my dream. I have to say though that in my dream you did look a little different, I can't pin down how exactly but I think that is why the sketch is you but 'better' as you put it, and that's not to take away from how you look now. Oh I don't really know what I'm saying, it's hard to explain, sorry.'

'No its fine I understand, now I think of it you looked a little different in the dream too, though like you say it's hard to explain. But the other sketches look exactly like the people I saw in my dream.'

'I'm glad you get it.'

'I do, and now I really want to see the paintings you've done.'

'I've only done you and the guy with the scar; I'll show you him first.'

After carefully turning the easel around to face Mary he stepped back to let her view the portrait of the man with the scar. She took it all in and then turned to look at him her face glowing with admiration.

'It's so damn good, its almost like looking at a photograph, I don't know how you do it, you have a real talent Aaron.'

'Thanks.' It was all he could think of to say, he was feeling a little overwhelmed by the intensity of her praise.

'Now I really can't wait to see your portrait of me.'

So the time had finally come and Aaron fetched the painting from where he had propped it behind his bedside table so she wouldn't see it as she came in.

The sight of her own face on the canvas literally took Mary's breath away and it was a couple of minutes before she could put her feelings into words.'

'Thank you Aaron, it looks so like me and yet not me at the same time, it's like you've painted the 'real' me.'

'Or the 'dream' you.'

'Yes, it is literally the 'dream' me, and the expression on my face, I look so calm and confident and I'm pretty sure I've never looked like that in reality' she said with a little laugh.

'I'm really happy that you like it.'

'Like is an understatement.'

'I really want to hug you right now but I'll get paint all over you' he said indicating his paint splattered t shirt.

'Take it off then' she said and then immediately blushed and stuttered 'I erm, oh, I didn't mean that like it sounded, I just meant, erm, sorry.'

'Its fine, I know what you mean, I should just take it off' he said 'and put a clean one on' he added laughing. Mary laughed too relieved.

Having relieved an awkward moment with laughter Aaron continued the comedy by slowly taking off his t shirt and then swinging it around his head in a mock striptease. Mary joined in the act by squealing and whooping like she was at a hen night party and then applauding as Aaron stood in a show-off pose with his hands on his hips, and his chest puffed out.

'Okay, show over' he said and walked over to the chest of draws next to where Mary sat to get a clean t shirt. Mary would usually have found that sort of situation mortifyingly embarrassing but with Aaron it had felt comfortable and fun, plus getting a glimpse of Aaron's slim but well-muscled torso and broad shoulders had been very enjoyable. Aaron was also feeling at ease, he was not usually such a showman but he felt more confident and relaxed around Mary,

'Now I'm no longer paint smeared how about that hug' he said.

Mary stood up and they embraced and then kissed; a long, deep, passionate kiss. They held each other a little longer and then parted a little so they were looking at each other. For a few seconds they just looked, drinking each other in until the silence was broken by a strange grumbling noise.

'That's my stomach' said Aaron 'I was so involved in my painting I forgot to eat lunch.'

'You must be starving; we'd better get back to my place so I can start dinner.'

'That sounds great.'

Max was driving home from his delayed trip to the supermarket when he spotted it. His mind was still full of 'Artfest' and his quick glance towards a familiar, but usually ignored landmark had given him a surprising answer to one of the major questions he had over the planning of his two-day trip.

His glance took in the largish second-hand specialist car dealership and as he drove past a vehicle on the forecourt caught his eye. He was past the dealership before he could fully process what he'd seen and what it meant and so was quite a way down the road before he made the decision to turn back and take a proper look.

Once back at the dealership he pulled into the entrance and parked in one of the visitor spaces. As he got out of the car he started to feel nervous. He'd never been to a car dealership before even to look around and now he was here possibly about to make a very large impulse purchase.

An hour later Max left the dealership having made a part exchange deal trading in his father's 1988 Jaguar Sovereign XJ40 for a blue and cream 1963 RHD Split Screen VW Camper.

He now needed to return home to get the necessary paperwork, then return to make the bridging payment and do the swap. He felt a little guilty about getting rid of his father's beloved car, but he also felt good about his decision.

The VW Camper was perfect for his 'Artfest adventure', obviously it was perfect for the nights of camping, but it also provided him with storage space for his recent sculptures which for some reason he felt compelled to take with him. And as for after 'Artfest' the VW was much more 'him' than the Jaguar and far more practical for his clay transporting needs so it would work out well he thought.

Max felt that maybe he was finally moving on to a new phase in his life.

It had taken a lot of phone calls and a lot of called in favours but Geth had finally found a place to stay for Artfest. Having had no intention of spending those two nights in a tent in a field he had contacted a large number of hotels and bed and breakfasts near Artfest venue but all had been fully booked. Frustrated and beginning to panic a little he had then turned to calling all his 'contacts' in the tattoo world to see if anyone could help him out.

This Artfest had become strangely important to Geth. Luckily Chris was being very helpful and supportive although Geth was fully aware his friend thought he was behaving very strangely. Chris' attitude also made Geth feel he was leaving the business in good hands which made things a lot easier for him.

Geth had eventually turned to the previously helpful Darren for help. He felt bad about 'using' the guy again but needs must and Darren had been eager to help stating that he'd do 'practically anything' to guarantee a free Geth Hudson tattoo as promised and Geth felt he fully deserved a freebee.

Darren's solution wasn't exactly perfect as it involved Geth sleeping on a stranger's sofa, but it included that night so Geth could travel later today, arrive this evening and then be rested ready for the following morning.

Now all he had to do was sort out which equipment and designs to take. His new designs were top of the list, they were the best he'd done for a while and he'd worry about their strange origin later, now he had work to do. For the first time in years Geth felt excited about something.

Clea was so excited she could barely contain herself. The morning had been spent in a flurry of activity and she was now almost ready to set off on what she knew would be a life changing journey.

Her bags were packed, her route planned and her nights stop over booked. It would be a long journey to the event venue but Clea was going in style. Parked outside her house was a newly rented Lunar 62 two berth RV. The vehicle had all the mod cons including a four-gas hob and full oven, fridge/freezer, TV, and a roll out awning with a small picnic table and two chairs.

Clea was rather enamoured of her temporary home. The RV was packed with her clothes and toiletries along with enough food for a family of five for a week and three extra folding garden chairs from her own garden. The food and chairs were obviously too much for one person but Clea was certain that she would not be spending the entire weekend alone which was why in amongst her own clothes she had also packed the four t-shirts she had now finished making and embroidering for the 'strangers' from her dreams.

The four strangers had come to her in dreams, as had the idea that she desperately needed to go to the event and Clea felt that this was no coincidence, she somehow knew that if she went to the event she would meet these people. Why was another matter, but she wasn't too worried about that as the moment, the reasons for it all would be made clear soon she was sure, and she was convinced the revelation would be amazing, she had a good feeling about it.

Taking a last look around her front room Clea's eyes alighted on the photo of Andrew. Darting across the room she picked it up and hugged it to her ample breasts. 'You're coming with me sweetheart' she whispered. Then picking up her handbag and keys she left the house with a beaming smile on her face.

After the slightly emotional scene of Mason's departure Sofia went upstairs with Eddie to help him finish cleaning the rooms. When they came back downstairs a couple of hours later their job finished they were surprised to find Phoebe and Mark in the kitchen having something to eat.

'How are things going?' Sofia asked them.

'Good thanks.' Replied Mark

'We thought we'd sleep here tonight if that's okay' added Phoebe.

'Of course its okay' agreed Sofia

And so the four of them spent the evening eating, talking and generally relaxing before retiring for a much-needed night's sleep.

When Aaron and Mary arrived at Mary's flat she suggested they have dinner first before showing him her poems. She used his hunger as an excuse, but she was stalling as she was still a little nervous about sharing her poems but if Aaron realised this he didn't let on.

During the meal, a simple pasta dish that Mary often cooked herself, they chatted easily avoiding the major issue until dinner was done and cleared away. Then finally it was time for the big reveal.

Mary was a little nervous of Aaron reading her poems, not because of the subject; she was just worried he'd think her poetry was rubbish but she couldn't stall any longer it was time to get it over with.

Nervously she handed him the pieces of paper on which she had neatly written out her poems a couple of nights earlier. She told him she couldn't bear to watch his face while he read them so she was going to take herself into the kitchen to do a bit more clearing up (not that any really needed to be done) and bustled off until she heard him call her to say he was done. It was time to hear his verdict.

'Well' he said, 'I'm no expert on poetry having never really read any before but I have to say that I love these.'

She let out a breath she hadn't realised she'd been holding as Aaron continued.

'And somehow I know which one relates to which face, though I guess the Seer is obvious being the only female, but the Gatekeeper is the guy with the scar right, making the other guy the Dreamcatcher?'

Mary nodded.

'Thought so, but where did you get these names from?'

'They told me those names in my dream; they each told me 'who' they were.'

'You didn't tell me that before.'

'I know, I was going to but then decided it was best to leave it to the poems, they say it best.'

'I guess they do. It's like we've captured the essence of these people between us. I captured their likeness and you captured their... I don't know... their purpose maybe. A likeness is easy to capture in such a short time, but how on earth did you get these words from just seeing someone in a dream?'

'I have no idea, they just told me 'who' they were and then later these words came into my head, I mean I could have totally made it all up, I have a very vivid imagination, a lot of my poems come from dreams, but these felt different, I can't explain it, they just seems so 'real', so strong. I guess I really am just a Dreamfreak'

'You're a what?'

'A Dreamfreak' said Mary a little sheepishly, she hadn't meant to use her secret word for herself, it had just popped out 'it's what I call myself sometimes and it seems even more fitting now with all this extra weirdness going on.'

'It does kinda fit but if you're a Dreamfreak then so am I'

'You're right it does, we're a pair of Dreamfreaks Mary was smiling now, glad it had slipped out, her link to this amazing man was just getting stronger.

'Sounds good to me, and maybe these other people from our dreams are Dreamfreaks too because whoever they are, wherever they are, they are real, they exist and I think we have to somehow find them.'

'Yes, but how? Unless, well maybe we'll dream of them again, get more clues about whom and where they are.'

'Wait, wait, I just realised something, our last strange dream was about Artfest right?'

'Right' agreed Mary.

'And although we didn't see them in that dream, they were there right? In essence they were with us.'

'Oh my god yeah, they were.'

'Yes, and this dream, it made me determined to go to the event, I mean you were already going, but remember I told you how this dream gave me this strong sense that I had to be at this event.

Well maybe it's because that is where we are gonna find these people. Maybe they're all going to the event too.'

'That's a great idea; I think you may be right.'

'Okay, I think we're on to something here, but the burning question now is why?'

'Oh Aaron, no, I thought we were getting somewhere, now we have to work out why, I really don't think I can handle any more right now, this is doing my head in, it's so beyond normal, I just don't know what to think.'

Mary was near to tears and Aaron couldn't bear to see her upset.

'I'm sorry, you're right, it's too much, we need to take a break and not think about this for a bit, come on, come here.'

And with that he wrapped his arms around her and pulled her to him. Mary pulled her feet up onto the sofa and curled up against him with her head on his chest, and enclosed in his arms she began to relax. She felt warm and safe and happy and all their weird problems could wait, for now she just wanted to be right here listening to his heartbeat and gentle breathing.

They were silent for quite a while enjoying their physical closeness. Neither of them felt the need to say anything. Aaron moved his hand up and began to slowly and gently stroke her hair and Mary couldn't help but let out a sigh of pleasure. She marvelled at how relaxed she felt around him, at how sure she was that this man she had only just met would never do anything to hurt her and it was the most gratifying feeling she'd ever felt.

Aaron felt like he was holding the most precious thing in his arms. He'd never met anyone like her and the connection he felt to her was so deep and so strong. She felt so warm and soft curled up against him.

After he placed a gentle kiss upon the top of her head Mary felt the need to see his face so lifting her head from his chest she slowly looked up to meet his gaze. After looking into each other's eyes for long seconds he bent his head and touched his lips to hers.

The gentle touching of lips soon grew into an intense and passionate kiss. Burying one hand in her hair he used the other to pull her onto his lap and as close against him as he could. She put one arm around his shoulders and her other hand on the nape of his neck where the tips of her fingers sunk into his hair.

Their breathing became heavy and when they finally broke from the kiss, he moved his lips to gently kiss her neck. The feeling of his lips and hot breath on her neck was electric and she let out a moan of pleasure before he again covered her lips with his.

Their passion growing they needed no words, there was only one way this was going and they both wanted it, wanted each other more than anything. The kiss was broken momentarily as in one easy, impressive movement he stood from the sofa with her in his arms. Mary pointed to show which door led to her bedroom and Aaron easily carried her towards it.

Their lovemaking had an intensity and passion to it that neither of them had ever experienced before. It was not just a joining of their bodies but another step towards the true joining of their souls. There was only one step left, and after the lovemaking came sleep, a sleep which would bring that final step in the form of the shared dream that would bind them together forever.

Talionis was spent and in pain. Having slunk away to Its dense, wooded hiding place It lay in the dark seething with frustration and anger, too weak to act on it.

The woman's mind had been different, not quite the same as the man he'd controlled, similar but not the same, and strong so strong and It had been defeated. It was still weak from that first attack. It was the fault of Its captors, the years of confinement and inactivity had made It weak, but It would find a way, a way to become what It was and what It should be, and then It would wreak Its revenge and no one would be safe.

CHAPTER 13

ARTFEST DAY 1

Sofia awoke with a start, her arms and legs involuntarily jerking her from her sleep. She was disorientated for a few seconds unsure what had awoken her. Then she remembered her dream and stifled a cry of distress as the realisation of its meaning hit her.

Sitting up she reached for her mobile phone on the bedside table but then paused with it in her hand. She needed to get her thoughts together before making a call, at the moment it was all a little jumbled in her head. She needed to make sense of things a little more first.

Glancing at the bedside clock she noted it was 5:36am. Getting slowly to her feet she walked a little unsteadily to the window and pulled back the curtains to let in the early morning light. She needed some light to diffuse the darkness of her thoughts. It didn't help much. As her thoughts began to unjumble she felt a moment of despair. If things had seemed bad before they had just got worse. But her falling apart wouldn't help things. I'm strong; I can deal with this she told herself. And now she had herself under control she needed to call the Somnium Foundation and she needed to call them now.

She dialled a number not in her phone, a number committed to memory. The emergency Foundation number, a direct line to the big bosses. They and only they could help her with this.

After only two rings the phone was answered with a simple 'yes, code please'. Sofia gave the unnamed person her personal emergency code and was told 'hold please'. After a few seconds there was a click and then a few more rings before she heard the familiar, cultured voice of her boss Cedric Neale.

'Good Morning Sofia, what's the emergency?' he said polite but to the point as usual.

'I have some disturbing news for you I'm afraid. When you spoke to me a few days ago regarding the death of Rita Deacon and the 'escapee' you said that it would not affect my work here, well unfortunately I'm pretty sure you were wrong.'

'Really, how is that?'

'I think 'It' has found its way here, and I'm pretty sure that It was the cause of the dreadful events regarding Claude. I believe the poor man is no crazed murderer but is in fact a victim himself.'

'I think I may know where you are headed with this but please go ahead and explain to me why you think this is the case.'

And so Sofia did, she told him in more detail how Claude had acted that first day, and then how he had been before he was taken away and then she told him what had happened to her out in the woods and how she had made the connection between it all.'

When she had finished there was a moments silence as the information was processed by her boss before giving her his measured reaction.

'Why do you think you were able to resist Its attack when Claude was not'?'

'I'm not sure, my talents are slightly different and maybe that confused It, made it harder. Or maybe It's just weak after the attack on Claude, after what It made him do It must have been exhausted.'

'Well, whatever the reason I'm glad Its attack didn't work and as startling and terrible as this news is I feel some good has come of it. What happened to Claude and to you is frightening and disturbing but at least we can now understand what caused Claude's terrible actions, which means we can more easily help him. Also, we now know It's approximate whereabouts so the search teams can be called off and we can send in trained employees to re-capture and detain It. We have Foundation members with the necessary skills for the job on standby it's just a matter of briefing them on the new developments and getting them to you, therefore I think it best to cut this call short in order to get things underway ASAP.'

'Okay, thank you sir.'

'No problem, speak to you soon, goodbye.'

'Goodbye sir.'

Feeling a little more relaxed after her boss's assurances Sofia went to get herself a cup of coffee while she waited for his return call. It was still very early and none of the others were up yet which was good, she needed some definite plans and positive news to give them along with the bad.

There was also something she wanted to discuss with her boss regarding Eddie. It was actually more of a request really, one that would mean breaking a long-held Foundation rule. It was a risk but she'd felt that the unusual situation they'd found themselves in possibly warranted it and now after this latest development she felt it was even more pertinent. If he didn't agree with it she at least hoped he could give her some advice in the matter.

Sofia was in the office waiting when the return call came about twenty minutes later.

Firstly, she listened as her boss explained that help was on its way in the form of two people equipped with the necessary skills and knowledge who would be arriving at The Gateway the next morning so she would need to make sure things were ready for their arrival.

He then asked her the situation with Phoebe and Mark wanting to know if they were in the house or out in the Factory. He was relieved to discover they had spent the night at the house as although he felt they were safe whilst in the Factory they would be at risk whilst travelling to and from it through the woods. He instructed her to keep them at the house for the time being until there was someone there who could escort them safely back to the Factory. It was then time for her to broach her request.'

'I need to ask you something sir?'

'Go ahead.'

'It's regarding The Warden Eddie Oakley. He has been exemplary in his work so far and I feel in the days to come he could be even more invaluable, but to truly help us I think he needs to be trusted with our 'secret'. I know this is a big ask but the alternative is that Eddie will have to be sent away almost immediately and apart from the logistics of that it would be very unfair on him. I understand that the needs of the Foundation as a whole come way before just one of its members, but I feel that the man can be fully trusted and that he would be an even bigger asset to us here in the coming days rather than being farmed off somewhere else.'

'Your points are very valid but this is a very important decision and it's not one I can make without serious consideration and without consulting others first, therefore I will give it some thought, consult with my peers on the matter and get back to you as soon as a decision has been made.'

'Thank you sir that is all I ask.'

'Then I think we are done for now unless you have anything else to discuss.'

'No, that's all sir.'

'In that case I will speak to you again when I have a decision for you. In the meantime please do not hesitate to contact me if any other urgent matter arises, or if the matter is less urgent please go through Barbara.'

'I will sir, thank you.'

'Goodbye Sofia.'

'Goodbye sir.'

After the call was finished Sofia would have liked to go back to her room for a quick shower and a change of clothes as she was still in her pyjamas, but she was afraid she'd miss Phoebe and Mark when they came out of their rooms. She was contemplating waking the pair up when Eddie entered the room.

'Hi, how are you this morning?' he asked.

'I'm pretty good thanks, how are you?'

'Rested and ready for a new day. So is there anything you need me to do.'

'Actually there is. Could you please wait here for about twenty minutes whilst I go and have a shower, I can't really go into details right now I'm afraid but I need you to stay here because if Phoebe or Mark make an appearance whilst I am away I need you to make sure that they do not leave the house.'

'Wow, sounds serious.'

'Yes it is I'm afraid. I will explain as much as I can to you all when I'm showered and dressed plus I have some more work for you to do.'

'Okay, fine.'

'Thank you Eddie I really do appreciate your help' she said as she left the room.

When Sofia returned to the office she found Eddie and Phoebe sitting chatting. She said hi to them both and then to Phoebe 'Any sign of Mark yet?'

'He's up, I heard him in the shower as I came out so he shouldn't be long.'

'Okay, good we have some important things to talk about. And Eddie I'm sorry to give you more work but I need you to prepare two rooms upstairs. I know you have just finished clearing them out for the new arrivals when they return with Mason but we are going to have to use them for two others that will be arriving tomorrow morning, therefore could you please make sure the beds have clean linen and that there are clean towels in the bathrooms. I'll explain more about what's happening later okay.'

'Will these people be gone before Mason gets back with the others only we won't really have room for everyone if not' asked Eddie.

'I'm not really sure at the moment; we will have to deal with that problem if and when it arises. All I can tell you at the moment is that the people who are coming have a very important job to do and that it is urgent.'

'Fair enough, I'll go and get it sorted.'

'Thank you Eddie.'

Just after Eddie left the room Mark emerged from the guest room his hair still wet from the shower.

'What's up?' he asked when he saw the two women waiting for him.

'There's been some developments' said Sofia 'and I need to fill you in on a few details. Firstly for the time being you are not to leave the house, it's not safe for you to travel through the woods right now.'

'Seriously?' said Mark 'That sounds kinda sinister, what's going on?'

'Why don't you wheel the desk chair over here and we can all sit and talk.'

When Sofia had finished updating the pair there was a few seconds silence as they digested the new information before Mark spoke

'This is some serious shit and I can't deny that it frightens me more than a little.'

'I totally understand' said Sofia 'but as long as we stay together we should be fine. As you know physically It is weak and can only do you harm if it is close but hidden, therefore we just need to be vigilant and to make sure none of us are ever alone, there is definitely safety in numbers where this particular threat is concerned.'

'Sounds good to me' said Phoebe 'but what about our work'

'You can use the art room in the house for now, I know it's not ideal as it weakens your output but it will have to do until the woods are made safe for you to travel.'

It was then that Eddie returned.

'All done' he said

'Thank you Eddie' said Sofia, then 'why don't the two of you go and get some breakfast, I just need to speak to Eddie for a minute.

There was still no word from her boss on her request regarding Eddie but for now she would tell him as much as she could. She told him that there was a very dangerous 'person' on the loose out in the woods and that they were all to remain confined to the house. She explained that the Foundation was sending two highly trained Foundation members to track and capture this 'person'. She also told him it was his job to keep an eye on Phoebe and Mark.

Eddie was aware that there was more to the story, but he was also aware of how the Foundation worked and so as long as he knew enough to be able to do his job properly, he was happy.

'I'll do whatever is needed of me Sofia, you know that.'

'I do Eddie and I want you to know that you are just as important to the operation as anyone else.'

'Thanks, that's nice to hear. Can I just make a suggestion?'

'Of course.'

'I know that those coming will be well equipped for whatever it is they have to do but can I just remind you that we have a really good surveillance system here. Generally we only use the Gate entry system part of it, but there are camera's all around the property and the perimeter wall. There aren't any intruder alarms as they would be a nightmare to operate since the residents are constantly coming and going out to the woods at all hours, but you can monitor the cameras via the computer screen on the desk. There's also a map of the Gateway estate somewhere which may be of help.'

'Good thinking Eddie. If you could find the map and then give me a quick lesson on how the surveillance system works then when the others get here we can have it all set up ready for them to use as I'm sure it will be of help.'

'No problem.'

Eddie found the map quickly and whilst he set up the surveillance monitors Sofia took a quick look at it.

The Gateway stood within 700 acres of land most of which was wooded. The Gateway itself was at the southern tip of the estate and was protected by a twelve-foot-high brick wall with the ornate iron gateway being the only entrance/exit.

The wall extending around the part of the estates land that was exposed to any roads or easy access but the boundary for the rest of the acreage consisted of ten-foot barbed iron fencing most of which were off the beaten track buried deep within hard to access woodland.

The rarely used surveillance cameras were mainly mounted on the boundary wall with only a few within the wooded areas. As she studied the map Sofia noted a small building in the northern most corner of the estate and when she realised what it was she was shocked. She'd been quietly berating herself all morning for not making the connection between what had happened to Claude and the news of the escapee but now thought that if she'd known that the place It had escaped from was so close she might have made the connection sooner.

She'd always known about the 'prisoner' but had never realised that It had been kept so close to the Gateway all these years. This could be looked upon as a huge mistake by the Foundation, but then they'd probably never envisioned the prisoner escaping. Where had they been searching up until now? They must have assumed It had left the estate somehow, but It hadn't, It had come 'home'.

She had no idea how much the two Foundation members who were coming to help knew about any of this so for now she needed to find out as much as she could about the estate's layout and security so that she could update them if necessary.

Once Eddie had finished showing Sofia how the security system worked they went to find Phoebe and Mark. They found the youngsters in the lounge / art room and with their work pretty much done for the time being they decided to join them in some therapeutic art.

Mark had found the biggest canvas in the workroom cupboards along with some acrylic paints and had already made a start on an abstract piece of work whilst Phoebe played a soothing classical piece on the piano.

Sofia and Eddie found themselves a sketch pad each and whilst Eddie used sharpie pens to draw cartoon versions of his companions Sofia found some charcoal sticks and began to sketch the view of the driveway and woods from the window.

The group spent several hours this way; their work productive in a way that only a group like this could be. It both helped relax them and help others.

Mary had woken early with a smile on her face, one that had broadened at the sight of Aaron as he lay sleeping beside her.

For a few minutes she'd simply lay gazing at him, her mind replaying the events of the night before. The best night of her life. And as her mind got to the end of its mental rewind she'd remembered something new. A dream. She'd had another strange dream, but this one had been far better than all the others. In this one it had been just her and Aaron, his face clear and his touch known.

She couldn't remember anything particular that had happened in the dream, just that they had been together during the whole thing, really together, in fact she thought the best way to describe it was that they had joined together in the dream and this thought made her very happy. Then, suddenly, the words had begun to come and she had to carefully sit up and reach for the notebook and pen she kept on the bedside table.

'Morning beautiful.' Aaron's croaky morning voice snapped her out of her daze and she turned to see him propped up on one elbow a soppy grin on his face.

'Morning handsome' she said

'What you up to?' he asked

'I just wrote a poem about the dream I had last night, about us.'

'You dreamt about us last night?'

'I sure did.'

'Me to.'

'You did?'

'Yeah, it was a great dream, not that I remember much detail, but I feel really good thinking about it now so it must have been great, I just remember that we were together, whatever that means.'

'I think we had the same dream Aaron; I think we dreamt it together.'

'That's kinda cool, but still another one to add to the weird file though.'

'Yeah, but this one's good weird.'

'It most definitely is. So can I read your poem?'

'Sure, my handwritings actually not too bad for a change so you should be able to read it okay.'

Mary handed him her notebook and this is what he read.

They are our Dream Mates,
Bringing love and friendship in our sleep.
Their love gives us comfort and understanding,
Strength and release.
They appear with different faces,
Some know, and some hidden.
They express our inner feelings,
And bring ecstasy to our dreams.

'Wow' said Aaron when he finished reading 'you got that from our dream, that's amazing, and so I guess that's us, we're the Dream Mates.'

'I guess so, though what the hell that means I have no idea.'

'Me either, so I suppose we just wait until Artfest and see if it somehow brings us the answers, speaking of which look at the time, we need to be at the event venue in about an hour and a half, that means I won't have time to go home and get changed so I'll just have to wear the same clothes again.'

'Errr minging' joked Mary laughing.

'Cheek' he said with a grin 'my t shirt was clean on yesterday afternoon so its fine, I'm just glad we woke up in time.'

'Me too because for some reason I was far too distracted last night and totally forgot to set my alarm' she said with mock innocence.

'How remiss of you' said Aaron in mock sternness making her laugh.

About forty-five minutes later they were both showered and ready to go and after a thirty-five-minute drive they pulled into the events employee / pitch holders' car park.

As they exited the car Mary felt her excitement level rise as she got her first proper look at the event site. The field before them was immense and dotted around it were several large, white marques. Scattered amongst these were a few smaller tents and somewhere near the middle Mary could just make out the top of a structure she assumed was the outdoor stage upon which the main music events would take place. And in amongst all this were scattered their fellow helpers along with the pitch holders all busy setting up for their first day.

Aaron walked around the car and took Mary's hand.

'Come on, we need to go over there' he said pointing to a small tent just to the left of the entrance from the car park to the site.

'That's the organiser's tent; we need to go and check in.'

'I hope they're okay about me helping.'

'I'm sure it'll be fine.'

And he was right, the organisers jumped at the chance of extra help and as an extra thank you in lieu of the fact that she'd already bought tickets they gave them some vouchers for the 'food market' so she could at least get a free lunch.

They were given their event pass wristbands and assigned to the modern art tent where they were to help set up the tables for the pitches and give any other help needed by the pitch holders. They set off with big smiles on their faces and big hopes for the day.

As Mary and Aaron were leaving the organiser's tent Geth was parking his Ford not far away from Mary's Corsa.

He'd slept surprisingly well and was ready for the day ahead. As he got out of the car his new, temporary flatmate was getting out of the car parked next to him. The man's name was Len and Geth had been pleased to discover that he was a decent guy and pretty good company.

They'd shared a takeaway pizza and friendly conversation the night before in Len's small, but thankfully clean flat. The man's sofa had been comfy enough but Geth had been less impressed by the tiny bathroom they'd taken turns to shower in this morning. Still it could have been worse.

Len was a volunteer helper for the event. He was in his late forties, with a solid build, thinning blonde hair and a chubby, friendly face. He was a car mechanic who liked to make sculptures out of used car parts in his spare time. As well as putting Geth up for the duration of the event he'd cheerfully helped unload Geth's tattoo equipment and personal luggage from the car the night before and then just as cheerfully helped load it all back in the car early that morning. He'd also explained that Darren had assigned him the role of helping Geth set up and pack away at the event and both men were happy with this arrangement.

'We need to check in at the organiser's tent and get our passes' said Len 'then we can get you set up for the day.'

As they walked toward the organiser's tent Geth took in his surroundings. The site looked a lot bigger and more impressive than he had imagined. The car park was starting to fill up now and as he walked he could detect the beginnings of a 'buzz' in the air as the excitement began to mount amongst his fellow artists. He had a good feeling about the day ahead and those to come. Exciting things were going to happen here. Bring it on he thought, I'm ready for anything.

At the same time that Geth was entering the organiser's tent Max was just setting off for the event. His sculptures were safely stored in the VW Camper, his other supplies packed, and the house all locked up safe.

He estimated that the journey would take him approximately an hour and a half and although he wasn't exactly looking forward to the drive itself, he felt excited and happy to be on his way.

It was strange how driving a VW Camper to a strange place made Max extremely nervous yet give him a mountain bike and an extreme bike trail to ride it on and he was in his element.

He'd always had this strange contradiction in his personality. On the one hand in his everyday life he was a very cautious and even nervous person, but on the other he had a passion for extreme mountain biking which was not a hobby associated with cautious people. This was on top of the contradiction of his calm, serious councillor persona against the manic sculptor. But it was how he'd always been.

He started up the vehicle but then sat for a minute taking long, deep breaths in an effort to calm his nerves. He thought again about the sculptures stowed behind him. It had been hard work getting them finished and fired in time and he'd only just managed it, but what he still didn't understand was why he was taking them with him. Yes he was going to an art event but it wasn't like he had a pitch or anything. But then perhaps that didn't matter, it was an art event after all and so what was strange about taking your art with you? Surely others would do the same. But then it wasn't like he could carry them around with him, there were seven of them and they weren't exactly light and portable.

Thoughts of his sculptures inevitably lead to thoughts of the weird dreams that had spawned them. But no, he wasn't going to go there, he must push these thoughts to the back of his mind. Right now he just needed to concentrate on driving an unfamiliar vehicle on a route he'd never driven before. He would need all his concentration so there was no room for these maddening thoughts.

With that Max took one last, deep breath, put the VW in first gear and set off, his heart pounding with a mixture of excitement and fear.

An hour and forty minutes later Max was sat in the queue for the event camping site. The queue was pretty long and rather slow moving but he didn't mind, it gave him a chance to calm himself a little. The journey had gone pretty well and he'd only got lost once, briefly, having taken the wrong exit on a roundabout. He'd soon realised his mistake however and after a brief panic had easily turned around and got back on track.

Now he was almost there and as the tension of the drive began to dissipate his excitement began to grow. Good things were going to happen here he was suddenly sure of it.

Several vehicles ahead of Max in the queue Clea was feeling a lot less stressed but a lot more impatient.

The last leg of her journey had only taken an hour to this point as she had planned it that way. The day before she had got the majority of the driving out of the way before stopping at a campsite for the night, and although the RV was completely alien to her she had slept well as usual. She had awoken feeling fresh and rested with only the short drive ahead of her, therefore, ensuring she had plenty of energy for the event itself.

But now she was stuck in the queue with the distant tops of the white tents taunting her, so near and yet so far. She really hoped that the walk from her parked RV to the entrance to the event wouldn't be too far. She didn't want to waste too much energy before she even got to the first tent.

From what she could see of the site it was huge, this definitely was the biggest art event ever staged and she couldn't wait to get in and see all the beautiful (and no doubt not so beautiful) artwork on show, but most of all she was looking forward to talking to the artists. She was sure there would be many interesting people here. She'd also now convinced herself that the four people from her dreams would be here, they had to be. The only problem would be finding them amongst the crowds. What she was going to say to these people when she found them she didn't know, but she would think of something. She would know what to do when the time came she was sure.

As the traffic ahead shifted a little she suddenly realised that she was almost at the entrance to the campsite. Her heart did a little skip as her excitement level went up a notch. She was nearly there; her adventure was about to truly begin.

As Clea was nosing her RV through the entrance Mason was entering the event itself along with the other early arrivals as the doors were opened on the dot of nine o'clock.

The Foundation driver had picked him up from the hotel early and dropped him at the site with plenty of time to find a good place to pitch his thankfully easy to assemble one-man tent and then make his way to the entrance to wait for the event to open.

Now for the hard part. Somewhere amongst all these hundreds of people he needed to find five individuals and he had no clue what any of them looked like.

Before leaving The Gateway, he had discussed this problem with Sofia. She had agreed it would be hard amongst such crowds but had assured him that it didn't matter that he didn't know what they looked like, that if he saw them he would 'know' them, or at the very least one of them. She said they would have a 'bond' and that this 'bond' would be strongest with one of the five in particular. He knew this must be true after all he'd been through something similar before, had felt this 'bond' with the other people who shared The Gateway with him from the moment they had come together so why not these others.

But things were a little different this time. The process had been rushed, had taken place under difficult circumstances and with less help than usual. Finding these people seemed an immense task, not to mention what he would need to do once he did find them and Mason was struggling a little to keep himself calm and not let the situation overwhelm him.

So Mason had made the best plan that he could which was to get there as early as possible and situate himself somewhere with a good view of the entrance so he could watch people arrive. Of course it was possible that one or more of the five may have a pitch at the event so would be there already but it was unlikely that would be the case with all of them. Anyway, he just needed one of them to come through and for him to 'recognise' them because if he could find that one all he'd have to do was stick with them then hopefully they would find the others themselves. That was how it should work.

Of course this plan all hinged on the fact that all five people were actually coming to the event. They had no way of knowing if their hard work over the last few days had paid off but Mason didn't really want to think about that. These people had to be here, they just had to.

Mary and Aaron had thoroughly enjoyed helping set up in the Modern Art marque. The atmosphere had been very upbeat and friendly, the work interspersed by art chat and best of all they'd never been more than a few feet away from each other. Artfest was turning out to be just as good as they'd hoped, if not better.

Now it was nine o'clock, their mornings work was done and they left the marque hand in hand free to enjoy the sights and sounds of the event proper.

Geth was pleased with the location of his pitch, especially as it had been a last-minute thing. He really did have a lot to thank Darren for. With help from Len his pitch was set up and ready for visitors well before nine o'clock which gave him time to check out the other pitches.

He'd seen a few familiar faces and had stopped for a brief chat with a couple, both of whom had been surprised to see him there. He'd checked out flash art of some of his fellow tattooists, they were all pretty impressive; the organisers had made some good choices.

During the morning Geth had felt the excitement in the marque building and as nine o'clock arrived he realised that he was feeling it too. Whatever the day would bring he was ready for it.

Max locked up the VW and joined the growing crowd heading for the entrance. He walked slower than those around him his nerves getting the better of him. He tried to tell himself there was no need to be nervous and he couldn't even think of a reason why he should be but that was how he felt. Everyone else around him looked happy and he was feeling that too, but right now those feelings were being dampened by his nervousness.

Max joined one of the short queues at the trestle tables set up just inside the entrance.

Once at the front of the queue he handed over his ticket. His ticket was examined briefly and then he was handed a blue wristband with the event name emblazoned on it in black lettering. He was told to make sure he wore it both days as it was now his ticket back into the event. He dutifully put it on noticing that everyone around him was doing the same only some had red wristbands. He assumed these were for those people there for the one day only.

Moving on into the field itself he came to another set of trestle tables from which people were handing out leaflets on which was printed the itinerary for the event. Taking one he walked on slowly looking around him. He needed to get out of the flow of people coming behind him so he could stop and get his bearings. Heading off to the side a little he managed to find a clear space a little way behind one of the trestle tables. It was a relief to stop for a minute and now he could take a good look at the itinerary and plan for the day.

As Clea slipped on her blue wristband she felt a thrill of expectation run down her spine. It was truly beginning now. What 'it' was exactly she didn't know, but she knew it would be amazing. Moving on she found herself taking in long deep breaths of air, breathing in all the sights and sounds around her.

She was offered a leaflet and took it with a thank you but was too busy gazing around her to really look at what she'd been handed. She walked slowly, her head turning from side to side. She saw the happy, excited faces of the event goers around her; she saw the big, white marques dotted around the massive site ahead of her.

And then she saw him. He stood slightly away from the incoming crowd, alone, his stillness making him stand out in the moving throng. A thrill of recognition passed through her making her gasp. For a minute Clea saw the visions from her dream superimposed over the view surrounding her. She saw the low, grey stone building with the symbols above its door. She saw the symbol she'd designed from the dream of this man. Then everything around her came back into focus.

Although part of her had known this would happen it was still a shock. She recognised that kind face, the long hair, the beard and the glasses. He looked a little different, a little less groomed his hair and beard scruffier, and although she couldn't see the colour of his eyes from where she was, she knew they'd be blue. It was him, he was here, he was real, a man from her dreams.

Someone bumped her arm and she realised she'd stopped dead in the middle of the moving crowd. Not a good idea. She started to walk, but not with the crown. She headed towards the still figure on its outskirts. This wasn't really a good idea either and she had to apologise to a few people as she crossed their paths, but she was too intent on her destination to really care.

She didn't head straight for him as she needed time to think of an approach. She figured there was little chance of him noticing her first as he seemed so intent on studying the leaflet in his hands.

Finding a clear spot about thirty feet from him she stopped to think. It was bound to be a shock to the man being approached by a complete stranger like this. But then the whole situation was so strange it was likely to freak him out however she did it. Would he recognise her too? That was something she hadn't really thought of before. Well there was only one way to find out. Deciding it was best not to plan too much, to just go with the flow Clea made her move.

Max was standing in a daze overcome with strange feelings. His head was foggy and he felt like his insides were being pulled in two different directions. It was very disconcerting and then all of a sudden there was a strange woman stood in front of him, smiling.

'Hello' she said

'My name is Clea, what's yours?'

'I'm... errr...Max' he replied startled.

'Nice to meet you Max.'

As she said these words a strange look came over Max's face and his skin turned from just pale to white as a ghost. For a second Clea thought he was going to faint but he managed to hold it together, just. It was obvious now that he recognised her too, that he was going through something like she just did.

And she was right. As recognition dawned Max saw the image of one of his sculptures superimposed over Clea's face. It was a perfect likeness; it was like his work in clay had come alive before his eyes. To say he was shocked was an understatement, but he didn't feel afraid. In fact he felt strangely comforted. He knew this woman somehow, he felt connected and this calmed him a little.

'It's okay lovey' Clea said reassuringly 'I know it's a shock but there's no need to be afraid.'

He seemed to relax just a little but it was obvious he was unable to speak so she continued.

'I realise this is all very strange but I'm positive that it's a good sort of strange. This was meant to happen, us meeting I mean. You realise that too don't you?'

Max was still too shocked to answer but he managed a little nod.

'Good, okay, so now I think we need to find a place to sit, maybe get a cup of tea or something.'

'Okay.' Max managed to say as the initial shock began to wear off. He then held out the leaflet he was holding to show her the map in the centre pages.

'The nearest refreshment tent is not far away' he said pointing to a little square on the map.

'Let's head there then' said Clea taking his arm, and together they set off, Clea looking happy, Max looking dazed, both unaware that they were being watched and now discreetly followed.

As planned Mason had been one of the first to enter the event. Upon entering he'd quickly found a spot just inside the entrance from where he would be able to see everyone who entered. Well, that was the theory anyway, although in practice he soon realised that the size of the crowd would make it difficult at times. Still he had no other choice. He just needed to keep vigilant and hope.

After only fifteen minutes scanning the crowd Mason began to feel a headache coming on. This was not good; he may have to keep this up for quite a while yet.

Just for a second Mason closed his eyes, he couldn't help it, he needed the brief respite. When he opened them again something caught his eye. It wasn't a movement, more a lack of it. Across a sea of moving bodies his eye had caught on a lone, non-moving figure. He saw it first in brief flashes between moving bodies until a small break in the crowd enabled him to get a better look. The lone figure was a man. He was dressed in scruffy jeans and a wrinkled looking beige t-shirt. The man had long hair, a beard and he wore glasses.

As the crowd thickened again Mason kept his gaze on this man and as he did the people and scenery around him seemed to blur across his vision bringing the subject of his gaze into sharp focus. He did not recognise this man, well not in the usual sense anyway, but he knew him, he knew who he was. As this realisation hit an old but familiar feeling came over him, a feeling that he had only ever experienced once but had never forgotten.

There was a pulling sensation in his chest, his mind felt clouded, and his senses felt dulled except for his sight which narrowed into sharp and clear focus on the bearded man. He also felt a profound sense of relief which released a lot of the tension that had built up inside him over the last few days. This was a really good start. This whole crazy scheme might actually be paying off.

As his senses began to return to normal Mason spied a blaze of colour from the corner of his eye, it was moving towards the subject of his intense scrutiny. As it moved into full view this riot of colour solidified into the figure of a woman. She was wearing a brightly coloured dress that skimmed her curvy figure and her long, red hair shone in the morning light. Wow thought Mason, another one; things were really working out now.

He watched as the woman approached the man, observing their first interaction, smiling to himself at the shocked reaction of the man and the apparent calmness of the woman. You wait, he thought, you think this is strange well it's going to get a lot stranger.

As the pair began to walk away Mason began to follow. It wasn't time to approach them yet but he needed to keep them in sight, now he'd found them he couldn't afford to lose them.

'Hi, I'm Darren, it's really great to meet you.'

The man standing before Geth had cropped blonde hair and a round, clean shaven baby face making it hard to judge his age. He was quite short and his body was a little soft and plump. At odds with his softness however most of the exposed flesh on his arms was covered in tattoos, and very good tattoos at that.

'Great to meet you too' Geth replied taking the proffered hand in a firm handshake.

'So how are you finding things so far?' asked Darren.

'Really good thanks. I really appreciate all that you did to get me here.'

'It was no problem; I was glad to help. Your pitch looks great.'

'Thanks.'

'Are you here on your own?'

'Yeah, I thought it was a bit short notice to shut the studio down for the weekend so I left my partner Chris holding the fort.'

'Well I'm around checking up on things so if you need a break or want a bit of time to go look around I'm sure I can find someone to keep an eye on your stuff for you.'

'That's great; I might take you up on that offer.'

'So do you have anyone lined up to tattoo here?'

'No, well except for you if you want me to tattoo you as promised, that is if you know what you want.'

'I would love for you to tattoo me today thanks, I have a good idea what I want but I don't have any artwork.'

'That's okay; I can draw something up for you.'

'I'll have to check what time is best as I have my duties as an event organiser, but I'm sure I'll be able to have a couple of hours off at some point.'

'Okay, I'll be here whenever so just let me know.'

'Great, will do, now I'd better get on.'

'See you later then.'

'Looking forward to it, bye for now.'

And with that Darren moved on to the next pitch to continue his duties.

Geth was glad he had a tattoo lined up for later as he'd not been looking forward to just sitting chatting to people who passed by all day, even if that chat was about his work or tattooing in general, Geth wasn't much of a talker. This event wasn't really his thing at all but for some reason he'd felt compelled to come here and until he discovered what that reason was he'd have to make the best of it. He had a feeling it was going to be a long day.

So, where to next?'

Mary and Aaron were just leaving the Fine Arts Marque where they had spent a good deal of time looking at the paintings on display and chatting to the artists. Aaron had been particularly drawn to the work of a fellow portrait artist. Mary thought the guy was good but nowhere near as good as Aaron. She'd told him so as soon as they were out of earshot of the other artist. He'd thanked her for the compliment and had even blushed a little.

They were having such a great time and this was only the beginning of the event. There were all sorts of things to look forward to. For now they were having a good look around, getting their bearings. Later on they hoped to watch a few demonstrations or even possibly take part in a workshop or two. It was time to move on to the next marque.

'I'd like to go to the Creative Writing Marque next' Mary said in answer to Aaron's question. 'Sounds good to me, I think it's this way.'

They headed off to their left and soon found their destination. Mary was really looking forward to this one though she had no idea what to expect, after all writing wasn't something you could display, not like paintings or sculpture.

As they entered the marque the first thing they noticed was that it was a lot less colourful than the others they'd visited. Instead of display boards full of paintings there were tables spread with books and several groups of chairs, some set around tables, others simply in a circle. The chair circles were there so that people could form little discussion groups on writing in general, or on specific authors or books. Most of these chairs were taken with their occupants deep in animated discussion.

Those set around the tables were for the most part empty and as Mary and Aaron approached the first one they realised why. On each table was a small board on which was written details of several writing mini workshops that were to take place throughout that day. In front of each board were sheets of paper on which people could sign up for the workshops. It was obviously on a first come first served basis as there were only eight places in each workshop. Each group of table and chairs was for a different genre of writing e.g. crime/thriller or romance and to Mary's delight one was for poetry.

'You should sign up for it' said Aaron

'I'd like to but what about you, it's not really your thing is it.'

'No, but I'm sure I can find a way to occupy myself whilst you take part.'

'Are you sure?'

'Of course, I know we wanted to spend this weekend together but a couple of hours apart won't hurt and besides we need to make the most of all the great stuff that's going on here. I'm sure I can find some sort of art workshop or demonstration to go to.'

'Okay, I'll do it.'

The next workshop started in forty minutes so Mary signed up for it and then they set off for the photography marque - which was a medium of art that they both enjoyed - to pass the time before the workshop was due to begin.

Clea's plan to visit her friends pitch first thing had totally gone out the window after her surprise encounter with Max. She had instead spent the first hour of her event experience sitting on a white, plastic garden chair drinking tea and having the most unusual conversation of her life.

She'd done most of the talking to start with as she suspected that even when not in a state of shock Max wasn't much of a talker. He sat smoking a scruffy roll up and looking nervous and Clea had decided that the best course of action was to try to act as normal as possible, to play down the strangeness of it all as best she could.

'So Max I take it you recognise me?'

'Yes I do, it's all so weird, but I do.'

'I know, you dreamt of me right, and not in the romantic sense but the actual sense?'

'Yes.'

'And I dreamt of you. I take it that you also dreamt of this event and then you felt the need to come here?'

'Yes.'

'Did you dream of other people too?'

'Yes, two men and a woman.'

'Right, me too.'

'Oh wait, I dreamt of another man too, right at the beginning.'

'Really? Okay, well that's different to me then, I only dreamt of four people.'

'You did.'

'Yes, but don't worry about it. How about I tell you about my dreams and then you tell me about yours?'

'Okay.'

So that's what they did, and after both had told their stories they were silent for a minute or two digesting the new information. Then once again it was Clea who took the initiative in the conversation.

'So I'd say we've both been brought here for some reason and that it was somehow destined that we meet. I'm also assuming that the other people that we dreamt about are here don't you think?'

'I guess so.'

'I could be wrong, after all what example do we have to go on, but I'm assuming those other people dreamt of us and each other too.'

'Do you think we should look for them?'

'That seems a pretty daunting task, this event is huge.'

'So what do we do then? This is all so weird; it's messing with my head.'

'It's okay Max, I don't know what's going on here either but I do know somehow that it's a good thing that's happening to us.'

'You think so?'

'I know so. As to what we do now I suggest we just go and enjoy ourselves at this amazing event and see what happens. I don't see the point in actively looking for these other people, I mean the logistics of that are mind boggling. I say we leave it all to chance.'

'But it's all so weird.'

'Listen Max, a few weird things have happened to me and I've learnt over the years that the best thing to do is just to accept the weird and get on with things.'

'Accept the weird?'

'Yes, it's kind of a motto of mine.' Clea laughed and was pleased to see a smile begin to tweak the corner of Max's mouth.'

'There you go' she said, 'that little smile that's creeping up on you, that's you accepting the weird.'

'Okay I'll go along with that' said Max his smile broadening.

Smiling back Clea was relived; it looked like Max was beginning to relax. It was time to start enjoying their strange adventure.

As the two new friends moved off into the crowd Mason followed. Two found, three to go.

Late morning Darren arranged for someone to keep an eye on Geth's pitch so that he could have a look around. Geth was impressed with the level of organisation and the diversity of the art represented. He spent most of his time in the Fine Arts Marque admiring the art on display.

As well as designing tattoo flash art he liked to paint when he got the chance. The themes and style of his paintings were still very tattoo orientated, for instance he liked to paint large koi or dragons in oils, but paint on canvas was still a very different medium to ink on skin and it was nice to change things up a bit.

After his tour Geth bought himself a burger and took it back to his pitch to eat. Then a little while later Darren showed up to discuss his tattoo. Darren explained his idea's to Geth and then went off to do some more organiser duties whilst Geth worked on the artwork. When Darren returned he was very pleased with what Geth had come up with, so Geth made up the tattoo stencil using the machine he'd brought with him and they were ready to go.

It wasn't a particularly large or complicated design but Geth was happy to be working. A few people stopped to watch him work and he was surprised to find that he quite enjoyed having an audience.

Although Mary had enjoyed her poetry workshop she was pleased when it ended and she could be with Aaron again. He had spent their time apart watching a demonstration on photorealistic portrait painting. He had enjoyed the demonstration as it was a technique he was interested in and would love to have a go at himself someday. He was also glad when it was over though and he could be with Mary again. The couple set off to get something to eat before continuing their exploration of the site.

Having paid a belated visit to Clea's friend Simon's pitch the new friends had spent a happy couple of hours wandering around the tents. The highlight for Max had obviously been the sculpture tent and for Clea a wander around the needlework tent had provided all she'd hoped for including a few familiar faces from her art fair days and now they were looking for their next experience.

As they wandered Clea suddenly stopped dead their conversation stopping with her. She stood staring ahead but her eyes looked glazed over and she appeared to be in what looked to Max like some sort of trance.

'What's up Clea?' he asked a little concerned.

For a minute Clea did not respond and Max was contemplating physically shaking her to try to snap her out of it when she suddenly snapped out of her trance.

Turning to Max she asked 'Have you ever considered having a tattoo?'

'No, never' replied a confused Max 'Have you?'

'No, well until now that is.'

'What, you go into some sort of weird trance and now all of a sudden you want to get a tattoo?'

'More like I'm considering it. As for the trance I did tell you that weird things happen to me sometime and that was one of them. I'd just caught sight of the Tattoo Art tent up ahead and suddenly everything seemed to stop and my vision went, and then I had an image flash into my mind of me sitting inside that tent having a tattoo whilst you sat watching, and then it faded and my vision returned and so now I figure in keeping with the spirit of our accepting the weird philosophy I say we check out the tattoo tent.'

'Okay, I guess we could' agreed Max a little hesitantly.

They headed for the tent and stopped just inside the entrance.

'So, where to?' asked Max

'I'm not sure' replied Clea scanning the room 'maybe we…. ooohh, hold on, yes' she turned to Max a big smile on her face 'over there, that's where we're going' she said pointing over to their left. Max looked in the direction she was pointing trying to spot what had caught her eye. Then his breath caught as he spotted what, or rather who she was pointing at.

The man had dark hair, receding slightly and a distinctive scar on the left side of his face. A scar that Max had recently portrayed in clay.

He turned back to Clea and was smiling too although in his case a little nervously.

'What do we do?' he asked.

'We go and say hello' said Clea and she was off, no hesitation. Max followed admiring her confidence.

'Hello there.'

Geth looked up from the design he had half-heartedly started work on after finishing Darren's tattoo to see a woman smiling down at him. A woman with long, red hair and friendly green eyes. He felt a jolt of recognition even though he knew he'd never met this woman before.

'Hi' he replied tentatively.

'I'm Clea' the woman said 'and this is Max.'

Geth shifted his gaze to this man Max. This time he physically blanched at the sight of another strangely familiar face.

'I know its weird lovey' said the woman soothingly 'but it's okay.'

'Just accept the weird' added the man a wry smile on his bearded face.

Geth looked from one to the other for a few seconds before it finally dawned on him where he'd seen them before. Instead of being a relief the realisation just made things seem stranger. He'd seen them in his dreams. The sentence seemed weird even in his head and there was no way he'd manage to say those words out loud, instead he only managed to mumble 'I know you.'

'We know you too' replied the woman he now knew as Clea.

'It's okay' she continued 'it's a good thing, I'm sure of it. We're meant to meet; we haven't figured out why yet but it'll be an adventure finding out right?'

'I guess'. Geth was still too shocked to think straight.

'Do you want us to go away for a bit and come back when you've had time to process things a little?' asked Max.

'No, no it's fine.' As gobsmacked as he was Geth didn't like the idea of these two leaving. 'Please stay.'

'Okay, good. So what's your name?'

'I'm Geth.'

'Nice to meet you Geth, I know you're a little freaked out so why don't we keep things more 'normal' for now. Why don't you tell us about what you do, show us some of your work?'

Mason had hesitated outside the tattoo tent for a while before making the decision to go in. After all he had a couple of tattoos himself and it was an art form he admired so it couldn't harm to go in. They wouldn't know he was following them and as long as he kept one eye on them so he knew when they were leaving what harm would it do to have a look around.

When he entered the tent he spotted them almost immediately. They had pulled chairs up to one of the pitches' and were looking through some flash art books. They looked like they might be there for a while which pleased Mason; it gave him the chance to have a look around.

After a few pitches' he came across some art he liked at a pitch a couple of places down from his quarry and as he turned the pages of a flash art folder he couldn't help glancing over at them. They were deep in conversation with the tattoo artist and he was about to look away again when a strange sensation came over him. His vision narrowed to focus on the group of three and a 'glow' appeared around them, then he observed what looked like fine silver thread weaving around and through the three of them linking them together.

After a few seconds the silver thread and the glow disappeared, his focus adjusted back to normal and he realised what his vision had shown him; he'd found another one, or rather they had. He felt a little more weight lift from his shoulders. He could relax a little now. This guy was more static than the other two, Mason would know where to find him, he could relax his surveillance and take in a little more of the event. He still had work to do there was no doubt of that but things were coming together nicely.

Mason decided to leave the tent and find somewhere to sit and relax and have something to eat, he would also give Sofia a call to update her on the good news then he could come back to the tattoo tent after. If the other two had left it wouldn't be a disaster, he knew where the tattoo guy would be all day. He gave the trio a last look before heading out of the tent.

After a quick lunch Mary and Aaron decided that having visited all the tents relating to the arts they were mainly interested in it was now time to check out those genres of art that were outside of their comfort zone. They felt it would be interesting to diversify and open their minds up to art forms they were less familiar with, and it would be good to experience these new things together.

After studying the guide pamphlet for a bit, they decided to head for the Music Stage. The act currently playing was a local punk band called The Ejected. Neither of them were really into punk so it fit in with their new experience philosophy perfectly. The band had just started their set when they arrived and after a couple of songs they found to their surprise they were enjoying their music.

They discovered that the band were a little more tuneful than they'd expected yet they still had that classic aggressive punk attitude. Their songs had the typical anti-establishment lyrics but there was also humour in them which Aaron particularly enjoyed.

They ended up watching the bands whole set; their first foray into the unknown a success. After The Ejected left the stage they decided to set off in search of their next new experience.

Max and Clea had been looking through Geth's flash art books for about ten minutes when Geth had a sudden idea. Picking up the rucksack he'd stowed under the table he got out the one folder he'd brought but not laid out on the table. It was the one that had his new designs in, the ones he'd drawn after he'd dreamt of the two people who now sat across from him (as well as the other two).

'These are my latest designs' he said handing the folder to Clea.

She took it from him and started to leaf through it. She was impressed with Geth's work so far but as she opened his folder her heart skipped a beat. Although they were in a different medium these designs reminded her of the drawings she had made after her dream, the ones she had simplified and embroidered on the t shirts she had made. Then she turned the page to the fourth design and her stomach did a little flip.

The design was beautiful and familiar. It was a beautifully drawn human eye but where the iris and pupil should be there was an orb containing a kaleidoscopic swirl of beautiful colours. She was amazed by it on more than one level.

'I want this one' she exclaimed.

'Which one?' asked Geth although he already knew the answer. Clea turned the book to show him the design and he nodded. 'Good choice.'

'So you're definitely having a tattoo then?' asked Max.

'Definitely now I've seen this design' said Clea 'have a look in there, I have a feeling you'll like one too' she continued handing him the folder.

Max took it feeling pretty sure that he didn't want a tattoo at all no matter how good Geth's designs were. Then he opened the folder and the very first design jumped out at him. It was a circle and within the circle there was a feather trapped inside some sort of web.

He looked at Clea in surprise and wonder, then he looked at Geth.

'You want that one?' asked Geth with a rare smile on his face.

'I think I do' said Max his tone and the expression on his face making Clea and Geth laugh.

'That's the magic of tattoo's' said Geth 'once you think up or see an image you fall in love with you just have to have it put on your skin forever.'

'Can you do mine now?' asked Clea.

'I don't see why not; I just need to make a stencil and we're away.'

After some food and a little time to relax Mason decided he should call in and update Eddie and Sofia on his news. He wanted to check how things were going with them too.

Eddie answered.

'How are things going mate?' he asked.

'Pretty well, I've managed to find three so far.'

'That's amazing news Sofia will be trilled.'

'Yeah things seem to be going to plan; the three of them are together in the tattoo tent right now which is really encouraging.'

'Great and they have a tattoo tent? You're making me wish I was there now; you know I love a bit of ink.'

'Yes my friend I do, this new guy is actually a tattoo artist.'

'I look forward to meeting him then.'

'Lets not get ahead of ourselves , I've got some work to do yet.'

'I have faith in you mate, things are going well so far right?'

'As well as can be expected yeah.'

'Good. So how are you doing in yourself, you okay?'

'Yes, a little tired but a lot better now I've found three of them. How are things your end?'

'Pretty good thanks.'

'So it's all under control then?'

'Yeah I think so mate.'

'Okay, good. Say hi to Sofia for me and I'll call back when I have more news.'

'Will do, and good luck.'

'Thanks, bye.'

'Bye.'

His call made Mason decided to head back to the tattoo tent.

On arrival inside a pleasing sight greeted him. The three of them were still together and the woman was now actually being tattooed by her new friend. This was a pleasing sight because it meant they would all be together in the same place for quite a while leaving Mason free to have a wander around the event for a bit giving him some time to form a plan of action.

Back at the Gateway Eddie's news of Mason's success was greeted with the expected relief and joy, at least something was going well. Sofia left the group briefly to update the Foundation on the good news before returning to her fellow artists.

It took Geth a little under two hours to complete Clea's tattoo. She had opted to have the tattoo on her left shoulder. With the help of Max and two mirrors Geth showed her the finished tattoo.

'It's beautiful' she said, 'I love it.'

'Good, I'm glad you're happy, and you sat really well.'

'Thanks, it actually didn't hurt as much as I feared.'

'Really?' asked Max surprised.

'Yes. I'm not saying it didn't hurt at times but not too bad.'

'Well it does depend on where the tattoo is done' said Geth 'the shoulder area is not too bad usually, it does also depend on the person though, some people have a higher pain tolerance than others.'

'I'm a tough lady' said Clea laughing.

'I get the feeling you are' said Geth.

'Your turn' said Clea turning to Max.

'So where are you having it? asked Geth.

'Where it hurts least' joked Max.

After a few minutes discussion Max decided to have the tattoo on his left arm just below the shoulder. He'd been a little unsure about having the tattoo to start with, but after seeing how Clea coped with the process and being impressed with Geth's skill and with the finished piece of art he actually felt quite eager to have his own. Geth's design was literally made for him and he felt compelled to have the image put on him for life. It was totally out of character, something he'd never considered having, but it felt like the right thing to do right then. So after a quick visit outside for a cigarette he was ready to go.

An hour and a half later Max's tattoo was finished. He'd coped well with the pain and thought the finished tattoo looked even better than he'd imagined. Geth was a genius. Max had a newfound admiration for tattoo art.

'You love it don't you' said Clea

'Yes I do which kind of surprises me, but then a lot of today has been surprising.'

'It sure has.'

'Thanks Geth' he said turning to their new friend 'you are a true artist, I'm very impressed.'

'I'm glad; if you're happy then I'm happy,'

The trio had been so involved in their discussion that they failed to realise that Geth's fellow tattooists had begun to pack up for the day and so they were surprised when Darren turned up to see Geth before leaving for the day. He was closely followed by Len who'd come to help Geth pack up and so the three of them made brief plans to meet up again the next day before Max and Clea left them to it.

As they strolled back to the campsite Clea and Max decided they'd spend the evening in Clea's RV. She would cook dinner and they would chat. First though they stopped off at Max's VW Camper. During their talk about their dreams they had discussed the art they had created from these dreams and Clea was eager to see Max's sculptures. Max showed Clea his sculpture of her first. The sight of her likeness in clay left her speechless for a minute or two. Finally she managed to speak.

'Oh Max it's incredible' she said 'It looks just like me, only better, you are so talented. I love it.'

Max blushed and mumbled thanks. Clea was equally impressed with the busts of the other three 'dreamers'.

'Amazing, they look just how I saw them in my dreams.'

Then max showed her his 'Jekyll and Hyde Trio'. Clea studied the three sculptures for a couple of minutes before speaking.

'Wow these are something else Max. So the last one is obviously you, and the first one is the other man you told me you dreamt of that I didn't, and the middle one is a weird mix up of both of you right?'

'I guess that sums it up yes.'

'There's got to be some strange meaning to this but I really can't imagine what.'

'No, me either.'

A short distance away the subject of the mystery sculpture was watching. He couldn't see what they were looking at or hear what they were saying but that was okay, he didn't need to, he just needed to keep them in sight. Now he knew at least one of their vehicles and where it was parked he would be able to keep tabs on them.

A little while later when Max and Clea moved on to Clea's RV to have dinner and share her dream artwork Mason followed behind. Once he realised they were settling in for the evening he decided he should return to his own tent to have something to eat and then get a good night's sleep. He figured he'd need to get up early and stake out the RV so he could trail them again. Tomorrow they would hopefully lead him to the others. As Mason made his way through the motley collection of RV's and caravans to the field where his tent was pitched he realised how hungry and exhausted he was. Around him the other event goers were forming little gatherings and parties, some of which would no doubt go on all night. But Mason just wanted to rest. He had a sandwich and a drink he'd picked up during the day and which he intended to consume the minute he got to his tent then he planned to settle down for what he hoped would be a good night's sleep.

As Mason headed to his tent Clea was giving Max the t shirt she had made for him. No one had ever 'made' anything for him before and he felt a little emotional about it, and the t shirt itself was so perfect. Clea was pleased with his reaction and the two spent a happy evening chatting before retiring for the night to prepare for another interesting day.

Leaving the event after a very enjoyable but tiring day Mary and Aaron were headed to Aaron's boarding house. They planned to spend the night at Mary's again but first they needed to pick up a few things for Aaron. He needed a change of clothes and some toiletries.

As he packed a few things into a small sports bag Aaron caught sight of his carrying portfolio and decided he wanted to take it with him. During the day he had spoken to a few fellow artists and they had expressed an interest in seeing his work so why not take a few things to show them the next day. He'd have a look through when they were back at Mary's and pick out a few pieces to take along. Mary agreed it was a good plan and then when Aaron suggested she took some of her poetry too suggesting she might want to read some at the poetry readings they'd noticed were scheduled for the next day. The thought of reading them out to an audience daunted her a little but it also excited her so she agreed.

On the way back to Mary's they stopped to pick up a Chinese takeaway and then after eating they sorted what they wanted to take with them the next day. Both of them included their recent 'dream' pieces as it was some of their best work even though they both felt unsure about sharing it with just anybody. Then the happy couple got ready for bed. Although they were both pretty exhausted and were looking at another tiring day ahead sleep wasn't the first thing on their minds and so the couple made love for the second time before falling into a contented deep sleep.

CHAPTER 14

ARTFEST DAY 2

It was early morning at the Gateway and Sofia and Eddie were in the office awaiting the new arrivals. Phoebe and Mark were in the kitchen finishing a leisurely breakfast before a planned return to the art room. Mark wanted to continue work on his painting and Phoebe to work on a piece of music she had started to compose the evening before.

Right on schedule the gate intercom buzzed heralding their guest's arrival and Sofia and Eddie were waiting at the door when the Foundation car pulled up to the house.

As the Foundation driver went to retrieve the bags from the boot the first of the newcomers emerged from the car and came striding towards them. She was tall, her slim, bony frame hidden under dark, loose fitting trousers and an oversized man's shirt. She looked to be in her late forties and wore her greying dark hair loosely tied back. She had a square jawed, handsome face, the weathered skin free of make-up.

'Good Morning, my name is Dorothea Atwood' she said extending her hand first to Sofia and then Eddie. Her grip was strong, her hand rough to the touch. She gave off a strong air of no-nonsense efficiency. Sofia and Eddie introduced themselves and then turned their attention to her companion who was now headed towards them carrying several bags.

Samuel Raven was a very striking looking man. He was in his early forties but looked younger and he was obviously not of British descent. His very long, straight, black hair, strong features and bronzed skin colouring told of his obvious Native American heritage. He was very tall at six foot five and his strong physique was defined by tight black jeans and a startlingly white t shirt. His movements were fluid and easy and he gave off a feeling of calm. He put the bags down in order to shake their hands and Sofia noticed that although his hands were enormous his touch was surprisingly gentle.

As introductions were made Sofia couldn't help but think that he was the most beautiful man she had ever seen. But this wasn't a social gathering for fun, the man was here to do a job and a very serious and important one at that, so it was not appropriate to dwell on his looks, they all had work to do.

Taking some of the bags Eddie showed the pair to the rooms he had prepared for them upstairs. As he was doing this Sofia went to the office to put in a quick call to Cedric Neale.

'I take it your new guests have arrived safely' he enquired after the initial pleasantries.

'Yes sir they have.'

'Good, good' and after a brief pause 'and now to the business you asked me about before regarding Eddie Oakley. We have discussed it at length and it has been decided that you are right the man should be told everything so that he can be of more help to you.'

'Thank you. I know that Eddie will be an even greater asset to us once he is fully briefed on the situation.'

'I trust your judgement Sofia, it's one of the reasons I have agreed to this. I suggest you tell him as soon as possible, and then the four of you can get to work as a team.'

'I agree.'

'Good. I will leave you to get on then but keep me updated obviously and call me if you need anything.'

'I will.'

'Goodbye Sofia.'

'Goodbye sir.'

After putting down the phone Sofia went in search of Eddie and the others. She found them in the lounge / art room where Eddie was introducing the newcomers to Phoebe and Mark having already given them a quick tour of the house. After introductions and a brief chat it was all business.

'Can you stay here with Phoebe and Mark for a bit' said Sofia to Eddie 'I'm going to take Samuel and Dorothea to the office and acquaint them with the security system, and then whilst they use the cameras to have an initial look around the property we need to talk.'

'Okay, no problem' agreed Eddie.

Before giving them the security system tutorial Sofia explained to Dorothea and Samuel that she had been given authority to fill Eddie in on the full story. They were a little surprised but when she explained the reasoning behind it and told them how well Eddie had dealt with everything over the last few days they understood that it had to be done.

After showing them the basics Sofia then left them to acquaint themselves with the security system and make their preliminary search and went to get Eddie. The pair then went to the kitchen and after making and delivering tea and coffee to everyone they sat at the kitchen table to talk.

The second day of Artfest dawned bright and dry and the thousands of artists and their appreciators flocked to the massive field for another day of revelling in their passion.

Geth, Mary and Aaron were once again amongst the early arrivals ready to set up for the day. Mary and Aaron looking forward to another day of bliss together and Geth with his newfound strange friends foremost in his mind.

Whilst they worked those strange new friends of Geths were again in Clea's RV, this time for a fortifying breakfast before setting out for the day. And outside the RV Mason, having thankfully slept well, waited.

Clea and Max's first destination of the day was of course the tattoo tent. Clea greeted Geth with a good morning kiss, Max with a friendly handshake. The three then made plans for the day. It was decided that Max and Clea would take turns to keep an eye on Geth's pitch so that he had more time to explore the event that day. Max was to take the first sitting whilst Clea and Geth explored together. Plans made the unlikely 'couple' set off leaving a slightly nervous Max alone on the pitch.

Max was feeling antsy. He'd been feeling it all morning and at times the feeling had been pretty intense. It felt like he had mild pins and needles all over his body and every now and then he felt a strange 'pulling' sensation in his gut. He'd not mentioned it to Clea or Geth basically because it was really hard to describe let alone understand. Maybe it was just stress, a reaction to him not quite 'accepting the weird'. Maybe he should discuss it with Clea and Geth when they got back; it would be hard but maybe they could shed some light on it. However, by the time Clea and Geth returned the feeling had faded, it was still there but weaker so he decided not to mention it.

Now it was time for him and Geth to have a wander whilst Clea looked after the pitch.

After following Max and Clea to the tattoo tent and taking a brief peek inside where he saw them chatting intently with Geth Mason decided it was safe to leave them to it for a while. He decided he'd go and check out the music stage, maybe sit and listen for a while, take it easy for a bit, he had a hard task ahead and needed to keep his strength up. He'd check back in a couple of hours.

So where to next?' asked Mary.

The couple had already paid another visit to the creative writing tent to see a poetry reading at which Mary had chickened out of taking part. And then they had visited a few of the artists Aaron had spoken to the day before. He had shown them some of his work which they had been impressed with, but he had not shown them his most recent work for reasons he didn't fully understand. And now back on the hunt for new artistic experiences they were outside one of the few tents they hadn't visited yet.

'Let's have a look in here' suggested Aaron 'I've quite fancied having a tattoo in the past but could never afford it or decide what I wanted tattooed, it's a big commitment so you've gotta make the right decision. I really admire the talent of a good tattooist.'

'I've thought about it too' agreed Mary 'though its more the pain than the cost that's put me off and I agree it's an amazing talent, and I could never decide what I'd like tattooed on me either.'

'Well maybe we'll get some ideas inside' said Aaron as they headed into the tent.

Mary's first thought when she saw the smiling red-haired woman sat at pitch number nine was 'she doesn't look like a tattooist'. This thought was quickly followed by 'but she does look familiar.' Then things got weird. The sights and sounds around Mary faded away and two images flashed before her eyes. The first was an image of the red-haired woman's face rendered in pencil strokes, Aaron's portrait sketch, then there was a grey mist and the same woman walked from it smiling in greeting, a flashback to a dream. Then suddenly sight and sound rushed back in making Mary stagger a little. She felt Aaron's arm encircle her waist and he pulled her to him. She looked up at him and saw the emotions she was feeling mirrored in his face.

'Did you just....' She stammered.

'Yes' Aaron replied not needing to hear the rest of the sentence.

They both then turned to look at the red-haired woman. She was looking right back at them. She smiled at them and waved.

'What the...?' said Aaron looking back at Mary.

Mary shrugged 'I guess we should go over'.

'I guess so.'

Mary's legs felt like jelly as they made their way over to the woman.

'Hello, you two, it's so nice to meet you. My name's Clea. Maybe you'd better sit down' she said indicating the two chairs set opposite her.

Mary and Aaron sat like two obedient children.

'It's okay' continued Clea 'you just take a minute; it's a shock I know.'

'You recognise us?' Aaron finally managed to say.

'Of course I do, the same way you recognise me and each other right? From dreams.'

'Well yes, I suppose we shouldn't be too shocked, after all it's happened before when Mary and I met.'

'So the young ladies name is Mary, and what's your name?'

'I'm so sorry, how rude, I'm Aaron.'

'Hello Aaron, hello Mary.'

'Hello, sorry, what did you say your name was?' asked Mary suddenly finding her voice.

'I'm Clea.'

'It's nice to meet you Clea.'

Clea gave the two another of her beaming, friendly smiles.

'I know you're feeling a little strange right now but it's okay, I can't explain all this right now but I just know that what is happening to us is a good thing, don't you feel that too?'

The young couple nod in agreement.

'That's good. If it helps the boys and I have kind of invented a mantra for what's going on, which is 'accept the weird'.

'The boys? Who are the boys?' asked Aaron.

'Ah, yes, well you two are not the first 'dream friends' I've met recently, there are two more of us. I take it there were two other people you dreamt of?'

'Yes, the guy with the scar' said Aaron.

'And the man who looks kinda like Jesus' finished Mary.

'That's right' said Clea with a little laugh 'I guess Max does look a little Jesus like, and the guy with the scar is called Geth. This is actually Geth's pitch; I'm just looking after it whilst he has a look around with Max.'

'So you're not a tattooist then' stated Mary.

'Oh no, I wish I had the talent for it, although my talent does include working with needles too, I'm a seamstress and embroiderer, and Max is a very good sculptor. So what can you two do, artistically speaking I mean.'

'I paint' said Aaron 'portraits mainly.'

'And I write poetry' added Mary.

'Well aren't we a talented bunch' said Clea 'I'd love to see your work Aaron and read your work Mary and I have something for you both, I can show you later, or to be more exact give you later.'

'Really, what on earth could you have to give two people you've never met before? Asked Mary.

'You'll have to wait and see.'

'Teaser' said Aaron smiling at Clea.

The three were silent for a few minutes not really knowing where to go from there until Clea said 'Geth tattooed Max and I yesterday, do you want to see mine?

Clea didn't wait for an answer she just turned around and pushed the left strap of her dress down to reveal a square patch of cling film taped to her skin. 'Just peel in back and take a look it's okay' she said.

Aaron gently did as she said and they both leaned in to take a look.

'That's beautiful' Mary breathed.

'Very impressive' said Aaron 'Geth is very talented.'

He gently taped the covering back in place and Clea pulled up her strap and turned back around.

'Yes he is, you should take a look at some of his designs' said Clea indicating the flash art folders on the table between them.

Mary and Aaron each picked up a folder and began to leaf through them.

'These are really good' said Aaron.

'I'm no expert, but I agree' said Mary.

'If you think they're good wait until you see these ones' said Clea handing Aaron the folder that included the designs for her's and Max's tattoos.

Mary leaned in to look as Aaron opened the folder. The first design was Max's tattoo which they admired accordingly. Then they turned the page to the next two. The two tattoos were basically different versions of the same image, that image being a bare branched tree silhouetted by the moon. One design was a stylised line drawing of the tree and moon within a circle, the other was a more detailed realistic representation without the outer circle.

'I love that one' they both said in unison, Aaron pointing to realistic one and Mary the stylised version. They all laughed, and it was at this point that Geth and Matt returned.

'Hello boys' said Clea 'let me introduce you to our new friends.'

As the group met it was like something 'shifted', they all felt it, it was like time stopped for a few seconds and when it re-set things were different. Things were 'better' somehow. Something had begun. They felt connected, and as strange as it all was if felt somehow natural and right.

Mason was practically on the other side of the event when the five 'dream friends' came together, but he felt it. It was like an echo of an experience he'd had years ago. He staggered and almost fell from the physical impact of it, but he'd never been gladder to feel anything in his life.

After taking a minute to steady himself he headed for the tattoo tent hoping that was where the actual event had taken place.

On arrival at the tent he was again shaken, this time with relief to see the five people gathered together at the tattooists pitch.

The three he'd already seen had now been joined by a young couple. The group was complete. The first part of his 'task' was completed but there was still work to be done.

Mason left the tent, he needed to call The Gateway with the news and then plan his next move. A little way from the tent there was a refreshment stall with seats. He would be able to keep an eye on the tent from there in case they left. It was the perfect place to sit and make his call and plan.

Unaware of all the turmoil going on back at The Gateway Mason made his call. Again it was Eddie who answered. His friend sounded a little distracted but was obviously very pleased at the news. He told Mason that things were going as well as expected at his end.

Next Mason spoke to Sofia. She sounded tired and stressed but Mason didn't think too much of it, that's how they were all feeling. His news seemed to perk her up a bit though. With the news catch up done Sofia and Mason went on to discuss how Mason should proceed with the next part of the plan.

After a brief discussion it was decided that he would remain an observer for most of the rest of that day giving them all a chance to process what had happened to them today before adding to the strangeness of it all, then he planned to approach the group at an opportune moment. The meeting could be tricky but it needed to happen. He could only hope that the meeting went well.

As Mason made his plans outside the tent, inside the five new 'friends' were getting to know each other.

Despite the strangeness of their situation conversation flowed. The group were definitely practising their newfound 'accept the weird' philosophy. How else could they deal with it all?

They took turns giving a brief autobiography and then began a long discussion on art. At one point the discussion came back to Geth's tattoo designs and both Aaron and Mary expressed their wish to have Geth Tattoo them with the designs they loved but explained they feared they couldn't afford it.

Geth explained that he'd already only charged Clea and Max 'mates rates' for their tattoos and would be willing to do Mary and Aaron's for free if need be. They protested that was too generous but Geth insisted. They finally agreed but on the proviso that they would pay Geth back in some way at a later date. It was decided that Geth would start their tattoos straight away.

'So who's going first then?' he asked.

'Ladies first' suggested Aaron.

'No, you go first, I'm a little nervous' admitted Mary.

'Ok fine' said Aaron with a little laugh.

'Max and I will go for a wander then' said Clea 'leave you too it, see you in a bit.'

'Okay' chorused Geth, Aaron and Mary.

So Clea and Max set off and Geth set to work making the stencil for Aarons tattoo.

When Clea and Max returned about an hour and a half later Geth was almost finished. They joined the small, admiring crowd that had gathered to watch a master at work.

When the tattoo was complete the crowd dispersed leaving the five of them together again. Geth stood up to stretch.

'Well done mate' he said to Aaron 'that was a tough one but you coped well for a first timer.'

'Thanks, I sort of enjoyed it really. I can understand how people can get addicted, especially when the results are this good, you did a great job Geth, I love it.' said Aaron as he studied the artwork newly adorning the inside of his left forearm.

'I love it too' said Mary.

'Good, so how do you feel about me doing yours after we have a little break?'

'I'd be lying if is said I wasn't still a little nervous but I know that any pain will be worth it so I'm confident I can bear it with that in mind.'

'Good girl, I'll be gentle with you I promise.'

Mary smiled at Geth; the man wasn't half as intimidating as he looked she decided.

'How about me and the love birds go and get us all some food, stretch our legs a little whilst you two stay here and look after my pitch.'

They agreed Geths plan was a good one so that's what they did.

After the meal break Max and Clea decided to stay and watch Mary get tattooed. Hers was a smaller, less intricate design than Aaron's and so wouldn't take too long.

The tattoo tent was filling up nicely, the air full of the buzz of machines and people talking. Mary had opted to have the tattoo low on her inner left forearm near her wrist and she found the noise of the tattoo machine strangely soothing as she watched Geth work.

She found the process quite painful at times but she knew what was causing the pain and that it would end quite soon so it was bearable. She also knew the end result would be worth it.

When the tattoo was finished she couldn't stop staring at it. It was beautiful. Geth couldn't help but feel proud of his work. He felt they were four of the best tattoos he'd ever done. His newfound friends were very happy with his work, what more could you ask for. He was shocked that he had made friends with these people so quickly and under such strange circumstance. He felt more at ease in their presence than he did with people he'd known for years. He'd decided not to analyse it too much, to just go with the flow which wasn't his normal course of action but nothing about this situation was normal.

After admiring Mary's tattoo a thought occurred to Clea.

'So' she said to Mary 'Geth has shown off his talent and when I intimated that I have something to show you later I can now say it is to do with my art. Max here also has something or somethings to share later but what about you two, do you have anything to show us?'

'Aaron has some sketches.' Said Mary

'And what about your poems.' Aaron responded.

'Delightful' exclaimed Clea 'can we see and read them please?

'I guess so, but can you go first Aaron' said Mary nervously.

'That's fine by me' agreed Aaron 'I knew there was a reason I brought them.'

And so after arranging themselves on chairs around the pitch Aaron passed around his sketched portraits of the people around him.

They all reacted much as Mary had, they were amazed and flattered, and Aaron had never felt prouder of his work.

'He's painted a couple of portraits too' said Mary proudly 'one of me and one of Geth.'

'How lovely' said Clea 'I'd like to see those sometime.'

Aaron smiled at her 'I'm sure that can be arranged, but maybe not yet, I intend to paint you and Max too and then I'll show you all four.'

Clea returned his smile. 'I'll look forward to that.'

And then it was Mary's turn. She felt a little nervous as she passed around copies of her poems.

Aaron's portraits had gone down well but his and the others 'art' was of a visual nature but poetry was different, her skill was with words, a totally different medium. It was also a medium not many people were fond of. It was very subjective; she just wasn't sure how they would react to her words.

Her hands shook a little as she handed them each the poem she had written after she dreamt of them. Aaron of course had already read the Dream Mates poem but she handed it to him anyway. He smiled at her and she realised he'd picked up on her nervousness and was trying to reassure her. She returned his smile and sat down.

Max was first to speak.

'So this is about me?' His voice wavered a bit. 'I'm a Dreamcatcher? But what does that mean?'

'I don't know' replied Mary 'It's just what came into my head after the dream I had of you.'

'And I'm the Gatekeeper?' said Geth.

'Yes.' Said Mary quietly.

'But the poems are good right, you like them?' asked Aaron as he put a protective arm around Mary.

'I don't really know anything about poetry' said Geth 'I thought they had to rhyme.'

'A lot of people do' said Mary the disappointment clear in her voice.

'I'm sorry' said Geth feeling bad 'you shouldn't listen to me, what do I know. What I can say is that I find these words intriguing, especially as they are about me.'

The group were silent for a minute, then Max said 'I've read a little poetry, and after a second read I think that it's really good. I couldn't appreciate that at first because I was dealing with the fact that you wrote it about me'. He smiled at Mary 'I'm not just saying that I mean it.'

'Thanks Max.'

'Can I read yours?' he asked Geth.

'Sure, let's swap' replied Geth who was still feeling bad about hurting Mary's feelings.

'Wow, you're a powerful guy' said Max to Geth after he'd finished the poem.

'And you're an important sounding man' said Geth making them all laugh a little and easing the tension. All that is except Clea who was still staring at the words Mary had written about her.

'Are you okay Clea?' asked Max when he realised she wasn't joining in, and when she didn't answer he repeated his question louder.

This time his voice got through to her and she looked up startled to see them all looking at her.

'I can't believe you wrote this' she said focusing her gaze on Mary. It's amazing, how did you know?'

'Know what?'

'That I see things in my dreams.'

'I.... I... didn't, I dreamt of you and then the words just came to me.'

'You see things in yours dreams? Asked Aaron. 'I mean other than the things we've all seen lately that is.'

'Yes, I've dreamt of things that have then happened a few times in my life.'

'Well that's impressive, and a little weird.'

There was silence again for a minute until Mary spoke.

'Remember our motto, let's accept the weird.'

This time all of them laughed. Mary's poems were passed around until they had all been read by everyone. They discussed them a little, and after the initial shock at her words had worn off were finally able to give her work some praise.

After the intensity of the poetry reaction it was decided by the group that they would get back to the relative normality of Artfest for what was left of the day. So Geth stayed with his pitch and now it was clear of his new friends he could interact with some of the other event goers. The others set off in their pairs to see some more art with a promise to check in on Geth at regular intervals.

As all but Geth exited the tent they were unaware that their 'watcher' was back. Mason had spent a relaxing few hours listening to music and had returned to the tattoo tent not long before. Seeing the four leave Mason decided to follow Mary and Aaron for a while not having actually seen the pair until now he was curious to observe them for a while. He had made a rough plan of action whilst resting but it was too early to put it into action so for now he would just observe.

As the event was winding down the five again converged at Geth's pitch and when it came time for the event to shut down they made plans to all pay a visit to Max's VW to see his sculptures and then to go to Clea's RV for some dinner and chat and of course so she could give them their, mystery 'gifts'.

Geth let Len know that he would make his own way back to the flat later if that was okay as he had plans with friends. Len said it was fine he'd see him later.

Then after helping Geth pack up the group set off for Max's VW.

Mary, Aaron and Geth were amazed at the likeness' Max had achieved of them in clay and were intrigued by the Jekyll and Hyde Trio.

'So who do you think this other guy is?' asked Geth.

'I have no idea' said Max 'I dreamt of him but it appears none of you did so I don't know what that means'.

'We can't know' said Clea 'but I've a feeling we'll find out soon.'

'Let's hope so' said Mary.

It was a little cramped but kind of cosy with all of them sat inside Clea's RV. First Clea gave Mary, Aaron and Geth the garments she'd made them. They were impressed with the craftsmanship involved and amazed at how perfectly the symbols she'd designed suited them. Their praise made Clea a very happy lady.

Next Clea set about cooking them dinner.

'I knew there was a reason for buying all this food' she said as she bustled about the tiny kitchen area. The food went down very well and conversation flowed.

After Sofia finished talking Eddie had needed time to process the new, startling information so Sofia suggested he go to the lounge / art room where he could sit and get his head straight and / or chat things through with Phoebe and Mark whilst she went to check on Dorothea and Samuel.

Before leaving Eddie with the youngsters, she quickly explained to them that Eddie now knew everything and that they were free to answer any questions he may have and then she left them to it.

Back in the office she'd discovered that her new colleagues had done a full camera sweep of the property and had seen nothing out of the ordinary. This was to be expected, it wasn't going to be that easy was it? So now a course of action had needed to be decided on.

After an intense, protracted discussion a plan of action was put in place. Then they had decided that a big group meeting to brief the others on their plans was needed.

The meeting took place in the kitchen after a quick meal prepared by Eddie who was feeling calm and strangely relived after mulling things over and then chatting to Mark and Phoebe. They had answered some questions he had, and their quiet but typically youthful candour and humour had helped him come to terms with the new knowledge. Now he was about to sit down with a group of amazing people to find a solution to their shared problem and he felt privileged to be part of the 'inner circle' of the Foundation despite the burden of such an important secret.

The briefing and resulting discussion went on into the evening and when all the plans were in place they decided on an early night as they needed to be well rested in order to deal with what was to come.

It was finally time for Mason to approach the group of new friends. He had called the Somnium Foundation to check a few things with them and to get their advice in order to help him form his plan. They had also taken details off of him that would help them locate these people again in case the plan failed, those details being the number plates of the two vehicles he had seen belonging to the group, the first names of all five which he had picked up whilst listening in as he followed them plus the surname of the tattooist as it was emblazoned on the guys pitch.

Now with the plans in place it was time to put them into action.

Mason's knock on the open door of the RV startled all those inside stopping their conversation mid flow and as he stepped inside the cramped space he was greeted with silence and shocked looks as expected. What he wasn't expected however was the fact that as well as shock their faces seemed to register recognition of some sort. He had expected it from the guy with the beard that he now knew to be called Max, after all they had a special connection, but he hadn't expected the others to recognise his face. Had they spotted him following them?

True to form it was the red-haired woman Clea who spoke first.

'Well hello there, I recognise that handsome face, come and join us, I have a feeling you may have a few answers for us. Squeeze up there Mary, let the man sit down.'

As Mason took his place amongst the group they seemed to break from their shock and before they could assault him with questions he held up his hand and spoke first.

'I know you're shocked and confused but if you're patient you will, in time, have answers to all you questions, but first I have a question for you, you all seem to recognise me although we have never met, can you tell me how that is?'

'That's down to Max' again it was Clea who spoke 'he did these amazing sculptures of us all and he also did one of someone we didn't recognise, but now we know that it was of you,'

'Ah I see, that makes complete sense now, thank you' and to Max 'I would love to see it sometime.'

Max just nodded. He should have been used to this by now having already met the other people from his dreams but this guy was different, he gave off such a feeling of what Max could only think of as power and it was overwhelming. The strange feelings Max had experienced earlier that day were back with a vengeance. He felt the tingling and the strange pull in the stomach and realised now that it was some kind of reaction to the 'power' that Mason was giving off. Max said nothing, would the weirdness never end?

'Okay, you've had your answer so now can we have some.'

Mason turned towards the speaker; it was the tattooist Geth.

'Well first off, let me start by introducing myself, my name is Mason Winchester and I am here to make you an offer that I hope you cannot refuse.'

The group remained silent, waiting and so he continued.

'I am part of an organisation called The Somnium Foundation. Although they are a major, global organisation I doubt very much that any of you have heard of them' the blank expressions told him he was correct so he continued 'the Foundation has been around for a very long time in one form or another and in this modern age it is run solely for the purpose of supporting groups of very talented and special people all over the world. The public face of the Foundation is that of a charity supporting the arts, but its real purpose goes deeper.

The real purpose is not something I can go into in detail right now, for now I will tell you about the more public aspect of the Foundation.

Scattered around the world there are numerous 'art communes', these communes are funded through and looked after by The Somnium Foundation. In each house there are a group of specially chosen artists, again I can't go into how and why these people are chosen at this point, its best I keep it simple for now, what I can tell you is that you have been chosen due to your 'special' talents to become the residents of one of these art communes.

I realise that this does not really answer many of your questions but to be honest this isn't really the best time or place to tell you the whole story. What I am proposing is that you join me tomorrow at a nearby facility belonging to the Foundation where you will find out much more. Your attendance is voluntary but I must stress how very important it is that you attend, myself and many others have put a lot of work into finding you and bringing you together and we wouldn't have done it just on a whim. I appreciate it is hard for you to grasp what is happening to you and that your minds are full of questions but I hope that the experiences you have had over the last few days mean that you are open to trust me enough to attend tomorrow.'

Surprising everyone it was Max who spoke first.

'I don't really understand what's going on here, but I want to find out. I'm not afraid to admit that I find this all a little daunting, but not in a bad way. I feel a connection to you which is puzzling but at the same time it feels 'right', so I for one will be wherever it is you need me to be tomorrow,'

Masons relief showed in the smile he gave to Max.

'Count me in too,' said Clea 'I'm intrigued. I get a good vibe from you Mason and I intend to be there tomorrow.'

Mary and Aaron were looking at each other, speaking without words. Mary nodded in answer to the question in Aaron's eyes and he answered for the both of them.

'We'll be there.'

That left only Geth. The group turned to look at him expectantly. Geth was feeling totally out of his depth, what the hell was happening here? But despite his confusion he couldn't deny the connection he felt to these people, or the strong sense of curiosity that was building in him. There was only one answer to give here.

'Okay, I'm in.' he said

Mason almost applauded he was so relieved and happy. His hard work had paid off and hopefully things would now get easier. And so, after giving them the address and directions to the meeting place for the next day it was decided that Mason would travel there with Max giving him a chance to view the sculptures in the morning before they left the camp site. He then spent a companionable hour with the group getting to know them a little before they decided to call it a night.

Clea was obviously staying in her RV for the night, Max returned to his VW and Mason his tent. Geth, Aaron and Mary returned to the near empty employee / pitch owners car park to retrieve their cars and return to Mary's / Lens for the night.

Once back at his tent Mason made a couple of quick calls. It was late but they were still up at the Gateway and there was always someone at the Foundation to answer the phone. He told both parties that it had gone well and that the plans made for the next day were in force. He then settled down for the night and slept well, his work done.

CHAPTER 15

INDUCTION

'Wow' exclaimed Mason 'the middle one is kinda freaky, but the first and last are easily identifiable as you and me, they're amazing in fact, you are a very talented man Max.'

The two men were sat in the back of Max's VW Camper with the three 'Jekyll & Hyde' sculptures out on the bench in front of them. Max was feeling nervous and a little in awe of the man beside him and he blushed at the praise he was given. Mason was aware of Max's nervousness and was doing his best to make the man feel more at ease.

'Can I see the others?' he asked

'Sure' replied Max and glad to have something to do rather than sit looking embarrassed he moved around the cramped space putting away the three sculptures already viewed and getting out the other four.

After viewing and admiring the rest of the sculptures they were stored safely for travel along with Mason's small tent and his few belongings, and then, before setting off the two men went to check on Clea and help her to pack up. Despite the early hour they found they were too late, Clea was already packed up and raring to go.

They joined the queue of traffic leaving the event grounds and headed to the Foundation facility twelve miles away.

Geth had spent the night at Len's again as had always been the plan, but now instead of heading home he was following the directions given by Mason to some 'facility' belonging to a charitable Foundation he had never heard of.

He was holding off calling Chris to say he'd be later back than planned because there was still a part of him that believed this whole thing would turn out to be a waste of time. He felt he was having a harder time than the others were when it came to 'accepting the weird' or whatever their little moto was. On the other hand he could not deny the strange sense of connection he felt towards the group and his rational mind desperately needed some sort of explanation. This is why he was headed to this meeting; he was hoping he would get some answers today at this Somnium Foundation thing.

Mary was driving with Aaron using her phone as a Satnav. Driving somewhere she didn't know always made Mary nervous but with Aaron and her phone giving her directions she felt a little calmer. They hadn't really discussed what was happening today much as the night before it had been late and they'd been very tired, and now they needed to concentrate on finding the place, besides what more was there to say, this wasn't the sort of situation where you could speculate on what was going to happen. They had decided on a let's just wait and see attitude.

'You have reached your destination' said Aaron echoing the satnav as they pulled into a small parking area making Mary smile. The parking area was big enough for seven vehicles and Mary was pleased to see that two of the three vehicles parked there were Max's VW and Clea's RV. The couple had worried a little that they may have been the only ones that turned up. She didn't know what car Geth drove so wasn't sure if he was here too.

Getting out of the car they headed for the building that the parking lot belonged to. It was a large double fronted Victorian house that to Mary looked more like a seaside guest house than the office block they were expecting. There were no signs anywhere to give any idea of the buildings name or use.

As they approached the door it was opened by a relieved looking Mason. They exchanged pleasantries and followed him inside and into the first room on the left. The room was large and airy and sticking with the guest house theme was furnished like a communal guest lounge with several sofas, chairs and coffee tables and a large TV on the wall above a beautifully restored fireplace.

Seated on one of the sofas were Clea and Max. They rose to greet the new arrivals with a polite hello from Max and big welcoming hugs from Clea. The small group then sat making polite chit chat until Geth turned up ten minutes later, then after greetings were made it was down to business.

Mason stood to address the group 'I am so relieved that you all chose to come here today and I promise you that you will not regret it. I expect you will find today a bit of a challenge as there will be a lot for you to take in and understand, but I can assure you that you will, in time, be very glad that you came' smiling reassuringly at the group he continued 'first I will tell you about this place. As already explained it belongs to The Somnium Foundation and I guess the best way to describe it is to say that it is a training facility with accommodation for new recruits.'

'And that's what we are, new recruits?' asked Clea.

'Yes, that's correct' said Mason.

'Hold on a minute, we're not being recruited by MI5 are we?' said Aaron with a cheeky grin making everyone, except for Geth, laugh.

'No, I can safely say that you are not being recruited by MI5' replied Mason still smiling at the joke 'but I guess there are similarities because it is important that whatever happens after today you must keep the things you learn here a secret. If we have chosen correctly, and I really hope we have, then this will not be a problem, but I just need to make you aware of how sensitive this information is.'

'Now I'm even more intrigued and excited' said Clea.

'That's a good thing' said Mason. He had a good feeling about Clea; it was obvious that she was the member of the group who was most open to what was happening to them which was very encouraging. He was pretty confident about Max, Mary and Aaron too, the only possible problem was Geth, he appeared a lot more restrained than the others, but only time would tell.

'Let me just tell you a little about this facility' continued Mason 'opposite this room is the training room, adjoining that room there are toilet facilities and a large storage area. Next door to the room we are in now there is a large, well equipped kitchen diner. You are free to use all these facilities at any time.

Upstairs there are five twin bedrooms and one double bedroom all en suite. They are small but comfortable. The Foundation use this facility to initiate and train new staff and for educational and self-improvement courses for existing staff. Most of these courses require several days' work which is why we have the guest rooms upstairs. A small team of staff make sure that the rooms are clean and tidy and that the kitchen is stocked at all times. The only other staff are the visiting trainers. Today is going to be a long and challenging day for you all so I suggest that we go to the kitchen for some refreshments before we start.'

The group were pretty quiet as they drank tea and coffee in the beautifully appointed kitchen. None of them were really interested in breakfast but Mason insisted they ate some toast at least. As they drank and ate Mason explained that although he would be with them all day their initiation would be undertaken by a specialised staff member and that she was in the training room waiting for them. And so after finishing their drinks Mason took the group to meet the woman who would answer all their questions.

The woman in question was Pam Weaver. She had been with the Foundation for years and had held two very important positions within it. The official title of her current role was Dreamteller, and it was her job to welcome new recruits and initiate them into the Foundation family. She worked with all levels of recruits from the basic entry level staff to the really important new members like the group that she was waiting for now. She had been advised that this group were a little different and had been fully briefed on the reasons why. This one was going to be a bit of a challenge but she felt she was up to it.

When the group entered the training room they all looked very tense and nervous, but after receiving a warm welcome from Pam they relaxed a little. She always had that effect on people which was one of the reasons she had been given her role in the organisation. She was small in stature but gave off strength and warmth. She had a friendly face which was framed by tightly curled dark hair which told of her Afro/European heritage. She also had a very melodic voice which people found soothing.

The training room had two distinct areas. The first was what you would expect consisting of a large table surrounded by twelve office style chairs, a row of filing cabinets and attached to the back wall a large white board. The second area was a smaller version of the guest lounge with comfortable seating and low tables. It was to this area that Pam guided them.

'Make yourselves comfortable' she said, 'we'll be here for a while but if any of you need a break at any time please let me know.'

Once all her 'students' and Mason were seated she chose a seat central to the group and made herself comfortable.

'Let's start with introductions, my name is Pam Weaver, I was recruited by the Foundation seventeen years ago. I spent the first eleven of those years at one of their art communes where I was free to immerse myself in my art. I am a classical cellist and along with five other artists I spent those years literally living the dream. Since leaving the commune six years ago I have had the privileged job of welcoming new people to the Foundation.

Now I know that you have all met and know a little bit about each other but for my benefit I would like you to each in turn tell me your name and a little about yourself.'

Starting with Clea they all made their introductions and then the focus was back on Pam.

'That's great; it's very nice to meet you all. Now, I'm sure you are all desperate for some answers and it is finally time for you to receive those answers. I have a lot to tell you and at the risk of sounding over dramatic what you learn today will blow your mind. As you listen I am sure you will have many questions but I must ask you not to interrupt me. Some of your questions will be answered as I continue but I will be pleased to answer any others you may have when I have finished.'

And so the Dreamteller began a tale that had been told many times but with a little editing in this case as she had been instructed to leave a few details out for the time being.

Do you wonder why you dream? What dreams are, and what they mean?
Well, it is simple really, DREAMS ARE THE SOULS DOMAIN.
Every human has a soul, and a soul never sleeps. So, whilst our minds and bodies rest our souls take control, and drawing from our resting minds all that has happened and all that we wish or fear will happen, it gives us ways to heal and learn and solve our troubles. It brings us insight and gives us wish fulfilment. It is not always clear to our waking minds what we have learnt from our dreams. Some barely remember what they dreamt at all and some dismiss what is remembered but believe me the knowledge is there and it always helps.
And now we come to a special few, those who dream deep and awake understanding, at least in part, what they have learnt. They find answers in their dreams and as they help them in life they also express what they learn through art because these special few always have artistic leanings. So out of all the great painters, musicians, writers or those who have a talent in any other artistic field there are a special few, and out of these few special people the elite will be chosen for a special task.

Primitive man dreamt but not as we do as their souls and the dreams they brought were as basic as their primitive minds. As the human race evolved they were watched. The watchers were of this earth but of a species far more evolved. They were 'spirit forms', their spirituality and intellect was higher but their physicality and numbers restricted. The weak dreams of the humans fed them, but poorly.

Over time however they discovered that a select few humans dreamt a little deeper. The souls of these special humans were stronger and they possessed skills that their fellow humans did not. These humans were the first to discover art, though primitive and restricted they stood out and the spirit forms were attracted to them as they dreamt, and after a while they decided that an alliance needed to be made. And so, when they felt the time was right they made themselves known to a select few of the more gifted humans through their dreams and gradually an amazing partnership grew.

The sprit forms fed the humans with their spirituality, heightening their dreams and therefore their waking lives. And through the spiritual energy produced from their art the humans fed them in return forming a partnership that benefited all.

Over time the partnership flourished, and they discovered together that they could enrich the life of all humans through their dreams.

The newly formed partners met with danger and resistance however from some who did not understand, and so another set of humans with their own unique talents were tasked with their protection, and over the years the spirit forms and their special humans went underground and became a secret that only their protectors knew of.

They spread in small groups across the world in order to better remain hidden and although the spirit forms did not increase in numbers their protectors did. And so with the help of their human partners they worked in secret to enlighten the human world through their dreams, enriching the souls and minds of the human race.

As with any group of sentient beings these protectors evolved over the centuries forming their own hierarchy and setting their own rules and procedures taking on many forms until now, in the modern world, they have become a Global Organisation. This organisation is known as The Somnium Foundation.

The Somnium Foundation was set up and is run by an incredibly old, extraordinarily rich and powerful family named Vecchini. This family have been prominent amongst those who protected the spirit forms and their human partners for centuries.

To most of the world the Foundation is an organisation that funds a network of art communes across the globe. Most people are unaware it exists at all as it does not advertise its work, and those who do know of it have no idea of its real purpose.

Outside of family members The Foundation employs a global network of lawyers, accountants, and stockbrokers who help raise funds to run the communes via investments in real estate, antiquities trading, small businesses and the stock exchange. Only its members are privy to its secrets and even then there are levels of knowledge amongst its employees. The Foundation has a strong Ethos with a solid hierarchy where everything and everyone has a name, a distinct identity and a defined purpose.

The name given to the spirit forms that are the heart of this amazing organisation is THE ETERNAL DREAMERS (Eternals or ED's for short). They do not have a solid form, and some believe them to be the embodiment of pure soul. They are immortal and with the help of their human 'partners' they enrich our dreams. Their human partners are needed to strengthen them by acting as a 'conduit' to bridge the gap between them and the human race. And so, in order to do their work, they must join with a special human being and these special people are known as DREAMBRINGERS.

These Dreambringers are people who have a particularly strong talent for dreaming. They are prolific dreamers who need little help from the Eternal Dreamers. They dream much more than others and their dreams are filled with vivid and diverse images. This is because when they dream they tune into the dreams of others around them as well as their own. These select few humans are also born with an artistic talent of some kind. Their dreaming talent is what connects them to the Eternals and their artistic talent is what 'feeds' them.

The energy created as they work on their 'art' enables the Eternals to enter and enrich the dreams of those who sleep during the day and at night the Dreambringers connect with them and together they join with our souls to bring us inspiration and insight, helping us to learn and grow.

A Dreambringer set consists of one of each of the five 'kinds' of Dreambringer. They are The Dreamcatcher, The Dream Mate (female), The Dream Mate (male), The Gatekeeper of Dreams and The Seer of Dreams plus five Eternal Dreamers. Within the set each Dreambringer forms a strong bond with one particular Eternal Dreamer and together they help to bring the kind of dream specified by their Dreambringer role. Outside of this paring they are all linked by an artistic energy that feeds the whole group.

The sets of Dreambringers are not joined with their Eternal Dreamers for life. The years they spend at their task varies, there is no set time they are expected to serve, no average time, each group is different.

There is one other kind of Dreambringer. They are called Dreamwishers and they have similar talents as the others, the differences being that they are not part of any particular set and are not joined to one specific Eternal Dreamer; they are able to link, on a lesser level, to any Eternal Dreamer. They are transient members of the organisation who travel around the different houses in pairs on a rota giving the group an extra boost every now and then. They are also used on rare occasions to fill in for those that are long term sick or who need to be away from a house for more than a day at a time.

Once a set of Dreambringers feel they have given all they can of themselves to the Eternals it is then their task to bring together a replacement group. This is almost always a joint decision made by all.

Once the decision has been made and agreed the Dreambringers, with the help of the Eternals, must contact their replacements through dreams. Prospective candidates are found quite easily as they stand out in the dream world. All current Dreambringers need do is send out feelers that will be picked up by their natural replacements in their dreams. Once the connection has been made the Current Dreambringer can begin to instruct the New Dreambringer in their new task via their dreams.

Once the New Dreambringers have been told what they need to know they are then told to reach out to each other through their dreams. Once the group has connected with each other they are given a meeting place where they will come together and where they will be initiated into the Somnium Foundation and told of their task. This initiation is undertaken by a member of the Foundation known as a Dreamteller. These Dreamtellers are ex-Dreambringers who have taken on the new role after retiring from their Dreambringer role.

The new recruits will then be brought to the home of their particular group. These homes are all large, impressive houses purchased over the years by the Foundation and set up as art communes. They live together in these houses for the duration of their time as Dreambringers. The Eternal Dreamers reside in a nearby dwelling that only the Dreambringers have access to as they are protected by a very unique security system. Once at their assigned house they will receive further instruction and be introduced to and joined with their Eternals ready to begin their task.

And now for their protectors.

All employees of the Foundation are carefully vetted through their dreams by a few special family members via the Eternal Dreamers. These special family members are known as MARSHALS. The Vecchini Marshals have existed almost as long as the Dreambringers and Eternal Dreamers themselves. Future Marshals are spotted at an early age by the current Marshals through dreams. They are first tested and if they pass they are then initiated into the family secret.

The Marshals have a dream talent too. Like the Dreambringers they are prolific dreamers and possess an artistic talent, however, their connection to the Eternal Dreamers is different as is their purpose. Whereas the Dreambringers have a strong connection to one particular Eternal the Marshals have a more general connection to all Eternals. The Marshals connection is in the dream world only; they cannot come into direct contact with the Eternals, only the Dreambringers can do that. The Eternals communicate with them through their dreams on a basic, instinctual level. They guide them by sending dream messages via emotions rather than instruction. This communication between Eternals and Marshals is needed in order for the Marshals to carry out their own task.

The Marshals task is as follows;

They must vet prospective new employees of the Foundation for trustworthiness. They do this with the help of the Eternals through dreams.

When a set of Dreambringers decide that their task is over they must contact their appointed Marshal who will then come to the house in order to ensure that the changeover goes smoothly. With the help of the Foundation they must make the necessary arrangements for the new Dreambringers to move in and the current Dreambringers to be moved out and all the many arrangements that entails. If there are any problems it is the Marshals job to sort them out either alone or with the help of other Foundation members depending on what the problem is. In-between change overs it is the Marshal's job to monitor the houses in their area to make sure things are being run well which includes regular visits.

There is one other important member of each house and that is THE WARDEN.

A Warden is appointed to each house after each set of new Dreambringers has been initiated. Their job is to look after the house and its inhabitants. They deal with any minor, practical problems at the houses, however, if any major problems arise, or if any big decisions need to be made then the Warden must contact the Marshal who deals with them, usually in person.

It is the job of The Marshal to choose the new Warden from amongst the most trusted of Foundation employees. They choose from those employees who have a higher dream/artistic talent than normal (but not high enough to make them a Dreambringer). They are let in on the secret of the Dreambringers without being told of the added existence of The Eternals and cannot access the nearby house where they live. Although they are aware that they have not been told everything and that the Dreambringers travel to a nearby place where they cannot go they trust their employers and accept this with no questions asked.

When a Dreambringers task has ended some choose to go back to normal life and others choose to stay within the Somnium Foundation in a different role. These roles range from menial jobs to skilled jobs that they had been trained for before their Dreambringer work (e.g. Doctors or Lawyers), to very specialised and important roles. Whatever role they take on they will remain part of something very special for the rest of their lives.

Pam had finished speaking a couple of minutes ago but no one had spoken yet as they were all processing the new information. She waited patiently for them to react and ask questions. Another minute passed before the first person spoke. That person was predictably Clea.

'My head is spinning and I really don't know where to start with my questions but what I can say is that I feel really happy right now. I knew when this all started that it was the beginning of something good and now I know it's not only good but amazing. I always knew I had a special talent for dreaming but never thought my talent could be such an important one. I can't quite believe that I am a Seer of Dreams, its sound so fantastic.'

'How do you know you are the Seer of Dreams?' said Pam surprised that she was asking a question of them before they asked her. The newbies didn't usually find out which kind of Dreambringer they were until they met with their counterpart at the art commune.

'Mary told us' answered Clea 'she wrote a poem for each of us after her dream and our Dreambringer names were in the poem.'

'Really, that's interesting I've not heard of that happening before.'

'Maybe it's because of the way they were called' suggested Mason 'it was pretty unconventional. I had to do it basically alone and faster than usual.'

'You could be right.'

'They know the symbols too.'

'Really?'

'Yeah, I believe Clea saw them in her dream, right Clea?'

'You mean the symbols I saw carved in the door, the ones I embroidered for my new friends?'

'That's the ones, yes. I was amazed when you showed me the garments you'd embroidered them on. Those symbols represent the Dreambringers and are centuries old.'

'This just keeps getting better' said Clea her cheeks rosy and her eyes sparkling with excitement.

'So I'm guessing that Mary and Aaron are the Dream Mates' said Pam smiling at the couple who were sitting close together and who she had noticed had held hands throughout the whole storytelling. The lovers shock at the recent revelations was displayed clearly in their wide eyes and flushed cheeks but they managed to return her smile and nod in unison in answer to her question.

'But which of you other two is which?' Pam asked looking between Max and Geth.

'I'm the Dreamcatcher' said Max in a quiet, wavering voice making it sound more like a question than the answer to one. Pam noticed that he was visibly shaking, not an unusual reaction in her experience. She gave him her best reassuring smile and received a shaky one in return.

'So that makes you the Gatekeeper of Dreams' she continued turning to look at Geth who was the only one not looking back at her. He sat with his head bowed scowling into his lap. So he's going to be the awkward one thought Pam. All new Dreambringers struggled in their own way to come to terms with what they were. Most embraced it pretty quickly after the initial shock had worn off, but some took a little longer to accept their new calling. She was confident he would be fine eventually but it was clear he was struggling more than the others and would need careful handling.

'I can see you are struggling Geth and I understand, I've been where you are now, and so has Mason and we're here to give you any help you need. Whatever you are feeling now you will get through it and come to see what a great life you have ahead of you. It can be stressful to start with but it will ultimately be very rewarding I promise you.'

Geth raised his head to look at her but the scowl remained as he spoke.

'I'm really not good with all this hippy dippy stuff lady. I realise that something unusual is going on in my life right now and up until this business with the Eternal beings I was doing okay but now it's a reach, I'm a pretty basic guy and this stuff is seriously messing with my head.'

'I know, and I'm sorry but I assure you that in time you will come to accept and embrace it all.'

'Well I'll have to take your word for it because I can't see it right now.'

'But you are willing to give it a chance?'

'Don't worry, I'm not going to storm off or anything, I'm aware that something important is happening to me I'm just not sure how I feel about it.'

'Okay that's a start anyway.'

'I'll help you any way I can' interjected Clea 'and I'm sure the others will too, we're a team now.'

The others nodded their agreement and the scowl on Geths face softened a little.

'I really need a drink' he said causing a ripple of nervous laughter.

'Then let's go have a drink' said Mason getting up 'I'm sure they must have something suitable in the kitchen as I'm sure you're not the first to have this sort of reaction.'

And so the group followed him to the kitchen in search of beverages to calm their nerves. Pam and Max were happy with tea (in Max's case after a trip outside for a quick cigarette) and for the others they discovered beer and wine in the fridge and a small stash of spirits in one of the cupboards. So Clea and Mary had wine, it was beer for Mason and Aaron and for the instigator of the booze hunt Geth it was Jack Daniels. Taking their drinks with them they returned to the training room to talk. Things had sunk in a little now and the group had questions.

'How exactly do we bring people dreams?' asked Clea

'You'll find that out soon enough but its not my job to explain that to you now, sorry.'

'Well that's helpful, thanks' said Geth sarcastically.

Pam and the others chose to ignore this remark and carry on.

'So we just live together in this house, work on our art and then somehow help bring dreams to people' it was more a statement than a question from Aaron.

'That's basically it yes.'

'Sounds a bit jammy to me, there must be a catch somewhere.'

'I assure you there isn't, not really. You are restricted regarding travel as you can't leave the house and its grounds for more than a couple of days at a time so no long holidays but believe me your time as a Dreambringer will be so rewarding this won't be an issue.'

'But we can go out a bit if we want, to do shopping, go for a meal, stuff like that?' asked Mary.

'Yes or course you can.'

'What if we get ill or have an accident? This question from Max.

'Then you will be looked after by Foundation doctors and if it involves a hospital visit then it will be arranged, that's where the Dreamwishers come in, and you'll get a much better service from the Foundation than you do the NHS.'

'That sounds like a bonus to me' said Aaron 'In fact it all sounds good to me, I'm just hoping this is all for real cos it sounds too good to be true.'

'I feel maybe I should interject here' said Mason 'If that's okay with you Pam?'

'Its fine with me, go ahead.'

'I understand how you're all feeling right now, I've been there. Its hard to take in but I promise you that the life of a Dreambringer is a good one. It sounds cushy, and to some extent it is, you are looked after, you can work on your art as much as you want and you have no money worries, but it is still a job when you get down to it. You do have commitments and restrictions but it's like no other job you'll ever have because the rewards are amazing. Your fellow Dreambringers will become far more than work colleagues, they will be your friends for life. Dreambringers don't just enrich the lives of others they enrich their own. You are very lucky to receive this opportunity and you'd be fools to turn it down.'

'Well I'm sold' said Clea'

'Me too' agreed Aaron.

With Max and Mary adding similar comments that of course left Geth.

'I'm gonna take a little more convincing' he said to no one's surprise.

'I have every confidence that you will be convinced' said Pam.

'We'll see.'

The group continued to discuss what they had learnt and as Pam listened her mind drifted to thinking about the parts of the story she hadn't told them. She had been instructed to leave the last part of her usual story out. The missing parts being another kind of Dreambringer, and a cautionary tale told to new Dreambringers to highlight the importance of knowing your limits and living by the mandates given by the Somnium Foundation.

The reason Pam has been instructed to leave these parts out was because due to recent events it is now more than just a cautionary tale, and this new group had enough to process as it was.

This is what she could not tell them;

Firstly there are actually six 'kinds' of Dreambringers, not just five. The Dreambringer that has been missed out is The Soulhealer of Dreams, and this is why.

Several hundred years ago there lived a man; he was a Dreambringer, a Soul Healer of Dreams to be exact. He was a very skilled Dreambringer and revelled in his task. Over the years however he grew very arrogant and self-important. This was not an unusual occurrence back in the days before the Foundation had stricter rules and fail safes in place, but what was unusual was the extreme actions that the man's arrogance lead him too.

He discovered that the others in his group were thinking of bringing their time as Dreambringers to an end as they had been in place for many years. He did not agree with them. The thought of being separated from his Eternal Dreamer and possibly never doing Dreambringer work again was too much for him. He also felt his Dreambringer talent was too impressive to come to an end. And so he decided on an extreme solution. He decided that he could make his link to his ED not only stronger but permanent by properly merging with it to become one entity.

Although he knew that this was something that had never been thought of before let alone attempted he was convinced he could do it. Deep down he knew that his Eternal did not agree with him but in his desperation and arrogance he decided to go ahead anyway.

His Dreambringer skill enabled him to project his spirit from his body and for it to merge with the spirit form of the Eternal, but he did not have the necessary skill to fully extract his soul from the earthly bond of his body and send it with his spirit. This and the fact that the Eternal Dreamer was not totally complicit meant that the spirit form instinctively resisted the merge.

There was a spiritual struggle as the Dreambringer was unable to complete the full merging but refused to let go the connection he had made. As the struggle continued his body without its essence began to die. When the Eternal finally began to eject the Dreambringer he began to return to his dying body but at the last minute he managed to increase his hold and instead of strengthening his attempt at merging he managed to pull the essence of the spirit form back into his body trapping it there with him, and a new hybrid being was formed.

In appearance this new 'being' took on the basic form of a man, but the spirit form within it shone through those parts of its body which had begun to die. This meant that from its eyes there shone a white light and a white glow emanated under the skin of its torso where the dying organs had been. The skin of its fingers and toes also glowed white and if it opened its mouth a white light shone from within.

Its brain was also transformed making it not quite human and giving it powers it was soon to discover. The more immediate discoveries made were that it could not see well, only in shapes and shadows, and it could not speak. Its movement was also impaired, partly due to poor sight but mainly because its limbs were leaden and hard to control.

When the other Dreambringers discovered this new creature they were understandably appalled and frightened. Word was immediately sent out to their protectors for help.

In the days before that help arrived the new being discovered it could communicate through telepathy. Although disconcerting at first the other Dreambringers were glad of the connection as It could tell them what had happened and how It was feeling but in turn as It probed their minds It discovered how horrified they were by what It had become, and how wary they now were of It. This knowledge made It nervous and a little angry.

Others arrived to help but were at a loss what to do as this was an unprecedented event. More help was sent for. And whilst they waited and discussed what to do It began to come to terms with what It had become and what It could and could not do and It discovered that It could 'control' those around It.

To start with it was just little things like putting thoughts in their heads about what they should be doing, but this only confused them. After a while It was able to control their thoughts and movements, first in little ways and then It learnt to take control of one of them totally for short periods of time.

When they discovered what It was doing there was widespread panic. The new being's powers could not affect the Eternals but they could not protect the humans from It and their own powers were suffering because of it. Therefore, when the new batch of helpers finally arrived they were met with chaos and fear. This new group were made up of a number of very powerful ex-Dreambringers. It was discovered that due to their stronger Dreambringer talent and there having been forewarned they were, with a little effort, able to resist the creatures mind control. Now armed with this new knowledge these protectors were able to make plans. The creature's mental power was restricted by distance and so It was taken by the three who could resist Its control the most to a remote property and as physically restraining the creature was easy a locked room was sufficient to contain It for the time being.

Back at the house where the creature had been born things would never be the same. Those Dreambringers who had been most affected by what they had been made to do under Its control were retired and replaced as soon as could be managed, with one notable exception. There was no new Soulhealer of Dreams. There could never be a replacement as the set were now missing the required Eternal Dreamer. Therefore, at this particular house there would from then on only ever *be five Eternal Dreamers and five Dreambringers. The short fall would be made up to some extent by regular visits from Dreamwishers, but this house would forever remain different from all the others.*

It was suggested by some that the creature should be killed but although it was likely they could destroy Its body they had no idea how this would affect the creature and it was thought possible that it may become stronger if freed from the body that was restricting It physically. And so, it was decided that It would need to remain imprisoned until a better solution was found. The temporary prison nearby was made more permanent and a dwelling was quickly built beside it in which the creatures captors were to live. They were given a new role and title within the organisation. They were THE CUSTODIANS and through the years many retired Dreambringers would take on this inherited role.

It had been established that the creature could not influence dreams, Its talent for mind control only worked on those who were awake and in close proximity. Therefore, their task was to ensure that the creature remained locked away to prevent It from encountering anyone susceptible to Its influence and to keep It secret and safe from outsiders.

At first the Custodians tried to communicate with the creature, to find out what it wanted and why it was so hostile, but after Its initial contact with Its fellow Dreambringers the creature became more and more unresponsive.

Gradually over the years less and less time and effort were put into understanding the creature and the Custodians job became one of simply monitoring and confinement. They made sure It stayed safely locked away and monitored It to make sure Its mind control talent did not evolve into something even more dangerous.

Also, less and less effort was put into finding a better solution until it was no longer something that was even discussed. The confinement of the creature simply became the norm as no other solution has even been found.

At some point someone gave the creature a new name. From then onwards it was known as THE SOUL STEALER.

As the new Dreambringers were being introduced to their new world and coming to terms with their new knowledge, the people at The Gateway were dealing with this remaining secret. They must re-capture and imprison The Soul Stealer.

Samuel and Dorothea had been chosen for the job due to their particularly strong Dreambringer talent. They were both ex-Soul Healers of Dreams who now held other roles within the Somnium Foundation. Dorothea had passed the screening process and was near to the end of her training to become a Custodian. In the normal course of things she was in line to be one of the replacements for William and Rita Deacon when they retired. The couple had been Custodians for just over two and a half years which meant they had been less than six months away from retirement when tragedy had struck.

Each set of Custodians (not always a couple as the Deacons had been) only 'served' for three years as it was a mentally demanding and isolating role. A role that required strength of mind and dedication both of which Dorothea Atwood had.

Samuel Raven held a singular role within the Foundation, one that he had basically created for himself. He had been the Soul Healer of Dreams at one of the Foundations American art communes. Having had a fascination with The Soul Stealer story since his induction he had asked that after retirement he be allowed to make a study of what had gone wrong all those years ago with The Soul Stealer with a view to possibly finding a solution to the centuries old problem.

Before agreeing to his request, the Foundation had tested him by putting him through the screening process and training for the role of Custodian. He had proven to be more than capable of the Custodian role and so having passed the training with flying colours his request had been granted. He was then allowed access to all the data that the Foundation had on the Soul Stealer and studied it thoroughly.

Once he had consumed all the knowledge available Samuel had embarked on a tour of Somnium Foundation facilities and art communes around the world where he met with all levels of Foundation members and Dreambringers to gather data and experience. It was intended that he ended the tour with a face to face meeting with the Soul Stealer itself, a visit that had not been planned to happen for a few months yet.

Samuel had been at a remote art commune in New Zealand when the news of the escape first reached the Foundation. The news had been kept amongst a select few to start with and their first action had been to send a small, specially skilled, covert team to track the escapee down.

Another team, which included Dorothea, had then been put on standby to be sent in once the escapee was found. But with no way of knowing which direction the escapee had taken, or how far it had got the search proved more difficult than first thought.

Over the next few days as a solution was sought more Foundation members were contacted for their input and advice until the news finally reached Samuel. He immediately requested he be allowed to join the search team, a request that was quickly granted and it was as he set out for England that Sofia contacted Cedric Neale giving them a lead on the Soul Stealers whereabouts.

On arrival Samuel was teamed with Dorothea, and after a short briefing they were despatched to The Gateway where their plan was now being put into action.

The group at The Gateway knew that the Soul Stealer could only control one mind at a time, and therefore no one was ever to be alone. Unlike Claude they were all aware of the potential danger they were in and so if one of them were to be attacked the other would know what was happening and be on their guard. They were all equipped with mobile phones and so they could call for back up immediately. Due to their natural talent and Custodian training Samuel and Dorothea would be immune to an attack, therefore if an attack took place it would be their job to locate and capture The Soul Stealer whilst the remaining three not effected would contain and assist the person who had been attacked.

With this in mind early that morning Samuel and Dorothea had escorted Phoebe and Mark through the woods to the Factory whilst Sofia and Eddie stayed in the office monitoring the security cameras.

It had to be Samuel and Dorothea because neither Sofia nor Eddie could 'see' the Factory.

The building referred to by the Gateway residents as The Factory was the home of their Eternal Dreamers. Over the centuries the Eternals had developed a way to cloak their habitats as a security measure. They always lived in a secluded building near to the more prominent art commune houses but used their abilities to shield these buildings from view of unwanted guests.

Passers-by would be unable to see the building due to an aura constructed around it by the Eternals combining mind control and optical illusion. Only those deemed worthy by the Eternal Dreamers could find these buildings and be allowed to enter. It was not known if the Soul Stealer would be able to locate and see the building, but it was known that the Eternals were immune to its control and were therefore safe.

Phoebe and Mark would be vulnerable to an attack if they were discovered, but it was important that they be with the Eternals as for now they were the only ones available to feed the Eternals enabling them to fulfil their purpose. If it was felt that the Eternals were becoming too weakened in the absence of their new Dreambringers temporary reinforcements could be sent but it was felt best to keep the numbers of people involved to a minimum for the time being. The pair were to call in on a regular basis to confirm they were safe.

And so, Phoebe and Mark led Samuel and Dorothea through to woods to the home of the five Eternals.

As they approached the building and it was revealed to Samuel and Dorothea, they could not help but be impressed.

Standing in a large clearing in the woods the building is a single story, unusually circular construction made from large stone blocks that are dark grey in colour and appear very old. There are large, white framed, arched windows set all around the building. It has a porched doorway with a huge arched door made of ancient, solid looking oak. The door has heavy duty iron hinges and a large cast iron escutcheon keyhole. But the most striking element of the door are the symbols carved deep into the wood.

There are six circles carved into the door in a clock face style pattern. In the top circle there is carved a basic representation of a bare branched tree. The next circle (going clockwise) contains another smaller circle containing cleverly carved marks making it clear after a little examination that the circle depicts the moon. In the next circle there is a lattice pattern with the bottom ends ending in points representing a portcullis gate. The next circle around holds a delicately carved representation of a feather caught in the centre of a web. A human eye stares out at you from the next circle, the pupil of which has as swirl pattern carved into it. The last circle is devoid of any symbol or pattern which in itself appears symbolic.

Weaving around these six circles there is a carved pattern that looks familiar. It is the same pattern as the one depicted in the iron gate at the entrance to the Gateway. A mess of vines undulate within the space inside the circle created by the symbols and then tendrils weave out from it winding between the circles with the five strange flowers/leaves at the end of them each pointing to one of the circles, the sixth vine being headless ends at the empty circle.

The group of four stood taking in the details of the door for a few minutes. Samuel was very impressed. The design wasn't completely new to him as apart from one fundamental difference he'd seen very similar designs many times before only in various different mediums. Some had been more impressive due to their age, some because of their size but this one was the most skilful he had come across. The workmanship was amazing, so detailed even in the more basic elements. Also, the slight difference to the others made it special, a one of a kind.

The difference was in the one circle that did not contain a symbol. In the others he'd seen there was always a sixth symbol in that circle, a symbol that was very dear to him, and the reason for that difference was the reason he was here. This sixth circle should contain the symbol for the Soulhealer of Dreams. That symbol being a basic human form with lines emanating from its centre to represent rays of light.

It had obviously been decided many years ago when this door had been carved that there being no Soulhealer the symbol should not be represented. Then he remembered another element of the usual design and searched the door for it. He found it in the top right corner, another smaller circle with yet another symbol inside. This symbol was a simple depiction of a crescent moon and a star. It was the Dreamwisher symbol. It was always there, somewhere discreet, a reflection of what it represented.

Although this wasn't the first time that Phoebe and Mark had seen the door they understood the effect it was having on the two newcomers and so they stood quietly and let them take it in. Dorothea was impressed with the workmanship, but she was done staring at it after a while and wanted to get on.

'Shall we go in now?' she said in her usual abrasive manor.

'Sorry' apologised Samuel coming out of his slight trance 'yes, let's get inside'

The inside of the building shared a little of the ancient feel of the outside with its bare stone walls, large grey slate tiled floor, and with the arched windows looking as beautiful from the inside as out.

The contents of its one massive, circular, mostly open plan room were decidedly modern however. To the right of the door as you entered there was a little cloakroom area with an ornate, old fashioned coat stand and under the nearest window a small, padded bench. Beyond that, in the right-hand corner, there was a large, wooden cabinet which held two foldout beds for the Dreambringers to use should they wish to spend the night (and which were now being used by Phoebe and Mark). To the left of the door along under the front windows there were several low wooden chests containing mainly pillows and bedding.

Each piece of furniture had been expertly made specially to fit the slight curve of the walls where needed.

For several feet into the enormous room there was just bare, slate floor but further in it became a bigger version of the front lounge area of the Gateway in that the central area was littered with work benches, easels and other art equipment and machinery, with the left-hand side taken up by a large stainless-steel sink and storage cupboards.

In the back left-hand corner a couple of large, comfy sofas and an ornate rug formed a lounge area and next to it was a small kitchen area with tea making facilities, a small sink with a storage cupboard underneath, a small fridge and a table holding a microwave oven.

At the back on the right-hand side were the only closed off parts which consisted of a small bathroom and a large, soundproofed room which contained various musical instruments and a small recording studio. Both rooms had slightly curved walls in order to blend better with the buildings circular shape.

The many large, arched windows along with several skylights in the high ceiling gave the room plenty of natural sunlight and even though the building was very old it has been fitted with a good lighting system. Good heating and electrical systems had also been installed. It was, therefore, surprisingly warm and bright for such an old, stone building, and there was plenty of electricity for powering the machinery and the recording Studio.

Samuel and Dorothea were very impressed but knew instinctively that the most astounding part of this building was not visible. They knew that hidden from view below the slate floor was the dwelling of the Eternal Dreamers. They were capable of finding the entrance to this dwelling but it was not their place to venture down there. The Eternals had acknowledged their presence telepathically and now that they had escorted the youngsters safely they must leave and carry out the next part of their plan. So, after saying their goodbye's Samuel and Dorothea set off into the woods. As they left the studio Samuel put in a call to the house. It was Sofia who answered.

'Hello Samuel, how did it go?'

'They're safe in the studio and we saw nothing on the way here. Anything on the cameras your end?'

'No, all clear so far.'

'Okay, we're going to start our sweep of the woods now. If you see anything call us immediately and we'll do the same.'

'Okay, will do.'

And so the pair set off into the woods in search of the Soul Stealer.

Talionis hides. It senses the presence of the new arrivals. It senses that they are strong and It is afraid. Its strength has returned, and It wants to roam, to enjoy Its freedom, to find company and join with a new mind. It remembers the joy It felt days ago when It was joined, when It walked in another body and enacted Its revenge. It wants that again but fears if It leaves Its hiding place It may come across the strong ones. It knows what they want; they want to lock It away again, to return It to loneliness. The thought is unbearable; It is in a torture of fear and indecision and Its hatred grows deeper.

Back at the induction centre the new recruits had finished their drink break and were gathered in the training room ready for the next stage of their initiation. This part would be a little less mind blowing but still hard to take in only in a different way.

It was now time for Pam to explain more about how the Foundation works and how it deals with the practical side of the transition from their normal life to that of the Art Commune. She began by telling them how the Foundations team of lawyers, accountants etc. would do all the work for them. They would assess each person's requirements and talk over their options with them before making the necessary arrangements on their behalf.

These arrangements consisted of the selling or renting of the new employees' property and the management of any businesses and their finances. Any money the Dreambringers have or receive from the sale/rental of their property when they first join the Art Commune is put into a good investment/savings account by the Foundation for the duration of their stay at the house. Some of the profit made on this money is used to help fund the many houses worldwide, the rest is put aside so that when the Dreambingers have finished their task and leave the houses to go back to the normal world the Foundation is able to help them find somewhere to live and give them back control of their now increased finances ensuring they are provided for for the rest of their lives.

Any Dreambringer going into the house with little or no money will still be well provided for when they leave as investments are set up for them when they enter the house. The accounts of all the art commune residents are also boosted by money made off any artwork that they produce and sell whist in the house.

The portion of profits that are funnelled into the art communes are used to provide a generous account for each house. These accounts are used to pay the household bills and buy food, clothes, art supplies and any other personal items the residents require. The Foundations employees who do all this work are kept loyal through good pay and working conditions. These people are unaware of the Eternal Dreamers or of the real work of the Dreambringers but subconsciously through their dreams the Eternals and Dreambringers let them know that what they do is important, and they therefore enjoy their work and remain trustworthy and loyal. The information given to these people, however, is split so that no one person knows too much in case they ever do turn on their employers.

Pam knew that this new information would be reassuring to some and worrying to others. It was now her job to deal with the questions and fears that this news brought. The group would probably have an easier time processing this more mundane information than they had the strangeness of the Dreambringer revelation and that it would therefore help to focus their minds. But it would also bring its own problems. She began by addressing the group.

'So now that I have given you the basic details of the life that the Foundation is offering you I need to know how you are all feeling about moving ahead. You don't have to sign on the dotted line right now so to speak, but I do need to know that you are willing to commit to giving this a shot.'

The group were silent for a few minutes as they all tried to put their thoughts into words.

Geth was the least comfortable member of the group when it came to the spiritual side of what was happening to them. He was also the least trusting member in general. This meant that again he was having the most trouble processing this new information. He had worked hard to get where he was and as a small businessman he had an inherent mistrust of large money-orientated businesses.

'Let me get this straight' said Geth 'if we join one of these communes this Foundation takes all our worldly goods off us?'

'Basically that is correct, yes, but not in a bad way' explained Pam 'I know it sounds a little frightening in principal but it's not taken without anything being given back, I promise you that you would benefit in the end.'

'But they take control and we have no say in anything?'

'You can have as much or as little say as you wish. For those of you who have little and/or have no expertise in finances The Foundation will simply do all the work for you ensuring that you have more when you leave than you did when you joined. But for those of you who own businesses or already have stock portfolio's etc. they will take over the running of them but with as much input from you as you would like. Everyone is different and they understand this and will work with you in whatever way benefits you best. It is understandable that the global finance side of the Foundation can be frightening but what you have to remember that at its heart the Foundation is the protector of an amazing human secret of extreme importance and everything it does is for the good of the world.'

'Okay, I get it they're not bad guys. I realise I am being offered an amazing opportunity here but I have a business, one I have worked hard at for years and which I love and I'm finding the idea of giving that up difficult.'

'I completely understand and I can assure you that no one will be forced to do anything they do not want to do.'

'I guess I have a lot to think about and it's a little daunting so I appreciate your understanding.'

'You are welcome Geth. You don't have to decide right now; you can think on it for a bit and I can give you more details to help you later, but first I need to find out how the rest of the group are feeling. So what about the rest of you? Any more concerns or questions?'

'Well I for one have nothing to lose because I literally have nothing, so if they want to give me a place to live and then set me up for rest of my life I'm up for it' said Aaron with a self-deprecating laugh lightening the mood a little.

'I'm glad someone's happy' said a smiling Pam

Aaron was still holding Mary's hand and turned to her now.

'How are you feeling about all this?' he asked her. He was feeling pretty good about it all, how could he not, it was new and exciting, and it gave him a future which was something he'd never had before. But he understood that Mary's life was different, she had a home and a job and she seemed pretty happy where she was. He knew that however much he liked the sound of this new life he wouldn't do it unless Mary agreed too.

Aaron was right Mary did have more to think about than he did but she was also very excited about this possible new life especially if it included Aaron. She was pretty much sold on the idea but had a few concerns.

'My flat is rented' said Mary 'and although it's my home and I've come to love it I'd have no problem giving it up for what to me sounds like a better deal' in fact Mary felt a thrill at the thought of finally be free from the hold her Mum and Stepdad had over her due to their financial support 'but what about my job? I'm due back in the day after tomorrow so what happens there?'

'Ah yes of course, I'm sorry Mary this process usually happens over a much longer period making this sort of thing a lot easier to organise. This situation is unprecedented in the Foundations history but I'm sure we can work it out. The situation regarding the rental on your flat will still be pretty straight forward and the Foundation will deal with that, but the job situation is a little trickier.'

'Well yes, I'd need to work my notice.'

'Working your notice is not really an option Mary, I'm sorry.'

'But I can't just quit with no warning, it's not fair to my colleagues and it's not good for future references etc is it.'

'It's commendable that you feel bad about leaving like this Mary, but future references are not something you have to worry about, not once you commit to your role within the Foundation that is.'

'But what happens whilst I'm still deciding if I want to commit?'

'You could always phone in sick' interjected Aaron

'That's not a bad idea' agreed Pam 'for now you can call in sick, that way if you decide not to join us there's no harm done and if you do decide join us, which I'm pretty sure you will, we can inform them you won't be back. We can work on the mechanics of it at a later date, the Foundation will help, it will be fine.'

'Okay' said Mary 'but I just need a good excuse for being off sick, I've never thrown a sicky before, what do I tell them.'

'Tell 'em you had a slight accident at Artfest' suggested Aaron 'Sprained an ankle or something.'

'Well, it sounds better that I caught a cold or got a stomach bug I guess' agreed Mary.

'Good, we'll go with that then shall we?'

Mary nodded her agreement.

'What about your family though? asked Aaron

Mary gave a little start at that. She was only just digesting the work thing and now this. She took a few seconds then cleared her throat before talking.

'There's just my Mum and Stepdad and we're not close, I doubt they'll miss me, I think I'll be more of a loss to my work colleagues.'

'Oh lovey that's sad' said Clea

'It's okay Clea, I'm fine with it, I won't miss them much either.'

'Are you sure about that?' asked Aaron

'Yes I am. I don't know what they're gonna make of me swanning off to an art commune though' Mary answered giving a little nervous laugh at the idea 'I take it we can tell them that much?' she added looking at Pam.

'Of course, that's fine; they can even visit occasionally if you want them too.'

'Okay, that's good I guess'

Mary knew for a fact that her Mum and Stepdad would be very unimpressed with her decision to give up everything and move to an art commune and she doubted they'd agree it was a good idea, but on the other hand she suspected the fact that she'd be out of their hair so to speak would appeal to them once they thought it all through. But it in the end it would be her decision and she didn't care enough about what they thought for it to influence her choice. She'd feel a bit bad for letting her employers down, but this new life sounded like it would be much more fulfilling and the fact that Aaron would be with her made it impossible to refuse.

'So I'm in too' she said her decision made.

'Wonderful.'

Clea was the member of the group having the least trouble getting her head around the spiritual aspects of what they had learnt. She had been extremely excited by the prospect of becoming a Dreambringer. It sounded challenging which didn't faze her at all but now at the thought of giving up her home she was feeling a little emotional.

'I have a small business' said Clea 'but it's one I can run from anywhere, or not at all I suppose. It will be a little harder to give up my home though. I love that house, I have happy memories there, although some not so happy ones too so I erm…' and here Clea paused and the others sensing her high emotion waiting patiently for her to have a little think before continuing. When she did continue she sounded a little tearful but positive.

'You said you can rent our properties, but to be honest I'm not sure I like the idea of other people living in our house either but it's an option I'm willing to consider. I will be able to return to my house when my Dreambringer time is done though?'

'Yes, it's completely fine if that's what you want to do. And as to the renting thing if that makes you uncomfortable we can look at other options, we can appoint a caretaker for instance to keep an eye on the place, make sure it's safe etc. but not really live there, kind of like a holiday home set up.'

'But whatever I decide now I can change my mind at any point?'

'Yes, that's correct. If you come to feel that you are comfortable with renting or even selling it can be arranged.'

'Okay, so I don't have to make any rash decision, that's good. I'd like to think that my house will still be there for me if I want to go back to it, but I have the option to start again if I choose to when my time is up.'

'Exactly.'

'Good, I'm fine to go ahead then' and with a little sniff she appeared to regain her composure a little 'now that little worry is dealt with I'm excited to see what happens next.'

'That's great, and so that just leaves you Max, how do you feel?'

How Max was feeling was basically a little shaky and indecisive. He had never been good at decision making when it came to his own life. He had always been better at listening to others and helping them deal with their problems than he had been at dealing with his own.

'I don't know right now, I have a little problem with change, it scares me' he said with his head bowed and his hands raking his hair.

'I think a lot of people fear change Max, and to have it thrust upon you like this is particularly hard, but I am here to help you and I'm sure your new friends are too.'

'Thanks, I think I'm going to need all the help I can get.'

'No problem. Why don't you tell me how you stand property and job wise and we'll go from there?'

'Well I have no job really; only volunteer work so that's not really a problem. Property wise I own my house, it's my family home which I inherited when my parents died. I guess I am quite attached to it, I've never lived anywhere else.'

'Okay, so we could go down the rental route, what do you think?'

'I suppose so' said Max making it sound more like a question than a statement.

'Can I butt in at this point?' asked Mason

'Sure, go ahead' agreed Pam.

'Speaking as someone who has already gone through what you are going through now I can totally understand all your concerns, but I want to help put your minds at rest. When I was recruited I had a newly established guitar making business and a great little house. I was a little reluctant to give that up but it turned out that I wasn't giving anything up, I was just moving on. I have continued my business from the commune and I love where I live. What I had to give up is nothing compared to what I gained. As well as a home I gained friendship, artistic fulfilment and purpose. Believe me when I say you will not regret accepting your role within The Somnium Foundation.'

'Wow, I should have let you give that little speech sooner' said Pam 'I think that's going to help these guys more than any of the reassurances I've just given. So Max, has that helped you at all?'

Max was staring at Mason and thinking about the connection he felt with this man. That feeling and the man's speech gave him that little push that he needed.

'I'm willing to give it a go then' he said quietly but firmly.

'Good, so that brings us back to you Geth. How are you feeling now?'

'To be honest I'm feeling completely mind fucked but don't worry I'm not a quitter. I need to understand this a bit more before I commit fully so I agree to continue and see what happens.'

'That's great, we're all on board. I think it's time for a break, I know I need one so let's get something to eat before we go on to the next step.'

As the group headed to the kitchen to eat Mason decided it would be a good time to call The Gateway for an update.

When Sofia answered Mason's call she sounded tired and irritated but he hoped his news would cheer her up a bit. It seemed to do the trick to start with until he mentioned a time frame for bringing the new Dreambringers to The Gateway.

'I think we're going to need one more day to give them time to get their head around things a bit more and to sort out a few practical matters, but I think we can be back with you the day after tomorrow' he said expecting her to be pleased, but instead there was a long pause before she spoke and then what she said was not what he was expecting.

'I'm sorry Mason but I'm not sure that's going to happen, there are things you don't know, things that have been kept from you and right now it would be a mistake to bring them here, it's not safe.'

'What the hell's going on, what haven't you been telling me?' he asked though her tone of voice was setting off alarm bells and he wasn't sure he wanted to hear her answer.

'There have been some developments here and we thought it best not to tell you, you had enough to worry about and we didn't want to add to your stress levels. But now things are going well your end we can update you.'

And so Sofia proceeded to tell him all that had happened since he left for Artfest.

What she told him was alarming and he couldn't help but feel a little annoyed that his short-lived relief had now been replaced by more worry, when would all the craziness end? But being an optimist Mason calmed himself by gleaning two positive points from the new information. Firstly, his friend Claude was exonerated, he was not after all a crazy or evil man, he was a victim as much as the friends he had harmed, it was no wonder the man had behaved as he had after the possession, what must he have been going through after what he'd been forced to do.

And secondly his other friend Eddie now knew everything, he was truly one of them now and Mason would never have to keep anything from him again. He knew however that no matter what good spin he put on it the news was still bad. He also now understood why the Soul Healer part of the induction had been left out. He'd been told by Pam that the Foundation thought that the speed of the group's induction meant they had enough to deal with as it was so the cautionary tale was being left out for the time being. Obviously, this was how the Foundation had explained it to Pam, but now he knew the real reason.

'So these new people, Samuel and Dorothea do you think they're up for the job?' he asked.

'I'm sure they are. They're out in the woods now searching.'

'Should I come back and help, with the Eternals I mean, they've been without us for a few days now and that can't be good?'

'No, you should stay with the newbies for now. Phoebe and Mark are doing a good job, it's not ideal but I can't detect any major problems from the Eternals, other than the threat of the Soul Stealer that is. I will keep you updated and let you know if we need you and when it is safe to bring the new recruits here. At least it will give them a little more time to get their head around the new direction their lives have taken and they can get a few practicalities out of the way before coming here.'

'That's true, it will help them and of course I will stay with them if that's what you think is best, I trust your judgement.'

'Thank you. I know I can rely on you.'

'Say hi to Eddie for me.'

'Will do.'

'Bye for now, speak to you soon.'

'Bye Mason.'

Samuel and Dorothea were in the densest part of the woods surrounding The Gateway. It was the least pretty part and the hardest to traverse as the ground was a lot more uneven. It didn't help matters that they were in the darkest part of the woods at a time when the natural daylight was starting to fade.

'We should have checked this section earlier when the light was better' stated Dorothea.

It was a true statement and Samuel did not feel the need to reply. The truth was he was kind of enjoying their trek through the trees and he particularly liked this part of the woods, it reminded him a little of home. That's not to say that he wasn't focused on their task, in fact his enjoyment of and affinity with his surroundings meant that his senses were even more honed and alert, you could say he was in his element.

Just then he thought he heard a noise and stopped dead to listen holding an arm out to halt Dorothea who was a few steps behind him. The sound was not repeated as the pair stood quietly looking around them. For a second he thought he saw a movement way off to the left, a faint blur of light, but it was gone in a second. He signalled Dorothea and they set off to the left anyway.

As they walked Samuel began to get a strange feeling. It was a little like the feeling of being watched but somehow more internal. He glanced at Dorothea but could tell from her expression that she was not feeling the way he was. Then he saw a brief blur of light ahead of them again. Dorothea's slight intake of breath told him she'd seen it too this time. Without speaking they continued ahead towards where they had seen the light.

The strange feeling stayed with Samuel for a short while but then gradually began to fade and they saw nothing. They tried changing direction but still nothing.

After another hour of fruitless searching the pair were beginning to tire and the light was almost gone. They had brought torches and searched for another half hour with the help of the torch beams but still nothing. But then what did they expect thought Samuel. The thing they hunted could be anywhere, it could even be long gone by now. They needed to rethink the whole thing; this mindless wandering was no good.

After a brief discussion the pair decided to head back to the house. They would sleep on it, and maybe their dreams would help, after all that was where their real skill resided, not out here in the woods. And as they walked an idea came to Samuel: he realised that a technique he learned on his travels may help and by the time they reached the house he was looking forward to what he hoped would be a productive night's sleep.

At the induction centre the new recruits had eaten and were back in the training room with more questions for Mason and Pam. The meal had been a subdued affair with everyone lost in their own thoughts but now those thoughts were being put into words.

Pam and Mason answered the questions as best they could, a few issues were laid to rest and a few practicalities were sorted. The group were obviously all going to spend the night and possibly more at the induction centre. Clea, Max and Geth already had changes of clothes and toiletries with them from their trip to Artfest and they could make use of the centre's facilities to do any clothes washing etc needed for the time being.

As for Aaron and Mary they could make do for one night again with the help of the centre's facilities. With Aaron and Mary opting to share the double room that left everyone else with a room to themselves. And so after a bit more talking Pam showed them all to their rooms to settle in for the night before retiring for the night herself.

CHAPTER 16

HUNTING AND GATHERING

He is walking through the trees. He see's landmarks he recognises and notes where he has been. He moves on searching for a light and after hours, or maybe just minutes he sees it. A brief glimpse but it leads him to where he needs to be. He enters a denser, more overgrown area. The thicker canopy of leaves above makes it darker but he sees clearly. The root and shrub strewn ground is uneven but he walks with ease. He comes to a stop beside a very old, large, oak tree. He walks around its expansive trunk and notes a darkness upon a patch of its bark. He looks closer and discovers the darkness is in fact a split in the huge trunk. An opening. He does not need to go any further he has found what he seeks.

Samuel opens his eyes and smiles. He has a big day ahead; they all do but now he is confident that it will go well. Today he knows where to look. It's still early so he decides he has time for a shower before he rouses the others to tell them the good news.

When he knocks on Dorothea's bedroom door he finds that she is already awake and informs him through the closed door that she will meet him downstairs shortly. On venturing downstairs he finds Eddie in the kitchen preparing a fortifying breakfast for them all.

'Morning Samuel did you sleep Okay?'

'Yeah, great thanks, you?'

'Yep good thanks. Sofia's awake and should be here in a minute.'

'Dorothea will be down soon too'

'Ok, I'll get on with breakfast then.'

Samuel decided to wait until breakfast was over to give them his good news. And so after the ladies joined them he tucked into the bacon and eggs and joined in with the subdued small talk. Then, once the dishes had been cleared away he made his announcement.

'I have some good news; I have a good lead on where our quarry is hiding.'

'Seriously?' asked Sofia 'How?'

'I found Its hiding place in my dream'

'Of course' said Dorothea

'Obviously, why didn't we think of that' said Sofia

'What?' asked Eddie looking from one to the other 'What's obvious?

'Sorry Eddie' said Samuel 'I forgot you are new to this sort of thing so let me explain as we all need to be clear on what's happening here. Generally as you now know when we dream the Eternals help us solve our problems and find inspiration but this is usually in a very general way and most dreamers do not consciously realise its happening. However for some experienced Dreambringers with a particularly strong talent it's possible to focus their dreams on a specific problem. It's not something that's in common practice these days, in modern times Dreambringers prefer the more relaxed style but years back it was more prevalent. In the past one of its uses was to find missing possessions so last night with the help of the Eternals I gave it a go and managed for find where The Soul Stealer is hiding.'

'So you can go right to It then?' asked Eddie

'Well not right to it, I have a good idea which area to search, and I know what its actual hiding place looks like. It'll still take a little searching but I'm confident I can find it pretty easily.'

'That's pretty impressive' said Eddie

'Yes, well done' agreed Sofia

'That's enough explaining and sentimental pats on the back' said Dorothea 'time to make some plans now we have the information we need.'

It was decided that the first course of action would be for Dorothea and Samuel to go out to the Factory and escort Phoebe and Mark back to the house. They then discussed what should happen after Samuel found the Soul Stealer. Once the final plan was decided on they then went over and over it until they all had it down pat.

As the Gateway residents were making their plans Mason was in the kitchen at the Induction Centre making tea for himself and the other early risers Clea and Pam. After a small discussion it was established that they'd all had a good night's sleep with only vague unremembered dreams and had woken up feeling refreshed and positive. Clea had expressed a little worry about the lack of dreams but Mason had reassured her that under the circumstances it was to be expected at this point. What he had not told her was that his own vague dreams had left him with a strong feeling that things were going well at The Gateway.

As they drank their tea and made small talk they were joined by Geth. He made himself a cup of coffee and then sat with them at the kitchen table.

'Did you sleep okay?' asked Clea

'Yeah, fine thanks.'

'Good and how are you feeling about things this morning?'

'Not sure yet, ask me again when the coffee kicks in.'

'Will do' said Clea smiling to herself.

'Anyone hungry?' asked Mason

'I'm fine with coffee for now thanks' said Geth

'I'm fine for now too thanks' said Pam

'I'm okay to wait until everyone's up and we can all eat together' said Clea

'Okay, good idea, we'll wait' said Mason.

They didn't have to wait long. They were joined first by Max shortly followed by Aaron and Mary and the group were soon tucking into a classic full English breakfast cooked by Clea.

They kept the conversation light as they ate then as they were clearing away the breakfast things Mason received a call from Sofia. The conversation was brief as there was a lot going on at The Gateway but the basics were that they had made a breakthrough in their search for the Soul Stealer and therefore if everything went to plan they would have the situation under control by the end of the day. She didn't have time to give Mason all the details but promised to call him with an update later that day. Mason was relieved and reassured by her news and so was feeling optimistic as he led the group back to the training room to talk through their plans for the next couple of days.

Mason started things off by explaining that they would be spending at least one more night at the centre possibly more before setting off for the new Dreambringers (potential) new home. He then asked if they were all still feeling positive about the new direction their lives were taking. He received a definite, excited yes from Clea, Mary and Aaron; a more subdued but positive reaction from Max and a hesitant but affirmative answer from Geth.

There was no need for any long-term plans to be made at this point, it was just about the next few days for now.

They tackled the easy options first with Mason and Pam making calls to the Foundation to make arrangements for the following: A member of the Foundation would be despatched to the centre in a small van, and they would follow Mary and Aaron in Mary's car first to Aaron's boarding house and then to Mary's flat.

At Aarons they would collect all of his possessions (as there weren't that many), load them in the van, inform his landlady that he no longer needed the room and pay what he owed her.

They would then travel on to Mary's flat where she would pack what she needed for the short term along with her spare keys as they may be needed by the Foundation at a later date. They would leave her car in her space in the communal off-road car park and again the keys would be given to the Foundation for future use. Mary and Aaron would then return to the Training Centre in the van along with their possessions driven by their Foundation helper.

Whilst they waited for the van to arrive the couple made some phone calls. Aaron called his boss to tender his resignation, a task he enjoyed immensely. Mick tried to make out Aarons resignation was an imposition but due to their lack of work at present and the fact that Mick had never liked him Aaron knew it was bullshit and even after Mick swore at him he resisted the urge to tell him so, though only just. On reflection though he was glad he didn't tell his old boss exactly what he thought of him, he never had to see or speak to the man again so why sink to the man's level and be abusive. It was enough that he felt a massive sense of relief when the call was done.

Mary's first call was to her Mum to give her a watered down, short term version of the truth. She told her that she had met a group of artists at Artfest who had invited her to visit their art commune for an impromptu workshop/mini break. Her Mum, as expected, showed little interest and asked no questions just commenting 'that's nice dear'. Mary felt her own sense of relief when she explained that she'd miss their next family lunch but although it was expected felt a little deflated by her Mums lack of interest in the exciting new development in her life and couldn't help but wonder if her reaction would be different when she learned that the mini break would become more permanent.

Next Mary called work with her fake sprained ankle story. She was relieved at first when the call was answered by one of the friendlier managers but the woman's sympathetic and understanding reaction also made her feel guilty.

After she finished her call Aaron and Pam did their best to make her feel better about it, reminding her how important her new role was and that she wasn't letting people down for selfish or trivial reasons. With their help she shook off the guilt and set her mind on the adventure ahead.

Whilst these calls were being made Max and Mason were making plans for their own little trip. It had been decided that they would travel together to Max's house so that he could pack some things for the coming days. They would use his VW Camper as it would have the room for his belongings along with the sculptures of his friends that it already carried as he did not want to leave them in the empty house.

Max had a call to make too. He needed to inform the Youth Centre that he would not be volunteering there for a while at least but as it was a voluntary role and he had made no firm commitment for the next day or two the call could wait. It was more important to get an earlier start on his trip home.

Once Pam had finished advising Mary on her call to her boss she liaised with other Foundation staff to make the more complicated arrangements for Clea and Geth.

Clea had no phone calls to make but there was the return of the rented RV to deal with. Also, as she lived furthest away from the Induction Centre a trip home for supplies would take much longer and needed more planning.

It was decided that a Foundation helper would drive the RV with Clea as a passenger and return it to the rental company. They would be met at the rental place by another helper in a van who would drive Clea and the RV driver back to her house where they would help her pack what she needed and load it into the van. Then the fresh helper would drive them back to the induction centre in the van dropping the other helper off on the way. The round trip would take all day but with the helpers sharing the driving it would be easier on Clea.

Geths trip wouldn't be quite as long but would still take most of the day. Initially he had wanted to go alone but Pam managed to persuade him that having someone along to share the driving at least would be a good idea.

When Geth voiced his feelings that the Foundations reasons for wanting someone to accompany him were more to keep an eye on him and make sure he came back Pam was honest and agreed that was an element of it. She added that his safety and comfort were still the main priority however as he was very important to the Foundation. Her honesty was what persuaded him to go along with the plans.

Before leaving Geth had to call his business partner Chris James. He had been due home the evening before and so he needed to let Chris know that he wouldn't be there when he turned up for work later that morning. He said that he would explain more when he arrived later in the day. The full, awkward conversation he needed to have with Chris would need to be done in person. There was no avoiding it as Chris would hear him moving about in the flat above the studio. Besides it wasn't his style to 'cop out'.

His story was that through connections he had made at Artfest he had been commissioned to do a large back and sleeves piece as a guest artist at another Tattoo Studio. The piece would take several days and with healing time added in before a second round of sessions he would be away for a couple of weeks at least. He would tell Chris he had agreed to do it because Artfest had rekindled his love of his art and he needed a challenge, plus it would be very well paid. The bookings he had at his own studio would have to be taken on by Chris or rescheduled.

He knew that Chris would be a little pissed off at first, but that once he thought it through and realised the extra work would be good for his portfolio and would also mean extra money for him he hoped he would come around to the idea. Geth would also suggest that their apprentice Rick take on any simple tattoos booked or from walk ins. Geth felt he was ready so it would be the ideal time to give the youngster a shot. Geth was as happy as he could be with the plan.

As usual the Foundation set the plans in motion very quickly and so by mid-morning Pam was the only one left at the Induction Centre where she set to work making the remaining arrangements for the day.

At the Gateway the plan to capture The Soul Healer was being put into action. Whilst Samuel and Dorothea were making the trip to collect Phoebe and Mark from The Factory Sofia phoned The Foundations to update them and to let them know what they needed help with. Meanwhile Eddie was loading his van with the few things that Samuel and Dorothea had brought with them.

When Phoebe and Mark got back to the house they were briefed on the plan and then they headed for the art room as their job remained the same; they must keep the Eternals strong.

After a last discussion of the plan Samuel and Dorothea headed out to the woods and as they left Sofia was back on the phone with the Foundation making arrangements. Eddie was now on standby: when he received an arranged message from Dorothea he was to drive the van to the planned location on the driveway, leave the doors open and the key in the ignition and walk quickly back to the house.

Out in the woods Talionis crouches in Its hiding place. It feels alone, afraid and so tired, but above all It feels anger, always anger. Although It knows that It is hunted It thinks that they search for It in vain. It feels Its hiding place is safe and so dares not move for fear of discovery unknowingly making Its hunter's task easier.

Samuel and Dorothea walked in silence through a dense part of the woods. The heavy canopy of trees blocked most of the afternoon sunlight giving more of a twilight feel to their surroundings. They had been walking for a while but now Samuel felt they were nearing their goal, he could feel it, the Soul Healer was near. He signalled to Dorothea to stop walking, he needed to re-orientate himself a little. He stood with his eyes closed conjuring the images from his dream in his mind. When the dream image was clear he opened his eyes and projected that image outwards overlaying it on the visual image of the woods around him. He shifted position slightly until the two images matched as best they could and then he pointed slightly to the left of where he stood indicating to Dorothea the direction they needed to take.

A few minutes later he spotted a familiar tree, he'd found it.

As Samuel and Dorothea drew nearer to their destination they slowed their pace and trod carefully so as to make as little noise as possible. When they came within a few feet of the tree they sought Samuel used hand signals to indicate which one it was to Dorothea. As in his dream Samuel realised that they were approaching the tree from the opposite side to the hidden opening in its truck and so as they got near they circled in different directions around the tree.

As they approached the undergrowth hiding the entrance they sensed movement from within. It knew they were there, how could It not, the leaf and twig strewn floor made it impossible for them to remain completely silent at that distance. The atmosphere was tense but Samuel and Dorothea were confident and felt no fear.

Their quarry on the other hand felt nothing but fear at this moment. Talionis' feeling of safety had been shaken as it heard their approach and then shattered completely as it sensed them directly outside. It was trapped; knowing It was no physical match for the two outside It had only one defence against capture.

Samuel and Dorothea felt a brief moment of disorientation as the Soul Stealer attempted to take control of their minds but that was all, they were prepared for the attempt and put up the defences that their training had taught them rendering their quarry completely defenceless.

The decision had been made earlier that Dorothea should be the one to extract the Soul Stealer from the tree if needed as being smaller than Samuel she would be able to get inside easier and so now Samuel pulled back the undergrowth as best he could to allow her as much access as possible. Crouching down she shuffled into the entrance. It was dark inside but she detected several small faint lights in the corner of the hollowed-out trunk. There was no sound. Then she detected a slight movement below the light and reaching out she took hold of something solid. It was a foot encased in what felt like a soft shoe or slipper. The foot moved feebly trying to shake off her grip. Using her other hand she found the ankle above the shoe and took a firm grip, then releasing the foot she used that hand to feel around until she found the other leg and grabbing the other ankle she then began to shuffle out of the opening dragging the feebly struggling owner with her. Once clear of the tree Dorothea remained crouched keeping a firm hold on the ankles whilst Samuel moved to pin their captive down by the shoulders.

Samuel and Dorothea had both heard descriptions of The Soul Healer before, but nothing really prepares you for the actual sight of it in reality.

At first glance it appeared to be an ordinary man that struggled weakly and silently in their clasp, his eyes tightly shut. He was of average height with a slight build, long, unkempt white blond hair and sallow skin. He looked to be in his late thirties and was dressed in a dirty brown sweatshirt and sweatpants with moccasin style slippers on his feet.

Then they noticed that the tips of the fingers it was weakly grasping at the undergrowth with glowed white and a faint glow also emanated from the strip of skin exposed where the sweatshirt had risen up in the struggle. The illusion of humanity was then completely shattered as It suddenly opened Its eyes and then Its mouth in a silent scream: and from those open orifices there emanated misty white beams of light rendering Its visage no longer human.

Although the sight before them was alien, shocking and invoked in them both a slight sense of pity for the creature they held they were prepared and fixed upon their task. And so after a few seconds hesitation they continued with the plan. Samuel changed his grip pushing the creature up into a sitting position so that he could wrap his arms around Its chest, then Dorothea let go of Its ankles so that Samuel could stand up straight bringing his captive with him. The strange being had now closed Its eyes and mouth and hung completely limdp in Samuels arms making it easy for the big man to readjust his hold once again so that he now held it as you would a sleeping child you were carrying to bed, and with just as much ease.

As they headed off through the trees Dorothea made a quick call to Eddie giving him the planned signal to carry out his part of the plan. Therefore when they emerged from the woods at the pre-arranged place they found the van ready and waiting for them. Dorothea got into the driver's seat and started the engine whilst Samuel climbed into the back with the prisoner.

When they arrived at the big iron gates Dorothea and Sofia had a short conversation over the gate intercom system before Sofia opened the gate for them and they headed off. Their destination was the nearby hidden facility where most recently the ill-fated Rita and William Deacon had lived and where The Soul Stealer had been imprisoned for years. The facility was being prepared for them as they travelled and Samuel and Dorothea were to be its new Custodians, for now at least.

'Everything okay back there?' asked Dorothea keeping her eyes on the road.

'Yeah, all good so far' replied Samuel keeping his eyes firmly on the creature slumped on the metal floor of the van's storage area. It wasn't going to be a comfortable journey but you couldn't really put a creature with glowing eyes in the front seat of a van, it could prove distracting for other drivers, not to mention bringing unwanted attention to them. So Samuel settled his large frame as comfortably as he could for the journey.

Talionis had retreated into Itself. The physical struggle It had put up, feeble as it was, had exhausted It and with Its attempt at mind control thwarted just as easily It was helpless. It sensed that Its new captors were even stronger than those he had escaped from and this frustrated and angered It. That's all It had again now, Its anger and all It could do was rest and wait, wait for any chance of escape, an escape It feared would never come.

Eddie had arrived back at the house before Samuel and Dorothea had finished their trek through the woods and reached the van so he was there to hear the intercom conversation with Sofia and to therefore know that the plan had gone very well. He felt such a sense of relief, and although he knew there was work ahead for everyone the massive threat that had hung over his beloved Gateway was now gone. Soon his friend Mason would be home and they could start to get things back to how they should be.

Sofia was also feeling very relieved. They had some breathing space now, but no time to relax. The Soul Stealer was Samuel and Dorothea's problem for now, her job was to sort out the problems left in its wake. She needed to speak to Cedric Neale first, to give him an update and check something with him before calling Mason to make arrangements for the transport and arrival of the new Dreambringers.

'Do we tell the New Dreambringers about the Soul Stealer? Sofia had updated her boss and now posed her question.

'I think not for now' answered Cedric Neale 'they have enough to deal with at the moment. It no longer poses a threat to them so I suggest we hold off a little longer. If they start asking awkward questions or become overly suspicious then I trust you to use your discretion and tell them when the time is right.'

'Thank you sir for your advice and trust.'

'Please keep Barbara updated on a regular basis and if there are any major problems contact me at once.'

'I will do sir.'

'Goodbye my dear and good luck.'

'Thank you, goodbye'

Mason was in Max's kitchen making them both tea whilst Max packed his things upstairs when he received a call from Sofia.

'How are things going?' he asked after they exchanged greetings.

'Well, it all went to plan and Samuel and Dorothea are now transporting their captive back where it belongs.'

'So the Gateway is safe once again?'

'Yes, it's safe. How are things your end?'

'All is going to plan here too, I'm with Max at the moment and the others are all out getting their things together.'

'Good, so do you think they will be ready to travel here tomorrow?'

'I don't see why not. They should all be back at the Induction Centre by this evening, then we can all get a good night's sleep then set off for The Gateway in the morning. I have to say I can't wait to get home.'

'And we'll be glad to have you back, not to mention the newcomers. Eddie and I will get to work and make sure everything is ready for your arrival.'

'Great. I'll be back at the Centre in a couple of hours so I'll get to work on the arrangements for travel tomorrow as you have plenty to do, and I'm sure Pam our Inductor will help me.'

'That's good. Call me later with all the details.'

'Will do.'

'Speak to you later, bye.'

'Bye.'

Max entered the kitchen then carrying an old-fashioned style suitcase.

'I wasn't sure what to pack but as I don't have much clothes wise I packed everything plus a few toiletries in here' he said indicating the case 'now I just need to decide what to take with me from my workshop.'

'Okay, I'll give you a hand.'

Before the group had gone their separate ways for the day they had all been told that a few of their various art supplies should be included in the things they packed. Mason had explained that part of the induction and training would involve each of them working on their art, he did not go into detail but said it would all be made clear to them when they reached The Gateway. So with Mason's help Max collected together a bag of clay and some basic tools to take along with his suitcase.

'This will do fine for now' said Mason 'anything else you may need can be purchased for you by the Foundation and the rest of your things can be collected and brought to The Gateway at a later date.'

'I have a room full of my work what will happen to them?'

'They'll be safe here for now and then when the time is right they can be transported to The Gateway.'

'Okay, but I can take the busts that I did of you and the others now right?'

'Of course you can, they're in the Camper already so it's not a problem. Let's just load the rest of this stuff lock up and head back to the Induction Centre.'

Max nodded his agreement and the pair got to work.

As Mason and Max were loading the Camper Aaron and Mary were on their way back to the Induction Centre driven by their helper Connor, a tall, thin young man with a close shaven head and a shy smile. He was around the same age as the couple, and they'd warmed to him immediately.

After gathering Aaron's things together Connor and Mary had loaded them on the van whilst Aaron went to inform his landlady he was leaving and pay her what he owed with money provided by the Foundation via Connor.

With Aarons business sorted Connor had then followed the couple on to Mary's flat. This would be a longer task. Mary needed time to sort out what best to take with her so whilst she'd headed for the bedroom to sort out clothes etc the two young men had headed for the kitchen tasked with clearing her fridge of perishables and bagging up the rubbish.

After filling a suitcase with clothes and toiletries Mary had filled a smaller case with other essentials, which mainly consisted of the hardback notebooks containing her poems. As she'd packed she'd wondered if she would ever return to her little flat. If things worked out it seemed to her that she wouldn't need to return as the Foundation would deal with it all for her and she wasn't sure how she felt about that. She loved her little flat but she'd often felt a little lonely there and now it seemed that she was headed for a new life in a place where she would never be lonely again. Aaron would be there along with her new friends not the mention the strange new creatures she would soon meet. How strange it all was, and how exciting. She'd been sitting on the bed contemplating when Aaron walked in.

'How's it going?' he'd asked

'I'm all packed I was just kind of saying goodbye to the place I guess' she'd replied looking slowly around the room.

'I expect it'll be strange for you, I'm used to moving on to strange new places on a regular basis, though none have been as strange as this one promises to be, but it's different for you, are you feeling okay about it all?'

'It is going to be strange but I feel good about it.'

'That's good then' and after a pause 'we've sorted the rubbish and Connor is just taking it down to the bins, he'll be back in a minute for your cases.'

'I'll just do a check in the other rooms then to make sure I have everything I need then I'm good to go.'

A short while later, the three of them had climbed into Connor's van and leaving Mary's car and flat behind had headed back to the Induction Centre.

'We're nearly there' Dorothea shouted back to Samuel without turning her head as she scanned the road ahead looking for the left turn. They were on a narrow country road and she knew that the turning was coming up soon but having only been there the once she wasn't sure exactly where it was. She knew what to look for though and so reducing her speed a little she kept a look out. When she spotted the small, weathered Private Road sign she braked and then steered the van onto the narrow lane. The lane was unpaved and had tall hedgerows on both sides.

'Hold on its going to be a little bumpy' she called.

'Great' mumbled Samuel who already felt a little battered from being bounced around a little in the metal box of the vans storage area. But it hadn't been a long journey and at least his fellow occupant hadn't given him any trouble. The creatures most unsettling features had remained hidden by it closed eyes and mouth and as long as you didn't look to closely at its hands it just looked like an exhausted, scruffy, sleeping man.

The road surface was a little uneven but at least it was relatively straight and Dorothea drove slowly so its occupants weren't buffeted about too much. After just under two miles she stopped at the expected iron gateway. It was a lot smaller and much more ordinary than the entrance gate to The Gateway but it served the same function. It led to a property that was actually within the expansive grounds of the Gateway tucked away in the northern corner furthest away from The Gateway house. She leant out of the van window and keyed a code into the gate entrance pad and a few seconds later the gates began to slowly open. Dorothea drove the van through onto a narrow but thankfully tarmacked road.

After about a quarter of a mile the road opened out onto a tarmacked driveway in front of a small, whitewashed cottage with a thatched roof. There was a car parked outside the house with two people sat inside. Dorothea acknowledged them with a wave which they answered with a thumbs up before the driver started the engine and headed off down the narrow lane that the van had just emerged from.

As she'd been there once before Dorothea knew to follow the tarmac surface around the left side of the house where it led to what appeared to be a large, modern brick-built garage. She also knew that the two men who had just left in the car had left the keys for the house etc just inside the unlocked garage door.

'We're here' she announced as she brought the van to a stop in front of the garage. Then, getting out of the van she went around to the back of the vehicle to open the back doors. Samuel clambered out unfolding his large frame from the cramped space.

'I'll get the keys and unlock the door then you can carry It through' she said.

'Okay' answered Samuel as he stretched his cramped muscles whilst keeping his eyes on the captive.

Dorothea pulled up the garage door revealing that all was not as it first seemed. The modern brick-built garage was basically just a shell and the concreted space inside the door was only about two feet deep before it ended in a much older stone wall. A large bundle of keys lay on the floor in the right-hand corner by the old brick wall. Dorothea picked them up and then after closing the garage door she walked around the side to a modern PVC door and after a couple of tries found the correct key to unlock it.

A couple of feet inside the door there was another door. This one was made of heavy, metal studded oak and was set in the old stone wall of the small building that was encased in the modern brick shell of the fake garage. She had no trouble finding the key to fit this door as it was, large, old and made of iron. Despite its age the key turned in the ancient lock with no trouble and she pushed the heavy door open.

In the light from the open doors Dorothea took in the strange sight within. The stone chamber was a strange mix of ancient and modern. The walls were whitewashed stone and there was only one small, narrow window set high up on the wall opposite the door. The slate paving slabs on the floor though newer than the walls were obviously not modern. In contrast the wood burner that heated the chamber was definitely modern as were the single bed, armchair and small wooden table that furnished it. Then it was back to old fashioned for lighting which would be supplied by an oil lamp placed in a niche in the stone wall. The whole thing gave off a strangely mixed impression of cosy and depressing.

Leaving both doors open Dorothea went back outside to the van.

'All set' she said to Samuel who nodded and then reached into the van, pulled out the limp body of the Soul Stealer and carried It back to Its prison where he placed It on It's bed.

It was only as Dorothea was locking the wooden door that she spied something and pointed it out to Samuel. There in the middle of the door there was carved a circle and inside the circle was a symbol. It was the symbol that was missing from the door of the Factory, the symbol that represented the Soul Healer of Dreams. And below it attached to a short 'vine' there was a single flower/leaf like shape. Samuel smiled, his symbol was represented after all and there beside it the symbol of the Soul Healers Eternal Dreamer. They had been left off the door to the Eternal Dreamers abode because neither a Soul Healer or its Eternal Dreamer dwelled there anymore and then put here where those two things, though changed forever, did live.

Once the prisoner had been locked safely in the stone chamber and its outer shell its new Custodians headed for the house. They entered the cottage via a white, stable style back door that led into the kitchen which had a slate floor and a cosy, country style. There was a round table with four chairs in the middle of the room and despite its old-fashioned look it was equipped with all the mod cons. The kitchen had also been stocked with food for them by the Foundation members they had waved to when they arrived. Luckily one of its modern adaptations was an increased ceiling height meaning that Samuel could stand up straight in the room which was a relief. He did have to duck to get through the doorways however.

The rest of the downstairs was made up of a small slate floored hallway leading from the front door off of which lead the doors to the kitchen, a small 'snug' which contained a couple of comfy, worn chairs, a TV and not much else and a larger sitting room with an inglenook fireplace and beamed ceiling. This room was more lavishly furnished with a couple of leather sofas and several bookcases, but it looked less lived in.

The beamed ceiling was a bit of a problem for Samuel and so it looked like it would remain unlived in whilst he stayed there. Upstairs there was a bathroom and two bedrooms, the slightly larger of which had a small en suite shower room. Both bedrooms had slightly sloping ceilings which was not good for Samuel, but he'd have to get used to it and they decided that Dorothea would take the large room as the en suite was a bit small for Samuel so he could use the main bathroom which was next to the other bedroom.

All of Rita and William Deacon's personal belongings had been removed from the cottage by Foundation staff and now with the sleeping arrangements made the pair went back down and out to the van to get their belongings.

The cottage wasn't ideal for Samuel and he didn't think Dorothea was keen either, but they'd have to live with it for the time being, their work was too important to let a little discomfort disrupt it.

Geths Foundation driver was called Justin 'See you in a bit' he said as he dropped Geth off outside Studio Ink. As Geth entered the studio Rick was sat at the reception desk taking payment from a client and Chris was clearing up his station. Rick gave his boss a quick wave hello as he chatted to the customer.

'So the wanderer returns' said Chris catching sight of Geth.

'How's business?' asked Geth

'It's a bit slow today, I haven't got anything else booked in so I was thinking I'd stick around for a couple of hours in case we get any drop ins then call it a day.'

'Fair enough, and its good you're free now because we need to talk.'

'Sounds ominous.'

'What does?' asked Rick as he approached having seen the client out.

'I have something to tell you both. Rick can you lock the door and put the closed sign up please, we'll go up to the flat and talk.'

'You're right it sounds ominous' said Rick to Chris as he went to lock the door.

Chris and Rick reacted to Geth's 'story' better than he'd hoped they would. They were a little shocked and both had their own concerns obviously, but the three men talked it all through calmly and plans were made. Rick was actually pleased with the arrangements as it meant that he'd finally get a chance to do his first tattoos. Chris grumbled a bit at first about taking on extra work, but after a little discussion he saw the benefits. He'd be totally in charge and when Geth agreed to let him stay in his flat whilst he was away meaning he wouldn't have to commute after his longer days' work he was happy. Geth couldn't help wondering how the pair would feel if the situation became permanent.

'I have a favour to ask before I go' Geth said to Chris

'Sure, what is it?'

'I'd like you to tattoo me'

'What, right now?'

'Yes now.'

Geth had made the decision in the car on the way there. After tattooing his other four designs on his new friends he really wanted his own design tattooed on himself and he wasn't sure when he'd get the chance next. He'd asked Justin if it would be a problem if the trip took a couple of hours longer. Justin had said he didn't think it would be a problem and so they'd made a little plan. Whilst Geth talked with Chris and Rick and then got his tattoo done Justin would go and get a leisurely bite to eat at a café Geth suggested nearby and then he would park round the back of the studio in Geths personal parking space where he could relax and maybe even have a little nap before the drive home. When he was done, and Chris and Rick had left he would let Justin in so they could pack up his stuff before leaving.

'What do you want done?' asked Chris

'I have a design in here' said Geth indicating the flash art folder he'd brought in with him.

'Give us a look then.'

Geth showed him his design, it was a black and grey drawing of a stone castle gateway with the portcullis gate lowered halfway.

'Great design Geth' said Chris and looking at it over his shoulder Ricky nodded in agreement.

'Where do you want it?' asked Chris

'Left chest.'

'Okay, sounds good and I have to say I'm very flattered you've asked me, there must have been several tattooists at the Art Event who could have done it for you.'

'To be honest I didn't have the time at the event and besides I know your work, I rate you as an artist, so I know you'll do a great job.'

'I'm chuffed mate' said Chris meaning it.

'Well get on with it then' said Geth in his usual abrasive manor to counteract the sentimental direction the conversation seemed to be going in.

'Sure, let's go downstairs and make a start' agreed Chris with a smile unoffended by his friend's manor, he was used to it.

As Chris worked on his tattoo Geth found conversation hard. He had so much going on in his head that he kept losing the thread of the three way chat and time seemed to be going slow. Chris and Rick didn't really notice though as Chris was concentrating on his work and idle chat was natural to them both.

Finally, the tattoo was finished and Geth went over to the mirror to check it out. He was very pleased with what he saw. Although he couldn't help but think in the back of his mind that he could have done it better Chris has done a really good job.

'Great job' he said to Chris 'and I really appreciate you doing it for me out of the blue like this.'

'No problem, I enjoyed it, it's a great design.'

'Cheers.'

The three men chatted for a bit longer before Geth handed Chris his spare flat keys and after going over a few details he sent the pair off home. Chris would move his things into the flat the next day but for now Geth needed to let Justin in so he could help him load up the car. He'd have rather done it all himself but he'd made the poor guy wait long enough and they needed to head back to the Induction Centre ASAP after the extended visit. So he let the guy in and led him upstairs.

His tattoo guns and the other equipment he'd taken to Artfest were still back at the induction centre so in terms of what he would need in the unlikelihood that he would be tattooing someone in the next few days he just needed to pack some extra ink. However, Mason's instructions to bring art supplies had given Geth an idea, he was hoping that instead of tattooing he would maybe get the chance to do some actual paintings. Therefore, he had decided to pack some of his art paper, brushes and paints too. Then lastly some clothes and toiletries.

As he packed up his things he couldn't help but wonder if he'd ever be back and he wasn't sure how he felt about it, he wasn't sure at all.

As Geth and Justin headed down to the car with Geths belongings Clea was just arriving at her home with her own helper. The young woman's name was Laura and the pair were getting on just fine having spent the drive from the RV Rental place chatting like old friends.

'You have a lovely home' observed Laura as she followed Clea upstairs to help her pack up some clothes.

'Thank you dear' she replied failing to keep the slight catch out of her voice.

Clea had known it would be hard saying goodbye to her home and with all the decisions she would have to make buzzing around in her head she was beginning to feel a little overwhelmed. What should she take with her now? Would she ever come back here? Could she give it up totally or let others live here until she came back home, and when would that be?

Up until now she'd been swept up in the excitement of the new life she was headed too but now with the familiar sights and sounds of her home around her the new direction her life could take seemed more frightening. When they reached her bedroom she sat on the edge of the bed and fighting back tears she asked Laura to give her a minute alone. Laura said it was no problem; she understood and would be down in the kitchen making them a brew when Clea was ready.

After a few minutes, and a few tears, Clea gave herself a mental shake and told herself to get it together. How could she even contemplate refusing the new, amazing life she had been offered. It was a wobble that's all, and totally understandable after the last few crazy days.

And so, after a brief visit to the bathroom to freshen up she headed down to the kitchen with a plan. She needed to be more organised, coming straight up to her bedroom had been a mistake. She would join Laura downstairs for a brew and compile a considered list of what she needed to take, and then Laura could help her pack it all up. They'd start with her embroidery stuff then the personal things as that would be the harder part.

Later, with the tea drunk and the plan made, they set to work.

For the first time since all the craziness had begun Sofia found herself with nothing to do. The Soul Stealer was Dorothea and Samuels problem now, Mark and Phoebe were back out in the Factory, Eddie was upstairs cleaning the rooms Samuel and Dorothea had used and she had updated the Foundation and finished making all the necessary arrangements for Mason and the new recruit's journey to the Gateway the next day.

Her job here was far from over but with the danger under control and plans all in place she figured it was time for a little relaxation although her (obvious) choice of relaxation was still very much part of her job. She was headed to the lounge / art room to immerse herself in her art for an hour or two.

'So what happens now, that's the question right' stated Mason as he stood in front of the group sat around on the sofas in the training room. Clea had been the last to return to the Training Centre about an hour ago and he had called them all together now to explain the plans for the next day.

'Well' he continued 'basically we're all going to travel to what will hopefully be your new home for several, happy years to come. Under normal circumstances you would receive more training here before travelling to your new home, but in this case, we need you there as soon as possible.'

'So the adventure begins in earnest tomorrow then' said a tired looking Clea.

'Yes it does. The Gateway art commune is a few hours' drive from here so we'll be setting off quite early tomorrow. We'll travel together in a luxury minibus provided by the Foundation. And don't worry Max someone will also drive your camper there too, we thought we'd use it to transport some of the other luggage as well as your sculptures.'

'Great, thanks' said Max.

'Regarding your car Geth we thought we'd leave it here for now' Mason continued 'we hope that's okay?'

'It makes me a little uncomfortable but I guess so' agreed Geth

'Good, as we're all travelling together I can fill you in on a few things on the way and so now I suggest we all relax a little before getting a good night's sleep as its going to be a long day tomorrow.'

'Will we dream tonight?' asked Mary quietly, almost like she was talking to herself 'the special type of dream I mean, of each other, only I haven't dreamt much since we got here and I kinda miss it.'

'Good question' agreed Aaron 'now we know what they're about I think I'd enjoy them more; you were all extra cool in my dreams.'

Aaron's comments caused a small ripple of laughter amongst the group and a few nods of agreement.

'You know what' said Mason 'why don't we try a little exercise tonight then, make it part of your training yeah, let's all try and meet up in our dreams.'

'Cool' said Mary 'How?'

'We're already linked in the dream world now so it should be pretty easy, we just think of a place to meet and all go to sleep thinking about that place and each other and hopefully that'll work. Our Eternals are far away and none of you are 'linked' directly to them yet but I believe you have enough talent to do it.'

'How about we all meet back in the Tattoo tent then?' suggested Clea

'Good idea' agreed Mason 'it's where you all met and connected and it's still fresh in our minds. So that's decided then, we'll all meet there tonight.'

'How exciting' said Clea

'I'll give it a go' said Max sounding a little unsure.

'I'm totally up for it' said Aaron

'Me too' agreed Mary and when he didn't join in to Geth she said 'Come on, join in ya big grump'

Geth's expression showed shock, then brief annoyance and then the cheeky grin Mary was giving him seemed to penetrate his hard shell and he cracked a little smile.

'Fine, you're all crazy but I give up, I'll meet you loons in my dreams' and then under his breath 'what the fuck have I got myself into.'

Mary giggled and Aaron leaned over and patted Geth on the shoulder.

'That's the spirit' he said, 'just accept the weird.'

This time Geth joined in the laughter, what else could he do?

CHAPTER 17

TO THE GATEWAY

Five people stand in a circle, two women and three men. Blurry human forms move around them, sound is muted. This is where they came together and this new meeting bonds them more firmly together. Someone approaches, a newer friend, he joins the circle and they move in closer. No one speaks, there's no need. They belong together.

Mary awoke to the sound of Aaron's gentle snoring and the warmth of his body heat against her back. She smiled. It had worked; they had all met up in the dream world just as they'd planned. The success of their little experiment gave her a little thrill and a boost of confidence. Excitement now outweighed apprehension in her mind giving her a more positive outlook on what was to come.

She felt Aaron stir behind her and rolled over to face him so that he opened his eyes to see her smiling face.

'Morning gorgeous' she said

'Morning sweetheart' he replied giving her a sleepy grin.

'We did it.'

'We sure did.'

Then brushing a strand of hair from her cheek he moved closer to give her a good morning kiss.

Downstairs Clea and Max were chatting over cups of tea after a similar but less romantic good morning greeting.

'How are you feeling about things this morning?' asked Clea.

'Better after last night, it feels more real now though I'm not sure that's the right word considering we're talking about something that happened in a dream.'

'I know exactly what you mean.'

'I feel less afraid of what's to come I know that much.'

'That's good. I have to confess I had a little wobble when I went home yesterday.'

'Really? I'm surprised; out of all of us you've always seemed the most accepting and excited about it all. But you're alright now though?'

'Yes, I'm fine now, especially after the dream.'

'I'm glad for your sake and also because I need you to help keep me strong, you've really helped me through all this you know.'

'That's so sweet' Clea said blushing a little 'I'm glad to have helped and you've helped me too you know.'

'Thanks, but I can't see how.'

'I like someone to look after, it helps me feel stronger.'

'That makes sense, I'm glad to have helped' said Max with a self-conscious little laugh.

Mason entered the kitchen then and joined the pair for a cuppa and more chat. He was closely followed by Geth who returned their greetings and went to make himself a coffee.

'It worked then' he said as he joined them at the table.

'It sure did' said Clea with a big grin 'has it helped you?'

'I guess' he answered with a slight frown rather than a smile.

'You are such hard work' said Clea making Max and Mason laugh.

'Sorry' said Geth not looking sorry at all but then Clea noticed a little smile pulling at the corner of his mouth.

'Ah ha' she exclaimed 'was that a little grin then?'

'Maybe' he replied.

When Mary and Aaron joined the group a little later they found the rest of their new friends in as good a mood as they were.

'Good morning my loveys' said Clea jumping up out of her chair 'now you're here I'll make us all a lovely breakfast to set us up for a new day of adventure.'

Over breakfast they had a little light-hearted discussion about their new titles to which Mary added a little hilarity by telling them all about her own word for what they were. But although they agreed that Dreamfreak was very apt for how they'd felt before they'd learnt the truth their true titles were much nicer.

After the initial bustle of setting off the atmosphere on the minibus was subdued as everyone was lost in their own thoughts. Then, after Clea's suggestion of a sing-along was vetoed by Geth and Max conversation started to flow. Everyone was in a good mood and the excitement level was high.

The journey was uneventful with a couple of quick comfort breaks and a longer one for lunch. After lunch there was a bit of a lull and the mood turned more reflective. Then after the last planned comfort break the excitement began to build as they neared their destination and they began firing questions at Mason about The Gateway.

He mainly answered these with variations of 'wait and see' not wanting to spoil their first sighting of their beautiful new home, plus he was a little preoccupied with his own thoughts. He couldn't wait to be home again; it was the longest he'd been away from it since his initiation. His joy at returning was tinged a little with sadness though due to the fact that Eddie was the only one of his friends that remained at the house and by the knowledge that in bringing the new Dreambringers to his home he would soon be leaving it again, and for good this time.

He couldn't let his mind dwell on where he would go after he helped the newbies settle in though. He knew that the Foundation would see him right, but his time as a Dreambringer had been cruelly and prematurely cut short. He wasn't ready to give it up and it was taking all his mental strength not to let his disappointment get the better of him. He needed to focus on the near future, on helping the transition go smoothly. He still had work to do at The Gateway, his job wasn't done yet, so he needed to push the worry about his more long-term future to the back of his mind.

Finally, the minibus pulled up at the ornate iron gateway and as they waited to be buzzed in Mason took pleasure from the exclamations over its beauty. The appreciation continued as they drove along the tree lined driveway and then when they arrived at the house everyone was buzzing at the sight of its Georgian splendour.

'I can't believe I'm going to be living in such a beautiful house' exclaimed Mary.

'How wonderful' said Clea.

'Cool' was Aaron's comment.

'It's magnificent' said Max.

'Very impressive' remarked Geth.

'Welcome to your new home' said Mason his voice cracking a little with emotion.

Max's VW Camper was already parked up in the triple garage over in the corner of the driveway having arrived earlier and been unloaded by Eddie. Now as they got off the minibus Eddie and Sofia opened the door and came out to greet them.

Eddie headed straight for Mason and the two friends greeted each other with a blokey half hug / shoulder slap. Then after greeting Sofia with a slightly awkward peck on the cheek Mason made the introductions and they all headed inside.

Eddie took the minibus driver through to the kitchen to join the driver of the VW for a drink and a break before they both headed off in the minibus and Sofia took the others into the lounge/art room.

'Make yourselves comfortable' said Sofia indicating the large sofas 'Eddie can give you a tour of the house after we've all had a drink and a chat so, who wants tea and who wants coffee?'

When Sofia returned with their drinks and Eddie the group had a little informal chat and then there were a couple of little details to talk over before Eddie could give them the promised tour.

'Firstly, we need to discuss the sleeping arrangements' Sofia began 'Usually the new recruits sleep in the guest rooms whilst the changeover is taking place but as with everything else in this case things are a little different. Two of the three guest rooms inside the house are already occupied, one by me and the other will now need to be shared by two other guests we have here at the moment. I will tell you more about them later, but now most of you will actually be able to get settled in your new rooms straight away as they have been cleared and made ready for you by Eddie. However, one of you will have to stay in the other guest room for the time being.'

'Of course, damn it.' muttered Mason realising what Sofia was getting at.

'Mason's things are still in his room' continued Sofia 'which means one of you won't be able to move your things in yet. Mary and Aaron, you have no choice which room you have as it is a slightly larger, shared room that is always occupied by the Dream Mates, but I'm sure that won't be a problem.'

'Sounds okay to me' said Aaron and Mary nodded her agreement.

'So' continued Sofia 'that means that when we have shown you all the rooms and you have all decided who wants which, whoever chooses Mason's room will have to stay in the guest room for now. We felt it only fair that Mason should stay in his own room for the time being as this is all as much an upheaval to him as it is to you seeing as this change has been forced on him rather than the choice he would usually have made when the time was right.'

'I totally understand' said Clea 'and I'm sure the others agree.'

The others did and Clea, Max and Geth all stated that they'd have no problem staying in the guest room. And with that little issue dealt with Eddie took the group on the promised tour.

Eddie felt proud as he showed them around the beautiful house but as Mason had earlier he was suffering a little inside at the possibility that he may soon have to move on. He wasn't sure if he would be allowed to stay on as Warden to the new Dreambringers, plus with his friends no longer living there with him, much as he loved the house, he wasn't sure he'd want to stay. He kept the turmoil to himself though and remained outwardly cheerful with the appreciative comments from the group helping him remain upbeat.

The house was impressing them all with Clea falling in love with the kitchen in particular. With the communal downstairs part of the tour complete they went upstairs to view what would be their personal rooms. The stairs led up to a wide corridor off of which there were five doors, two to the left and three to the right. At the back end of the corridor there was a patrician wall behind which were the stairs up to the attic.

Aaron and Mary's room was the second on the left and they were more than happy with their shared room. It looked out over the lawn and woodland at the back of the house and was a really generous size. It had a beautiful, spacious en suite bathroom, a king size bed, a cosy seating area with a tv and an ornate feature fireplace. There was also ample storage in the form of two chest of draws and two large wardrobes.

The group were told that there were other pieces of furniture stored in the attic that they were free to use as well as or in exchange for what was in the room already if they wished. And then once they were settled in they would be supplied with new bed linen and towels of their own choosing and the Foundation would arrange for them to make any changes to the décor in their rooms that they wanted to.

Mason's room was the first on the left. It looked out over the driveway at the front and although it was smaller than the Dream Mates room it was still a very good size with its own en suite, a double bed, chest of draws, wardrobe and small seating area and fireplace. Across the hallway the other two rooms were basically the same as Mason's, one with a front outlook the other at the back. In-between these two rooms there was a spacious, walk-in linen storage / laundry room for them all to use. The room at the front had belonged to Claude and the one at the back to Mahesh.

After viewing all the rooms, the group gathered in the hallway to talk about who wanted which room. Mason already knew who would choose which. Although they'd made it sound like the group (apart from the Dream Mates) had a free choice he knew from experience that they would automatically choose the room of the Dreambringer they were replacing.

It had happened with his group, and he had been told after his group made their choices that it happened that way every time; it was the first test. If they were right for their new role they would know as soon as they entered their predecessor's room that it was the one for them.

The Dreammates test was a little different, their room was assigned but it was their reaction to sharing that room that confirmed their roles. Most Dreammates arrived at the houses already a couple but their relationship would be very new and so a shared room could be a shock. If they were right for each other and for their role they would accept the arrangement without question or doubt.

As expected the room assignment were decided quickly with no arguments, and the correct choices were made. Clea chose Mahesh's room and Geth chose Claude's. And of course, Max chose Mason's room.

'I'm sorry Max' said Mason 'that means you get the guest room for now.'

'It's no problem' replied Max 'the guest room looks great and I'm fine with it, honestly.'

'Thanks for understanding.'

Sofia was of course aware of the importance of the room assignment and so when the group re-joined her she was pleased to find they had all passed their first test. Hopefully the rest of the changeover would go as smoothly. The rest of the day would be about settling them in physically, then tomorrow they would start with the initiation in earnest.

Now taking charge Sofia addressed the group.

'As you will have seen earlier Eddie put all your bags in the office downstairs so now we'll help you carry your things to your new rooms and leave you to unpack and settle in for a bit. We'll meet back in the kitchen in a couple of hours for a meal and we can talk a few things through then. You don't need to stay in your rooms until then though, feel free to have a wander around the house if you like; you could even sit out on the patio as it's a nice evening. I'll be in the office and Mason and Eddie will be about if you need them.'

The group spent the next couple of hours acclimatizing in their own ways.

After unpacking a few things Clea went downstairs and knocked on Max's guest room door and invited him to come out and sit on the patio with her for a cuppa and a chat.

Geth was feeling a little restless after unpacking his bag and so after watching the departure of the two Foundation employees in the minibus from his window he went for a wander. He walked into the office, saw that Sofia was on the phone and walked out not wanting to invade her privacy. He then found Eddie and Mason in the kitchen. The two friends were chatting as Eddie prepared the dinner after having found some extra chairs so they would all be able to sit around the table. He was about to leave to give them their privacy too when Eddie spotted him and invited him to join them.

'I don't want to interrupt' he said.

'You're not' replied Eddie 'in fact Mason just told me that you are a tattooist and as you will see' he said indicating his heavily inked arms 'I'm a fan of your chosen art and would love to chat to you about it.' So, he joined them.

Aaron and Mary were taking their time unpacking and getting used to their new room. Mary loved the room but as she put her things away, she was already making plans for little changes she wanted to make and Aaron was teasing her about it.

'Don't laugh at me' she said giving his arm a playful slap.

'I can't help it, your adorable' he replied making a grab for her and pulling her to him 'I think we're going to be really happy here' he continued planting a kiss on the top of her head.

'Me too, I feel at home already.'

'Yep, the whole things a bit surreal but I feel strangely comfortable with it all.'

'I know what you mean, it's like strangeness abounds and although I'm having a bit of trouble processing it all on some level somewhere inside me it all makes sense and I've accepted it already; it feels right.'

'Exactly and that's obviously why we're here, why we were called, we were destined to become Dreambringers and on some level we've always know it.'

'We are Dreambringers, amazing but apparently true.'

'I can't wait to find out more about our new life.'

'We should find out more soon, we've got about an hour before we're due to meet up with the others so let's finish unpacking and then go for a wander before dinner.'

'Okay.'

Downstairs out on the patio Max and Clea had just finished having a similar conversation to Mary and Aaron and now decided to head back inside. They entered the kitchen to find Geth and Mason sat at the kitchen table chatting with Eddie as he bustled around the kitchen preparing dinner.

'Sorry to disturb you boys' said Clea 'but we fancied another cuppa.'

'No problem' said Eddie 'I'll put the kettle on.'

'No need for you to worry about it lovey' said Clea 'I'll do it, you have enough to do, in fact I can lend you a hand with that too if you like.'

'I have the dinner all under control, but thanks for the offer. I'll take you up on your offer to make the tea though.'

'Okay, good. So, who wants tea?'

Geth declined, but the other two men said they did.

'I'll go check if Sofia wants anything' added Mason.

When Mason entered the office, Sofia was just ending a phone call. The poor woman always seemed to be on the phone he thought as he waited for her to finish. Sofia finished her call and putting the phone down she looked up and smiled at Mason.

'Hi there' she said

'Hi, still busy as ever I see.'

'Yes, a Marshals work is never done.'

'Well why don't you take a break, Clea's making tea, if you fancy one, or I'm sure she'd make coffee if you prefer.'

'Tea sounds good, thanks.'

'Are you gonna come and drink it with us, we're all in the kitchen except for Aaron and Mary.'

'I'd love to come and join you; I'm done here for now.'

'Good, but before we go I need to ask you something.'

'Go ahead.'

'When are we going to tell them the full story about what happened here, and the full Soul Healer history that got left out at the induction centre?'

'I've been thinking about that, and I think it's only fair we tell them ASAP. We kept if from them initially because we were so unsure how things were going to go here, but the danger is over now and there's no real reason to keep it from them any longer. There is a risk that this information will scare them off but at this stage I think that's unlikely.'

'I was hoping you'd say that, they need to know everything before we can move onwards with their induction.'

'It's decided then, we tell them after dinner.'

'Yes, good.'

With the decision made they joined the others in the kitchen. A short while later Aaron and Mary made an appearance and soon it was time to eat.

The atmosphere over dinner was lively and friendly with everyone complimenting Eddie's cooking. Then after the dinner things were cleared away the whole group moved to the lounge/art room.

There was plenty of room for everyone and once they were all seated there was a brief silence before Sofia started to speak.

'Your induction and training will start in earnest tomorrow, but before that you need to know a few things. Firstly, you must understand that your calling has come about in a slightly different way to how it should have done, and this is due to circumstances never before encountered in the history of The Somnium Foundation. Now I don't want you to be alarmed by this, everything is fine now, but things have been a little strange around here and you need to know what has been happening.'

Before continuing Sofia glanced around the group to gauge how they were reacting. Clea was looking at her with what looked more like excitement than alarm, Max looked more apprehensive as to a lesser extent did Aaron and Mary and Geth was scowling a little, but Sofia felt it was safe to go on.

'This particular commune is already historically different to all the others across the world. The difference is that for many years there have only been five Dreambringers here whereas everywhere else there are six' and after a pause for them to take that in she continued 'When you had your initial induction your Trainer was told to leave a part of the history out for the time being and so now I'm going to tell you the part she left out.'

And so, Sofia told the tale of the Soul Stealer.

When she had finished there was a short silence before Aaron was the first to speak.

'Bloody hell, that's really freaky' he said managing to sound both appalled and fascinated.

'And this happened a long time ago?' enquired Clea

'Yes, a very long time ago'

'And this hybrid thing has been kept locked up all this time?'

'Yes' answered Sofia and then reluctantly added 'well almost.'

'Oh Jesus, I don't like the sound of that 'well almost' bit' said a pale looking Max.

Sofia found herself having to stifle a laugh. It wasn't really funny, but for some reason Max's comment on top of her own nervousness made her feel like giggling. It was childish and ridiculous but luckily, she managed to control the urge before she carried on.

'Over the years many pairs of Custodians have successfully kept their charge safely locked away but recently tragedy struck. One of the custodians was suddenly struck ill and died whilst carrying out her duties and her partner was so distraught at her death that he let his guard down completely and their captive escaped. By some sort of instinct, it found its way back here to where it came from.'

Sofia then went on to tell them what had happened at the Gateway from the Soul Healers possession of Claude, to the arrival of Phoebe and Mark and the creatures subsequent capture by Samuel and Dorothea making sure it was clear that they were all now safe.

Again, there was a brief silence and this time it was Mary who spoke first.

'Those poor people, and Mason and Eddie this must have all been so hard for you.'

'It's been pretty tough yes' answered Mason with a little catch in his voice whilst Eddie just nodded looking emotional.

'So, we weren't supposed to take over from you all yet then?' asked Max

It was Sofia who answered as she thought the subject was too emotional for Mason and Eddie to deal with.

'No, it would have probably not happened for several years yet if at all.'

'What do you mean 'if at all'?' asked Clea frowning.

'Well in a few years' time things are likely to be different in your lives and you may no longer have been the ideal candidates to take over.'

'So, it's not set in stone then, the succession?'

'No. I expect you have already been told that the length of time served by each set of Dreambringers varies and that the decision to end their term must be a joint one. Once the decision is made together they set about calling their successors. What hasn't yet been explained to you is that at any given time there are numerous potential candidates scattered all over the world. When the current Dreambringers send their spiritual feelers out into the world of dreams it is the strongest of the current candidates, the ones who are the most ready and able at that particular time who pick up on the signal.'

'Does that mean that some of these potential candidates miss out on their chance to be a Dreambringer?' asked Clea.

'A lot of them do, yes.'

'That's sad. So, if this terrible thing hadn't happened here we would have all missed out on becoming Dreambringers because if Mason and his friends had served their full term we wouldn't have been ready when they called for their successors?'

'There is a chance that one or two of you may have yes, but not necessarily. All potential candidates are obviously born with the Dreambringer talent but the periods of time within their life span where they are suited to the Dreambringer lifestyle varies. It depends on individual life experience and the course their lives take them on.

Those candidates that lead very free lives, with no responsibilities or dependants, are therefore much more likely to be called as their time span will be longer. Whereas those who have spouses and or children are obviously only suitable for the Dreambringer life up until they make those sort of lifetime commitments.

Over the years we have realised that of those born with the Dreambringer talent the strongest tend to be those who live a more solitary life whether through choice or circumstance as this seems to concentrate and elevate their talent to dream. For those less solitary types we have found that their potential to be called is only strong when they are young and have not therefore made any strong commitments yet, or later in life when their circumstances may have changed through, sadly, relationship breakdown or loss.'

'Oh' exclaimed Clea at that last bit, and then a little tearfully 'that's me. A few years ago, when my husband Andrew was alive I wouldn't have been ready for this, but now I'm alone I am.'

'Exactly' said Sofia 'And I'm very sorry to hear that you lost someone so close' she added giving Clea a sympathetic smile.

Clea nodded her thanks feeling a little too emotional to answer. This news put a new spin on things and she didn't know how she felt about it. Her time with Andrew had been the best years of her life and his death had been by far the worst thing that had ever happened to her. And now after years alone this new and excited twist that her life had taken suddenly felt kind of bittersweet as it would never have come about if her Andrew was still alive. Life had a great knack of giving and taking away she thought as she tried to hold back the tears that were threatening to overwhelm her.

This new bit of information was also making the others reflect on their own lives. It made sense to them all. Clea was the only one in the group who had ever been married and none of them had children.

Geth had always been a loner with no family to speak of and very few close friends which meant he had always been free to live his life as he chose. His only commitment being his business.

Max had been close to his parents but had always been a bit of a loner with few friends growing up and since losing his parents at nineteen he had spent his adult life outside of work pretty much alone.

After escaping his unhappy childhood home as soon as he could Aaron had led a very free, nomadic but ultimately lonely life and this amazing opportunity had come about just as he was contemplating a more settled, committed lifestyle.

As for Mary although she had her Mum, and more recently her Stepfather, they had never been close, and she had lived alone for a while now. But now she had found Aaron and this amazing new life was opening up before them this new information brought up a question.

'Would Aaron and I have met if we hadn't been called together by Mason?' she asked Sofia.

'It's impossible to say for sure, but it's very likely that you would have, after all one of the reasons you have been brought together is because you are soulmates. You will definitely have met in the dream world as that's part of your talent, but in real life it's harder to say. I will say that you probably wouldn't have met this soon in your lives if things had been different here.'

'Do the Dream Mates ever meet before they get called and arrive already an established couple' asked Aaron.

'Not that I've ever heard of no. They do however more often than not meet each other a little while before the whole group come together. Their bond is obviously stronger, so it takes less time for them to find each other. The calling dreams seem to set off a sort of hormonal homing beacon in each other.'

'But me and Mary were living really close to each other when this all happened, isn't that strangely convenient? I was even thinking of putting some roots down and getting a permanent job and home as I was getting tired of the nomadic lifestyle.'

'I didn't realise that' said Sofia 'I had no idea where any of you were when Mason sent you the first dream. Now I know that I can only assume that your dream connection was already bringing you to each other so it's more than likely that you were destined to meet, but there's still no way to know how long it would have been before that happened.'

'So, we could still have been destined to take over from Mason and his friends, but it would have happened a few years later?' asked Mary.

'Possibly yes' said Sofia 'or you may have been called by another set of Dreambringers, or met, got married and had kids and therefore missed your chance to become Dreambringers altogether. As I've said it's all about right time, right place.'

'Its mind boggling is what it is' said Max his tone of voice and the confused look on his face making Aaron and Mary laugh and the others – apart from the ever serious Geth – smile.

'It sure is' agreed Mason 'and I apologise 'cos it's not usually this confusing for newbies, you usually get more time to digest this stuff. This all happened much quicker than it should've done, sorry.'

'No need to apologise lovey' said Clea 'It's not your fault.'

'Cheers for that Clea and I just gotta say that I really admire you lot for how you're dealing with it all, you're a great bunch on people and I'm proud to be the one who brought you together.'

'Thanks lovey.' Clea was close to tears again as she continued 'and I for one think you've done a great job under the circumstances.'

There were mutterings of agreement amongst the others and Mason smiled and nodded his thanks.

'I totally agree that Mason has done an amazing job' said Sofia 'usually the calling takes place over a matter of weeks, sometimes even months. Each pair of Dreambringer and Eternal send feelers out into the dream world in search of the perfect candidate. The strongest candidates stand out and over several nights each pair makes their choice. With the choice's made they then begin the process of sending the chosen candidates dreams of each other, bonding them together even before they meet in real life.

Then when they feel that the dream bond is strong enough, they start to send dreams about a meeting place and on top of the dreams of each other this impels the group to seek out the meeting place and each other. In this case although Mason had the help of all the Eternals he was the only Dreambringer and he had to complete the task a lot quicker. It was very intense, stressful and exhausting, but he did it and I for one am very proud and impressed.'

'You did your bit too' said Mason feeling a little embarrassed by all the attention and praise 'you've been great, I couldn't have done it without you. And Eddie you did great too mate.'

'Hold on a minute' said Max 'how does the fact that we were called differently than normal affect things? I mean if the choosing phase was pretty much cut out were we just the first ones Mason came across or something and he was like okay they'll do?'

'No, it wasn't like that at all' said Mason 'you five were simply the strongest candidates at this time. I connected with you that first night so quickly and easily Max it just couldn't have been anyone else. And connection wise the rest of you were surprisingly easy too in the end. I was worried I'd have trouble connecting with you as only Max was my direct successor but you all stood out, so you were easy to find. The difficult part was whether you would accept what was happening and let your dreams lead you to each other.'

'If anything, Max' added Sofia 'I think the fact you came together like this means you are some of the strongest candidates we have ever found.'

'Yeah, Yeah, Yeah, we all did amazing, but can we cut all the lovey dovey shit now' interrupted Geth 'I want to know more about what happens next.'

'Don't be such a grump Geth' said Mary.

'He does have a point' admitted Sofia 'it's probably time I told you a little of what is going to happen in the next few days. I suggest you spend the rest of this evening relaxing and getting used to your new surroundings, then get a nice early night and dream well because the work starts tomorrow' Sofia paused briefly before continuing 'You will spend the next couple of days working on forming a stronger link with each other, and also with your Eternal Dreamers. I'm going to be honest here and admit that again things are going to have to be done a little differently and I'm not sure exactly how it's all going to work myself.'

'Well that reassuring' said Geth sarcastically.

'I realise this is worrying but although things are a little uncertain I'm confident they will work out, it's really down to logistics and it's my problem to sort it, not yours.'

'Okay, so how do we work on forming these bonds then? Asked Clea.

'Basically, by doing the two things you are all best at – dreaming and art' answered Sofia

'Sounds simple' commented Max.

'Well some of it is simple, the rest shouldn't be hard exactly, but it will seem very strange to you' explained Sofia 'Tomorrow we will start off here in the lounge with a group art session, the art being the simple part. What this art session will achieve is the strange part.

All artistic endeavour creates energy and in the case of you as Dreambringers the energy you produce is what fuels your work, that work obviously being helping to bring others dreams. As you have been told you do this with the help of the Eternal Dreamers. Your artistic energy is what feeds the Eternals and therefore links you to them and the link you create with them is what enables you all to help bring dreams to everyone.'

'So, all we have to do is work on our art? That's it? Asked Aaron.

'That's the basis of it yes, but that's not all.'

'For fucks sake just tell us what we have to do' said Geth 'and as for these Eternal buggers where the hell are they?'

'Well that's the other part or forming a link with them, after your art session you will be sent out to find a special place.'

'What the hell does that mean?' asked Geth 'Sent out where?'

'Basically, one by one, you will be sent out into the woodland surrounding the house having been given general directions and if your link is successful you will find it easily.'

'And if it's not?' asked Geth looking increasingly angry.

'I really don't think that's anything to worry about, I'm confident you will all find your way with no problems.'

'I'm not' Mary interjected quickly in an effort to head off another angry comment from Geth 'I have a terrible sense of direction' she added with a little laugh intended to lighten the mood.

'Don't worry' said Sofia giving Mary a grateful smile 'I promise you that a sense of direction in the way you mean it is not needed.'

Seeing that Mary's efforts hadn't really worked and that Geth was about to make another hostile comment Clea decided to head him off by asking a politer version of what she assumed he was going to ask.

'So, what is needed?' she asked.

'I'm really sorry if you are feeling frustrated with what I am telling you' said Sofia looking at Geth, and then addressing the whole group she continued 'but it is very difficult to explain, and I am doing my best. I know it's a lot to ask but I need you to trust me when I say that everything will come clear over the next couple of days.'

What Sofia didn't want to say was that being sent into the woods was a test and because it wasn't the sort of test you could practice or revise for it wasn't a good idea to let on that they were being tested. It would only cause extra pressure and stress. Once the new recruits passed this test all would be revealed, and tensions would ease, but getting to that point was proving tricky.

'I realise you have all had a lot to deal with over the past few days' Sofia continued 'and I will answer what questions I can, but some things just aren't explainable, some things you just have to experience for yourselves,'

'I trust you' said Clea 'and I'm willing to wait to find the answers to my questions. It's a little nerve wracking but also exciting so I'm up for it.'

'I'm okay with it too' said Aaron 'I'm looking at it as an adventure, so I say bring it on.'

'I'm with Aaron' said Mary 'but I have one little question, do me and Aaron go into the woods together or separately?'

'You go together' answered Sofia making Aaron and Mary smile.

'At the risk of sounding like a wimp I'm a little jealous of Mary and Aaron being able to go into the woods together, but I'm in all the same' said Max with a shy smile.

Then everyone was quiet as they waited for Geth to speak. He looked less angry now but still far from happy.

'I'm not very comfortable with any of this' he said 'but I'm not going to be a complete dick about it. I'm still half expecting all of this to be some elaborate joke, but I'm going to play along for now because I realise that if this is all for real then it's going to be worth it.'

'That's great' said Sofia looking relieved, as did the rest of the group.

Now with the tension dissipated the group fell into a more relaxed conversation. There was even a little laughter as they chatted and although he didn't join in with the laughter Geth did join the conversation and become more relaxed as the evening went on.

After a couple of hours, the group decided it was time to retire for the night and they all headed to their (in most cases) new rooms with varying expectations of a good night's sleep.

CHAPTER 18

MAKING CONNECTIONS

When Sophie entered the kitchen, she was surprised to find Eddie sat at the table nursing a cup of tea. It was very early, and she had assumed she was the first up.

'Morning Sofia, can I get you some tea or coffee?' said Eddie beginning to get up.

'No, don't worry, you sit, I'll get it myself thanks. How come your up so early?'

'I slept like a log for a few hours but woke up early and couldn't get back to sleep, too much on my mind. How about you?'

'The same really, although I'm usually up pretty early. So, what's on your mind? I've been meaning to have a word with you actually, to see how you're doing, the newbies aren't the only ones who've had some new information to process.'

'It's not the new information itself that's playing on my mind, I mean it's not a huge leap from what I already knew to what I've learnt. Its what's gonna happen to me once the new guys are all settled in that's playing on my mind.'

'That's understandable'

'Don't get me wrong, I know that the Foundation will see me right, but it's all so unexpected and sudden. I've lost friends and its more than likely I'm gonna have to leave my home. I know I'd have to leave sometime anyway but I always thought it'd be my decision, or at least that I'd have time to get used to the idea.'

'I don't know exactly what is going to happen to you and you friends now, but I can reassure you on one level, you won't be rushed into anything. The last few weeks have been crazy but now things are more settled I think the Foundation will take its time re-assigning you. It's my opinion, and it will be my recommendation, that you stay on here for a while. I feel that the newbies will benefit from having someone experienced as their Warden, at least to start with.'

'I'd like that, just for a few months so I can get my head around the changes to come and I do wanna help these new guys. It's gonna be weird here without Mason and the others though.'

'I'm certain that the Foundation will give you this transition period. We also have to consider the fact that you are more than just a Warden now, you know about the Eternals and this is unprecedented, it opens up more avenues for you in the Foundation.'

'I hadn't even considered that side of it.'

'The Foundation have a lot of things to sort out, but I think some positive will come from all this.'

'And then there's Mason and the others. Gina and Blake have been physically harmed and Claude mentally, what happens to them now? And Mason, he's not ready for his Dreambringer term to end,'

Before Sofia could answer another voice interrupted.

'Are you two talking about me? asked Mason as he entered the kitchen.

'We are mate' said Eddie 'we're discussing your future, and mine and our friends.'

'So, what does my future hold?'

'We hadn't really got that far.'

'Okay, good, I can join in then. I have something I need to ask you Sofia.'

'Go ahead' said Sofia as Mason took a seat at the table.

'Once things are more settled here I would like to visit my friends. I know the Foundation keeps us updated, but I want to go and see how Gina and Blake are doing myself, and I want to go and see Claude too.'

'I'm sure that can be arranged' said Sofia

'Thanks. And about Claude, I want to know if he knows what happened to him, has someone explained that what he did wasn't his fault?'

'I don't know exactly what Claude has been told, but I am sure he is receiving the appropriate treatment. But I can find out more for you if you would like me to.'

'Yes, I'd appreciate that, and one more thing, I was wondering what's happening regarding Mahesh's funeral.'

'Okay, I will make some calls later when I get a few minutes and find out what I can. I'll get an update on Gina and Blake too and get permission and make arrangements for your visits.'

'Thanks.'

'I hope that puts both your minds at rest for now because for the next couple of days I need you to concentrate on getting our new Dreambringers settled in. We need to get their links with their Eternals established ASAP because I'm a little concerned about how being disconnected from their Dreambringers has affected them. I believe that Mark and Phoebe are doing a really good job and I have contributed what little I can but it's no substitute.'

'I think that the new guys being here has helped a little already, I could feel it in my dreams last night' said Mason 'we do need to get things moving though. It's going to be a little weird giving up my link for Max to take over,'

'I understand the transition is always a little strange and this one will be even stranger, I'm sorry' said Sofia.

'It's not your fault. What about the links between the others though? I assume Mahesh's was severed when he died, but are the others still linked to their Eternals and if so how do they release the connection if they aren't here?' asked Mason.

'Well as you know the further away physically you are from your Eternals the weaker the link becomes which is why Dreambringers aren't allowed to be away from their base for longer than a day or two at a time. Therefore, what with the time and distances involved Gina, Blake and Claude's links will be severely weakened, especially as they have also suffered physical and mental trauma. I have learnt through my own contact with the Eternals and from my conversations with Phoebe and Mark that this is the case, and that Mahesh's Eternal is suffering from the loss. Phoebe and Mark have done what they can, and this has averted serious problems, but we must move quickly now. We have a lot of things to work out, but I think we have a good, strong set of new Dreambringers here and with your help Mason I think the transition will go well.'

'Well all we can do is try our best. I do believe it will work out, but I can't help but have a little nagging worry after all we've been through.'

'That's perfectly understandable. So, let's just go over the plan for today and talk a few thinks through before the others get up shall we.'

Clea woke up in her new surroundings, stretched and smiled to herself not phased at all by waking up in a new place. At first, she couldn't remember dreaming at all, then she realised it was because she had dreamt differently. Instead of the little mental movie memories her dreams usually left her with she had awoken to memories of feelings alone. The strongest of these feelings was a feeling of belonging. Her dreams had contained no sights or sounds and no other people and yet she had not felt alone. It was both strange and comforting. She lay enjoying the remembered feelings for a while before getting up and heading for the bathroom.

After showering and dressing Clea headed downstairs. Halfway down the stairs she noticed the front door was open. As she reached the bottom step she noticed a figure sitting on the front doorsteps and as she drew nearer she saw it was Max. He was staring out across the driveway to the woods and smoking one of his occasional little roll ups.

'Good Morning lovey' said Clea as she sat down next to him.

'Morning' replied Max.

'I'm not sure it's good for you sitting on a stone step' said Clea as she felt the slight morning chill of the step through her clothes. 'Why didn't you sit out on the patio to smoke?'

'I could hear people talking in the kitchen' he explained 'and I didn't want to attract attention, I just needed fresh air and a minute on my own.'

'Oh, do you want me to leave you alone then?'

'No, its fine' he said as he put out the tiny stub of cigarette on the step next to him.

'How did you sleep?' she asked

'Pretty good, you?'

'Yes, good thanks. I had weird dreams but woke up feeling good.'

'Me too. It was like I was just floating all night. Not sights or sounds, just floating free but feeling connected, though to what exactly I don't know.'

'I had a similar experience.'

'It's a Dreambringer thing then I guess.'

'I expect so.'

The pair were silent briefly, contemplating. Then Clea broke the silence.

'Shall we join whoever's in the kitchen then and get a cuppa.'

'Sure.'

Mary and Aaron woke up wrapped in each other's arms which is how they had spent the whole night both physically and in the dream world. Like Clea and Max they had experienced nothing visually or aurally, they had just felt the link between themselves as well as a strange general belonging.

They discussed it a little upon waking before taking turns to shower and get ready. They headed downstairs wondering aloud what was in store for them that day.

They met Geth in the hallway. He returned their greetings but did not join in their conversation as he descended the stairs behind them.

Geth was in a strange mood. The frustration he'd felt the day before had dissipated overnight and he'd woken up to memories of vague unexplainable dreams that despite their strangeness had left him feeling calmer than he could ever remember feeling in his life. With everything that had gone on calm is the last thing he'd expected to feel. As he followed the loved-up couple downstairs to the kitchen he decided not to analyse things too much, this feeling of calm was very alien to him but he kind of liked it.

After breakfast Mason and Eddie stayed in the kitchen to clear up and Sofia went with the others to the lounge/art room. Once there she told them all that they should continue with their artwork for an hour or so whilst she made a few arrangements, then she went across the hall to the office. First on her to do list was a call to check on Phoebe and Mark. They were fine and confirmed everything was ready for the next stage of the newbie's induction. That done she then made a call to the Foundation to give them an update and get an update on Claude, Gina and Blake. Then after checking in with the artists she set off to find Mason and Eddie. She found them still in the kitchen sat at the table drinking coffee and chatting.

'All set?' asked Mason when he spied her approaching.

'Yes, everything's ready, but before we make the final plans for today I have the promised update on your friends.'

'Great, how are they doing?'

'They are all obviously receiving the best care the Foundation can offer and are making some progress. It has been explained to Claude what happened to him and that he was not to blame, and I'm told it has calmed him somewhat, but although he is physically well even after these reassurances, he is understandably suffering mentally over what the Soul Stealer made him do.

Gina's arm is healing well as is her head wound, but she is very worried about Blake and has been having anxiety attacks. It was decided late yesterday that they will start to bring Blake out of his coma later today, they will take it slowly so we may not have any real news of his condition until tomorrow. That's all I can tell you for now.'

'Thanks for that Sofia' said Mason 'what about my request to visit them?'

'They will discuss that and get back to us tomorrow,'

'Okay, thanks again, and Mahesh's funeral?'

'The funeral has been put on hold as the Foundation realise that you and possibly your friends would like to be there. For now we have other things to concentrate on, I hope you understand'

'Of course, I get it, and you're right I want to be at my friend's funeral so I'm happy to wait.'

'Good, now we need to concentrate on plans for today. We need to decide what order we are going to send the newbies out to the woods.'

So, they discussed the order for a while and once that was decided Mason set out for the Factory. Usually each of the retiring Dreambringers set out slightly ahead of their new replacement so that the group gradually built up in the Factory until they were all there. In this case Phoebe and Mark were already there and Mason would join them, so they would be a welcoming party for the new recruits as they arrived.

Sofia and Eddie then headed to the lounge/art room. Eddie would stay in the room with the remaining recruits as Sofia took them each out and sent them off.

To keep the process the same as usual in the one way that they could it had been decided that Max would be first on the heels of his predecessor Mason.

When they entered the room, they found everyone hard at work. They were all continuing the work they had started the day before and were finding their work easy and enjoyable. There was a great atmosphere in the room that seemed to be growing in intensity as they worked, and the longer they worked the easier things seemed to flow.

Mary sat in one of the large armchairs with her legs tucked up as she wrote furiously in her notebook. The words were flowing this morning.

Clea sat in a similar position on one of the sofas with paper and colouring pencils scattered around her as she worked on a new embroidery design. This new design was larger and more ambitious than any she'd done before. It was a little complicated and would take a while to perfect on paper before she was ready to sew but she was enjoying every minute of it.

Aaron had an easel set up over near one of the large windows and was working on an oil painting of Clea – much to her delight. He was working from the sketch he'd done after his dream and it felt so good to have the time and space to take his time and perfect his work.

Geth sat at one of the long wooden tables with a large sheet of quality paper he'd found in one of the cupboards laid out in front of him. He was sketching out a large Japanese style dragon design that he hoped to then paint. It was a complicated design, and he was relishing the chance to do something more than flash art.

Max had another of the worktables to himself. He had retrieved the small amount of clay he'd brought with him from his VW Camper and had moulded most of it into a foot high vaguely human shape. He wasn't really sure what it would end up being yet, but his hands kept moulding and shaping and he was confident his vision would clarify soon.

Max was the first to see Sofia and Eddie as they entered the room, but it was Clea who greeted them first. Once she had everyone's attention Sofia began to explain what was going to happen. She told them that they would be continuing with their artwork but that they would be doing it elsewhere, and that it would be the place they spoke about last night, the one they'd have to 'find' themselves.

Sofia explained that the place they were going to find was affectionately called The Factory by Mason and his friends because its where they went to do a lot of their 'work' but that there was nothing factory like about the place.

She then told them they would be going one at a time in the following order – Max first, then Clea, followed by Geth, and Aaron and Mary would go last. When Max heard that he would be the first to go he blanched a little unable to hide his nervousness.

'Don't worry, you'll be fine' Sofia reassured him. She then went on to explain that he would need to take his art supplies with him. This was another deviation from the usual. With more time to plan etc the Factory was usually kitted out by the retiring Dreambringers with supplies for the recruits in advance. Having to carry their stuff with them on this initial trip wasn't ideal especially in Max's case, clay was heavy, so Sofia searched for a solution.

'Is there anything else you can take, just for now?' she asked him 'Only what you're working on looks a bit heavy. It can be brought over for you in an hour or so, but for this initial journey I think it would be best if your burden was lighter.'

'I could take that instead' Max suggested pointing to the much smaller quantity of clay still left in the bag. 'I could try working on something else for a bit, I'm a bit stuck on this larger piece anyway.'

'Okay, sounds good, Eddie will help you get things together then you can meet me on the back patio, and whilst we're doing that if the rest of you could consider what it is you need to take and what can wait and then start to get packed up ready. There is no set timetable for each departure, you just need to be ready for when it's your turn.

Sofia then left them to get organised with Eddies help and headed out to the patio to wait for Max. He arrived clutching his bag of clay and another bag containing some small tools and looking very apprehensive. Sofia tried her best to calm his nerves with reassurances, but he remained tense as she gave his instructions.

'You need to head straight down the lawn' she said pointing straight ahead of them at the sloping sweep of grass 'and then enter the woods at the bottom. The precise point of entry isn't important but once you are amongst the trees you need to head to your right. Again, this doesn't have to be exact, just head a few yards into the trees and them turn right. There will be no discernible path, just walk straight ahead until you come upon a small stream cutting in front of you. You need to jump across the stream, but don't worry its very narrow. Once on the other side of the water you need to follow it deeper into the woods. After a short walk the stream will disappear underground next to a large fallen tree stump. This is as far as I can tell you. I suggest at this point you sit on the tree stump to rest a little and take stock. After this rest you will know what to do.'

'That's it?' his voice was shaky 'I sit on a stump and then I'll know what to do?'

'Yes, that's it. Don't worry, you'll be fine.'

There was nothing else Sofia could tell him. It was all she knew herself. Her link with the Eternals was in mind only she would never be able to find the Factory herself. The directions she'd given him had been given to her by Mason. It was up to Max now. If he truly was Mason's successor, he would find the Studio.

'Okay, off you go then' she said feeling like a mother leaving her child at the school gate on his first day of school.

Max hesitated, looked like he was going to say something but changed his mind and then set off down the sloping lawn. Sofia watched him until he entered the trees then turned and went into the house. She paused in the kitchen to send a quick text message to Mason to let him know Max was on his way before joining the others to wait. Mason would text her when Max arrived at the Studio and it was therefore time to send Clea. There was no way to estimate how long it would take Max to reach his destination, Mason said that once you knew the way it was only a ten-minute walk though it took a little longer on the first trip but how much longer varied for each person. The wait would be a strain on everyone's nerves, so she hoped it wouldn't be long. If this first one went okay she felt it would give her more confidence that the others would too.

Max was relieved to find that Sofia's directions – as far as they went – were easy to follow and it wasn't long before he found himself sat on the tree stump wondering what to do next. He was breathing a little fast and heavy, partly from the exertion of the walk but mainly from nervousness. He took a few deep breaths in an effort to calm himself and after a couple of minutes, with his breathing returning to normal, he began to look around him.

Trees, that was all he could see, on every side trees and of course the little stream he had followed to this point. Getting to his feet Max began to turn in a small circle as he scrutinised the woodland around him, but as hard as he looked, he could not see any discernible path and definitely no sign of a building of any sort.

Then a strange sensation came over him. At first, he thought he was a little dizzy from turning around but when he stopped turning he didn't feel unsteady or off balance. He stood still and let the sensation wash over him. Part of him wanted to resist the alieness of it, but the urge to welcome it was winning. The sensation had started in his chest as a strange sort of vibration and then had begun to spread throughout his body making his limbs feel rubbery and causing a pleasant sort of light headedness. There was also a sound.

At first, he thought it was just the wind in the trees, but it had a different sort of rhythm, it sounded more like whispered voices, it was like someone was talking to him not using words. Then he began to feel a slight tingling sensation throughout his body but strongest in his hands and feet. These sensations began to intensify and then just as they reached a point verging on intolerable they ceased, the light headedness, the sound, the tingling all gone in a second. Feeling a little wobbly Max took a few steps back and sat back down on the tree stump.

For a minute or two he sat stunned, his mind blank, his eyes seeing but his vision blurred. Then suddenly his vision sharpened, and the surrounding trees came into super clear focus, and then there it was, a path, not in the expected sense, but it was a path he was sure.

Instead of a worn track amongst the soil and greenery on the woodland floor the path appeared to him as a ribbon of fog floating a few inches off the ground. It started about three feet in front of him and wound its way off through the trees over to his left. He stared at it for a bit, half expecting it to disappear. When it didn't he decided there was only one thing to do – follow it.

After a short distance he glanced behind him to see that the path behind him had dissipated, but ahead the ribbon still undulated clearly through the trees.

After a few minutes more walking the strange path led him out of the trees into a small, grassy clearing. Here the ribbon extended from where he emerged into the clearing then circled the edge of the tree line until it came back on itself and joined the ribbon at his feet. So now instead of the ribbon of fog winding through the trees it circled the small clearing.

What now? he thought. There was nothing here but a patch of grass surrounded by trees. Without being conscious of making the decision Max found himself taking a few steps forward so that he was standing in the middle of the clearing. As he stood the semi-circle of trees in front of him began to shimmer. Then they began to move as if there was an unseen force pushing them backwards and over like an invisible machine clearing a path. Instead of falling to the ground however a few feet above ground level they simply disappeared and were replaced by lush grass. And as the last trees fell an amazing sight was revealed. There, at the far end of the now extended clearing stood the most unusual building that Max had ever seen.

The building was made from large, dark grey stone blocks and looked to Max like a circular castle that had been half buried under the grassy ground leaving only the top storey showing. Slowly he began to walk towards it awed by its strange beauty. He reached the large, wooden door of the building and stood taking in the ornate carvings on its surface. Then it was time for another decision – should be knock or try the ornate handle? Before he could decide, a loud clang sounded from the other side of the door and then it began to open. Max's heart hammered in his chest and he tensed ready to run if need be, but then a familiar face appeared in the open doorway.

'Welcome' said Mason, a large, relieved smile on his face 'you made it, well done.'

Sofia gave a little start when her phone gave out its message bleep. She'd been deep in conversation with Clea and had managed to forget to phone watch for at least five minutes. Apologising to Clea for the interruption she swiped her phone and Clea watched the tension visibly leave Sofia's body as she read the message.

'Okay Clea' she then said, 'your turn next.'

Clea set off with a lot more confidence than Max had. This was partly down to her more positive general outlook but she also benefited from the more positive vibes coming from Sofia. The vague directions did not phase her at all and she set off at a fast pace eager to solve the mystery of a secret location.

Clea spent less time at the tree stump than Max had and she embraced the strange sensations when they came more readily. As she followed the ribbon of mist Clea's excitement grew and then when her destination was revealed she felt a jolt of recognition followed by immense joy and relief. The building before her was the one from her dream, its image in her mind the beginning of this exciting adventure. She spent a few minutes studying the carvings on the door, running her hands over those symbols that were now very familiar to her and when Mason opened the door she greeted him with a hug.

'I'm home' she said as she entered.

Sofia smiled as she read the text message. Two passes, now for the next one,
'Come on Geth, it's your turn' she said
'Good luck' said Mary as a reluctant looking Geth stood to follow Sofia.
'Cheers' it was said a little sarcastically, but Mary chose to ignore that being used to Geth's grumpy attitude by now.

After giving Geth the basic directions Sofia heard him mutter 'for fucks sake' under his breath but like Mary she was used to his abrasive nature and took no notice. She watched him trudge slowly down the sloping lawn and she couldn't help but feel a little nervous. Geth wasn't embracing his new life as well as the others and she wasn't sure how he'd react to this test. She had to hope that the link between him and his Eternal was strong enough to overcome his doubts.

Geth found the tree stump at the end of the stream as easily as the others had but instead of sitting on it to rest and contemplate, he gave it a kick before starting to pace backwards and forwards in front of it muttering expletives.

He'd managed to stay calm whilst working on his art, had even enjoyed it but he'd got more and more agitated as he walked through the woods. Now he felt angry. He hated not being in control, not knowing what to expect. He was breathing fast and heavy now and then when a sudden wave of dizziness come upon him, he relented and sat down heavily on the tree stump. Resting his elbows on his knees he put his head in his hands and tried to slow his breathing.

When the strange sensation began, he worried for a minute that he was having a stroke or something and when the whispering noise began he lifted his head to look around him for the source, paranoid suddenly that he was being watched. He saw no-one and then as the sensations intensified, he realised that rather than amping up his agitation they were actually soothing him. He could feel the tension leaving his body despite the growing intensity of the unusual sensations. Then the tingling and whispering were gone. He felt dazed but calm and then when he saw the ribbon of mist winding through the trees, before he could even register what it could be, he was up and following it.

When his destination was revealed to him Geth was relieved. It was just a building, albeit a strange one. It was solid and real, and he could deal with that. And when the big oak door was opened by Mason, he was even more relieved. He almost hugged the guy, but only almost, it wasn't really his style.

Sofia was so relieved to hear of Geth's arrival that she gave a little yelp of delight.
'Everything okay?' asked Aaron
'Couldn't be better' she replied, 'now it's your turn.'
Mary and Aaron managed to set off holding hands even though they were carrying art supplies (mainly for Aaron) making Sofia smile as she watched them go. Then she went back inside to await the last message before she could get on with other plans.

'It's beautiful here' said Mary as the pair followed the stream through the trees.

'Yeah but I bet it's a bit spooky at night'

'It's weird how that works, trees are beautiful with sunlight through their leaves but become threatening without it.'

'Good thing we're doing this in the daylight then.'

When they reached the tree stump, they put their bags down and sat still holding hands. They didn't speak, just waited. As the sensations took hold, they remained silent with only a look passing between them to indicate they were both feeling the same. Their silence continued as they followed the ribbon of mist and was only broken when their destination was revealed to them.

'Wow, that is one unusual house' said Aaron 'if you can call it a house.'

'Looks more like a castle to me' said Mary 'a small, half hidden castle.'

'What do you mean half hidden?'

'I'm not sure, it's just how I see it I guess.'

'Okay, lets go and see who's at home.'

Mason answered the door to the couple and led them inside where their new friends were waiting along with Phoebe and Mark. They greeted Max, Clea and Geth like they'd not seen them for days and they all laughed at themselves. Then Mason introduced the newcomers to Phoebe and Mark before excusing himself for a minute to call Sofia.

'They're all here safe and sound' he said when Sofia answered.

'That's great, I'll update the Foundation and get their view on how best to proceed. I think it might be an idea if you send Phoebe and Mark back here after the others are settled in, with any luck their work is done for the time being but for now at least I think they deserve a break.'

'Sounds good.'

'Keep me posted on our newbies'

'Will do'

'Bye for now'

'Bye'

Returning to the group Mason helped Phoebe and Mark finish showing everyone around. He then explained that all they needed to do now was continue with their artwork and get acclimatised to their new surroundings.

'So that's it?' said Geth 'all this mystery for just another place to do our artwork.'

'For the minute yes. There is more to it but I think you've had enough to deal with today. You just need to relax and indulge in your art, there is a point to it, but I can't reveal all yet.'

Geth didn't look happy with that answer but it was Max who spoke next.

'What about these Eternals then, Sofia talked about us forging a link with them or something, but where are they?'

'All I can say right now is that they are nearby' answered Mason. Max nodded but Geth wasn't so accepting of the answer.

'Typical, more evasiveness' he said with his usual venom but somehow he didn't really feel it. Since he'd entered this new studio the frustration he'd been feeling had started to dissipate. His snide comment had come from habit more than anything.

'I'm sorry Geth, I know it's frustrating but I promise you it won't be long now before you know everything.'

'Okay, whatever' muttered Geth turning away from Mason a little embarrassed now at his negative attitude but not wanting to admit it. He noticed Mary watching him and when he saw the expression on her face he had an uneasy feeling that she could see right through him and knew exactly how he was feeling.

'What are you looking at?' he snapped before he could stop himself. But Mary just smiled and nobody else seemed to be taking any notice so he turned away to hide his embarrassment.

Mason dismissed Geth's little outburst understanding the pressure the man was under.

Nobody else seemed bothered by the lack of information and so as they got on with settling in he took Phoebe and Mark aside to tell them they should go back to the Gateway for a rest. He saw the relief on their faces even though they tried to hide it. They'd done a great job of standing in for him and his unfortunate friends and it must have been exhausting for them, but they were still upbeat and he knew they'd have continued without this break if necessary. They said their goodbyes and set off for the well-earned rest.

With Phoebe and Mark gone and the others getting on with their artwork Mason took himself off to the seating area at the back of the large room and sat on the sofa where he could look over the others and sit and contemplate for a minute.

What he hadn't been able to tell the group of artists was that they were only feet away from the Eternals and were forging their links without being totally aware of it. Mason could sense the Eternals stirring below and the feeling of finally being close to them again himself soothed him. In a few hours, before it got dark, he would send them back to the house whilst he stayed behind for the night so he could communicate with the Eternals both to give them back some of the strength his absence had lost them and to gauge their reactions to the new recruits.

He felt pretty certain that they'd all pass the test and there would be no rejections, but he couldn't know for sure. If all went well tonight the final reveal would happen the next day. His own first meeting with the Eternals was still clear in his memory, you don't forget something so amazing easily. He envied them the new life they'd be embarking on and wondered what sort of life he was headed for. But now wasn't the time for contemplation, now he needed to help get the Eternals strength back up.

Getting up from the sofa he headed towards the workbench where his own equipment was still set up from before all the trouble began. Some of his friend's artwork was still stored in the cupboards around the room, he'd done the unpleasant job of storing them himself recently and he would have to take it all back to the house at some point, but that was a job for later. Now he picked up the half-finished guitar and turning it over in his hands inspected his own work. He'd felt it was his best work the last time he'd worked on it and now, looking at it he still felt the same. With a little luck he'd get to finish it before he had to leave the Gateway for good, And so he set about his work and was soon engrossed and at peace for the first time since the trouble began.

Samuel and Dorothea had spent their time at the cottage so far getting acclimatised to their new surroundings and establishing a routine. Their new job as Custodians was a demanding one, especially after the drama they had just gone through and it was taking some adjusting to. The cottage was very alien to them.

For their predecessors the Deacons it had become a home and they had made it their own over the years and although their personal belongings and knick-knacks had been taken away by the Foundation the cottage still felt like someone's home, and that someone wasn't Samuel or Dorothea.

Their new routine was easier to get their heads around but was still demanding. Being a Custodian to the Soul Stealer was a very strange job even by Dreambringer standards. Their charge didn't need much physical maintenance as it did not eat, drink or defecate, therefore their job was purely mental vigilance and monitoring.

The first thing they'd had to do was put up a mental barrier around the Soul Stealer to prevent it from influencing anyone who may by chance wander nearby. The skills needed to perfect this protection came from a combination of their innate Dreambringer talent which had been honed over their years in the job together with specific mental training they had received after their time as a Dreambringer had come to an end.

The training was intense and so only those with the strongest Dreambringer talent were chosen to take it on. Once a Dreambringers time was over they no longer had a direct link with a single Eternal so it meant having to learn to make a strong dream-link with as many Eternals as they could in order to draw on the Eternals strength to boost their Dreambringer talents to a level where they could contain the Soul Stealer. It was difficult to achieve mainly because it was a reversal of what they were used to. As a Dreambringer they worked to give strength to the Eternals but as a Custodian they needed to draw on the Dreambringer given strength of the Eternals. Dorothea had been an excellent student, second only in the current standby Custodians to Samuel who had excelled at it which is why he had been allowed to follow his research into the Soul Stealer.

Once this initial 'barrier' was established it was the Custodians job to maintain it and to monitor the Soul Stealer. Firstly, the monitoring entailed paying a short, daily visit to the creature to check for any physical changes. Over recent years there had been very few but it was felt necessary to keep it up.

After the initial few days this job only required one person but after the recent events Samuel and Dorothea had decided to make it a two-person job. Only one person needed to go into the room with the creature so whilst one went inside to do the check the other would stay outside for extra security. The reason for this extra precaution was not because they thought the creature might harm them but because of the circumstances of the escape. Rita Deacon had been doing the daily check alone when she had suffered a stroke leaving her charge free to flee.

The rest of the monitoring was done remotely and was a lot more difficult because it was mental monitoring.

Over the years various sets of Custodians had tried to understand and communicate with their captive, to find out exactly what they were dealing with. They would try to reach it through telepathy, but little had been achieved. The creature's thoughts were readable in as much as anyone trying would be met by a wall of anger, hate and resentment tinged with confusion and self-pity. But any attempt at actual communication always met with failure. Many had tried to reason with It, to tell It they could help if only It would comply, but with no success. It was frustrating work and however enthusiastic a new Custodian started out they were always beaten down eventually by failure.

Samuel was sure that over the years the Custodians tired of trying and kept their monitoring to a minimum and who could blame them, but he was determined to get results. His research and training had been cut a little short by the escape but he was convinced if anyone could make a breakthrough it would be him.

Samuel and Dorothea had kept their monitoring light to start with giving the creature time to calm down and themselves time to read up on the Deacon's notes to see if they held any insights. They hadn't so far and now the reading was nearly done Samuel planned to make his first major attempt at communication the next day. The wait had been frustrating but necessary and so he was very much looking forward to it especially as he intended to break with tradition and do it face to face.

Dorothea had taken a little persuading and had insisted on checking with the Foundation first, but Samuel had been given free reign by the bosses, after all this is what he'd been training for and after recent events his work was now high priority rather than just the whim of a talented Dreambringer.

After all the extra training and research he had done Samuel had come up with a very different approach to the current confinement and monitoring protocol. In his opinion a more permanent solution needed to be found because if the creature remained as it was now it would always be a problem, one that could possibly even evolve into something more dangerous and/or put the secret work of the Somnium Foundation in jeopardy. He believed there was another way; he wanted to understand and help the creature, to find out why it was so hostile and work to change that. This would be the starting point and his level of success would then dictate where the plan went from there. He had the last of the Deacon's note's to go through and then he intended to have an early night and get a good nights dreaming in before facing the Soul Stealer in the morning and putting his plan into action.

'Anyone want a cup of tea?'

Clea's loud voice cut through the silence startling the other artists. Realising what she'd done Clea apologised but they all laughed it off making fun of themselves for being so wrapped up in their work. They all took her up on her offer and deciding to take a break they all joined her in the seating area to chat whilst the kettle boiled.

Noticing the time Mason told them that after their little tea break they'd only have about another hour and a half before they needed to start packing up as they'd need to set off back to The Gateway before it got dark. They were a little disappointed that they would have to finish for the day soon as they'd all been enjoying a particularly productive session, but no-one fancied walking through the woods in the dark so they didn't protest.

Mary had written two new poems earlier in the session and she was pleased with them. They were in the same vein as the ones she'd written after her dreams of her new friends. They expressed the extra knowledge she had recently acquired about other Dreambringers. This is what she had written;

Soulhealer of Dreams
He is the Soulhealer of Dreams,
Creating sounds that heal,
Music that casts joy spells,
And Conjures peace.
He has no power once you wake,
So cannot ease your earthly ills,
But as you dream,
He binds your wounds,
Enchanting and soothing those souls in pain.

Dreamwishers
They are the Dreamwishers,
Working magic in your dreams.
Showing you your heart,
Bringing you what you want and need.
They will sing to you of hope,
That you may carry when awake,
Giving you in dreams,
What your waking life cannot bring.

The poems had come easily with very few amendments needed and so she had finished them very quickly and had sat for a little while at a bit of a loss what to do next. But then after glancing back through her notebook she'd discovered some notes she'd written weeks ago about an idea for a novel. She hadn't written much, just the germ of an idea, but now looking at it again that little germ had started to grow.

She had spent the rest of the session making copious notes as the ideas began to flow thick and fast almost filling her notebook, she'd have to check the cupboards for paper soon at the rate she was going. She'd thought about writing a book for so long now, but her ideas had never gone beyond a few little notes, so she was very happy with this sudden flood of inspiration. As she drank her tea and chatted with the others her head buzzed with words that she'd need to get down on paper ASAP.

Geth was getting on well with his drawing. It had started out as a large but quite simple design, but after starting on it that morning it had grown in complexity and become a very intricately detailed piece. He didn't know where the inspiration had come from but he was enjoying the freedom of it and the luxury of being able to take his time. He was looking forward to the painting part but he still had a way to go until then, besides he didn't have the paint anyway. He'd have to talk to someone about that, it would be awful to get the drawing finished and not have the paint ready to carry his work on.

Another artist running low on paint was Aaron. His portrait of Clea was coming on well. The abundance of time he had meant he could paint it in his favourite ultra-realism style and he was relishing every minute of it. He felt this could be his best work yet.

He had felt strangely guilty earlier in the day that his finest work would not be of Mary. The portrait he'd painted of Mary after the dreams had been very good, he knew that, but he'd felt the need to finish that one quickly so had not been able to do it in his favourite style and so he'd felt that maybe he should have done another portrait of her first. He'd voiced his concern to Mary but she'd reassured him he was doing the right thing. She'd told him his portrait of her would always be special and that he'd have plenty of time to paint her again in whatever style he wanted, but for now he needed to finish the work his dreams had given him, he needed to portray all of the new Dreambringers, get them all on canvas, then when that was done he could paint her again. And so he had carried on guilt free.

His progress had been wonderfully slow, so he still had a way to go before he ran out of paint totally, but a couple of colours were running low. He'd checked all the cupboards here and back at the Gateway for extra paint as he'd never been able to afford a large stock, but he'd not found any. He wasn't sure how to approach it but he'd have to find out how to get more supplies soon.

Max was working with a smaller amount of clay than he was used to but he was enjoying the challenge of taking his work in a new direction. Instead of a bust or a full body study of the human form he was working on a small, intricately detailed scale model of the place where he was working. His very accurate depiction of the unusual stone building was finished and he was now adding a few trees around the edge of the round base it was mounted on.

Although this new style of work was challenging Max had found that his approach to it had been a lot calmer and controlled than his usual manic style. He knew that once he had more supplies he would most likely revert back to his old ways, but for now he was enjoying this new way of working with clay.

Clea had decided to break for a cup of tea after having a little revelation of her own. After stopping to take a look at her work so far it had come her. Her design resembled the pattern in the iron gate at the entrance to The Gateway and then more recently she had seen the same vine like pattern on the door to the Factory. With the design almost finished she now needed to decide about what material to use, what garment to make from that material, what colours to use and where to place the design. It was a large design so it needed some thought and planning but there was no rush, it would all come to her in time.

Glancing around him at the new Dreambringers as they drank tea and chatted Mason could feel the positivity emanating from them all and it made him happy. He'd had a great session too, his guitar was looking good, a real beauty if he said so himself and it had felt so good getting back to his work. He had missed this so much, the feeling of working at your art was always good, but in this place, so near to the Eternals influence it was always even more intensely productive and fulfilling. These five artists didn't quite understand why their work today was so special, but they would soon learn why and how this was the case.

When the tea break was over they all got back to work. Mason set an alarm on his phone knowing how easy it would be to get carried away and lose track of time. His work would carry on but the others would need to finish for the day soon.

After an hour when Mason's alarm went off he told them to all start packing up. They were a little reluctant but knew it had to be done.

Before they set off for The Gateway Mason gave them no directions telling them they wouldn't need them and they'd accepted his word showing their growing faith and that they were 'accepting the weird' as Clea liked to say. But now it was time for him to pay a visit to the Eternals to see how they were doing.

It seemed a little strange walking down the stone stairs to the Eternals abode after being away for what seemed a long time, but once amongst them he felt at home. He communed with them for a while, learning that they were pleased with the newbies so far. He could sense the change in them since he had last visited. They were thankfully a lot stronger and happier. He made a quick trip upstairs to get what he needed before heading back down to spend the night with the Eternal Dreamers.

CHAPTER 19

FORGING A LINK

They are in the woods. Gathered around the carved oak door. They each place a hand on the symbol that belongs to them. They feel warmth and light shines between their fingers. Suddenly they are through the door. Before them in the floor a set of stone steps lead downwards. They descend the steps to the light that awaits them.

All five of the new Dreambringers remember the dream when they awake only as far as the light shining through their fingers. They know there was more to the dream, that they learnt something, but none of them remember what it was.

Aaron and Mary try discussing it but find nothing to discuss. None of them are really bothered that they can't remember, they sense that whatever knowledge they learnt is still with them, inside somewhere. They leave the dream behind and start their day.

Phoebe and Mark awake in their now shared spare room after a nice, long, dream filled sleep feeling re-fuelled. They have enjoyed their time at The Gateway, it's been different, exciting, challenging and exhausting but they wouldn't have missed it for the world.

Eddie awakes from a dream filled night feeling better than he has in a long time. The memories of his dreams are fleeting and vague, but it doesn't bother him. The feeling they leave is one of belonging and that's enough.

Sofia awakes feeling relieved, her communes with the Eternals during a dream filled night having confirmed that the newbies have all passed the tests so far. Things are looking up at the Gateway.

Mason awakes feeling refreshed and happy and rises to go and prepare for the newbies next, important visit.

Breakfast is a busy affair. Clea and Mary cook the breakfast, and everyone is happy.

When breakfast is over and everything is cleared and put away the group convene to the lounge/art room and once everyone is seated Sofia lays out the plans for the day.

'Eddie, Phoebe, Mark and I will stay here at the house. I have calls to make and things to arrange. I will find out what the Foundations plans are for you two now' directed at Phoebe and Mark 'but for now you can work here or just chill out if you like. And Eddie I understand from a few comments people have made to me that a trip out for art supplies is called for, and I believe we also need to stock up on food. So could you please check with everyone and make a list of what they need and then check what we need food wise that would be great.

For our five new recruits it's another trip out to the Factory so if you could first give Eddie your list of requirements and then get the supplies you have ready to take with you today. The fact that some of you are low on supplies won't be a problem today as your artwork will play less of a part in what happens. Again, we will ask that you all make the journey separately. We have to make sure that you can each find your way there again. I'm confident none of you will have a problem but it will be different this time, a little less magical and more instinctual. You can decide amongst you what order you go in and Mason will be there to greet you. You need to leave about thirty minutes between each of you departing. Does anyone have any questions?

Nobody did.

'Okay, good so let's get going then. I will be in the office if anyone needs me.'

With her instructions given Sofia left them all to it and headed to the office to begin her own work. She needed to seek some wisdom and advise from senior members of the Foundation. The newbies would meet the Eternal Dreamers today and all being well stronger links would be formed, but in order to link to their Eternals properly a ceremony would have to be performed.

This ceremony was usually a simple affair, but normally both the retiring Dreambringers and their replacements took park. In this case however, four out of the five retirees could not be present, therefore she needed to seek advise on how best to proceed without them. It was a totally new situation, so no-one could know exactly what to do but together they should be able to come up with a plan. Only time would tell if they could pull this off without the missing Dreambringers.

Having spent the night close to the Eternals Mason awoke feeling rested and strong. He could tell that the Eternals had benefited too.

After a trip to the bathroom to freshen up he made a call to Sofia to check how things were going. She told him everything was fine and that the first of the newbies would be on their way shortly and he told her everything would be ready for them. She also gave him an update on Blake. He'd been successfully brought out of his coma and was doing well. There appeared to be no serious brain damage, but he was a little groggy so would be monitored carefully for a few days to be totally sure there were no deficits.

Mason was understandably relieved and could now concentrate on the day ahead. After the call he began to tidy up and prepare for the first arrival. He was feeling a little apprehensive about what needed to be achieved today but it was the days to follow that concerned him more, he knew Sofia was on the case regarding the ceremony 'problem', so he tried to push it to the back of his mind and concentrate on the job ahead.

Eddie had noted everyone's requirements and now he was in the kitchen turning the jotted notes into an organised shopping list. Once this was done, he popped into the office to let Sofia know he was leaving before heading out the door. There had been one little snag in that they'd realised his van was still with Samuel and Dorothea but Max has suggested he use the VW Camper and so he headed for the strange vehicle eager to get going. It felt good to be doing something useful and normal.

As Eddie was setting off for the shops the new recruits were deciding which order they would head out to the Factory in. Clea wanted to go first, she felt fidgety and excited and was eager to set off. No one had a problem with that so that was agreed. Aaron and Mary were enjoying a chat with Phoebe and Mark and so were happy to go last so they could continue their conversation. So that left Geth and Max. Neither of them expressed a strong preference so Clea made the decision for them. Max would go second and Geth third and so with the decisions made Clea went to inform Sofia before setting off.

Clea walked down the sloping lawn with a spring in her step and no doubts in her mind. Today was going to be a good day, she could feel it. She was starting to feel at home in this amazing place and the dream she'd had that morning had only cemented her growing feeling of belonging.

She followed the stream as before and arrived at the tree stump. This time no ribbon of fog appeared, but after gazing around her for a minute or two she knew which way to go. It was like she had taken this journey hundreds of times before and the way through the trees was permanently implanted in her mind.

There was no dramatic tree felling moment this time, she just found her way through the trees to the clearing, and there it was, the strangely wonderful stone building. As she approached, she did notice a slight shimmer in the air between herself and the building but she walked forward and through it with no hesitation feeling a tingling all over as she passed through the shimmer. It was a strange but pleasant feeling, like she had passed through some sort of invisible barrier. She continued unphased by it and stood before the beautifully carved door. She didn't knock, she just admired the carvings as she waited until Mason opened the door. He invited her in and led her to the middle of the room. He took her bag of supplies from her and placed it on the nearest workbench, then stood before her.

'I need you to find something' he said 'it is near to you but hidden. Please take your time, concentrate and follow the signs that you are given.'

Clea nodded her understanding and Mason backed away to stand a short distance from her. She took a deep breath and began to scan the vast space around her. So, what was it she needed to find? In normal circumstances she would assume it was an object and begin looking in the many storage cupboards, but this wasn't normal circumstances and she instinctively knew it wasn't an object she was supposed to find.

So, after discounting the cupboards where should she start? The answer was obvious really, start from the doorway. She walked to the door and then turned to face back into the room. She was on the right track she could feel it. She took a few steps to her right and stopped, no, that wasn't right. She backtracked to the door and then took a few steps left, yes, that felt better. It was almost like that child's game Hot or Cold where you searched for something and the person who had hidden it told you if you were nearer or further from it by saying hot or cold. But in this case, there was no one telling her this verbally, it was more of a feeling, almost like a physical sensation of hot and cold.

As she'd walked right, she'd felt cold and now stepping left she felt warmer. She took it slow, moving a step at a time now, letting the feeling guide her feet. After each step she looked around her, her eyes seeking something, but what. Then, as she took her next step she looked down and something caught her eye. It was like a quick flash of light seen out the corner of her eye and then it was gone but stepping forward a little to the right she thought she saw something, yes, there on the floor. Taking one more step she looked down in front of her feet, and there it was, etched faintly in one of the dark slate paving slabs, a symbol, her symbol.

'I've found it' she said quietly, then looking up and finding Mason where he stood near the middle of the room 'what do I do now?'

Mason smiled at her 'Open it' he said.

Clea frowned and looked down at her feet. Open what? She looked around for the obvious means of opening something – a handle or a latch maybe – she couldn't see a handle or anything like that but she did notice that either side of her symbol were etched the other symbols belonging to her friends. Inching forward a little in her search her toes touched the edge of her symbol and the curve of the outer circle where her foot touched brightened as if a light was being shone underneath it. Clea moved her foot further onto the symbol and more of it lit up. Realisation dawned, and she glanced up at Mason who smiled and nodded.

Reassured that her strange instinct was correct she moved forward so that she stood with both feet on her symbol. Beneath her feet the whole symbol lit up. She felt a slight vibration through her feet and heard a brief grating sound. Then several of the large slate floor slabs before her dropped down a few inches before sliding back underneath where she stood. And now instead of a solid slate floor before her there was a set of stone steps leading downwards into darkness. She felt a jolt or recognition and gasped as the forgotten part of her dream came back to her. She'd seen this stone staircase in her dream. Should she descend the steps? She glanced up to find Mason walking towards her.

'Not yet' he said 'soon, but not yet.'

She nodded her understanding but couldn't help taking another look down the steps and wonder what was at the bottom.

'Well done' said Mason 'you passed the last test.'

He then told her to step away from the staircase and explained that the hatch would close automatically in a few minutes.

Max embarked on his second trip into the woods with a lot less confidence than Clea had. He had visions on himself wandering lost in the woods for hours, he'd always had a terrible sense of direction. He was therefore very relieved and astounded when his instincts lead him to the Factory without any problems.

He had a little wobble when he noticed the shimmering veil in the air just beyond the trees though. He thought it was his glasses at first and took them off the wipe them clean on his t-shirt. When the shimmer was still there however, he managed to convince himself it couldn't be a bad thing as he obviously needed to pass through it to get to the studio and he was sure someone would have warned him of anything dangerous. He practically ran the few steps to get through it though and was pleased when he made it through with only a slight tingling feeling to show for it. At the door he was warmly greeted by Mason and Clea and he felt safe again. Until Mason explained what he had to do that was. Or rather didn't explain. What the hell was he supposed to find?

It took him a little longer than it had Clea to realise it wasn't an object her was looking for. He went to one of the cupboards first and stood holding the doors open gazing at the contents uncomprehendingly. Then something connected, his brain seemed to change gear with an almost audible click. He walked to the door and stood facing inward as Clea had done, and as with Clea his instincts took him left.

He moved quicker and more furtively than she had however and went as far as the left-hand corner before backtracking more slowly. He found his symbol, though he was unknowingly facing the wrong way, and like Clea on Mason's prompting he accidently stood on the symbol whilst looking for an opening giving a little start as it lit up.

He gave another, bigger start at the sound of the moving slates and then turned to discover the descending staircase. He was less eager than Clea had been to descend the steps into darkness so was glad when Mason told him he didn't have to yet. He was equally relieved to hear that he had passed the last of the tests even though he didn't quite understand what those tests had been.

Geth barely registered the shimmer in the air as he strode purposefully towards the stone building. His logical mind assumed it was some sort of play of sunlight and he dismissed the tingling sensation as a reaction to his coming from the cool shade of the trees into the sunlit clearing. He nearly lost his new-found calm however when Mason told him he had to find something without telling him what it was. What the fuck was that supposed to mean? But Clea sensing one of his outbursts managed to calm him with a few reassuring words and a warm smile.

To start with Geth wandered aimlessly amongst the worktables glancing around him. Then he stopped and seemed to stiffen as if he was listening to something the others couldn't hear. Then, like Max and Clea before him he went to the door and from there turned to his left. He paced backwards and forwards a few times making the mistake of looking up and not down before finally looking down and finding the symbols.

'Fuck me' he exclaimed as the staircase was revealed. And when Mason informed him that he'd passed the tests he looked unimpressed although what he really felt was relieved.

Mary and Aaron held hands once again as they strolled through the woods enjoying the beautiful surroundings. When they reached the shimmering barrier, they stopped and chatted about what it could be.

'I think it's some sort of force field' said Aaron 'to keep unwanted visitors out.'

'Yeah, and if you're bad it zaps you when you touch it' added Mary.

Despite laughing about their not completely serious suggestions Aaron and Mary were a little nervous of the see-through barrier, so Aaron volunteered to pass through first. After walking through with no ill effects, he was tempted to fake a bad reaction as a joke but decided that would be cruel and inappropriate, so he just told her the truth, that it felt a little strange but it was safe. So, Mary passed thorough and they continued to their destination.

Watching the strange hunt for the fourth time Mason felt proud of his new friends. They'd passed these tests just as easily as him and his friends had years ago but under much more stressful circumstances.

Aaron and Mary chatted together as they searched, working as a team. They followed the same route as their predecessors dismissing the idea of the search being for an object and then starting their search from the door. They discovered their symbols sooner than Max and Geth but not as quickly as Clea. When the slates began to move Mary gave out a little squeal and grabbed for Aaron's hand. They glanced down the steps and then looked at each other.

'It's like our dream right?' said Mary.

'Yeah, the bit we couldn't remember' agreed Aaron.

'What's down there do you think?'

Aaron shrugged but before he could think of a possible answer Mason interrupted.

'Come and join the others' he said, 'you'll find out what's down there soon enough.' And as they stepped away informed them that they had passed the tests.

'Yay for us' said Mary making them all smile.

Now they had all passed the test it was almost time for them to meet their Eternal Dreamers, but first Mason had to prepare them a little. So he gathered them on the sofa's so he could talk them through a few things.

'Okay guys' he began before having to pause and clear his throat, he was a little nervous 'It's finally time for you to find out pretty much all the answers to your questions. The next stage of your induction is about to happen and it's a very important one. I need to explain that your solo trips here and the little search you have just been on were all tests to see if you were fit to continue. You may feel that I'm stating the obvious or you may not have seen these things as tests, either way I apologise for any deception and assure you that it was necessary' he paused to gauge their reactions and wait for any comebacks, but no-one spoke and none of them looked unhappy so he continued.

'This building is very special; it is pretty old – on the outside at least – and it has a big secret. Its more than just a great place for you artists to work. Because of this secret it is well protected, for starters there is the obvious protections of it being on private land which is surrounded by a boundary wall and by the entrance gate controlled by a state-of-the-art security system. This keeps pretty much everyone who shouldn't be here out. But just in case someone does get into the grounds there is another level of security, and this one is much less conventional. As I'm sure you will have all seen today this building is surrounded by what we refer to as the 'Shimmer Wall' their nods of agreement showed him that they knew what he meant so he continued 'This Shimmer Wall is a mental rather that a physical barrier, only Dreambringers see it as just a shimmer in the air, anyone else will see it as a dense, unpassable section of trees and undergrowth that hide the building from their view and prevent them venturing nearer. So now you're thinking who put up this barrier, how and why? Well the who and the why are basically the same answer, that answer being the Eternal Dreamers and the why is because this is their home.' He let this information sink in for a minute noting that he had everyone's rapt attention. 'The existence of the Eternal Dreamers must be kept secret from all but a special few because despite the good they do there will always be people who would want to exploit or harm them. Now you are some of those chosen few and you have proved your worth so their secret dwelling has been made known to you. You are about to meet your Eternal Dreamers' he paused again and this time someone spoke.

'So I take it that the staircase we all had to find leads down to where they live' said Geth.

'Yes, they live in the lower chamber of this building.'

'The half-hidden castle' said Aaron quietly to Mary who nodded 'that's what you meant; you knew on some level that there was an underground part to the castle.'

'Yeah, and you sort of guessed about the shimmer wall thing' said Mary.

'Did you have a question?' Mason asked them not having heard what they said.

'No, sorry mate its fine' said Aaron 'we were just talking, sorry for being rude.'

'No its fine' Mason assured them.

'I have a question' said Clea

'Yes?'

'Are we going down there now?'

'In a few minutes, yeah, but I need to prepare you a little first. The Eternal Dreamers are very special creatures the like of which you have never come across before. I know that strangeness can be frightening but I can assure you that you have nothing to fear from them.

Once you meet them you will know this, but I want to alleviate any fear you may initially feel as much as I can. The Eternals do not communicate through speech but they will communicate with you. Through your dreams and the artwork you have done whilst here you have already forged a link to them and this will only grow. You are linked to them all but each of you will feel a stronger connection to one particular Eternal. We will all go down together, no more individual trips, you and your Eternals are now a team. I'll give you a few minutes to prepare yourselves then we'll make our way to the entrance.'

A few minutes later Mason gathered the new recruits near to where their symbols were etched into the floor. Then from one of the wooden storage chests along the wall under the window he produced LED lanterns which he turned on and handed out one for each person. He then lined the newbies up so that they each stood behind their own Dreambringer symbol where it was carved in the slate floor.

'When I give the signal' he instructed 'all step forward so that you are standing on your symbols. The hatch will open and then I will lead you down.'

The signal was given, the steps were taken, and the hatch opened. The staircase was only wide enough to accommodate two people side by side so Mason took the lead, followed by Max and Clea, then Aaron and Mary with Geth bringing up the rear. They descended slowly, the powerful LED lights adequately lighting the way.

As their heads went below floor level the staircase began to spiral to the right, then after a hundred and eighty degreed turn the staircase straightened out again continuing down to finally terminate at a small stone chamber with a wooden door set in the roughhewn stone wall facing them. It was a smaller, unadorned version of the door upstairs.

'I need you to wait here for a few minutes' said Mason as he opened the door, 'the hatch above will close itself soon so don't be alarmed by the sound and if you really do get panicked that lever there opens it again okay.'

The lever he was referring to was set into the wall on the right-hand side of the door. It was old looking, made of iron and set in a vertical slot carved in the stone wall.

In the moment before Mason closed the door behind him all the newbies were able to glimpse of what was inside was darkness. They waited nervously, the clang of the closing hatch making them all jump even after the warning, until he reappeared after the promised few minutes.

'Okay, come on in' he said opening the door wide.

The chamber they entered was about half the size of the rooms upstairs, but it was also circular, with the walls, floor and ceiling all roughhewn in stone. It was a marvellous feat of engineering; someone had basically carved a perfect circle into solid rock.

Dotted all around the wall from floor to the high ceiling were numerous stone shelves and recesses of various sizes. These shelves and recesses contained works of art of all kinds – paintings, sculptures, books and any number of other weird and wonderful artistic creations. These treasures were illuminated by small but powerful LED lights dispersed amongst them. Their light, plus that from the lantern that Mason had placed near the centre of the room gave the stone chamber a soft, comforting glow.

In the centre of the room there is a circular depression carved into the stone floor. It is three feet in circumference with the depth gradually deepening from the outside in until it's about a foot deep in the middle but the spiral pattern carved into the stone gives the optical illusion that the circle is in fact deeper. Arranged around this central circle are six rectangles. Five are large rectangular blocks made of stone. They are each two foot high, seven foot long and are three foot wide at one end narrowing to two and a half foot at the other. On top of each block of stone there is a fitted wooden frame encasing padded purple velvet cushioning. The sixth is just a rectangle of equal length and width carved into the stone floor.

The six rectangles are set in a radiating pattern reminiscent of a clock face with their narrowest end nearest the centre circle.

The five stone rectangles each have a pattern etched into the side at their wider end, or 'head' but the rectangle carved into the floor is blank.

On the floor at the head of each stone rectangle there is a slightly raised stone circle about a foot in diameter and like its adjacent stone rectangle the sixth circle is a plain flat circle carved into the floor. Each of the other five stone circle has a pattern etched into the middle of it.

The symbols etched in the stone rectangles are the Dreambringers symbols and the patterns etched on the stone circles represent the inhabitants of the amazing chamber, The Eternal Dreamers. They are the symbols depicted in the Iron Gate and on the carved oak door, the flower/leaf like symbols at the ends of the vines. Each one subtly different.

The newbies aren't really taking in these symbols right now though because although the chamber itself is an amazing sight something else has grabbed their attention; the inhabitants of the chamber are even more amazing than their surroundings.

They stand, or rather float, one at the wider end of each of the stone rectangles.

The Eternal Dreamers.

Each figure is roughly seven feet tall and has a vaguely human shape with an elongated head and limbs. But it is the substance they are made of that is harder to take in because they are definitely not made of flesh and blood.

They are not solid, yet not transparent, they seem to be made of smoke and light. Their white, ghostly shape is constantly shifting with little specks of white light moving within swirls of white mist. There is no definition to them, no facial features. They have an aura of soft, white light and are in constant but gentle motion, ever changing and mesmerising to behold. As they gently move and change shape slightly there is a hint of what could be flowing hair or a delicate hand, but it is all fleeting.

Their new Dreambringers stare at them in awe all lost in their own thoughts as they try to comprehend what they are seeing.

'*I should be afraid*' Mary thinks '*but they are so beautiful*' and she knows they won't hurt her.

Max is thinking along similar lines but wonders if he could touch them and how they would feel if he did.

Aaron thinks they look cool, like ghosts or aliens.

Clea thinks they are the most beautiful things she has ever seen and senses their goodness.

And Geth doesn't know what to think, his logical mind can't comprehend something so different, but despite this he feels no alarm or fear.

Watching them to gauge their reactions Mason can't help but remember his own first meeting with the Eternals, how he felt awe and astonishment but never fear of worry. After the initial shock he had felt surprisingly calm and judging by the looks on their faces his new friends were feeling the same way.

No one had moved or spoken for quite some time. Mason stayed silent too, he knew what would happen next and he could sense it was going to happen any second now.

And then there it was, all five of the transfixed humans suddenly jolted like they'd received a minor electric shock. He felt what they did too but he was used to it, and what they'd felt was the first real communication from the Eternal Dreamers. It was an unnerving but not entirely unpleasant feeling. It started with that little jolt like an electric shock to the chest, then a little flash of light in the mind followed by a light and tingly feeling all over. Then came a low, thrumming sound which they heard, or rather felt, not through their ears but from within them. They had all experienced something similar before, in the woods when they were guided to the Eternals home, but this was more intense. Mason was pleased to note that although they all looked confused no-one looked worried.

Then the sound/feeling changed, and they began to detect patterns and understood that these patterns were like words but not words. They were receiving a message and although the message was not in words as such they all understood it. And the message was;

'Welcome, please join us.'
The Eternal Dreamers were speaking to them without voices.

As the new Dreambringers were communicating with their Eternals for the first time Samuel was making his first attempt at real communication with the Soul Stealer. Dorothea had found a comfy garden chair and had stationed herself outside the fake garage where it was her job to keep her Custodian protective shield strong so that the Soul Stealers mind was contained and to protect Samuel as best she could as in order to do what he intended he would have to drop his own shield. It was risky but Samuel had studied and trained for this for years and his confidence in his abilities reassured Dorothea.

And so Samuel entered the creature's abode alone.

When he entered the Soul Stealer was laying on Its back on the bed. It was a position that according to the monitoring records It spent a lot of time in. Its eyes were shut and it was hard to tell if It was sleeping or awake. Its faintly glowing hands were resting down by its sides. It made no sign that It was aware of Samuel as he sat in the only chair in the room, but Samuel knew that this was normal. He also knew that those that had gone before him had preferred it this way noting that on the occasions when the creature had been more active and had Its eyes open the sight had been disconcerting. Samuel felt differently, he would have preferred to see It in Its full glory as it were. Having glimpsed It that way when they had captured It he had been fascinated and wished he'd had the chance to study It more.

Samuel had decided that he would try to communicate verbally first. He didn't expect the creature to answer, It had never spoken once in all the years that anyone was aware of, he just wanted to gauge if there was any visible reaction to his voice and to explain what he was doing despite not knowing if it would even understand.

'Hello' he kept his voice gentle, but clear 'my name is Samuel Raven. I am an ex Soul Healer of Dreams and I am now one of your new Custodians. I know that you have been through a traumatic experience recently and that I may have contributed to your trauma, but it was necessary for your safety as well as others, not that I expect you to see it that way.'

There was no sign at all that the creature could hear or understand him but he continued.

'I know that you must have suffered a lot over the years and I want to help ease your suffering, but in order to do so I need you to help me, I need you to co-operate with me. I understand this may be hard for you but I ask you to please try.' Still no response, but he hadn't really expected any, so he continued doggedly on.

'I know you cannot speak so I'm going to try another way, one that I'm sure you are more comfortable with. I am going to use my mind to try to communicate with you in a similar way that I would communicate with an Eternal Dreamer. I'd really like it if you could meet me halfway.'

Now Samuel prepared himself for his first attempt to connect with the creature. He was a little nervous, but mostly excited. It was finally time for him to put his years of training to the test.

First, he put the Dreambringer talent that his original Eternal Dreamer had honed within him into use by relaxing his body and opening himself up to receive communication. He then let his thoughts flow freely, sending them outwards to be received by anyone with the talent to 'hear'. He sensed Dorothea nearby monitoring him and giving him support.

Concentrated harder he searched for the mind of the creature. And then there it was, the mind of the Soul Stealer.

As Samuel had expected from what he knew from his studies the creature's telepathic thoughts were strong but incoherent. It wasn't relaxed and therefore it wasn't controlling and projecting its thoughts into words for others to understand, it was just emitting undirected emotional noise.

Now Samuel brought his extra training to the fore. He concentrated all his higher-level telepathic skills on the swirling mess of the creatures chaotic emotions in an effort to make some sense of them. He didn't try for full comprehension, not yet, but instead aimed to isolate specific emotions within the turmoil. It was hard going be he persisted. He detected that there was one emotion stronger than the others so he concentrated on that first. With a little effort it came to him. Anger. The creature was angry, well that wasn't really news, its actions were all about anger. And so he probed deeper, what else was the creature feeling that would be more telling. There, another emotion, what was it? Frustration. Okay, very akin to the anger. What else? There was something there, underlying the anger. He almost had it, wait, yes there it was. Self-pity. And then he caught a hint of something else. Then he had it. Confusion. So the creature felt angry, frustrated, confused and sorry for itself, he could work with that.

Samuel now switched tactics a little and instead of reading the creatures emotions he attempted to project his own. He knew that in the past the creature would have picked up on the negative emotions of those around it. Over time the creature had triggered fear, disgust and anger within those around it and in later years indifference had been added. But Samuel felt none of these, what he felt, and therefore what he wanted to convey to the creature was curiosity and compassion. Along with these emotions Samuel tried hard to communicate calmness and trustworthiness.

'You are safe, let me help you' he transmitted over and over.

After a few minutes Samuel sensed a little shift in the creature, he hoped it wasn't just wishful thinking but he thought the creature's feelings were calming a little. Maybe he was getting through to It a little.

Samuel decided it was time to move on to the next stage of his plan. A simple question. When reading all the Custodians notes both in the Foundations archives and those left by the Deacon's he had realised that although in the past the creature had been bombarded with questions he felt they'd always been a little aggressive and complicated. He had thought that asking the creature what it was and what its intentions were had been pointless, It probably didn't really understand that itself, so Samuel intended to use a different, gentler approach with easier questions. And so he began with his first question.

'My name is Samuel, what is your name?'

Normally this would be the easiest question for anyone to answer, for the Soul Stealer it may be a little more complicated but it was still the simplest of questions he could ask it. It was a more complicated question in the Soul Stealers case because the creature had once been two separate entities, one human, one Eternal Dreamer. Samuel was one of the few people who knew Its human name, he had read it in the oldest of the Soul Healer manuscripts in the Foundations library in Rome. Would the creature even know its name? And if so would it tell him?

There was no immediate answer which was expected, so Samuel repeated the question with as much mental force as he could using all the skill that his years of training had given him. He projected the question at the creature forcefully but without menace.

'What is your name?' he enquired over and over.

After doing this for a few minutes Samuel felt himself begin to weaken. It was taking a lot out of him but he wasn't done yet, he was determined to get an answer.

Then he thought he sensed something, a little shift in the creature's mind. He sensed for the first time that It may finally be hearing him, but did it understand? He continued to project the question. He sensed a slight lessening in the creature's feelings of fear and anger but a rise in Its confusion. Was It trying to answer the question? He asked again and felt another shift, this one more dramatic, all the creatures strong, negative feelings were receding and Samuel could sense something moving in Its mind, something crystallising. Then suddenly three words were blasted into Samuel's mind with a force that rocked him physically as well as mentally, and those three words were;

'I AM TALIONIS!'

The force of the words broke the connection and Samuel came back to the physical world with a jolt. He was slumped in the chair, physically and mentally exhausted but elated, he had done what no one else had, he had communicated with the Soul Stealer. The creature still lay as it had before but Samuel sensed it too was exhausted by the effort their communication had taken. His task was done for the day, he had made a breakthrough but was too drained to take it any further for now, but it was enough.

Samuel knocked on the outer door signalling to Dorothea that he was ready to come out but Dorothea had already sensed this and was there ready. She had felt that something had happened but wasn't quite sure what. She noted Samuels fatigue immediately though.

'Let me lock up' she said, 'you go and find a nice comfy chair, I'll make some coffee then you can tell me what happened before you go lie down for a rest.'

He nodded his agreement and headed for the cottage.

A few minutes later Dorothea joined Samuel in the cosy lounge and after handing him his coffee she sat in the chair opposite him.

'So what happened?' she asked.

'It answered me' Samuels voice was quiet and thick with emotion 'I asked It Its name and It answered me.'

'That's amazing, what's Its name?'

'That's the weird thing, I know what its human name was but that's not the name it gave me.'

'So what name did it give.'

'It says Its name is Talionis.'

'So it gave you a false name?'

'No, I don't think that's it, I think it gave me Its name, I think Talionis is the name It has given itself, which kinda makes sense if you think about it. It's not been just human or just Eternal for a very long time, It's a new thing, a new entity and so why shouldn't It have a new name, It may not even remember Its old name.'

'Well, whatever the reason you got an answer and that's the main thing. You did really well and now you need to rest; this was a great breakthrough but there is more work to be done.'

'I need to phone the Foundations and update them; this news can't wait. Then I'll rest.'

Mason was feeling both sad and happy. Things were going really well with the first meeting; therefore he was happy, but the sadness came from fact that he now felt a little left out. These people were at the beginning of their journey but his was coming to an end, and he had no idea what sort of ending was in store for him.

The group had recovered quickly from the initial shock of the Eternals unconventional method of communication and had embraced it wholeheartedly. They had each moved towards an Eternal knowing instinctively which one they had the strongest link to and had effortlessly followed the unspoken instruction to lie down on the stone bed sporting their Dreambringer symbol.

As Max had approached his Eternal Mason couldn't help but feel a small jolt of jealousy. He still had a strong link to that particular Eternal, one that he would soon have to relinquish. He would always have a connection with the Eternals through his dreams, but it would never be the same as the new Dreambringers were receiving their first lesson from their Eternal Dreamers.

The basics of this first lesson were the same but for each kind of Dreambringer there were slight variations. The differences were to do with which kind of dreams they helped bring. Each kind of Dreambringer had their specialities and although they could help in other areas these were the ones they were taught, the ones dictated by the Dreambringers personality. This meant that Aaron and Mary, being the Dream Mates, would be taught the same things. They lay on their beds and relaxed ready to receive their first lesson. And so the Eternals began to impart their knowledge.

To Aaron and Mary it was both calming and exhilarating at the same time, and they were soon immersed in their lesson which went as follows;

You are the Dream Mates and you will bring dreams of family, friends and lovers. You will take on the form of those that the dreamer knows and those that they have yet to meet. You will help the dreamer explore their feelings for those people and so to process any problems they are experiencing with them. You will help them explore wishes and feelings for those they hope to meet or become others for them to help process their relationships. You will also bring them erotic dreams. You have been chosen to be Dream Mates because of your capacity to love even though until now you have been shown little yourselves. Your character is what makes you a Dream Mate, but your newfound love for each other is what gives you the strength to do your Dreambringer duty.'

For Geth, the Gatekeeper of Dreams his lesson was as follows;
'You are the Gatekeeper, you will guard dreamers from their deepest primal urges and fears, those that are common to all. You will only show them to those dreamers that are strong enough to learn from them, if they do not feel ready you will guard them from themselves until such time that they are strong enough to face them. Until then you will give them dreams of confidence and strength so that one day they will be ready to tackle their darker side. Your own strong, guarded character is what makes you The Gatekeeper.'

For Max, the Dreamcatcher, his lesson is as follows;
'You are the Dreamcatcher bringing dreams of risk and daring. You bring dreamers the gift of flying and the freedom to do things their physical selves will never achieve. But you must also keep them safe. Should the dreamer fall you must catch them or wake them before they hit the ground. You are also the bringer of nightmares but you bring them so the dreamer may learn from their fears. You must help them to run or to hide and wake them to scream if the nightmare is too frightening. The duality of your character is what makes you the Dreamcatcher.'

For Clea, the Seer of Dreams the lesson is as follows.
'You bring dreams of the future, giving those with the ability premonitions. You help dreamers solve problems through their dreams so that they wake with answers or inspiration. You lift their spirits bringing them dreams of happiness and hope. From you they receive the will to continue into a future both known and unknown. Your own foretelling talent and your empathy and nurturing nature make you the Seer of Dreams.'

And the message to them all;
'We will be with you every step of the way as together we bring dreams to as many souls as we can. Together we will enrich the lives of dreamers as we enrich our own.'

Once the Eternal Dreamers had imparted all the knowledge their new Dreambringers could possibly need at this stage they had let them know that the day's session was over. Mason had led the reluctant group out of the chamber and had settled them all in the seating area upstairs. They needed time to come back to their normal state, to take in what had just happened and absorb the new information.

The group were very quiet, lost in their own thoughts. Mason knew how they were feeling and left them to it. He quietly made them all tea and after handing out the mugs sat with them in silence until they were ready to move on.

To everyone's surprise it was Geth who spoke first.

'I can't put into words what just happened or how I feel about it' he said 'but I just want to let you know that I get it now, I won't be the doubter anymore, I'm in.'

Mason half expected the others to give a cheer at this, but they just smiled, and Aaron who was sat nearest to Geth gave him a friendly slap on the back.

'So does that mean you won't be grumpy anymore?' asked Mary, her tone playful.

'I didn't say that' answered Geth making them all laugh.

The group lapsed back into a comfortable silence. There wasn't really anything to discuss now, they had all learnt the answers to their questions and were content for the moment to sit in quiet contemplation.

Mason left them to it for a bit longer before breaking the silence to suggest they all go back to The Gateway for food and rest.

Tomorrow they would return for a longer session with the Eternals.

Samuel and Dorothea were sat at the kitchen table eating a beef stew that Dorothea had cooked. The meat was a bit tough and the vegetables had been cooked to mush but Samuel chewed away without really noticing. He'd made his report to the Foundation and now felt tired and distracted. He needed a good night's sleep but he was too wired to think about sleep right now, his mind was too full of plans for the next stage of his work.

Dorothea kept quiet knowing Samuel had things to think through and so didn't want to disturb him. She was impressed with how well he had done so far and couldn't help but feel a little jealous of the role he had to play. The work he was doing with The Soul Healer (or should she say Talionis) was new, exciting and ground-breaking. But she also knew that she didn't have the talent to do what he was doing and that she had her own part to play. It was basically just a support role now, the mundane part of which was things like cooking for them (which she wasn't very good at) and looking after the day to day running of things so that Samuel was free to get on with his work.

The other part of her support role was more to her liking and worthy of her talents so she wasn't unhappy. She was there to back Samuel up by supporting him with her mental strength and dream talent. She was there to carry out the usual tasks of the Custodians, that of protecting dreamers from any adverse influence Talionis might try to impose on their dreams and to ensure that It remained locked up. It was also her job to keep an eye on Samuel to make sure he wasn't adversely affected by his exposure to Talionis, both for his protection and for others.

She had been training for this role for years and with the recent events her work was turning out to be even more important than she'd ever imagined. She was part of a new chapter for The Somnium Foundations and she was determined to play her role in it to the best of her ability.

So now, even though physically she was doing the mundane chores of cleaning away the dinner things and washing up, mentally she was on alert for any sign of unwarranted mental activity from their captive.

After her chores were done she intended to spend a little time on something artistic. Her artistic talent was writing. She was a successful novelist having had eight novels published. She wrote historical drama, mixing her love and knowledge of history with her passion for fiction. She had just started work on her ninth book so had plenty to work on.

As a Custodian she wasn't linked to any Eternal Dreamer in particular but the energy she created would feed the Eternals at The Gateway and then as she slept tonight, they would repay her through her dreams so that she awoke ready for her tasks the next day.

She would suggest to Samuel that he join her for a short while at least. She knew he was tired and had a lot to think about but she felt that a bit of music would do them both good. Samuel was a very talented musician and could play many instruments and she knew that amongst the few possessions he had brought with him was a guitar and she was looking forward to hearing him play it.

Dorothea had a sense that things were going well at The Gateway, but she would know for sure in the morning as she would be able to tell by the strength of her dreams if the Eternals and their new Dreambringers were finally linked.

That night the inhabitants of The Gateway and The Cottage slept deeply and dreamt well. The most unusual Art Commune in the Somnium Foundation was finally getting back to its full power.

CHAPTER 20

BONDING

The Gateway residents were in high spirits as they ate a hearty breakfast together. They discussed the vivid and plentiful dreams they had all had. There were no strange, shared dreams just the normal weird and wonderful dreams they were all used to and had sorely missed.

The new Dreambringers knew they still had work to do but the mysteries were solved, their doubts were gone, and they were looking forward to beginning their lives as Dreambringers.

They would head off to the Factory after breakfast where they would spend the morning at their Art which would be even more satisfying now they all had fresh supplies. Then in the afternoon they would spend time with their Eternals.

For Phoebe and Mark their work at The Gateway was done. They would leave that morning and head off for a few days well-earned rest before receiving their next assignment. They knew they'd never get an assignment like this one again; even if they returned to the Gateway as a future assignment it wouldn't be the same. It was back to holiday and sickness cover for them. This wasn't a bad thing; they had enjoyed their time at The Gateway but were glad to be going back to their normal lives. They enjoyed their roving lifestyle and the work they did, this had been more exciting than usual but it had also been more stressful and at times frightening. No, all in all they would be happy to leave and get back to normal.

For now Eddie would continue in his role as the Warden at The Gateway and he intended to continue to do it as well as he always had. He would keep himself busy because that was the only way he could keep the worry and fear about his future at bay.

Sofia would be staying on for the time being, she still had work to do. There was still the question of what was going to happen to Mason and Eddie once the new Dreambringers were fully settled in and the Foundation wanted her to stay until this was decided, they also wanted her to be nearby to keep an eye on the goings on at the cottage for them and to lend them a hand if need be.

She planned to pay Samuel and Dorothea a visit when she got the chance to see for herself how things were going. She had been updated by the Foundation on the progress that Samuel had made, the man's Dreambringer talents were impressive, and she was intrigued by what he would do next.

The main problem however was that in this case the usual next step after the first few more bonding session between the new Dreambringers and their Eternal's was going to be a problem. How would the Bonding Ceremony work with Mahesh dead and Gina, Blake and Claude indisposed? Obviously with Mahesh gone his link was already severed and bearing in mind the physical and mental state of the others not to mention the time and distance they had been away from the Gateway their links must be severely weakened. But still it needed to be clarified. Mason had expressed a wish to visit his friends and so Sofia had an idea this could be worked into the plans, she just needed to run it by Cecil Neale.

She had told Mason she would speak to the Foundation about his visits whilst he was at the Factory today which pleased him. He wanted to see his friends to judge for himself how well they were doing rather than rely on the brief updates Sofia had so far been given. He wanted to see Claude in particular because he felt he owed his friend an apology. He knew that it had already been explained to Claude that he wasn't to blame for the damage he had done to his friends and that no-one held him responsible, but Mason wanted to apologise for the way he'd treated Claude after the terrible events.

At the time he'd felt his treatment had been fair, even too good in light of what (they thought) Claude had done, but now with the knowledge that he wasn't to blame for his actions he felt the need to apologise, not so much for their physical treatment of him (they'd done their best in that respect) but for the feelings of anger and even hatred that Claude must have sensed coming from himself and Eddie at the time. He needed to reassure his friend that he no longer felt that way and neither did Eddie or anyone else for that matter. He hated to think how bad Claude must be feeling about what he had done, no wonder he had been in the state he was when they'd found him. Mason just wanted to do all he could to ease Claude's pain.

Sofia would also spend some time speaking to various people in The Foundation to see if anyone had any ideas how to proceed with the ceremony if the outgoing Dreambringers couldn't be present. It was another case of new territory for everyone in the Foundation and needed careful thought. And so once everyone had finished breakfast Sofia headed for the office to begin making plans and Mason and the new Dreambringers got their things together and headed off to the Factory.

Eddie stayed in the kitchen to clear up the breakfast things whilst Phoebe and Mark went to pack having already said their goodbyes to the group headed for the Factory. A Foundation car would arrive in about an hour to collect them. After seeing them off Eddie would keep himself busy cleaning the room they had vacated then he was sure he could find other things to do to fill the time before the others returned.

By the time the group reached the Factory Mason's mood had been lightened by the infectious high spirits of the newbies. They set to their various art projects (boosted by new supplies) with energy and enthusiasm. Although intense concentration was needed at times they still found time for chatting and laughing and they made sure that Mason felt included. They sensed that he was feeling a little unsettled and were well aware why. Max felt it more than the others due to his link with the outgoing Dreamcatcher. So the group did their best to keep Masons spirits up.

At lunchtime they would finish their artwork for the day and head downstairs to commune with their Eternals. The session the day before had been about them asking questions and finding out the basics, today's session would be more of a lesson; today they would begin to learn how to join with the Eternal Dreamers to influence people's dreams. The atmosphere in the art room was thick with expectancy and excitement.

It was early when Dorothea went downstairs to get her morning cup of coffee, but she found Samuel already at the kitchen table with this own morning kick start cup.

'How are you this morning?' she asked as she poured herself a cup and joined him at the table 'Did you sleep well?'

'I'm good' he answered, 'I slept better than expected, how about you?'

'Yes, good thanks.'

They lapsed into silence, Samuel was preoccupied with thoughts of his next session with Talionis and Dorothea sensing this didn't want to interrupt.

After about fifteen minutes Samuel seemed to shake himself out of a daydream.

'Well I better get on with it then' he said getting up from the table and going to the sink to wash up his cup.'

After the breakthrough of learning the name the creature had given itself Samuel hoped that he could now progress further. His next goal was to try to get Talionis to explain to him how it was feeling, to get some idea what drove it to do the things it did. The basic reason was fairly obvious – anger – but what Samuel wanted was to get to the root of these feelings. Why exactly had the creature's behaviour been so destructive right from Its creation? Why was it so angry? No one had really harmed it, especially not right at the beginning. It had been aggressive from the start for no apparent reason. The formation of the creature had been down to its human side, so was it the human that was angry because things had not turned out as planned or the Eternal Dreamer because it had been trapped? Which part of Talionis was in control, the human or the Eternal Dreamer? Was the Eternal trapped and basically helpless, or had it been affected by the power of having a corporal body and was controlling the actions of that body? It was important for Samuel to know this in order to help Talionis.

There had been speculation over the years; many people had tried to work this out some believed one theory, some the other but no-one had proved it either way. There were also some who believed that neither side was dominant but simply that the combination of the two beings had made something new and that something was bad. But how could two beings that had been basically good when they were separate entities and who shared a link that worked for the good of others be so bad when merged as one? Many Eternal Dreamers had been asked through their Dreambringers what they thought but they had no more answers than the humans did.

Whatever the answer was Samuel was determined to find it and he felt pretty confident that he could succeed.

'I'm ready to begin' he said to Dorothea

'Okay, let's go then.'

When Samuel entered the stone room he found Talionis sitting on its bed facing him. It was like it was waiting for him, not in a friendly, welcoming way but in an expectant, wary way. Its eyes were open and the light shining from them obscured the details of its face slightly. It was more than a little disconcerting but Samuel hid his discomfort well.

'Hello again, I hope you had a comfortable night' Samuel's voice was clear and calm but the creature did not react in any way to his words.

'I'm gonna spend a little time with you again today' he continued as he moved further into the room. 'I mean you no harm, I just want to help you.' There was still no reaction from the creature and so Samuel felt it was time to switch communication tactics. He had managed to ask a question and get an answer from Talionis the day before, now he needed to form a stronger telepathic link so that he could find out more about the creature.

He sat in the chair opposite Talionis who hadn't moved at all since he'd entered and after getting his body as comfortable as possible and closing his eyes he began to relax and focus his mind before going in search of the answers.

He encountered Talionis' emotions quite easily. They were still the same, anger, frustration, self-pity and confusion. In return Samuel sent out a telepathic message stating his intentions. '*I will not harm you; I want to help you; you can trust me*'. He kept this up for a while to get the message through, he needed It to trust him so gave It time to (hopefully) understand where he was coming from.

All the time he was sending he was also receiving, monitoring the creature's emotions for any change. After a while he thought he noticed something different. It was faint so he concentrated on it. What is that? He willed the creature to show him more. He tried harder. And then he got it. Curiosity. Good, the creature was curious about him, it was a start. Now it was time for a few simple thought questions.

'How are you feeling?'

'Is there anything you need?'

'Do you have any questions for me?'

Sending these three questions out on a loop he was careful to keep his own thoughts calm and friendly. It was hard work but Samuel was determined to get results.

After working tirelessly for several hours with no results to show for it Samuel decided to take a break. The creature hadn't responded to any of his questions and he was feeling very disappointed. After the breakthrough of the day before it was frustrating not to have got any further.

When he opened his eyes he found that at some point Talionis had laid down on the bed. Its eyes were closed and It did not move as Samuel got up to leave. Dorothea opened the outer door for him having sensed the session was over. They passed in the little anti-room so that she could lock the inner door then she followed him out locking the outer door after them.

They didn't speak until they were sat at the kitchen table with the kettle on, and even then there was no need for Dorothea to ask how it had gone. So she asked him what he wanted for lunch instead.

'I don't mind' he said 'I just need a short rest and some fuel and them I'm going back in.'

Dorothea just nodded and set about making sandwiches and heating soup.

At the Factory they were breaking for lunch too but in a much more buoyant mood. The group were looking forward to spending more time with their Eternals.

This time when the group entered the underground room they knew what awaited them. Each hurried to be near their Eternal, the silent communication started and the learning began in earnest.

At the moment the new Dreambringers were only performing half of their Dreambringer duties, that half being producing the art energy needed by the Eternals to help people benefit from their dreams. They were unable to perform the other half of their duties yet as it wasn't possible for them to do so until they were properly bonded with their Eternals. Mason, and for a short time Mark and Phoebe, had been carrying out this part until now. This second part of their task was the part where they joined the Eternals in the Dream Realm in order to help bring dreams. And so now was the time they learnt how this would work. And this is what they learnt;

A Dreambringers night's sleep is split up as follows; for the first hour to hour and a half their bodies are relaxing and then when fully rested their soul takes control. At this point the connection between their souls and the Eternals takes hold pulling them into the Dream Realm.

The Dream Realm is not a physical place, it is the Souls Domain. Its everchanging landscape created by the souls who inhabit it in their dreams. In the Dream Realm normal dreamers do not have a physical form their souls are simply represented by vague, white, misty human shapes. The Dreambringers however have more of a physical presence. Their souls appear within the ever-shifting dream landscape as ethereal forms of their physical selves. They are a ghostly and insubstantial yet perfected version of themselves. Their forms appear frail yet are smoothed of all their imperfections and their attributes are enhanced. They are their dream selves.

Along with their Eternal Dreamers the Dreambringers souls interact with those of the dreaming souls, learning what they need from their dreams and helping them to achieve it, becoming what the dreamers need them to be.

Whilst the Dream Realm is not a physical place it does have its own unique type of geography. It does not have physical territories and boundaries as such, but dreaming souls tend to inhabit the same area of the Dream Realm as others who live/sleep in the same physical area of the world as them.

Dreambringers are able to 'travel' to any area in the Dream Realm and help the dreaming souls there, but if all the Dreambringers were to roam wherever they liked it could be chaotic and some areas/dreamers may get missed. This is why it was decided many years ago that rather than travel erratically through the Dream Realm the Eternal Dreamers and their Dreambringers should split off into smaller groups and disperse to different areas of the world and for each group to keep to the area inhabited by the local dreaming souls in order to properly cover as much of the worlds dreamers as possible.

These groups would later become the art communes of today and so for many years Dreambringers have helped those souls who live/sleep in the physical area surrounding their commune and this has meant that these days a Dreambringers talent tends to become stronger within the area of the Dream Realm where local dreaming souls are as they are physically as well as spiritually near them. This also makes distance travel withing the Dream Realm not only unnecessary but less effective.

There is one slight exception, and that is when Dreambringers are 'calling' their replacements. It's a different thing to Dreambringing itself but the 'call out' can reach further than a Dreambringers area of the Dream Realm. The call goes out to the nearest suitable candidate and its unlikely all the candidates for one group will come from the same area. The candidates are likely to be in the same country as the Dreambringer they are to replace but distance can vary and although they have been known to come from another country it is rare.

Dreaming souls are unaware there is such a place as the Dream Realm when they are awake and whilst there, they cannot travel within it, but then they have no need to. Their 'local' Dreambringers interact with them giving them dreams in which they can then interact with their fellow dreamers either known, unknown, nearby or far away.

After five or six hours of this work the Dreambringer's souls are pulled back into their still sleeping bodies. Then for the next couple of hours they can enjoy their own dreams enriched by the Eternals before waking fully.

Dreambringers are by nature good sleepers who rarely wake during the middle hours of the night. On the rare occasion that a Dreambringer wakes or is awoken during their Dreambringer hours their time in the Dream Realm is over for that night, they cannot return until the next night. This would not be a good thing and is why it is so important for Dreambringers to have a good sleep routine.

This Dream Realm part of their task is the part that Dreambringers will miss once their duty is done. They will still dream well and commune with the Eternals in their dreams, but they will not be so present in the Dream Realm once their bond with one particular Eternal is broken. They can no longer help other dreamer as they once did. There are however a few extremely talented Dreambringers who are still able to maintain a stronger presence in the Dream Realm even after their bond is broken. These particularly strong Dreambringers are the ones who are then trained up to be Custodians or given other important roles within the Foundation. Samuel and Dorothea being two recent examples of this.

All this the new Dreambringers are now learning each of them excited by this new knowledge and eager for the day when they can fulfil their destiny and become a strong presence within the Dream Realm.

As he headed back to Talionis' abode Samuel sensed something, like electricity in his mind. He soon realised what it was and smiled, at least something was going right. With a little effort he caught more of a sense of the happy gathering nearby. The new Dreambringers and their Eternals were bonding well which was expected but still good to know. Now if only he could get some results then they really could be happy.

After almost five hours Mason led a reluctant group up to the art room for a short wind-down break before heading back to the Gateway. There was lots of chatter to start with as they compared their experiences and marvelled at it all. Mason made tea and coffee and let them chat his mind wandering. He wondered how Sofia had got on with the Foundation regarding his plans to visit his friends and if any decisions had been made about the bonding ceremony. He was eager to get back and find out but needed to give the newbies time to come back to the real world. So he left it as long as he could stand before telling them it was time to leave.

Eddie was relieved when he saw the group walking up the lawn towards the house, not because he'd been worried about them but because now he'd have something to do. He'd cleaned the room Phoebe and Mark had vacated and then found a few odd jobs to do, including making lunch for himself and Sofia, but for the last hour or so he'd been pottering unsuccessfully trying to find something to occupy his mind. He'd spent a little time in the art room working on a new cartoon but had found it hard to concentrate. There was so much going through his head right now. He'd thought about quizzing Sofia on a few things at lunch but she'd been quiet and preoccupied so he hadn't felt it was the right time. She'd spent most of the day in the office as usual making and receiving calls and doing whatever else it was she did. He'd been on his own in the house at times before in the past but had never felt as lonely as he had today.

The others were back now though so he would soon be busy making them dinner and talking to them about their day. He quickly went to the office to let Sofia know the others were back and then went to greet them.

The group's good mood was infectious and Eddie soon cheered up. The newbies kept him company in the kitchen as he started on dinner, but after a brief hello Mason had gone to the office to speak to Sofia who hadn't come out to meet the returning party.

As Mason entered the office Sofia was just ending a call. Looking up she gave him a tired smile.

'How did it go today?' she asked.

'Really well, the newbies are eager and are connecting well, they're very happy.'

'That's good.'

'What about you, how have you got on?'

'You'll be glad to know that the Foundation have okayed your visits to your friends and have decided that it should be very soon. In fact they want you to go tomorrow if possible because the Foundation think you need to visit your friends before we make the final decision on how to proceed with the bonding ceremony. They need you to see your friends to help ascertain what sort of bond if any they still have with their Eternals and if there is any likelihood that any of them would be fit enough and willing to return here for the ceremony.

You are to liaise with their various doctors and find out how your friends feel about it in order to help the Foundation decide on a course of action. Of course the doctors and other Foundation staff could talk to your friends but you know them a lot better and that fact along with your request to visit them means they think it best you talk to them. Before its confirmed though I need to decide after talking to you and our new recruits if today was successful enough for them to continue for a couple of days on their own. It's not ideal to have them continue without you but we have to weigh up the benefits of having you here against you talking to your friends ASAP.'

'I'm so pleased my visit has been agreed and I believe our new recruits will get along fine without me but you must obviously check with them.'

'I can't see it being a problem either but I have to make sure everyone is happy. Once I get the okay from the group I can confirm the plan with the Foundation and they will set things going pretty quickly. I expect they'll send a car for you tomorrow morning but let's worry about it a bit later, I need a break, we'll have dinner and then have a chat and go from there.'

Samuel was exhausted. He'd spent another four hours with Talionis and made no progress. He'd received no answer of any sort to any of his questions and apart from a few fluctuations in the already perceived emotions had discovered no new ones. His own main emotion was now frustration which he had tried hard to keep the creature from detecting. But it was hard to know what, if anything Talionis understood of the thoughts he was himself projecting.

Back at the cottage he ate another poorly cooked meal without really tasting it and was now stretched out on the sofa whilst Dorothea sat in an armchair both of them staring off into space lost in their own thoughts. Dorothea could sense the frustration he felt but didn't know what to do to help him. Then a thought occurred to her.

'What we need is something to lift our spirits and I know just the thing. I understand you are an accomplished musician and I know for a fact that you brought a guitar with you and although it's not my forte I can hold a tune. So how about we have a little music.'

'I'm not sure I'm in the mood'

'Oh come on its just tiredness talking, you'll love it once you get going. Music is one of the things that gives us so much, it can calm and soothe, or excite and uplift, it just generally brings joy. We could give it a go at least.'

As she spoke Dorothea saw the look on Samuels face change from tiredness and defeat to doubt and then brighten into something else. She thought it was him realising she was right and being cheered by the idea of music making, but she wasn't quite right.

'You are a genius' he said.

'Hardly, everyone knows music does you good, I was just stating the obvious.'

'Yes but you've hit on something that'll help us.'

'I know, it will help us relax and cheer us up, that's what I said.'

'No, you're not seeing it' Samuel had a big grin on his face 'it'll help me with Talionis. Don't you see, I can play It music.'

'Oh' said Dorothea realisation dawning 'the music may calm It, make It more receptive to you.'

'Exactly. I mean it's not a forgone conclusion but it's definitely worth a try. I read in the Foundation archives that the human side of Talionis was a talented musician, he played the Viola well and also the more unusual Hurdy Gurdy, so he would be receptive to music surely.'

'I would think so yes.'

'I doubt Its even heard music, not properly, for years. The couple that were here before us weren't musicians and although they may have played CD's or had the radio on in here I doubt Talionis would have benefited much from it if at all. But if I play to It, actually sit with It and play specifically for It I mean that's special right?'

'Your right it's always nice to have someone play to you alone, it makes you feel special.'

'Precisely. It brings you closer to that person as you both share the pleasure of giving and receiving.'

'It's a good way to try to win It over.'

'Let's hope we're right. We don't know if It can actually hear properly but it may still reach It somehow. Thanks for giving me the idea.'

'You're welcome, though I can't really take the credit for it, all I did was suggest we have a sing-along to cheer us up.'

'But the suggestion is what gave me the idea, besides that's a pretty good idea on its own. I say we have that little sing-along, just the two of us, then tomorrow I'll take my guitar in with me to play for Talionis before I try asking It anymore questions, see if it helps.'

'Sounds like a good plan to me.'

At the Gateway, after dinner was finished and everything cleared up they all congregated in the lounge / art room. From their attitudes and conversation at dinner Sofia could tell that the new Dreambringers were settling in well, but she still had to ask the question.

'I need to run something past you all' she addressed the group 'you all seem to be adapting well to your new roles but it is still very new to you so I want to gauge how you feel. Mason has something he needs to do which involves him leaving for a couple of day, so do you think you can manage on your own for a while?'

'I don't see why not' said Clea.

'It depends on what's expected of us' added Max 'I mean what is it we need to do next?'

'Well for the couple of days Mason is away all you need to do is what you did today only without him there with you.'

'Well I guess that's okay then, I'm sure we can manage that'

'It'll be no problem' said Clea.

'We'll be fine' agreed Aaron and Mary nodded her agreement.

'Fine by me' said Geth.

'That's good' said Sofia 'because what Mason has to do is important and it can't really wait.'

'What exactly is it he's got to do' it was an obvious question from Geth and so Sofia explained about Mason's planned visits and why he needed to make them. Then it was Mason's turn to address the group.

'I have every faith in you but I need to give you a little guidance. You need to spend the next two days just like today. What I mean is you will be tempted to spend more time with your Eternals but it's important you keep the balance. Mornings working on your art, a break for lunch, afternoons with your Eternals and then evenings here for dinner and relaxing. If you stick to this routine things will run smoother now and in the long run, okay?'

They each nodded or murmured their agreement and Mason was happy.

'With the new Dreambringers agreement now given Sofia excused herself to go and call the Foundation so that the plans could be set in motion. When she returned everyone was relaxed and chatting amongst themselves. They all spent a pleasant evening together and went to bed happy.

The inhabitants of the cottage went to bed a little happier after their sing-along. It had been a short session because Samuel was exhausted, but it had done the job.

Talionis was confused. The one who kept pushing at Its mind was one of 'them', one It hated so It did what It always did and hid from him. But then this one also seemed different. It sensed different emotions from this one. It sensed calmness with no fear and no hate. But the constant bombardment of Its thoughts and the repeated questions were exhausting.

This one was strong like all those who had held him captive over the years, but his strength was different and this difference confused Talionis. Part of It wanted to communicate with this new captor, something It had never wanted to do before, but the other half could not put down Its guard. Because of this new captor the two entities within Talionis were at war like never before, the weaker side trying harder than ever to exert Its will. It was a conflict that made Talionis afraid. It had a need to be understood but was fearful of letting Its guard down. It needed to rest, It didn't know when he would be back or what to do when he returned. This was new and so, so confusing.

CHAPTER 21

VISITING

Mason was the first one up; he'd even beaten Sofia for the first time. He had slept well for a few hours but woken early. He'd dreamt well too but his dreams had felt a little different, it was another blow, with his bond to his Eternal weakening as Max's strengthened his dreams though strong and good would never be the same.

After finding no one else was up he made himself a coffee and took it back to his room; another thing he would be giving up soon. He began to pack for his trip focusing his mind on that instead of the impending end of his life at The Gateway.

Max awoke with Mason on his mind. The man had been in his dreams, like a shadow, but not in a sinister way, just there beside him as he dreamt.

He felt bad for the man and a little sorry for himself. None of the others had to deal with having their predecessor around. It wasn't that he resented Mason being there, he liked the man a lot, but he felt the extra pressure of witnessing the pain the soon to be ex-Dreambringer was going through because of Max's presence.

Clea had talked the day before about the sadness she sensed from her Eternal over the death of her predecessor and Aaron, Mary and Geth had said they'd sensed the same from their Eternals over what had happened to the other Dreambringers, but it wasn't the same. He had to deal with the human emotions of the man himself. He was also the only one who couldn't get settled into his new room yet. Again he didn't have ill feeling toward Mason because of it and the room he was in was perfectly comfortable, but it was still hard. He knew that his fellow newbies understood and were sympathetic, but he was still struggling a little.

The whole thing was such a culture shock that any little complication made the transition harder. When they'd found out that Mason would be away for a few days he had felt a little nervous at first at the thought of being left without a mentor, but then he had felt relief. Max gave himself a mental shake; enough of this wallowing, he needed to get up and get on with it. First on the agenda a nice long shower.

After packing his bag Mason returned to the kitchen where he found Sofia and Eddie chatting over coffee. He joined them for a bit before Sofia excused herself to go and find out the details of the plans the Foundation had made for Mason. She passed Max on her way and they exchanged good mornings. When he entered the kitchen Max almost turned and walked out again. Mason and Eddie appeared deep in conversation and he didn't want to intrude. He had started to back track when Eddie caught sight of him and it was too late.

'Hey Max, can I get you some tea or coffee?'

'Errrmm, tea please.'

'Okay, sit yourself down then and I'll get it for you.'

Max sat at the table a couple of chairs away from Mason.

'I'm sorry for interrupting' he apologised.

Mason smiled 'Its fine, we were only chatting about what to have for breakfast.'

'Oh, it looked more serious than that.'

'It wasn't believe me,' said Mason.

'Oh, I don't know; I thought our discussion about bacon was pretty serious' said Eddie not sounding serious at all. Max smiled feeling more relaxed and a little foolish; he really needed to lighten up sometimes.

By the time Sofia returned the menu had been decided and Eddie was sorting the ingredients ready to start the first batch of cooking.

She sat between Mason and Max and began to tell Mason the plans. A car would pick him up in two hours' time and take him to the Foundation hospital where Gina and Blake were. He would have the whole day to spend with his friends and consult with their doctors. A conference call would then take place early evening between himself, the doctors, Sofia plus Cedric Neale and a couple of Foundation members to discuss the likelihood of Gina and/or Blake returning to the Gateway for the bonding ceremony. Mason would then spend the night at a nearby Foundation facility.

Early the next morning a car would take him on to the facility where Claude was being looked after. Again, he would spend the day with his friend and those caring for him before another conference call to assess Claude's fitness and willingness to attend the ceremony.

Mason felt a great relief. He was going to see his friends at last. But his relief was also tinged with worry. How would they be? Would seeing them relieve his worries or make them worse? Would they be fit enough to return? Would they even want to? How would Gina and Blake feel about seeing Claude? Even knowing that it wasn't really Claude who hurt them it would still be traumatic seeing him again surely. There were so many questions but it was useless letting them fill his head now, he needed to shake them off and not worry about them for the time being, he had two hours to fill and then a car journey before he could even start to find the answers.

Samuel propped his guitar against the chair and then sat in it. Talionis lay on the bed Its eyes closed. Samuel didn't bother speaking he just got comfortable and fell easily into the required meditative state. He wanted to gauge the creature's emotions before he played It music and then again after to see if there were any changes. He was met with the usual mess of emotions, anger, frustration, confusion and self-pity.

'How are you today Talionis?' he gently probed.

As usual there was no answer.

'I want to try something new today. Do you like music?'

Still no response.

'I love music and I have a feeling you do too, or at least you used to, am I right?'

Again nothing. But that was enough now, no need to waste any more time on questions, he'd gauged the creatures mood, now it was time for music.

After bringing himself back to the physical Samuel picked up his guitar. He'd decided to start with some gentle, old fashioned folk songs, some he'd learnt as a boy and some he'd picked up on his recent travels. Most he just played on the guitar, but a few had simple lyrics so he sang along. His voice wasn't the best but its deep tone was pleasant and he could hold a tune. After a while he moved on to some more modern tunes with a faster tempo, again some instrumental others with simple lyrics. Samuel was enjoying himself and he sincerely hoped that Talionis was too.

After over an hour playing Samuel decided to stop. Now he would gauge the creatures emotions again. Revisiting the turmoil that defined Talionis he probed Its emotions for any signs of change. He noted with satisfaction that the creatures emotions appeared a little less fraught. It was subtle but there was definitely a small difference.

'Did you like the music Talionis? Would you like to hear more?'

No reply.

'Well I enjoyed it so I'm gonna play some more'

And so that's what he did. He played a mixture of songs letting the music take him where it wanted. He played until his fingers were sore and his voice was getting hoarse. Then it was time to see if his efforts had any effect.

180

Again, he detected a subtle change, a slight calming of the creatures emotions. He concentrated harder trying to expand on the change. Were any of the emotions diminished? Were there any new emotion? He reached out to the creature with his mind and soul, willing It to tell him something. He was almost certain his music had soothed the creature a little but was desperate for some validation of this.

Wait, what was that? A little tinge of something, but what was it? A little tickle of a feeling. And then he got it. Curiosity. The creature was curious about him, about his music. The creature wasn't forming any mind words yet but on a basic level curiosity meant asking What? Or Why? So Samuel decided to answer questions that hadn't really been intermated let alone asked because maybe it couldn't, maybe it was finding it hard to put Its feelings into mind words. So he would help It.

'I'm playing my guitar because it brings me joy and I was hoping it would do the same for you too, its what music does. You can trust me Talionis, I'm here to help you in whatever way I can. Please tell me how I can help you.' He waited but still no reply came so he changed tact. Maybe if he directed It to ask the questions that would help It.

'Is there anything you want to ask me?

This time he felt a little spike in the creature's curiosity and was briefly hopeful of some sort of communication, but it didn't happen. He was getting tired now after hours of guitar playing on top of the monitoring and probing so he decided to bring the session to an end. He did have hope though, the creature was definitely reacting to the music so he would stick with it. He needed to build trust and that could take time but he was determined to get through to Talionis even if he had to spend weeks or even months serenading It. He'd do whatever it took.

Back at the Gateway Eddie and Sofia had waved Mason off and having no other jobs to do they had settled in the art room and were finding it to be a very productive morning. A strong vein of inspiration had crept in and they were hard at work, Eddie on the beginning of an ideal for a graphic novel, something he'd always wanted to do but had yet failed to make any real progress on, and Sofia on a rather good set of drawings of the new inhabitants of the Gateway.

Out in the Factory the new Dreambringers were also hard at work in the best possible way, and it was maybe their influence that had infected Eddie and Sofia.

When Mason arrived at the Foundation run hospital he was taken directly to the office of the doctor in charge of Gina and Blake's care.

The hospital was small but well equipped and very clean. The doctor's office was compact and sparsely but comfortably furnished with a sofa and coffee table as well as the expected desk, chairs and filing cabinets. The doctors name was Eden Harris. He was tall and very slim with neat, dark hair and a long, slightly gaunt face. Mason judged his age at around the mid-fifties.

The doctor rose from his chair behind the neatly arranged desk and held out a long-fingered hand for a welcome handshake. After the handshake and polite introductions Mason sat in the chair placed opposite the doctors and the man began to fill him in on the current condition of his friends.

Physically Gina was doing well, her arm was healing well as was her head wound and the doctor pointed out that in other circumstances she would have been discharged days ago. Not that she'd have been discharged to go home though, she was still very nervy and anxious and so she would have been moved to a facility where they could help her emotionally.

Her mental state had improved a little since Blake had come out of his coma but the fact that she refused to leave his side for anything but essential bathroom needs and became severely distressed if away from him for too long the move had been thought unwise. The hospital had sought advice from their psychiatric counterparts and were treating her accordingly.

Blake's physical injury had obviously been much worse. As Mason already knew he was doing well since being brought out of his coma. Since the last update given to Sofia more tests had been done confirming that Blake had suffered no serious brain damage. Although physically weak his speech was fine, and he was able to walk with a little assistance. His higher motor functions were a little impaired, but the doctors were confident they would improve with time although they couldn't know if he would get them back one hundred percent. He remembered little of the actual attack but other than that his memory was intact. The physical improvements were encouraging but the mental side was always going to be a problem.

Before he left Sofia had told Mason something he hadn't realised. Gina and Blake didn't know the real reason Claude had attacked them. The staff at this facility didn't have clearance for this information, they were on the same level within the Foundation as the Wardens like Eddie so they knew about the Dreambringers but not the Eternal Dreamers and therefore not the story of the Soul Stealer. So now it would be down to Mason to explain about Talionis.

He wasn't sure if finding out a frightening creature had got loose and taken over your friend in order to attack you was better or worse than thinking your friend had done it of his own accord. There was no way to know how they would take the news. Any hopes that Mason had held of the couple returning to the Gateway were fading fast. This was going to be even harder than he'd expected but he still desperately wanted to see his friends,

All the rooms in the hospital were private and therefore single occupancy but from the beginning Gina had insisted on being in the same room as Blake. Luckily the rooms were spacious so even with the two beds in the room was comfortable. The beds and the monitors were obviously hospital issue but the bed linen and furnishings were more in line with a basic but decent hotel.

When Mason entered the room Blake was sat up in his bed and Gina was sat in a comfy armchair placed between the two beds but facing Blake. They both looked very pale and Blake particularly a little gaunt. Gina's arm was in a cast and there was still faint bruising visible on her forehead and although there was no outward sign of Blake's injury it was clear he'd been through a lot.

The trauma they'd experienced had clearly sapped their vitality. Although now in their mid-forties the couple had always looked and acted younger, their blond good looks never fading, but now some of that youthful vitality was gone and it made Mason sad.

'Hello Mason' Blakes voice was a little croaky but strong and he gave his friend a welcoming smile.

'Mason how lovely to see you' her voice was a little shaky but Gina managed a smile too.

'Hey guys, it's great to see you too.'

'Have a seat' said Blake indicating an identical chair to Gina's placed on the other side of his bed. Mason pulled the chair a little closer and sat down.

'How are you both feeling?'

'Pretty good considering' answered Blake 'I'm not completely back to myself yet but I'm getting there, Gina's doing well too aren't you love?'

Gina gave a little unconvincing nod.

'I'm glad to see you're doing well.'

'Thanks' said Blake 'and how are you?'

'I'm good thanks.'

'How are things at home?' Blakes voice shook a little on the word home 'how's Eddie?'

'Eddie's fine, he sends his love and things are going well considering.'

'They haven't really told me anything since I woke up and Gina says they haven't told her much either, so what's been going on?'

'A lot has happened since I saw you last' with the small talk done it was time for Mason to tell them everything and he was nervous about how they would react 'and a lot of it is going to be hard for you to take in, but please let me first reassure you that everything is okay now, it's all under control, you are fine and you will continue to be looked after well, okay?'

They both nodded and so it was time to start. He noticed Gina reach out to take Blakes hand and Blake give her hand a reassuring squeeze.

'First of all I need to explain that what Claude did to you was not his fault, he was as much a victim as you.'

'How do you figure that' Blake said frowning. Gina began to nervously bite her lip and looked on the verge of tears.

'Do you remember' asked Mason 'back when we were inducted we were told the cautionary tale of the Soul Stealer?'

'Vaguely' said Blake and Gina gave a hesitant nod.

'We were told about the Soul Stealer as a warning not to get above ourselves and to explain how The Gateway was different from the other art communes right?'

'Right' again it was Blake who answered, 'it seemed like some sort of urban legend at the time, although we never thought the Foundation were lying, it was just a really old story.'

'Yes, well the Soul Stealer is the reason this terrible thing happened to you, to all of us.'

And so Mason told them the whole story. They listened in silence and although she made no noise Gina was visibly shaking the whole time and fat tears rolled down her face. Blake was more composed but the shock showed on his face at times. Mason was relieved that the couple stayed relatively calm whilst he spoke but now it was getting to the part where he had to ask them if they were willing to return to the Gateway for the Bonding Ceremony. He wasn't sure how to approach the subject so decided to give them a little time to digest what he had told them so far.

'Do you have any questions?' he asked

'This creature is definitely safely confined now? asked Blake

'Yes, the new Custodians are the best possible people for the job and new protocols are in place so that his tragedy is never repeated.

'So the new Dreambringers are safe?'

'Yes, they're perfectly safe'

'Did we miss Mahesh's funeral?'

'No, it hasn't happened yet, they knew we'd all want to be there so they're waiting until that's possible.'

'Where's Claude now?' this from Gina her bottom lip quivering.

'He's at another Foundation facility being looked after like you. He suffered badly emotionally after what he was made to do to you. I understand its hard but I hope in time you can forgive him.'

'I can forgive him now I know the truth, but its forgetting I'm not so sure about.'

'I completely understand, even though you now know he was being controlled in your mind's eye you still see Claude attacking you and Blake.'

'Yes, and I still feel afraid of him.'

'Hopefully in time the memory will fade and it will be easier, how about you Blake?'

'I don't remember the attack itself but in my mind Claude killed Mahesh and like Gina that memory is still vivid, but to be honest I think I've suffered physically more than emotionally. Now I know the truth I don't feel any hatred for or fear of Claude.'

'That's good.'

'So what happens now?' asked Blake.

'That's kind of why I'm here, but before we get into all that why don't we take a break, have something to eat, give you two time to absorb all the new information.'

'Sounds good' said Blake and Gina nodded her agreement.

'I'll go and get some food organised then, won't be long.'

After tracking down a member of staff who could help Mason sent them to the couples room to find out what they wanted to eat and then found an empty room where he could sit alone for a while before returning to the couples room.

None of them ate much and conversation was sparse. After clearing away the remnants of their meal Mason couldn't put it off any longer. He didn't go straight in with the main question though but started off gently.

'So how have your dreams been?'

'I think I did dream whilst I was in my coma but I don't remember anything specific. They were very weak dreams I know that much. Since I've woken up they've been better, but strange.'

'In what way?'

'It's hard to explain. They've been as strong as ever but however good the dreams are I've had an overriding feeling of being lost, or maybe untethered describes it better, oh I don't know, they're just different.

'No, it's actually a pretty good description of how my dreams have felt' said Mason 'or at least I kinda get what you mean.'

'Me too' added Gina 'I had nightmares the first two nights after the attack for the first time in many years. Then the dreams got really weak and I couldn't remember anything about them when I woke up, then lately they've been unusual, like you just described.'

'The nightmares are understandable' said Mason 'we were all separated and in turmoil. Then the weak dreams were because I was the only Dreambringer fit for my task and me and the Eternals were concentrating our energy on calling the replacements. As for the strangeness of our dreams now that is something we need to talk about. You have been away from your Eternals for a long time, as has Claude and so your links to them have been weakened.

Now the new Dreambringers are at The Gateway the Dream Realm is enriched again but we find ourselves in an unusual situation. The new Dreambringers have started to bond with the Eternals but at the same time we are still bonded to them however weak that bond may be.

Usually before the newbies begin to make a strong bond a ceremony takes place at which the outgoing Dreambringers relinquish their bonds, they never usually overlap like this. Hence the strength but strangeness of your dreams.

This is a totally new situation and as such it calls for a change to the normal procedure. The problem is no one is sure exactly what the procedure should be. So I am here to gather your thoughts and feelings on the matter, and then tomorrow I'm going to visit Claude to do the same. I need to ask you and Claude one important question' Mason paused before finally asking 'do you feel able to return to the Gateway in order to take part in the Bonding Ceremony?'

'If the doctors think I'm well enough then I'd consider it but I'll only do it if Gina does too.'

Both men then looked at Gina who had lifted a shaking hand to cover her lips and had a panicked look in her eyes. She didn't have to answer, both men knew it was a no.

'It's okay' Blake reassured her 'Mason isn't saying you have to do it. Its fine, we won't go' and then to Mason 'Sorry mate, like I said I won't go if Gina won't.'

'Its fine' Mason had expected a no but it was still a bit of a blow. So they definitely needed a plan B, so he had another question for the couple.

'If we can think of a way for you to take part in the ceremony either from here or somewhere else a bit nearer to the Gateway, would you be willing to take part?'

'Of course we would' said Blake and then to Gina 'you can manage that can't you love?'

Gina nodded 'Yes, I think so.'

'Good, thank you. I'm going to leave you alone for a bit now and go speak to your doctor to see if he thinks you're fit to travel, then we can go from there. I promise you that you won't be made to go anywhere you don't want to but we are still going to need your help. After I've seen Claude tomorrow we'll know where we stand and will need to make a plan.'

'I won't have to see Claude?' asked Gina

'No, not if you don't want to.'

'Okay, I'm not sure I'll be any help but I'll try.'

'I've actually been thinking that we could try something today. The new Dreambringers are with the Etetnals right now learning how to use their gift so maybe in a little while the three of us could put ourselves into a relaxed, sleep like state and see if we can commune with them from here. It'd be a kind of experiment, are you up for it?'

'Sure I'll give it a go' said Blake

'Okay I'll try' agreed Gina

'Good. So you both rest for a bit and when I come back we'll give it a go.'

Leaving the hospital room Mason went in search of the doctor. He found him in his office.

'How did it go?' the doctor asked

'Pretty well, but I need to check a couple of things with you.'

Mason was aware that the staff at this facility were on the same 'level' as Eddie had been in that they knew that the Dreambringer patients that came to them were special and to some extent why they were special but they didn't know about the Eternal Dreamers, therefore Mason has to adapt what he told the doctor now.

'Firstly Gina, Blake and I need to take part in a mental exercise so that I can assess how their injuries have affected their dream abilities. They both feel they are up to it. Secondly it may be necessary for them to leave this facility for a short while in order to help with some Foundation business. So the question is do you feel they are well enough to do these things?'

'Well for the first part I'm sure if they feel capable then this is fine with me. Regarding them leaving in Gina's case physically she is well enough to leave us and I'm confident that you will make sure she gets any help she needs emotionally so I agree to her leaving. As for Blake we are still keeping him under observation to be on the safe side as his head injury was quite severe. I would like to keep him here for at least one more night, I will assess him in the morning and if his vitals are satisfactory I would be willing to let him leave for a day or two but only if I know that a medical professional would be allowed to go with him to monitor him.'

'I'm sure that can be arranged. We can discuss it with the Foundation later when we have the conference call, but I just wanted to hear your thoughts on it. I'm going to let them rest for a while and then we'll need total privacy with no interruptions in order to carry out the mental exercise.

'That's fine, just tell me when you start and I'll make sure you're not disturbed.'

'Thank you. Is there somewhere I can rest up for a bit myself?'

'There's a staff lounge just down the hall but there will be people coming in and out, but I'm about to do my rounds so it will be nice and quiet in here for a while so you can stay here for a bit, the sofa is very comfortable.'

'That would be great, thanks.'

'I'll leave you to it then.'

The sofa was indeed comfortable and Mason half sat; half lay on it whilst he gathered his thoughts.

When the doctor returned Mason said he'd like to have a walk around and then get some fresh air if that was okay. He was told it was fine to wander the corridors as long as he didn't disturb patients and if he wanted fresh air there was a little courtyard garden the patients used and he was welcome to sit out there if he wished. He was given directions and set off.

After stretching his legs he found his way to the thankfully empty garden and sat on one of the small benches. It was a small, well-kept garden with raised beds full of colourful flowers. A very peaceful place, perfect for a spot of fresh air and thinking.

Mason reluctantly left the garden a little while later. It was time to try out his idea and so after letting the doctor know he was about to start he headed for Gina and Blakes room.

After a morning of artwork and a quick lunch the new Dreambringers had eagerly made their way downstairs for their afternoon session with the Eternals.

The group were midway through their session when Max and his Eternal were the first to notice it. Max felt a strange sensation like someone was standing directly behind him, he looked even though he knew there wasn't anyone there. He knew that his Eternal could feel it too.

'What is it?' Max asked without speaking

'It's a friend' answered his Eternal

This relaxed Max a bit and that was when he got it and just as realisation hit he received the message.

'Hi Max, it's me Mason, how are you?'

'I'm good, how are you?' Max was surprised at how easily he answered with his mind 'Where are you?' he enquired feeling a rush at the discovery of this new talent.

'I'm with friends, we're trying something out, I hope you don't mind.'

'No, its fine with me' and Max felt his Eternal respond in the same way.

Aaron was the next to experience this strange communication. Unlike Max however he did not know the person who spoke to him telepathically and he was a little confused. His Eternal knew them though and Aaron couldn't help but be affected by the acceptance and joy that the Eternal felt. The message came from someone called Blake and after a little while Aaron knew all he needed to know about who Blake was.

Mary's experience was very similar to Aarons and with her Eternals help she soon embraced this new form of communication and was soon enjoying a three-way telepathic conversation with her Eternal and Gina.

After a short while the other two Eternals picked up what was going on and conveyed this to Clea and Geth and soon the whole group were connected. It wasn't lost on Clea and Geth that two minds were missing from the get together. They couldn't help but notice the note of sadness felt by their Eternals, Clea's in particular, about the absence of two members of the group. Despite this the main emotion was joy. Mason's experiment was a success, and they all knew it was a big help to what lay ahead.

After a while Mason reluctantly brought the session to an end. He could sense that Gina and Blake were tiring and they'd done enough for this first try. Goodbyes were said and Mason, Gina and Blake's essences withdrew. The new Dreambringers continued with what was left of their session as Mason, Gina and Blake's consciousness' returned to their bodies.

Mason felt tired but happy. It had gone really well, he had real hope for the first time that things would work out. He could tell that the session had tired the couple considerably but he also knew that they were much happier now than they'd been since all the trouble started. Even without the mental connection you could see it in their faces. Gina looked calmer, less nervy and they both had more colour in their cheeks. Mason would have some good news to tell at the conference call and he was so relieved.

'How amazing was that?' said Mary. She was making tea for the group up in the art room kitchenette as they wound down from their session before heading back to the Gateway.

Clea smiled 'It just keeps getting better'

'Who knew we had that in us' said Aaron 'I mean we're Dreambringers and we can communicate telepathically with people and other lifeforms, its literally mind blowing.'

'Get a grip' this comment from Geth temporarily dampened the mood until Mary went over to him and playfully punched his arm.

'Don't be a grump' she said.

For a second he looked angry but Mary raised her eyebrows at him and his face softened.

'You guys just need to calm down a little' he said.

'So you don't think we achieved something amazing? Asked Max

'Maybe, but I just don't like all the hysterics about it.'

'Who's hysterical?' asked Clea 'we're just happy, you should try it now and then.'

'Let's not argue' said Max

'He just enjoys being a grump' added Mary laughing and the briefly charged atmosphere was cleared. Geth was just being Geth, Mary understood him the most and was conveying it to the others. They would get used to his ways and he theirs. They were a unit now and it was important they got on.

The conference call was taking place in Dr Harris' office. Mason and Eden had been joined by Sofia and the three of them were chatting whilst they waited for Cedric Neale and two other members of the Foundation to join the call. Once Cedric and the others were on the line they got down to business quickly.

The doctor gave them his report first and then he was asked to leave the room before Mason could give his own report. Eden Harris wasn't offended by this; he'd worked for the Foundation for a long-time and was well aware of the hierarchy and like all Foundation members he accepted his place within it.

Mason's report was received well, although there was a slight note of disapproval from Cedric Neale over Mason going ahead with his 'experiment' without consulting the Foundation first. Overall though everyone was very pleased with the progress he had made.

Sofia told them that the new Dreambringers had returned to the house just before the conference started and she had spoken to them briefly. They had told her what had happened and she reported that they'd been very excited and amazed at what had been achieved. This was obviously good news. Cedric Neale then moved the conversation on with a question for Mason.

'I take it you propose to try the same experiment with Claude tomorrow?'

'Yes I do'

'Fine, fine, whilst you do that I will look into possible sites to use near the Gateway then this time tomorrow when we know where we stand with all three we can plan our next move.

'Should we tell the new Dreambringers to expect another communication from outside tomorrow?' asked Sofia.

'That's a good question' said Cedric 'Is it better for them to expect it, or would it be better if it comes as a surprise like today. There are arguments for both scenarios. What does everyone think? Will knowing its coming make it easier or are we better leaving it as more of a test to see how it works with no warning?'

The group discussed this for a while and finally concluded that Sofia would let them know to expect it as in theory if they knew it was coming and were prepared things would go smoother and it would also help establish a routine for future use of this new Dreambringer skill. Because that's what it was, a new skill. With no Dreambringers up until now ever being away from their Eternals for long a connection across distance had never been tried (apart from in dreams) there had been no need for it. This was a new chapter for The Somnium Foundation and it's most important members across the world.

With that decision made the conference came to an end and the three Foundation members signed off. Sofia stayed on the line a little longer to chat with Mason then they said their goodbyes and Mason went to find Eden Harris to tell him his office was free again.

That night every dreamer in The Gateway's dream radius received stronger, more satisfying and soul strengthening dreams. The deficit of the past few weeks was over and their lives would once again be more enriched.

The Foundation facility where Claude was being looked after was totally different to the one Mason had visited the day before. It was a lot smaller for a start. The hospital was a large, purpose-built building, but this facility was a house. A large Victorian house yes, but still a house.

The door was answered by a middle-aged lady wearing a tweed skirt, an old-fashioned blouse and a friendly smile.

'Hello, you must be Mason Winchester, my name is Linda Michaels it's nice to meet you.'

'Hello nice to meet you too' answered Mason as she ushered him into an entry hallway that had the look and feel of a slightly run down but clean and handsome bed and breakfast.

'This way please' she said leading him towards the back of the house and through a door on the left. The room they entered was a strange mix of lounge and office with mismatched furniture consisting of a large antique looking desk with a modern office chair on one side and a basic plastic one on the other, an old metal filing cabinet and two upright armchairs, one upholstered in an old-fashioned tapestry print, the other a worn burgundy velvet. The carpets and wallpaper were both floral print but again a mismatch. Linda indicated that Mason should take the burgundy armchair and she sat in the other one and once they were settled she began to talk.

'We have an unusual set up here so I thought I'd give you a little information about this facility before I take you to see Claude.

This facility is mainly used as a kind of halfway house for retired Dreambringers. All retiring Dreambringers find the transition hard but some have more trouble adjusting, mainly those who came to their calling later in life. We help them make the transition. For most it's a reasonably brief stay, others stay a little longer and a few have been here quite a while and will probably remain here for the rest of their lives.

We're not the only facility of this kind within the Foundation but this is the oldest. We have five en suite rooms here, two of which currently have permanent residents. There is a communal lounge, a staffed kitchen and this office. I run this facility and there are six other members of staff: two cleaners, a cook, a caretaker and two mental health nurses. I myself am a psychologist and councillor. I live on site; the others work different shifts. The cleaners, cook and caretaker are on the basic Foundation level, the mental health nurses are on the same level as the Wardens at the art communes and I being a retired Dreambringer myself am on the same level as you. This obviously means that I am the only one here who knows the details of what happened to Claude; therefore we can speak freely but only when we are alone.'

'So you were the one who told Claude that what he did was the Soul Stealers fault and not his?'

'That is correct, the Foundation informed me and I told Claude.'

'How did he take it?'

'Well as you know he was in a terrible state when he arrived here. His physical injuries were minor and easy to deal with but his emotional problems were another matter. The Foundation didn't really know what to do with him having never dealt with such a crime being perpetrated by a Dreambringer.

I kept him lightly sedated to start with and had a few sessions with him. He was wracked with guilt and so confused and terrible as his supposed crimes were I could only feel sorry for the man. If it hadn't been for his own confessions I would have thought there had been a miscarriage of justice.

Of course we did then find out that in a very strange way that was the case. So to answer your question when I first told Claude he was not to blame for his actions he went very quiet and then I could see in his face as realisation dawned, it all finally made sense to him and his relief was visible. But then his expression clouded over and he raised his hands and said, 'but it was these hands that injured, these hands that killed and it was my weak mind that let it happen' so now the confusion was gone but his guilt and horror were still in force.'

'But you explained that he wasn't weak, that he'd been ambushed and that it could have been any of us and the result would have been the same.'

'Of Course I did but he remained inconsolable. But rest assured that since then I have worked with him every day and over time he has begun to forgive himself a little. Apart from a mild sedative to help him sleep he has refused any medicinal help but he is improving, slowly.'

'Does he ask about Gina and Blake or mention Mahesh?'

'He has enquired about Gina and Blake and I have kept him up to date with their progress. The fact that they are doing well has helped him recently. As to Mahesh he never mentions him, I think it's too painful,'

'And what about his dreams, does he dream, does he tell you what he dreams?'

'The first time I asked him about his dreams he said he didn't deserve to dream and wouldn't discuss it. I asked him again more recently and his exact works were 'I dream only the small weak dreams that my withered soul can manage' I haven't dared ask since then.'

'I don't blame you, that's pretty dark. Does he interact with the other people who live here at all?'

'No, he hasn't left his room since he got here, I can't even persuade him to get a bit of fresh air out in the garden. I bring him his meals and make sure he eats them. The only other people he sees are the cleaners when they do his room, he keeps himself clean but resists their visits as much as possible and won't speak to them whilst they are in his room. I'm always in the room with them just in case he does start to say anything he shouldn't though.'

'What does he do all day? Has he asked for supplies so he can paint?'

'He's never asked for supplies. I take him books and he has a television and a radio in his room both of which I know he uses.'

'Did he know I was coming?'

'No, I thought it best not to tell him.'

'Okay, well I think that's all my questions answered and I just want to say thanks for looking after him.'

'There's no need to thank me it's my job.'

They were quiet for a minute or two as Mason absorbed all the new information and then he asked one more question.

'Can I see him now?'

Claude's room, like the lounge cum office was very eclectic with a patterned carpet and floral wallpaper. There was a single bed, a small wardrobe and a chest of draws with a tv on. At the bottom of the bed opposite the tv there was an armchair similar to the ones downstairs, and in this armchair sat Claude reading a book. Linda had entered first and Mason stayed in the doorway as she approached his friend who looked up from his book.

'Hello Claude, dear, you have a visitor.'

Claude hadn't spotted Mason yet and first he looked puzzled and then his expression changed.

'I don't want any visitors' he said managing to look and sound both angry and scared at the same time.

'But he's come a long way and he really wants to see you'

'Who has? Who is it?' and then he noticed Mason in the doorway. For just a second a smile lit up his face and Mason saw his friend again, but then his expression returned to anger and fear. He didn't say anything as Mason entered the room properly, he just stared.

Mason noticed that Claude had definitely lost some weight and he looked pale and shaky and seemed to have aged ten years. Claude has always been a happy, gentle sort of man and it was breaking Masons heart to see him like this.

'Hello Claude, it's good to see you old friend.'

Claude just stared at him; his expression now less intense but still fearful.

'I understand Linda has been looking after you. It seems like a nice place here.'

Still no answer.

'I hope you don't mind me turning up unannounced like this but I really wanted to see you. Is it okay if I stay for a chat?'

Claude gave a small nod. Linda took this as her cue to leave.

'I'll leave you two friends to it' she said

With the door now closed Mason noticed a folding chair propped against the wall behind the door so he brought it over so that he could sit by Claude.

'How are you doing Claude?'

'Fine' answered Claude not sounding fine at all.

'First of all Claude I would like to apologise to you on behalf of myself and Eddie?'

'You apologise? What for?' Claude looked baffled 'I'm the one who needs to apologise, to you and to Eddie and to.......' And there his voice broke up.

'There's no need Claude, honestly, its fine now, everyone knows it wasn't your fault, please don't worry, and Eddie says to say Hi mate.'

'He does?'

'Yes'

'But what is it you think you need to apologise to me for?'

'For the way we treated you after we found you on the driveway.'

'Well I don't remember much about that to be honest, but from what I do remember I was treated fine, especially in light of the terrible things I'd done.'

'That's just it though, you hadn't done anything terrible, something terrible had been done to you.'

'But I did do it Mason, I was weak and I let that creature in, I let it overtake me.'

'You're not weak, it would have been the same for any of us.'

'I am though, I have always been a weak man.'

'Nonsense, you are a Dreambringer and the system doesn't let weak people become Dreambringers.'

'You'll never convince me it wasn't my fault; I just have to learn to live with this guilt and shame. I need to be left alone, outcast and forgotten about, I don't belong here, I have no place in the Foundation anymore.'

'That's not true, we need you Claude, your work as a Dreambringer is not done.'

'What do you mean? Of course it is, how can I be trusted now.'

'You are trusted and we do need you.'

'What do you need me for?'

'The Bonding Ceremony Claude, we need you to take part, to release your bond with your Eternal to your replacement, it's how it works remember.'

'But surely the bond is already broken, my Eternal must have disowned me, I have shamed It and everyone.'

'I assure you that isn't the case, your Eternal misses you like we all do.'

'That can't be true'

'It is. Have your tried making contact since you've been here.'

'No, of course not'

'That's one of the reasons I've come to see you, you need to try.'

'I can't'

'Why, what's stopping you?'

Claude didn't know what to say to this he just shook his head.

'You say you feel guilt and shame right?'

Claude nodded

'So wouldn't you want the chance to redeem yourself? Don't you think that helping us now would make you feel a little better?'

'Maybe'

'Isn't maybe a good enough reason to try?'

'I guess so'

'So you'll give it a go then?'

'I can do it from here?'

'Yes, to start with at least'

'What do you mean to start with, I can't go back to the Gateway I really can't go back there'

'You don't have to, I'm sorry I need to explain this to you better.'

'Yes please do'

'Firstly we need to establish how strong your link is from here, then I need to know if you would be prepared to move somewhere nearer if need be. I then have to report back to the Foundation so that a decision can be made on how best to proceed. I've already done this with Gina and Blake.'

At the sound of these names Claude blanched.

'How are Gina and Blake?'

'They're good, and this experiment went well with them?'

'Are they going back to the Gateway?'

'No'

'Do they hate me?' this said quietly'

'No, they don't hate you Claude'

'Are you sure? You've asked them?'

'Claude I'm going to be really honest with you here okay. Blake doesn't remember the attack at all, (Mason decided to omit mention of Mahesh) but he's been told what happened and he doesn't hate you at all, he feels bad for you. Gina doesn't hate you, in her heart she knows it wasn't you who hurt them so she forgives you, but in her head she still sees you brandishing that tree branch and she will never forget that.'

Claude had flinched at the mention of the attack and Mason worried that he'd gone too far but he had to continue.

'I don't think either of them will be able to be in the same room as you again for a while but I promise you that though they can never forget they can forgive. They don't blame you Claude and they don't hate you and Eddie and I definitely don't hate you.'

'Eddie would see me?'

'Yes, Eddie would definitely see you, in fact he would have come with me today if he could.'

'Really'

'Yes'

'I would like to see Eddie'

'I'm sure that can be arranged sometime soon, but for now we need to deal with the ceremony problem. Are you willing to give this a go now?'

'You want me to try to contact my Eternal?'

'Yes'

'And It won't reject me?'

'No, it will be happy to commune with you again, they bear no malice, you should know that about them'

'Yes, yes you're right sorry'

'So you'll do it?'

'I'll give it a try, yes'

'Good man. I suggest I go and find Linda and arrange for some tea then we can relax a little before giving this a go, okay?'

'Yes'

And so Mason headed off to find Linda.

Samuel was playing a song called 'Phoenix' it was by a singer/songwriter called Dan Fogelberg and it was one of his favourites both to play and to listen to. It was hard to know what Talionis would like so he'd started to work through some of the songs he loved the most.

It was a shame he only had his acoustic guitar; he'd have to contact the Foundation to arrange for some of his other instruments to be sent to him. His drums and piano were a bit impractical but he could definitely use his violin, steel guitar and his banjo. It would be good to change it up a bit. All his instruments except his guitar were in storage along with most of his other belongings. He'd only brought the basics he'd been travelling with to the Gateway. The Foundation would sort it no problem and he was sure that now they were settled Dorothea would like to rest of her belongings too. He'd get her on the case when he finished this session with Talionis.

At the beginning of the session when he'd monitored Talionis he'd found Its emotions much the same as the day before, now after a couple of hours of music he decided to give communicating with It another try. He was a little disappointed to find that there was no perceivable change. Yes the creature still seemed calmer and the little note of curiosity was still present, but nothing had really changed. So Samuel went back to playing his music.

When he went in at the end of the session to check Talionis there was still not perceptible change. This was definitely proving a challenge.

After their tea break Mason took a nervous Claude through some relaxations exercises before getting him to lay on his bed whilst he took his place in the armchair. Then the two men used their Dreambringer talent to go into a light sleep before sending their spirits out in search of the Eternals. Mason took it slow and hoped that Claude was following him.

'*Mason is here again*' Max told the group without speaking, something that was becoming more normal to them all now. They'd just started that day's session when Max had suddenly felt Mason's presence just like the day before.

'*Anyone else got a visitor?*' asked Clea

Aaron and Mary said no and Clea told them she hadn't but Geth didn't say anything.

'*Geth?*' prompted Clea

'*Wait*' he replied. They waited. Then after about a minute '*I think there's someone here*' another pause, then '*Hello*' it was a hesitant query as if he wasn't sure of an answer, then again '*Hello*'.

To Geth it was sort of like he was getting a phone call but the line was bad. Someone was there but he wasn't hearing them properly. He turned to his Eternal for help '*what should I do?*' and the Eternal replied with '*welcome him*' and so that's what he did and he was rewarded with a tentative '*Hello*'

'*Someone's here*' he informed the others and then he enquired, '*Who is this?*'

'*I'm Claude*'

And then he didn't have to tell anyone anymore, they all knew Mason and Claude were with them. They greeted each other and then conversed as a group. It was another success and it made them all happy and proud.

When the session ended and Mason and Claude came back to reality Mason noticed a change in his friend immediately. Claude had a little colour in his cheeks and he was even smiling a little.

'That went well' said Mason

'It was amazing' said Claude 'I was a little rusty to start with but I did okay I think'

'You did well mate, well done'

'So I've helped?'

'You bet you have'

Claude was really smiling now, the short contact with his Eternal had done him the world of good, he had been welcomed and hadn't noted a trace of bad feeling from the Eternals or the new Dreambringers.'

'I can do it' he said 'I can help with the ceremony; I want to help'

'That's great'

But then the smile on Claude's face disappeared as something occurred to him.

'Oh no I just realised this is nearly the end for us isn't it? I mean my time should end, I don't deserve to be a Dreambringer anymore, but you and Gina and Blake you have to give it up now too, I'm so, so sorry'

'Firstly no you don't deserve to have your time as a Dreambringer cut short anymore that the rest of us do. As for myself personally I'm not gonna lie, I'm not really ready to give this up but I know I have to and I don't blame you for it. Everything's a little uncertain right now but I'm sure the Foundation will see us right so please don't worry on my account.'

Claude gave a little nod of understanding but Mason knew he would still hold himself to blame no matter what he said.

'Let's not worry about all that now anyway. You need to rest now whilst I go and update the Foundation. They're gonna be really pleased this went well. I'll come and see you before I leave'

'Are you going back to the Gateway today?'

'No I'm staying somewhere nearby tonight then heading back early tomorrow, at least I think that'll still be the plan'

'Okay'

'Don't worry we'll see each other again soon I promise'

'That's good, and Eddie too?'

'Yes you'll see Eddie too'

The two men chatted for a few more minutes and then Mason left Claude to rest and went to find Linda. She wasn't in the office so he went for a wander and found her in the kitchen. The kitchen was large with outdated dark wood style cabinets and a table that looked antique in keeping with the rest of the house, but he noticed it had all the mod cons too.

'How did it go?' asked Linda

'Good, thanks.'

He then told her about the little experiment he'd tried with Claude and that it had gone well adding 'I think it helped him a little, proved to him that there's no ill feelings for him from anyone. Claude is resting now but he did good.'

'I'm so pleased. Maybe he can move forward a little now, this could give him the little push he needs to set him on the road to recovery.'

'Let's hope so'

'So what happens now?'

'The conference call is due to start in about an hour and a half so we have a bit of free time before then so you tell me'

'Are you hungry?'

'Now you mention it yes I'm really hungry'

'The cook will be here to do the residents meals in about an hour but I'm quite capable of a simple meal so how about I make us something?'

'That would be great, thanks'

They ate a leisurely meal and then cleared up after themselves. It was then time for them to go to Linda's office and set up for the conference.

The conference went much the same as the last one. Now Mason's job was pretty much done, and it was over to the Foundation to sort out a suitable place, or rather two suitable places to send the three outgoing Dreambringers to take part in the ceremony from.

Mason would return to the Gateway to explain things to the new Dreambringers, and he would play his part as the only outgoing Dreambringer to be on site for the ceremony.

As well as finding the sites the Foundation would have to find staff to go with Gina and Blake and Claude. They would have to be of suitable level and skill to lend a hand. There was always a Marshal on site for this ceremony so with Sofia already there that was one problem solved anyway.

These things to be sorted were relatively simply, it was the details of the actual ceremony itself that were uncertain. Mason's experiments with his friends had proven that their links were still viable and that they could commune with their Eternals from a distance, but could they actually relinquish their link this way? As the link was mental rather than physical it would seem very possible, but it had never been done so no-one really knew for sure that it would work. All they could do was plan the best they could and hope it worked.

Now with the jobs everyone had to do arranged the conference was brought to an end.

As promised Mason went to see Claude before he left. He explained to him what was going to happen and what was needed of him. Claude was a little distressed that Mason wouldn't be with him for the ceremony, but he pointed out that at least one of them should be there in person and that Claude would have plenty of support.

He did what he could to boost his friend's confidence and repeated his promise that he and Eddie would visit as soon as possible after the ceremony took place. He knew that Claude was still anxious but he felt that his visit had helped his friend and he left him in a much better state than he'd found him in. He left Claude with a goodnight that the Gateway group had used often and it brought a smile to Claude's face now'

'See you in my dreams friend'

That night in dreams old friends came together. There was no fear, no blame, just reunion, and when new friends joined them it became a powerful thing. Their positive energy radiated to dreamers everywhere benefitting all and beginning to heal deep wounds.

Gina awoke from her dream feeling refreshed. Claude had been in her dream but it had been dream Claude and she hadn't been afraid of him. She knew that the fear would return as the day wore on but she felt it wouldn't be as strong. She rolled onto her back and releasing her arms from the covers she lifted her uninjured arm up as if pointing to the ceiling. No shake. The healing power of the dream at work.

She heard Blake stir and turned her head to look at him.

'Good morning'

'Good morning beautiful, how are you feeling?'

'Better after that dream, you?'

'Same, it was a good dream and I feel pretty good'

'Look no shake' she held out her hand to prove her statement.

'That's great, things are going to get better now I know it'

She returned his smile.

Linda actually received a proper greeting and even a smile for the first time when she paid her morning visit to Claude.

'You're in a good mood today' she said

'I dreamt of my friends and we were happy'

'I'm glad to hear it'

'Can I tell you about them? You met Mason but I'd like to talk about him and Gina, Blake and Eddie'

'Of course you can'

He'd never wanted to talk about his friends before except to say how bad he felt about what he'd done to them so this was progress. She noted that there was still no mention of Mahesh but she was sure that would come in time now that Claude seemed to be moving forward. It would be a nice change to note some progress in his file for once.

The kitchen at the Gateway was very noisy that morning. Eddie was cooking one of his massive fry ups and the newbies were chatting loudly about their dreams of Mason and his friends. Eddie had dreamt of his friends too and joined in the chat. Sofia had dreamt too but she preferred to listen to the others. Mason would be coming home soon and she had a few things to arrange but for now she was happy to listen to the lively chatter and relax for a bit.

When Mason saw the big iron gate he felt relief at being home again. His trip had been important and had gone as well as could've been expected but he was glad to be home. Eddie met him at the front door and gave him a massive hug.

'Welcome back mate'

'It's good to see you Eddie'

'Come into the kitchen and tell me all about our friends. I know you've related it all to the Foundation and we've been told the highlights but I want to know everything. Do you want a drink or something to eat?'

'A cup of tea and a sandwich would be great and I'll tell you anything you want to know' Mason followed his friend smiling.

The newbies were out in the Factory and Sofia had gone for a walk so the two men had the place to themselves. It took Mason a while to eat his sandwich as Eddie inundated him with questions but he didn't mind.

Sofia joined them just as Eddie was running out of questions.

'I only have one more question' he said 'and now Sofia's here she can help answer it. When is the ceremony gonna take place?'

'I don't have a definite date yet but really soon is my guess, I'd say the day after tomorrow is likely unless any problems crop up'

'And what do we do until then?'

'I think we should all do what we can to boost the Eternals energy as much as possible by working on our art, the Dreambringers in the Factory and the three of us here. We all need to get plenty of sleep and the three of us should do what we can to assure the newbies that they can do this, we stay positive.'

'Good plan' agreed Mason

'Let's do it then' said Eddie getting up to head for the art room. He liked the plan as he was eager to do some more work on his new graphic novel and now he'd have company whilst he did it.

Earlier that morning Samuel and Dorothea had also shared the friends dream. Samuel was pleased, it meant things were working out regarding the Bonding Ceremony. Now he was on his way to his next session with Talionis.

When he entered the room he found Talionis sat on the bed facing him as he entered Its eyes open, the white light beaming from them like headlights through fog. It gave him a little start but he recovered himself quickly. Was this a greeting? Was it progress?

Samuel sat himself in the chair, his guitar propped beside him. The creature hadn't moved, Its strange gaze was still set on the door.

'How are you today Talionis?' he asked to see if the sound of his voice elicited movement. It didn't. Okay, so he'd see if this seated position was reflected in the creature emotional state. Putting himself in the required meditive state he went in search of answers once again. He noted the visual emotions present but after a little monitoring he detected slight changes in levels. The anger seemed slightly reduced as did the frustration and self-pity. That was a good sign. And then he noticed that the little glimmer of curiosity had grown, another good sign. Encouraged by these changes he probed further. Something else was different but it was so subtle he couldn't quite get it so he tried some thought questions.

'How are you feeling Talionis?'

No response.

'Is there something you want to ask me?'

Nothing. No wait, what was that? A little shift. Was it trying to answer? He waited. Then it was there, one word, faint but decipherable.

'Music'

Samuel held down his excitement and hoping for more communication asked *'Do you like the music? Are you saying you want more?'*

He paused expectantly and then just when he was going to give a little prod it came again, this time stronger.

'Music' and before he could react once again *'Music!'* even stronger.

'I'm gonna take that as you wanting more music' he told It hoping for a more informative reply but as he waited he noted a change. He perceived something, not an emotion exactly but it was clear, tiredness. The effort of that little communication had weakened the creature. So Samuel came out of his meditative state and picked up his guitar. He noticed that at some point during their exchange the creature had moved because It now lay in Its usual position on the bed, Its eyes closed. It was ready and so he began to play.

After a couple of hours he did the usual monitoring. This time there was a detectable difference. There was still turmoil within the creature but it was different now. It wasn't that the ever-present emotions of anger, frustration, confusion and self-pity were any less, it was more that other emotions were surfacing. He couldn't put a name to any of them though, they were too faint and in some cases fleeting. But something was definitely going on with the creature which he took as a good sign. He withdrew hoping that a couple more hours of music would help clarify these new emotions.

After another long music session it was time for Samuel to monitor the creature again. He was trying to stay positive without building up his hopes too far.

As expected the creature emotional state hadn't altered perceivably since a few hours before but he pushed harder to see if he could get a reading on the faint traces of new emotions.

'Please tell me what you are feeling' he pleaded gently over and over.

He concentrated on the new emotions. They seemed to come in little pulses with tiny peaks that then receded. He tried to read them at the height of the peaks but to no avail. It would have to be enough for now that his music seemed to be having an effect. It was time to end the session, he was exhausted.

Dorothea had arranged things with the Foundation and so his other instruments and the rest of their possessions were being delivered the next morning. The van they'd borrowed from the Gateway would be returned too. Maybe a change of instrument would help, a bit of variety would be good from Samuels point of view at least; he was getting a little bored of these long guitar sessions.

Talionis was changing. A part of it that had lay dormant for years was awakening. An old battle was re-emerging. Something new had come into Its life, something good, something that spoke to this gentler side of It, the part of It that had retreated long ago, beaten down by the stronger element. It was now gaining strength, a strength It had received from the simple joy of music. It had made Its voice heard over the anger and self-pity of Its dark, dominating side and It was clamouring for more attention. The fight was on, It had been silent too long.

Late in the afternoon Sofia received a call from Cedric Neale and as she'd predicted the ceremony was scheduled to take place early in the morning on the day after tomorrow. So that left them a day and two nights to prepare. It should be enough, it had to be enough.

When the newbies got back shortly after Sofia's call they were told the basics over dinner and then afterwards Sofia took them through what usually happened at the Bonding Ceremony. This is what she told them:

The five new Dreambringers and the five outgoing Dreambringers all enter the Eternals chamber together. The new Dreambringers lay on the stone beds. The Eternals 'stand' on the stone circles at the head of the beds and the outgoing Dreambringers stand at the foot of their replacements bed. The Dreambringers then put themselves into a meditative state as they have been taught by their Eternals their aim to form a strong telepathic link with their specific Eternal and the Dreambringer they are replacing forming a three-way communication. They then commune this way for a while to strengthen the circular link.

Then the outgoing Dreambringers begin to slowly withdraw from the circle letting go of their connection to their Eternal, and as their link weakens the new Dreambringer's link becomes stronger.

The outgoing Dreambringers being more experienced do most of the work along with the Eternals, all the new Dreambringers have to do is keep their minds receptive to their Eternals.

Withdrawing from their Eternals is not hard for the outgoing Dreambringers as such, but it does cause them sadness as once their telepathic link is severed it is gone forever. They will still commune with their Eternals at times when they sleep but their strong link is now being taken over by another.

Once their links have been severed the outgoing Dreambringers leave the chamber and their replacements remain a while in order to strengthen their new two-way link. When they emerge from the chamber their time as a Dreambringer really begins.

With the usual procedure explained Sofia then moved on to the differences, which to be honest everyone knew but it still needed saying with a few added details. Obviously Mason would be the only outgoing Dreambringer in the chamber. Gina, Blake and Claude would join the ceremony remotely. It would work much like it had when Mason and the others had visited them only this time they would need to forge a stronger link and they would need to do it alone.

There was no guarantee that it would work this way, but they would all do their best. The other abnormality was the one outgoing Dreambringer would not be present at all: Mahesh. With

Mahesh's death his link to his Eternal had already been broken. This meant that the ceremony would be different for Clea. With no third-party link to break Clea's link to her Eternal was already stronger than the others so her job would be to reinforce that already strong link. Clea wasn't fazed by this, she knew the sadness the man's death had caused her Eternal and she told them she would work to heal that sadness as she felt that would strengthen the link.

'Will severing their link hurt Mason and his friends?' asked Mary

'No, not physically anyway. As I've said emotionally it can be hard for them but they've usually decided that their time is over so they're ready for it.'

'But that's not the case this time' Mary said looking at Mason with a concerned expression 'they're not ready.'

'Don't concern yourself' said Mason 'I believe in our own way we are now ready. Gina, Blake and Claude have no wish to continue as Dreambringers, its over for them, they'll be fine I promise.'

'But what about you, are you really ready?'

Mason hesitated a little before answering 'A couple of days ago my answer would have been no but after visiting my friends I feel differently. It wouldn't be the same without them and over these last two days I've come to accept that my time as a Dreambringer will soon be over. I can't deny that I will find the ceremony hard but I am resigned to it and I am ready.'

Not knowing what to say to this Mary rose from her chair and walked towards Mason with her arms outstretched. He understood and rose to his feet to accept her hug.

'I know I'm leaving the Gateway in good hands' he said to everyone and Mary hugged him harder. There were a few more hugs and some more chat before the group settled down to work on their art and the evening passed quickly and pleasantly.

The next day the Foundation put the wheels in motion. Gina and Blake were taken to the remote farmhouse of a retired Dream Mate couple a few miles away from the Gateway. A retired Soul Healer of dreams who'd trained as a nurse within the Foundation was sent with them along with the necessary equipment for her to monitor Blakes condition. They arrived late morning, were warmly welcomed by the couple and were soon made to feel at home.

Claude was sent to the equally remote home of an ex Seer of Dreams. Linda went with him; the Foundation having arranged cover for her at the halfway home. They too were welcomed and made to feel at home. Linda had worried how Claude would cope with leaving his room having not set foot outside of it since he got there, but so far he appeared to be coping well. So now everyone was in place ready for the next day.

At the Gateway the new Dreambringers had left for the Factory after breakfast. Mason decided to stay at the house with Eddie and Sofia. Everyone worked on their art and it felt like the air was almost electric with the energy they were creating.

Later, when the Dreambringers communed with their Eternals they learnt more what was needed of them the next day deepening their understanding and helping lessen their stress.

The Foundation kept Sofia up to date with their plans and she in turn passed the information on to Mason and Eddie.

Samuel entered the room with his violin in one hand and his steel guitar on its strap around his neck. Talionis was again in Its sitting position.

'I have something new for you today' he said standing in Its eyeline 'I hope you like it, but first let's see how you're feeling shall we.'

How Talionis was feeling was conflicted, that was immediately clear to Samuel. He couldn't really explain the feelings he was getting from the creature; it was in no way clear and it wasn't like anything he'd come across before. All he could make of the whirling mass of the creatures emotions was that sense of conflict. He decided not to probe into it at this stage, he'd try music first to see if that clarified things. Of course the music could make things worse, but there was only one way to find out.

197

Again when he came out of his meditative state he found that Talionis had lain down on Its bed. Samuel got to his feet and took up his violin – preferring to play standing – and began an uplifting classical piece.

Playing violin took it out of him more than playing guitar so after a while Samuel switched to his steel guitar, at least he could sit down to play it. He kept to tunes that were upbeat but not too manic with a few slower ones thrown in. It felt great to be playing something different and he hoped his audience was appreciative.

After the usual couple of hours it was time to check on Talionis.

Conflict was still flowing from the creature in waves but this time Samuel tried to interpret the conflicting emotions. It was a little overwhelming and after a few attempts he still hadn't made any headway so he tried a question.

'What do you want? Are you trying to tell me something?'

He waited, ever vigilant for an answer however faint. And there it was, a little sensation, faint but perceivable and interpreted as one word *'Help'*

'That's what I'm here for, to help' he returned *'how can I help you?'*

Again a little ripple of one word.

'Help'

Samuel tried a few more times to get more of an answer but received nothing else. So after sending out a hopefully comforting message that he would help he withdrew and went back to playing music.

Maybe these one-word messages were all the creature was capable of thought Samuel as he played, or maybe the conflict he perceived was the creature deciding if he could be trusted or not and so it was both trying to communicate and stopping itself from doing so. How would he know which?

After an hour more playing and thinking Samuel was beginning to tire. He decided to end the session after a quick monitor in case of any change. There was none and he didn't have the strength to search deeper. So after giving more assurances of help he ended the session. He needed a rest and a think. Maybe a new approach was called for. He'd sleep on it and hope the magic of dreams brought him a solution.

It was a very harmonious day for those at the Gateway in general but each of them had moments when thoughts of the next day intruded tinging the day with worry. How could they not worry, they were about to attempt something that hadn't been done before. But then it wasn't the first time, everything that had happened since Talionis attacked Claude had brought change to a well-established system. On the plus side they had managed to find a way to make things work every time and this ceremony was just another obstacle that they would find their way around.

Eddie stood at the kitchen sink looking out on the sloping lawn and the woodland beyond. He was the first one up, or at least the first one downstairs. It was very early still and he'd slept well just not for very long. His dreams had been bright and strong, no strange, shared dreams, just the old normal plentiful ones.

He was contemplating the day ahead, it seemed like he was the only one who didn't really have a role to play. Well he had his role of Warden as usual; he would make sure they were fed and watered and do anything else he could for them but he had no special extra role and he wasn't sure how he felt about it. On the one hand he felt a little left out, but on the other he was relieved he wasn't under the extra pressure the others were. What would he do whilst the ceremony was taking place? Sofia was going to lie down in her room and use her Marshal skills to monitor the ceremony and help in any way she could if need be. He could work on his graphic novel but he would be alone again the thought of which depressed him a little. Hearing a noise behind him he turned to see

Sofia entering the kitchen. His time for reverie was over, for a while at least, it was time to begin his small contribution to the day.

'Morning Sofia what can I get you?'

She wanted coffee and toast which was a little disappointing but Eddie got on with it. Mason was next to arrive. He wanted tea and Eddie persuaded him to have a bacon sandwich too.

An hour later everyone was in the kitchen and their various breakfasts had been eaten. Eddie was clearing up with the help of Clea who had insisted even though Eddie had protested. The mood of the group was positive but quiet. Conversation was subdued and the subject of the ceremony avoided. The ceremony was due to start in a little under two hours and they were doing their best to keep the conversation and the atmosphere light.

After the breakfast things were cleared away the group dispersed. They all needed a little time to do their own thing before things got started. Mason stayed in the kitchen with Eddie chatting. Sofia went to the office to check things were okay with Gina, Blake and Claude. She was told that all three had a good night and were still willing to go ahead with the ceremony. She was given the final time check for when they should start and returned to the kitchen to share the information

Mary and Aaron went back to their room where they lay on the bed spooning. They weren't saying much, there was no need to, they knew pretty much what the other one was thinking. It was a side product of the telepathic skills that connecting with their Eternals had given them. It wasn't that they could read each other's mind exactly they could just sense what the other was feeling, kind of like how a couple who have been together for many years know each other. And that was also how it felt to them, like they'd known each other for a very long time. It was a comforting feeling, and the support they gained from each other eased their stress.

Clea and Max were in Clea's room trying their best to relax on the comfy sofa. Clea was mainly talking and Max mainly listening. This suited them both. The conversation was casual and to anyone listening a bit boring but it was what they needed.

Geth was the only one who chose to spend the time alone. He had always been a loner and his newfound friends would never fully change that. He did enjoy their company more than he'd expected to at first and definitely more then he'd ever enjoyed anyone else's company, but he still needed some alone time. After that first encounter with the Eternals he'd found it much easier to deal with this Dreambringer thing but he was still fundamentally the same grumpy, unsociable bugger he'd always been.

Samuel awoke feeling physically refreshed but his mind was a little clouded. When a shower failed to clear his thoughts he went in search of coffee. Dorothea had already been up for about an hour after waking to dream acquired inspiration. She had scribbled a few notes whilst sitting up in bed then quickly washing and dressed before heading downstairs. After putting on a pot of coffee she'd set up her laptop at the kitchen table and got to work.

'Good morning' said Samuel as he entered the kitchen.

After a brief pause Dorothea returned his greeting then returned to her writing. Samuel understood, she was in the zone. He helped himself to coffee and leaving her to it took it to the lounge.

The coffee helped clear his mind slightly and after a little contemplation he decided to hold his next visit to Talionis off until later in the day. The Bonding Ceremony was taking place that morning and he wanted to be available to hear how it went. There was another reason too. An idea was crystallising in is mind. An idea he knew had come from a dream. It wasn't clear yet because his mind was still processing the information from his dream. But it would come, he just had to relax and wait.

That morning after undergoing a few health checks Blake had been deemed physically fit to go ahead with the ceremony. After the tests he and Gina had been pretty much left to themselves to prepare. Like Mary and Aaron the couple didn't need to speak much, in fact after years together their telepathic link was even stronger. And as with Mary and Aaron they gave each other strength.

Like his replacement Claude chose to spend this time alone. He wasn't the loner that Geth was but being alone now felt right. After assuring Linda that he was fine she had left him to his own devices. He sat in his room and used some meditation skills he had learnt over the years to help keep as relaxed as possible. He had a chance to redeem himself a little today and he was determined not to fail his friends a second time.

After this period of rest everyone began their preparations. The Dreambringers and Mason headed for the Factory, Sofia went to her room, Eddie headed for his room having decided to work on his art there rather than the large, empty art room. Gina, Blake and Claude went to the rooms that had been prepared for them and lay down ready.

As the scheduled time to begin approached Mason and the others entered the Eternals chamber. Its occupants already 'stood' on their stone circles waiting as the humans took their places.

And then it was time to begin.

First the new Dreambringers made a connection to their Eternals just like they had done for the last few days. That was the easy part. Next Mason joined in. His connection was still easy and with Max being aware of him joining them the two Dreamcatchers and their Eternal soon formed the circular three-way link.

Now for the first potentially tricky part.

Gina and Blake needed to join their Eternals. The practice that Mason had initiated now proved invaluable. It took some effort but everyone felt it on some level when the Dream Mates made their connections. Mary and Aaron did their bit now encouraging their counterparts to link with them too. It took a few minutes but it was achieved, the circular links were in place. It was then Claude's turn. It took him a little longer than it had the Dream Mates but the desired link was formed. The first phase was complete.

There was relief all round, but everyone knew that having done this part to some extent before it was the next part that was unpredictable. It was time for the outgoing Dreambringers to relinquish their link. Everyone was aware that the Eternals did most of the work at this part. They were the ones who initiated the link so they were the ones who began its ending. First they sent reassurances, vibrations that the retiring Dreambringers felt throughout their bodies and interpreted as words. Words like '*I will always be with you. I will see you in dreams and help you to act upon them. But now I release you, and you must release me.*'

At this point Mason perceived his link with the Eternal as physical. In his mind's eye he saw two cords of swirling white mist extending from the Eternal to himself at the chest and head, a manifestation of the link between two souls. A link he must now let go of. He did what was asked of him and began to let go. He felt a sensation as if he was falling slowly backwards although he knew that his body still stood upright and unmoving. It was a little disconcerting but he went with it, he knew he had to. As the feeling of falling continued he saw the cords of mist begin to evaporate. He could still feel the presence of the Eternal in his mind but it was becoming weaker. For a few seconds he felt the urge to fight, to halt this mental feeling of falling, but although fainter the message from the Eternal was clear '*you must let go*' and so he did.

Gina, Blake and Claude were experiencing things a little differently. For a start all three having opted to lay down for the ceremony their sensation was more one of sinking than falling. There was also no cords of mist the distance making this perceived manifestation of a physical link unfeasible. The messages were also fainter so that they had to concentrate more to understand, but they managed it, and the command was clear '*You must let go.*'

Unlike Mason none of the other three felt even the slightest impulse to fight. Their links were already weaker and their trauma's meant they were more ready to relinquish their Dreambringer lives. And so it was now time for the four friends to '*let go.*'

For Gina, Blake and Claude the uncoupling was a release and a relief. They experienced it as a flickering light dimming and then disappearing from their minds, like a gladly lost memory. They sighed; it was done.

Mason experienced things differently. First the sense of falling abated and he saw the cord of mist completely dissolve. Then he felt a jolt shudder through his body and his vision dimmed for a second. Next he felt a strange sensation like a great weight was being lifted from him, but not in a good way. He felt light but empty. And then he was falling for real. His legs felt like jelly and he collapsed slowly to the floor where he lay physically unhurt but emotionally bereft. Then he heard a voice in his head, not the vibrational contact of the Eternals but a human voice, and he recognised the voice, it was Max and his message was simple

'*Thank you*'

Immediately Mason's mood lifted a little. He gained control of his body again and got to his feet. Max lay before him, eyes closed, his Eternal hovered behind him and there were the cords of mist again, this time coiling from the Eternal to Max. He looked around and saw identical cords of mist connecting each new Dreambringer to their Eternal Dreamer.

It was done, the Bonding Ceremony was a success.

Mason was lying on the sofa in the Factory art room. With his part of the ceremony done he'd left the Eternals chamber and was now taking a minute or two to rest. He needed to get himself together a bit before calling the Gateway to confirm it had gone well. He felt a bit mean holding off telling them the good news but then they would sense that things had gone well anyway so they could wait. He was battling mixed emotions right now and didn't trust himself to hold a conversation without those emotions coming through.

Sofia got up from the bed slowly. As Mason had thought she was aware that things had gone well and that she had done all she could for now. After taking a minute or two to come fully out of her dream state she set off to find Eddie. She could tell him she felt things had gone well and they could wait together for a call from Mason to confirm this. She understood that it may take Mason a little while to be in a position to make that call so wanted to give Eddie early assurances.

When the call came Sofia found that despite her own confidence in good news the relief at the confirmation was still immense. Mason told her he was going to wait for the new Dreambringers to finish their final bonding session and then come back with them. There was no way to know how long that would be, but he felt he should wait.

When she told Eddie the news she saw the relief in his face too. She then phoned Cedric Neale to tell him all was well. He was a very calm and controlled man whose emotions were often hard to read especially over the telephone, but she could detect the relief in his voice too. She asked him what happened now? Was there anything he needed her to do? He suggested that they all take a day or two to relax and make sure that everything was definitely on track. She was to stay there for now as were Mason and Eddie then in a couple of days they would start to talk about what was to happen next.

After telling Eddie what Cedric had said she asked him to phone Mason to pass the info on. Sofia was so glad that everything was back on track, but what on earth was she going to do with herself for the next couple of days? Then she had a thought, no-one had spoken with Samuel and Dorothea for days. With everything that had been going on it hadn't occurred to anyone to check up on them. A phone call was definitely needed so that she could pass on the good news from her end and find out what was going on at theirs.

She quashed a slight feeling of disappointed when it was Dorothea who answered.

'Hi Dorothea, I just wanted to let you know that the Bonding Ceremony went really well so things are really back on track here.

'That's great news.'

'Yes it's a real relief to everyone. How are things going with you?'

'We're settling in well and the creature is still contained so I'd say things are going well but if you want to know how Samuels doing with his work you'd best ask him' as usual Dorothea was brief and to the point.

'Is he free to talk now?

'Yes I expect so, I'll just go and get him'

'Okay, thanks'

After a couple of minutes wait Sofia was pleased to hear Samuels voice on the line.

'Hi Sofia, how are you?'

The sound of his voice sent a little thrill through her body which she tried to ignore. What was it about this man that made her feel like this?

'I'm good thanks' she said managing to keep her voice steady 'how are you?'

'Tired but okay thanks'

'I phoned to let you know that the Bonding Ceremony was a success and as we haven't spoken for a while I also wanted to check in to see how you were doing and if you needed my help with anything.'

Samuel was obviously pleased with her news and then she listened intently as Samuel told her about his music idea and the minor but important progress that he'd made. She was impressed and told him so, he thanked her saying there was a long way to go before real congratulations were called for. He then informed her that he was formulating a new approach to the creature that he was hopeful would provide results. He didn't want to go into details but said he would update her on his progress in a day or two bringing their conversation to an end. They said their goodbyes and Samuel ended the call. Sofia felt ridiculously bereft and then immediately embarrassed. She was a grown woman not a teenager with a crush, she needed to get a grip.

Samuel hadn't wanted to go into details about his new approach because he was still ruminating on it and now that he knew the ceremony was over and had been a success he could really get down to working it all through in his mind. His approach up until now had been through telepathy using the skills he'd learnt as a Dreambringer. It was the way the Dreambringers and Eternals communicated whilst the Dreambringers were awake. It was a direct link that combined the mind and the soul when the mind was in control. But the other form of communication they shared was different. It was the communication of dreams and this was done when the soul was in control whilst the Dreambringers slept. It was how they communicated as they worked together to bring dreams.

When you are dreaming and your soul is in control you are on a different level to the real world. You see things differently, feel things differently and express things differently. Samuel knew that over the years of monitoring the Custodians of the Soul Stealer had found no sign that the creature could influence the dream world in any way, there weren't even sure that it slept let alone dreamt. But Samuel had not found any report where someone had really delved into this, they had simply scanned the dreams of those in the creatures radius and found no signs of its influence and then remained vigilant for signs of it appearing. They had never really tried to reach the creature in the Dream Realm, had never tried to communicate with it this way. If the creature really did not dream then maybe it wasn't possible but Samuel decided it was worth a try.

During his tour of Foundation art communes he has visited one in China where he had met a Dreambringer named Xiu Bo who had a fascination with some odd dreamers that he had come across in the Dream Realm. He had discovered them lurking at the fringes of the Dream Realm and referring to them as 'Dark Souls' had made a study of them.

After weeks of study and attempts at communication he had concluded that either through their own dark personality or because of severe trauma these Dark Souls could not or would not dream. The would nots were those people who had such a disturbed personality and consequently warped soul that they would not allow themselves the luxury of dreaming, it was not in their nature. They would not accept the interaction of the Dreambringers and especially not the Eternals and did not want to dream the way others did, therefore they could not be helped.

After studying the evolution of the Dreambringer in Foundation lore Xiu Bo had made a connection between these Dark Souls and the formation of the Foundation itself. Back in the day when the Foundation had first formed in order to protect the Eternal and the Dreambringers it had been Dark Souls like these that they had been protecting them from. Although harmless within the dream world when awake the owners of these unresponsive type of damaged souls had been the ones to persecute the Dreambringers and Eternal Dreamers as something they did not understand and so were afraid of. These days the persecution had been eradicated by the Foundations work to keep the Dreambringers and their Eternals a secret, but the Dark Souls still existed.

Having discovered that those who chose to resist were not reachable Xiu Bo decided it was worth trying to help the could nots, those poor, damaged souls who due to severe trauma simply could not dream.

Samuel had joined this Dreambringer on a few of his attempts to help these people. Samuel had found the experience a little unsettling but fascinating. With a normal dreamer a Dreambringer would make a connection with the dreaming soul in order to learn what it needed from its dreams so that is could help the dreamer achieve more from those dreams. These Dark Souls could not dream but they still had a decent soul and so Xiu Bo would connect with these souls to learn what was stopping them from dreaming.

He claimed he had a knack for picking out those most receptive to help and that through simply communing with them he had managed to make their dream lives a little 'brighter'. They still could not dream exactly but Xiu Bo said he was working on that. He also claimed that the little help that Samuel had been able to give had helped and that once he had perfected things further the help of other Dreambringers is what would ultimately be needed to properly help all these Dark Souls.

Having not come across these non-dreamers before Samuel was unsure how true this was but he had no reason to doubt the man. Like all the other exceptional Dreambringers that he'd met on his travels Samuel had learnt what he could from this man in order to enhance his own skills. Now he was wondering if this knowledge would help him with Talionis. Surely the creature could be classed as a damaged soul so maybe It haunted the fringes of the dream world. He didn't think those who searched for the creature in the dream world in the past had knowledge of these Dark Souls so if the creature was present there they would have missed it. But he now had this knowledge and intended to use it to search for signs of Talionis. It was worth a try a least.

The problem was when would be best to try this? If the creature slept, when did it do so, it seemed impossible to know. During the day the Eternal Dreamers roamed the dream world mostly alone. Made strong by the Dreambringers art energy they dealt with those who dreamt during the day. At night when the dream world was most active the Dreambringers joined them to help with the extra load.

The system was geared to the natural human cycle of sleep as it was unrealistic and unhealthy to expect the human Dreambringers to alter their sleep patterns. A quick daytime nap was not sufficient to fully interact in the dream world and benefit from it.

Some groups of Dreambringers did work the odd daytime 'shift' into their routines but it wasn't a widespread practice. Samuel had come across one of these groups whilst in South America and he had tried a couple of daytime sleeps himself as part of his self-appointed task to gain experience in every kind of Dreambringer 'work'. He had enjoyed these daytime experiences, relishing the newness of it. The dream world was a slightly different place during the day, less populated and so less lively it had different things to offer. With the Eternals on top of things a Dreambringer could observe more and intervein as much or as little as they wanted to. Samuel had particularly relished the observational side of it. And this is what he intended to do now, well, not now exactly, he wasn't tired enough for a proper daytime session yet.

His music session with Talionis that day would be starting later as he'd been holding it off until the ceremony was done, so it would therefore go on later. He would then stay up for most of the night and start his sleep session in the early hours of the next morning. He could of course have looked for Talionis in the night-time dream world but felt it would be easier in the less populated daytime. If the creature was there it would stand out more in the sparser atmosphere. He could always try a night-time venture at a later date. He would need to take things easy for the long day ahead. He needed to be tired enough to sleep in the morning but not too exhausted that he fell asleep too soon. Therefore his session with Talionis would be a gentle one. He would play music but take breaks, and when he monitored the creature it would be a basic scan, no hard probing. Obviously if the creature had different ideas and was suddenly eager to communicate he would go with it, but he thought that scenario very unlikely. So now his plan was finalised he went to find Dorothea to tell her what he intended to do.

When the new Dreambringers finally emerged from the Eternals chamber they looked both enlivened and tired. Their eyes were bright and their voices high with excitement, but the languid movements of their bodies betrayed their tiredness. Mason knew how that felt. He'd spent most of the time waiting for them in a half sleep state and had experienced some crazy vague dreams, the effects of being so close to the bonding. The group didn't really have time to have much of a winding down session before setting off back to the house as it would be getting dark soon, besides the tiredness would really set in before long.

When they arrived Eddie was ready as ever to get them anything they wanted. They were all too tired to be hungry so it was hot drinks all round and a planned early night. There was talk of a celebration but they decided to put it off until the next day as no one was in a fit state to party.

Now he was back at the Gateway and his head had cleared Mason needed to make a couple of calls. He needed to know how his friends were now it was all over. He couldn't rest until he knew they were okay.

He spoke to Claude first.

'We did it Claude, how are you feeling?'

'Good, I'm feeling good' and he sounded it too. Mason noticed a note of tiredness in his voice but he sounded positive and happy.

'You did well, we couldn't have done it without you'

'Thank you and I just want to say I'm so glad that you persuaded me to do this. It's what I needed and I now feel that I've atoned at least in part for the terrible things I did'

'You know that I don't think you have anything for atone for'

'Yes, I know, but it's what I feel, though after this I feel so much better'

'I'm glad Claude, really glad'

'You will come and see me again soon won't you?'

'Yes, as soon as I can, I promise'

'I'll see you soon then'

'Yes, and until then I'll call you often okay'

'Great, yes, thanks'

'Bye for now Claude'

'Goodnight my friend'

Gina and Blake were similarly thrilled at the day's outcome. As with Claude Mason could tell that their success had given them the boost they needed. Blake told him that the Foundation were sending them back to the hospital the next day so he could be checked over but that he was confident they could soon leave the hospital and start their new life. Not that they knew exactly what that new life would entail yet, but they were in a positive frame of mind which was a good start.

Mason felt that Claude's road to a new, happy life would be longer, that he would be at the halfway home for quite a while yet, but he'd get there. Mason re-joined the group for a quiet wind down before they all retired for that planned early night.

They went to bed relieved and happy and slipped into restful sleep until it was time for the Dreambringers to join their Eternal Dreamers in their first proper task of Dreambringing.

Coming together for the first time as Dreambringers in the Dream Realm they marvelled at the beauty of their dream selves and at the amazing landscape around them. The Eternal Dreamers let them get their bearings for a short while before introducing them to the first dreamers in need of their help. And so the new Dreambringers truly began their task.

Mason, Eddie and Sofia were up early as usual, but it was a while before the others joined them. It was their first proper night as Dreambringers and they were making the most of it. They each slipped into as many dreams as they could and worked their magic. It was exhilarating and hugely satisfying knowing you were helping people manage their lives and fulfil their potential.

When they finally emerged from their rooms they were buzzing. The house was full of voices and laughter. A celebration was definitely in order.

They made their plans. Mason and Eddie would go out in Eddie's now returned van and get provisions as they were low on both art supplies and food. Lists were compiled and the two men set off. Eddie was in high spirits having so much to do. He was also glad of the chance to spend some time alone with Mason having missed the company of his friend greatly. Time with Eddie was also what Mason needed to lift his spirits and the two friends were happily deep in conversation as Eddie drove down the long driveway.

Sofia was to stay at the house, she would check in briefly with the Foundation and then spend some time on her artwork until Mason and Eddie returned when she would help them put the provisions away and prepare for the planned party.

The new Dreambringers would of course be going to the Factory. For today they had decided it would be a shorter day than the previous ones though. They would spend an hour or so on their artwork, then they would spend a couple of hours as a group with the Eternals before returning to the house for the party. It wouldn't be anything special, just some party food and drink, some music and (Clea's suggestion) a bit of dancing. A celebration between friends with lots of chat and laughter.

Sofia felt it was a shame they couldn't invite Samuel and Dorothea, but they couldn't leave the cottage, not both of them together anyway and inviting one and leaving the other out didn't seem fair. So it would just be the eight of them. It would be fun, a release after all the stress of the last few weeks. A release they all needed and thoroughly deserved. They had, together, pulled off something amazing against the odds. Sofia was proud of them all.

It was finally time for Samuel to sleep and he was more than ready for it. It had been a very long day. As planned he'd kept his daytime session with Talionis easy going. He'd played his various instruments in half hour sessions with breaks in between. During some breaks he'd left the room to get fresh air or food and drink, during others he'd stayed to observe Talionis.

Since the day they'd caught It out in the woods he hadn't seen the creature move at all. It only ever moved when he wasn't able to witness it, was this on purpose? Did the creature move much when it was alone? Although restricted Its recent exploits had proved it could get about if it needed to. He was surprised no-one had thought to put cameras in its room to monitor its movements. Another sign of the recent apathy towards it he guested. The monitoring he'd done in between the music sessions had been brief and light and had produced no new information. He'd returned to the cottage late evening for some food and had then used various distractions to keep himself awake. Whilst Dorothea was still up they'd chatted and played a few card games. Then he'd watched some tv, listened to some music and read a book. It had been a struggle at times but he'd managed to stay awake. Now he was ready to try the new approach.

The first step was easy, he needed to fall asleep. It took him less than five minutes. It would be a while before he entered the dream world, his body would go into sleep mode first. Then once his body was relaxed and his brain was in resting mode his soul would be released.

After the required rest period Samuels soul broke free and entered the Dream Realm. As he had planned the Dream Realm was at the quietening down stage. The local Dreambringers had finished for the night and after enjoying their own last dream had vacated their dreams to wake to the new day. That left the Eternals and the late sleepers. Samuel began to traverse the realm of dreams, taking it slow and easy as he got used to its terrain. He would take his time, get his bearings and then seek out any signs of Talionis.

He also took time to commune with the Eternals he came across. He told them why he was there and they not only accepted his presence with pleasure but said they'd help if they could. In order to forge a link with them that would then help him in his search he helped them with a few of the dreamers. It was great to be back in Dreambringer mode again. The lack of a permanent Soul Healer of Dreams in this area meant that his help was particularly appreciated.

After a while he began his search for the creature. He sensed the energy the Eternals were sending his way to help and he was grateful. He headed for the fringes and the Dark Souls that lurked there.

In the Dream Realm Samuel was an extremely impressive presence. His dream self appeared even taller, his long, silken hair flowing around him, his skin tone warm and vibrant, his sculpted face and brown eyes even more beautiful. He was a sight to enrich anyone's dream.

The dream representations of the Dark Souls could not have been more different, however. They are simply represented by a dark, vaguely human shaped mass with occasional sparks or eddies of light moving within it. There was nothing to identify them as the human they were. This was a little troubling for Samuels quest; how would he recognise Talionis? Still, he had a gut feeling about this, if It was there, he would know it.

Coming across the first few Dark Souls Samuel tried to engage with them as he had been shown by Xiu Bo. He needed to get a feel for who these souls were in order to tell if one of them was Talionis. It was hard to communicate with them but he got enough from each to know that they were simple, damaged human souls. And so he searched on. He searched for what felt like a long time and then he began to sense his Dreambringer session coming to an end.

A Dreambringer instinctively knows when they're getting near to the end of their nights work and it's time to leave in order to enjoy their own dreams for a while before waking. Samuel had decided that he would forgo his own dreams this once so he resisted the pull to sleep so he could search for longer. And so he continued to search.

His search had still proven unfruitful when the pull became to hard to resist and he began to withdraw from the Dream Realm. But just at the last moment he saw something; another Dark Soul, but this one was different. This Dark Soul was larger than any of the others and there was something else within it that the others didn't have. As well as the usual eddies of light at the core of the dark shape there was a lighter mass, it looked like a whirlpool of silvery smoke with flashes of while light within it.

Could this be Talionis?

But before he could study the strange soul further he felt the inevitable happen, he was returning to the physical world.

Samuel awoke with a jerk and the word 'No' on his lips. His heart was racing and his head hurt, it wasn't good for him coming out like that but what could he do. This was important work, and he had been pulled away just when he was getting somewhere. It was very frustrating. He would have to wait hours before he could go back and find out if it had been Talionis. That was if he could find the same dark masses again next time.

The question was what should he do until then?

Sofia was bored. She'd had a taste of what Eddie's last few days had been like and she wasn't enjoying it. She'd had a text from Mason about half an hour ago to say they still had a few shops to go to and so would probably be another hour and a half at least, but that was all the contact she'd had with anyone for far too long. She looked down at the sketch she'd half-heartedly been working on, it was an uninspiring view of the driveway and the woodland outside the art room window. Surely she could think of something more interesting to draw.

She let her mind wander and then she had an idea. Ripping off the page she threw the boring sketch onto the coffee table and then got comfy on the sofa with the nice clean sheet of paper on her lap. Touching charcoal to empty page she began a sketch of a strong male face crowned by long, black hair. The next hour flew by as she worked on several sketches of her new muse and before long she heard the sound of tires on gravel and Mason and Eddie were back.

By the time the group returned from the Factory the crack team of Eddie, Mason and Sofia had put away all the new art supplies and prepared all the food for the party. The tables in the art room had been moved against the wall under the windows and covered with tablecloths that Eddie had dug out from somewhere. One table was laden with food, one with drink and another held crockery, cutlery and glasses. Eddie had sorted out a selection of CD's and placed them by the CD player in the corner of the room. He told everyone that they were welcome to add any of their own music to the play list.

It was decided that before the party began they would all go and freshen up and get changed. It was a party after all, why not dress up a bit. Sofia didn't really have any party clothes with her so she just changed into her least work like blouse and some jeans.

Eddie's wardrobe only consisted of jeans and band t-shirts so his before and after looked pretty much the same, but he chose his favourite Motorhead t-shirt for the party.

Geth and Max's party looks weren't much different from their everyday looks either, but Clea happily noted that they both chose to wear the t-shirts she had made for them.

Aaron replaced his t-shirt with the only shirt he owned – a blue western style shirt that Mary told him he looked amazing in. She also complimented Mason on how handsome he looked in the loose-fitting white shirt and black jeans he put on.

Mary herself owned no real party clothes but had brought a top that was basically a long-sleeved t-shirt but with flared sleeves and a flattering round neckline, it was black and purple (obviously). Clea was the only one who really looked dressed for a party in a bright green dress that billowed around her ample figure perfectly. But then Clea always looked ready for a party in her wonderfully colourful dresses.

So, with everyone ready the party could begin.

Before the party got into full swing Mason pulled Max aside for a quick word.

'I made a decision today' he said 'I'm going to move my things out of the room tomorrow so that you can move yours in.'

'You don't need to do that' protested Max 'I'm find where I am.'

'No, it's been decided, you're the Dreamcatcher at the Gateway now, that room is yours. Eddie is going to help me box up my things, I'll take the essentials to the spare room, and we'll put the rest in the attic for now. I'll be leaving soon Max and I might as well get the packing done. Things move fast in the Foundation once decisions are made, its best to be ready.'

'Do you know where you're going yet?'

'No idea mate.'

'Well, if you're sure about the room'

'I am'

'Okay, thanks I appreciate it'

'You're welcome'

And the two men re-joined the party which was getting progressively rowdier by the minute.

Whilst the Gateway party was going on Samuel was in with Talionis for another music session. This time when he monitored the creature he detected a slight shift in Its emotions. Or rather an addition to Its emotions. He detected hints of two different emotions, one being hope, the other fear and took this as another sign that the creature was conflicted.

He decided to play It some music first before asking any questions. It would hopefully lull it a little, reduce the fear maybe making it more likely to communicate with him. These music sessions did seem to be having an effect but what Samuel really wanted to do was get back to the Dream Realm and find the strange Dark Soul again. He was pretty sure that it had been Talionis but he was keen to find out for certain and so the delay was frustrating. Although he was making some progress here he felt that communicating with Talionis in the Dream Realm would provide better results.

Having played for nearly two hours it was now time to see what effect, if any, his music was having. He didn't expect much and he was right not to. Things were pretty much the same as two hours earlier. He had a feeling that any questions he asked would go unanswered and so he decided to leave it for the day, saving his and the creatures energy for later. In the morning he would sleep and go in search of Talionis again.

He had told Dorothea what he was doing but hadn't informed Sofia or the Foundation. He wanted to know for sure if his hunch was right before he made a report. Now he just needed to keep himself occupied until the morning.

CHAPTER 22

BRINGING DREAMS

Eddie was in his element, after a big shop the day before and then the party he was now helping Mason and Max swap rooms.

The group at the Gateway had spent a leisurely morning over a big breakfast but now everyone was busy again. With the bonding ceremony over and the new Dreambringers now properly established in their roles there was no longer any need for all five of them to spend the whole day at the Factory. They would soon establish their own routines splitting their time between the art room at the Gateway, the art room at the Factory and the Eternals Chamber.

For today the group would split with Mary, Aaron and Clea going to the Factory for a few hours whilst Max and Geth stayed at the house taking it in turns to help with the move and work on their art. Mason and Sofia would be lending a hand with the move also, but Eddie was in charge. He had a plan that included a thorough clean of both rooms so there was plenty for everyone to do.

At last it was time for Samuel to enter the Dream Realm in search of the strange Dark Soul he believed to be Talionis. He was soon asleep and communing with the Eternals as before. He worked with them for a short while but was eager to start his search and they understood.

It wasn't like a normal search; he couldn't go back to where he'd seen the Dark Soul last time because of the constantly changing landscape of the Dream Realm. But at least this time he knew what to search for. There was the possibility that It wasn't there now but he couldn't let that stop him. He'd asked the Eternals if they'd ever seen this strange Dark Soul but they admitted that they took little notice of those souls who inhabited the fringes as they could not help them. They told him that they would look out for it now though and alert him if they came across It.

After what felt like a long-time searching Samuel received a message from one of the Eternals. He transported himself to where they were in the dream landscape. The Eternal communicated that it had caught a glimpse of something that might be what he was looking for in the misty outskirts of its current position. Samuel thanked the Eternal and set of in the direction indicated.

The fringes of the Dream Realm were just vast patches of nothing with a fog like atmosphere and the Dark Souls stood out within it. Samuel came across a couple, but they were not what he was looking for.

Then through the mist he caught a glimmer of fast-moving light and his spirits lifted. This could be it. He drew nearer so that he could see it clearer. And there it was, the strange dark mass with the lighter one within it. The light and pulses within flitting through both light and dark. Now he had to see if he could communicate with it. Using the techniques that Xiu Bo had taught him Samuel tried to make a connection between his dream soul and that of the Dark Soul. Even if the soul could not or would not answer his enquiries he hoped that he would at least be able to tell if this was Talionis.

'*Is that you Talionis?*' he probed concentrating hard on picking up any sort of reply. His Dreambringer skills were also automatically kicking in, searching the soul to find out what it needed from dreams. The pulses of light within the Dark Soul became brighter as he watched and he was beginning to feel something coming from them but it was like static on a badly tuned radio. After a while the static began to clear a little but then it seemed like there were two messages coming through but they were garbled and mixed together so he couldn't make any sense of them. It was hard to focus but he persisted. And then he was rewarded as out of the distorted mess one short message came clear.

'Music man?'

He knew it was a question rather than a statement, so he gave an answer.

'Yes Talionis it's me, music man'

It had to be Talionis, his hunch had been right.

'I'm here for you Talionis, I want to help' he conveyed with all the vigour and sincerity that he could.

'Music man, help'

The message was weak but understandable, Samuel was elated, he was getting through.

'Yes I'm here to help you, tell me what I can do to help you'

He thought an answer was coming through, but it was even weaker than the last one and he couldn't decipher it.

'Try again' he encouraged *'tell me how to help you'*

There it was again, a little stronger and this time he thought he understood. He thought it was conveying the word *'trapped'*

'Are you trapped?' he queried *'How are you trapped?'* but no answer came clear, the static was back. It was so frustrating.

Then something seemed to shift and he received another message, this one loud and clear.

Go Away!'

Samuel reeled a little with the force of it. Such a strange shift, from weak but responsive to this loud negative retort. The last message definitely felt different and Samuel thought he understood why. A theory had been forming within him since he'd first come across this strange dark and light soul and now this exchange had proved he was on the right track. Still there was no harm in trying to get more information.

'I'm not going anywhere right now. There's no need to fight me, I mean you no harm, let me help.'

'Go away' the message was the same but weaker this time.

'You don't really mean that, deep down I know you want my help'

'No' getting still weaker.

'Why are you resisting?'

This time the reply had no words, but Samuel sensed fear and anger.

'You don't need to be afraid of me, I won't hurt you, or let anyone else hurt you, you can trust me.'

Static again and then that strange shift as the light pulses with the figure changed once more.

'Please help' and it was back to receptive again.

'How?'

The light pulses were shooting around now, bright and frenetic. And then the experience got even stranger for Samuel as two messages assaulted him at the same time both loud and clear.

'Release'

'Nooooo'

It was very jarring and left Samuel reeling.

After a short time Samuel recovered enough to notice that the lights within both the dark shape and the lighter one within had dimmed. The exchange had taken it out of all involved. There was still so much Samuel needed to know but he could feel his time in the Dream Realm coming to an end. This time he wouldn't resist the pull, he'd need his own dream time to recover from this encounter. There was just time for more assurances.

'I have to go now, but I will be back, and I will help you. You can trust me, I promise.' And then he was drawn away into his own healing and inspiring dreams.

When Samuel awoke he had some answers. He had, at least in part, solved an old mystery. He knew now that within Talionis two beings vied for control. It had not become one being, the two sides of it still existed. He couldn't be sure, but he was pretty certain that the receptive part of the creature, the one that wanted help was the Eternal side and the part that was angry and afraid and was resisting him was the human side.

He needed time to think this all through and get it straight in his mind. He would assemble all he had learnt first to get a clearer picture of it all for himself, and them he would make a report for the Foundation. With their help he would then work out where to go from there.

A few hours later Samuel had ordered his thoughts, made notes and then typed up his report on his laptop. The report consisted firstly of an outline of each of the sessions Samuel had with the creature stating his methods and any progress made. This was followed by a statement of the conclusions that he had come to after these sessions. This is what it said:

After spending time with the creature known as the Soul Healer and named by itself Talionis both in the waking world and the Dream Realm and considering all I have learnt about It from the Foundation archives I have come to the following conclusions:

Within It's human shell the creature is still two distinct souls. For the most part I feel that the human soul is dominant and this is likely to have been the case since the souls were merged. The Eternal Dreamer can exert itself at times but I believe it finds this difficult and is quickly exhausted. The conflicting emotions I have detected can be divided between the two souls and I believe they are divided as follows:

Human = anger, frustration, self-pity,

Eternal = curiosity, hope

I feel that the feelings of fear and confusion can be attributed to both. In my opinion it is the human side that has resisted communication all these years and that the Eternal has become weak, or too disheartened over time to make any real effort to make its own feelings known. I believe that the human side is most likely responsible for the terrible recent events and that this has maybe woke the Eternal from its apathy. I also think that my music may have given the Eternal the strength to be more assertive, after all they do feed on art energy.

I believe the Eternal has intimated that it is trapped, I assume by the human. I also have a theory that the creature exists in both the waking world and the Dream Realm at the same time. I cannot say exactly what leads me to this theory, only that it may be another explanation for why it has been so hard to communicate with the creature in the waking world. The Dream Realm approach had never been attempted before and I achieved more results that way, the soul always being more receptive than the mind. Also, the Eternal was able to communicate better in the Dream Realm as that is their domain after all.

I intend to continue both with my music sessions and with the Dream Realm sessions. Regarding the Dream Realm I will try a night-time meeting next to test my theory of It being present there at all times. My aim during these sessions will be to encourage the Eternal side of the creature to be more assertive and to win the trust of the human side so that it relinquishes Its hold a little. This will then enable me to better assess the creature and therefore how to help it.

Any feedback on my conclusions so far will be welcome, as would any ideas on how to proceed. Although I cannot give a time scale for the work I am doing here I am hopeful of a breakthrough soon.

Once he had checked the report through several times Samuel asked Dorothea to read it. He wanted her to both check the report was written clearly and to give him her thoughts on its content. She read it through carefully before assuring him that his points were clear. She then read it through again and gathered her thoughts before giving her views on its content.

'I think that the conclusions you have come to all make sense given the information you have so far. Although your theory about the creature existing in the two realms simultaneously obviously needs proving. Overall though I'm very impressed, you've done more in a few days than many have done in years and I have to commend you for that.'

'Thanks, I'm sure others could have done the same if they'd only tried.'

'Maybe, but I think it needed someone like you, someone with both the talent and the inclination to try.'

'Someone had to do it at some point, the creature has been neglected for far too long. I know It's done some terrible things, but nothing will be solved by locking it away again for years.'

'Very true.'

'Do you have any ideas on how to move forward?'

'To be honest no, not right now, but I will give it some thought.'

'Thanks.'

Now with the discussion over Samuel e mailed his report to Cedric Neale. He considered copying Sofia in but decided it should be left up to Cedric Neale to decide who read the report and when. That done Samuel began planning his next move. It was late evening now and he wasn't sure when his report would be read or when he would receive a reply, but he would make his plan anyway, any changes could be made later.

His first problem was sorting out his sleep pattern so that he could try finding Talionis in the Dream Realm during the night-time. On his current routine he wasn't due for sleep for another five or six hours, but he really needed to go to bed before then.

Would he be tired enough though? He decided to split the difference, he'd try to sleep in about three hours' time and see what happened. It would still mean entering the Dream Realm several hours before his previous two times which was good enough for now.

With the timing now decided it gave him the next few hours to think of a strategy when approaching the creature. Maybe the mental energy it would take would help him sleep.

Things were changing within Talionis. The part of It that had lay dormant for many years had been awoken by the music man.

The Eternal Dreamer had been a silent witness to the atrocities done by the human It was trapped within. Its inertia first brought about by shock and then over time facilitated by a weakness caused by the lack of art energy It received. It could not die, but this lack of energy to feed upon coupled with It no longer having proper access to the Dream Realm had left It weakened and in silent despair.

Now this man had brought music back into Its life and restored both Its energy and Its hope. It was still trapped though, Its jailor the human It still loved despite it all. It could sense that the music man had reached the human too but that It was resisting. Now It had some strength back It must convince Its partner that the music man was trying to help and persuade It to become open to that help. Its human companion was very damaged suffering from Its solitude and lack of dreams. It knew that deep down Its human side was tired and afraid, but that anger and hatred ruled Its behaviour. It must endeavour to calm Its human so that It would be prepared to communicate with the music man. Then maybe It would come to see that this man could help.

And so the Eternal set about using Its restored energy to persuade Its human that communicating with the music man would be a way for It to express all It felt and had suffered and that this may lead to a better life for them both.

The human was a little unnerved by the Eternals newfound strength at first but was soon persuaded that this was a good thing. It was harder to convince It to put Its guard down a little and communicate with the music man though.

The Eternal persisted claiming that no harm could be done by letting this man know how It was feeling. And so, in the end it was agreed; the human would communicate Its feelings to the music man but promised nothing more. The Eternal was happy with the progress made. It believed that the music man was the key to ending the suffering that It and Its human had endured for so many years. It could only hope that Its human would allow them to receive that help.

Mason and Eddie were relaxing in the kitchen with a cup of tea. The move was completed and Max was in his new room sorting his things as he wanted them. Geth was in the art room (having declined tea) and the last time they'd seen Sofia she was on the phone in the office. Their light conversation had lapsed into companionable silence when Sofia entered the room.

'I have some news' she said joining them at the table.

'Good news I hope'

'Yes. The Foundation have made a decision on your future and I think you'll be happy with it'

Eddie sat up straighter 'Let's hope so' he said.

'Eddie, they want you to stay on here at the Gateway but in exactly what role is actually up to you.'

'How do you mean?'

'They're giving you two options. You can stay on here in your current role for the duration of this group of Dreambringers stay, but because you now know more than someone in your position usually does, and because they feel you have done such a good job during all the troubles, they are offering you more'

'More?'

'Yes. As you now know the group here have been missing a Soul Healer of Dreams for many years and so the Foundation have been sending Dreamwishers on a regular basis to help make up the short fall. Well, what they are now proposing is that you are trained as a Dreamwisher so that this site is better covered on a permanent basis. So what do you think?'

Eddie didn't really know what to think and he understandably had a few questions.

'Am I really qualified to become a Dreamwisher?'

'A while back, before asking the Foundation if I could bring you in on the secret of the Eternals, I monitored you and consulted with the Eternal and from that and your conduct throughout this whole business I believe that you have the potential yes and the Foundation agree. You will have to be tested and trained but they are willing to give it a try if you are'

'And if I fail do I still get to stay here as Warden'

'Yes, or course'

Eddie looked at Mason 'What do you think mate?'

'I think you'd be great; I believe in you'

'Actually' said Sofia 'this does affect you too Mason. If Eddie decides to do this he will need to go away for a bit for his training and so someone will need to do his job whilst he's away'

'And that someone is me?'

'If you want it to be yes. Don't misunderstand, you're not being demoted, this would not be a long-term thing, the Foundation just feel that in light of what's gone on here a new temporary Warden would not be ideal. Plus it will give you and the Foundation time to decided exactly where you want to go from here. So boys what do you say?'

'As a temporary solution it sounds great, so I agree,' said Mason

'I'm in' said Eddie with a big grin on his face.

'Fantastic' said Sofia 'I'll go and let them know it's a go, and then when the others get back we'll update everyone.'

Samuel was back in the Dream Realm on another search for Talionis. A lot more souls inhabited it at this time and these souls included the new Gateway Dreambringers. Samuel left it to the Eternals to explain his presence to them, he had work to do. And so he began his search of the fringes.

There were more Dark Souls lurking on the fringes than on his previous visits but if Talionis was here he would spot It easily. The question being was Talionis here this time.

It took a while but finally he was relieved to spot the larger Dark Soul he was looking for. The creature was here giving some credibility to Samuel's theory.

He approached the Dark Soul and made his presence known. It appeared the same as before, the smoky whirlpool that was the Eternal Dreamer moving within the darkness of the humans soul. There was no way of telling just by looking at it which of the two entities was in control right now. There was only one way to find out.

'Hello Talionis' Samuel sent his greeting with as much warmth as he could 'how are you?'

Lights pulsed within both the dark and light but he received no message in return.

'I would like to communicate with you both' Samuel was letting them know he thought of them as two separate beings 'so who wants to be first?'

There was a pause, and then

'Go away.'

'Ah it's you. Why do you want me to leave?'

'Hate.'

'Why do you hate me, I've done nothing to you.'

'Hate your kind.'

'But you are one of my kind, we are the same, I too was a Soulhealer of Dreams.'

Silence. Was it thinking what to say or had the short exchange tired it? Either way Samuel was happy he'd got something more out of It at least.

And then:

'I was rejected.'

'You did something they did not understand.'

'I was imprisoned.'

'You did bad things.'

'I've been treated badly.'

'I understand where you are coming from and I agree to some extent that you have been treated badly, but you hurt people and they are protecting themselves.'

'I feel such anger.'

'You have to let the anger go for your sake and for others.'

'I cannot.'

'Why?'

'It is what I am.'

'It is what you were, it's not what you have to be now. Let it go, I will help you.'

'Then what will I be?'

'I do not know.'

'How do I let it go?'

'I believe you only need to dream.'

'I have not dreamt for many years; it is my torment.'

'I understand and I will help you.'

'How?'

'I am not quite sure but I am formulating a plan, I just need you to be willing to try. Are you willing to let me help you?'

'I do not know.'

'What can I do to make you trust me?'

'I do not know.'

'Does the Eternal Dreamer within you trust me?'

'Yes.'

'Surely that tells you I am worth your trust.'

'It is hard.'

'I understand that but I can only prove you can trust me if you let me help.'

'Help how?'

'Help you to dream.'

'You can do that?'

'I can try, but only if you trust me enough to let me. Can I speak to the Eternal within you?'

'No.'

'Why not.'

'It was decided it is my turn.'

'I see, It is letting you have your say first.'

'Yes, it was agreed.'

'And when will It have Its turn?'

'Another time.'

'Is there anything else you want to ask me?'

'Why do you want to help me?'

'I have been fascinated by your story for years. You are unique in the Dreambringer world and that intrigues me. I think that you have been neglected for years and I want to remedy that. I want to learn from you. Ultimately I am a Dreambringer and it is in my nature to help people become the best they can be through dreams. I want to do this for you.'

'I must decide if I believe you.'

'I understand.'

'I grow weary now.'

'Then I will leave you to think about my offer of help, but I have one last question.'

'What is it?'

'Are you always here and at the same time within your earthly prison?'

'My soul lives here and my mind within the stone room. It is hard being split in two.'

'Thank you and I'm sure it must be. I will return here when I can so we can talk some more, and I will continue to play music for you if you wish me to.'

'Yes, music please, we both like it.'

'Then I will play for you soon.'

'Goodbye for now.'

'Goodbye Talionis.'

And so Samuel left the creature to its thoughts. He was amazed and pleased by the progress that had been made and the fact that his theory had been proved. He was sure that he could soon gains its trust. Now he could really start to plan how to help the creature.

He still had a little while before his time in the Dream Realm was over for the night, so he happily helped some dreamers before being drawn back to sleep and dream his own dreams.

At breakfast Sofia told the Dreambringers about Eddie and Masons new roles. They were all pleased. She then had a surprise for them.

'Whilst we have been dealing with settling you all in and getting through the bonding ceremony the nuts and bolts side of the Foundation has been working as usual. With the bonding now a success you are officially Dreambringers and so the next stage of your transition to Gateway residents has been put into action.

We are going to receive two deliveries today. Two vans are due here in about an hour and two more later on this afternoon. The first two will be deliveries for Mary and Max, the second two are for Geth and Clea. They will be delivering the bulk of your personal possessions. Foundation staff will have been to your old homes and packed up the rest of your clothes and small possessions such as CD's, books, photos etc. You can sort through your stuff when it gets here and if there's anything not there that you would like please let me know and I will pass the message on.

As you know when it comes to furniture and bedding etc this house is already well equipped but if there are any pieces of furniture that have special sentimental value that you would like brought here it can be arranged, again just let me know. Max I have been asked to let you know tha all your sculptures will be brought here today but the Foundation have decided that rather than bring your kilns from home they will supply you with a new, better model if that's okay with you?'

'Erm, yes that's fine' said Max looking a little stunned 'it's very generous of them, thanks.'

'It's no problem. They're sending you a catalogue so you can choose which one you'd like. It will mean a bit of a wait while they order it I'm afraid.

'I can't complain about that can I, I get to choose a new kiln what could be better.'

'I'm glad you're happy.'

'What about my mountain bike?' Max asked then 'is that coming too, only I was thinking I might take to riding it in the woods on occasion if that's allowed?'

'I'm pretty sure it will be, but if not, you can request it's sent, and as to riding it in the woods I don't see that will be a problem.'

'Great, thanks.'

With that answered Sofia moved on to Clea.

'For you Clea, on a similar note to the kiln, they are bringing your sewing machine and your supply chest as you may be attached to the machine and the supply chest is a good piece of equipment, but they are offering you a new machine if you would like it, either now or in the future.'

'How super. I'm tempted by a new one I must admit but my machine is like an old friend so I think I'll stick with it for now.'

'Fair enough, but the offer is there for the future.'

'Thank you'

'Now Aaron there will be no delivery for you today as I understand you brought all your possessions with you the first day.'

'Yeah, I travel light.'

'Well the Foundation want you to know that you have a real home now and so you no longer need to keep your clothes to the minimum, you can have whatever you need or want now. Once things have settled down here a bit more you will be able to take a shopping trip and buy those things you never could.'

'I don't know what to say to that'

'You're not offended I hope?'

'No, it's fine. I'm kinda used to my capsule wardrobe but it's been hard sometimes not being able to buy things cos they'd weigh me down.'

'That won't be a problem anymore. I think you're lucky in a way not having any baggage, almost literally, it's so much easier for you to start again now.'

'I agree, I am lucky, like you said I have a proper home now and no loose ends to tie up. It's all good.'

'It is. Now as for the rest of you there are loose ends to tie up. And so in light of all this at some point today you will each receive a phone call from a member of the Foundation staff who will go over things with you regarding the selling or renting out of your property and any other assets. They will find out which route you wish to take then make the relevant arrangements and draw up the necessary paperwork on your behalf. Again, I'll emphasise that you don't need to decide today, if you're still unsure you'll just be taken through your options for now. This also means that the four of you will need to stay at the house today. That just leaves Aaron. Mason has said that he would go to the Factory with you if you wanted, or you can stay here with the others.'

'I'll stay here unless you think someone should be at the Factory'

'Here's okay as long as you all work on your art when you can during the day it'll be fine.'

'No problem, with all the lovely supplies Eddie got us I'm itching to get painting.'

'I'll be here if you have any questions and as Mason has been through this process himself he can give you advise or information if you need it.'

And so another busy day began at the Gateway.

Samuel woke in a great mood for obvious reasons. He wasn't sure what had changed but Talionis had been much more receptive and so real progress had been made. He would get something to eat, see if he'd had any answer from his previous report and then update the Foundation on the new information. Then he would put in another music session with Talionis. He couldn't be sure how much his music had contributed to the recent results but he had a feeling they were a lot to do with it. He could also check to see if the creatures new compliance was evident in the waking world too.

Dorothea was pleased and impressed when he told her of his success.

After turning on his laptop he discovered that Cedric Neale was also singing his praises and he hadn't even heard the latest developments. Cedric Neale also said that regrettably no one had any ideas to help him as yet, but Samuel didn't mind.

He typed up another report giving an account of the latest encounter with Talionis and sent it off. He was a little worried about the Foundation's reaction to the slight inference that they had done wrong by the creature, but he wanted to remain truthful. Now it was time for sustenance. He'd have a leisurely, late breakfast giving the Foundation boss time to read his latest report and maybe get an answer before he set off to play some music for Talionis.

He had an answer even before he finished his meal. Cedric Neale was very pleased with his progress and said that although no one there could help him regarding ideas on how to proceed the Foundation would help him in any way they could, he need only ask. Samuel replied with a thank you and said he would keep them fully updated.

After he finished eating Samuel headed for the garage cell with his instruments. He was excited to see what he could pick up when he monitored the creature this time. He was hoping for more clarity and communication.

When Samuel entered the room he found Talionis sat on the bed facing him which wasn't unusual, but as he moved towards the chair he realised that Talionis moved It's head fractionally as if to follow his movements. Progress already, a good sign.

'Hello Talionis, how are you feeling?'

He received no reply but the creatures strange eyes were still directed towards him. He wondered what those eyes saw. Maybe he'd ask.

'I'm gonna play you some music soon but first let's see if we can have a little chat'

Settling himself into the chair Samuel put himself into the required meditative state and went in search of Talionis. He detected a change in the creatures emotions immediately. There was no longer conflict within it and the anger had definitely lessened. Also, now that he knew that the creature was still two distinct entities it was easier for him to understand the emotions he was detecting. He could also tell which emotion belonged to which entity. The (reduced) anger was coming from the human side as were the now low-level feelings of frustration and self-pity. He also detected a new emotion and interpreted it as indecision. There was also still a tinge of fear. From the Eternal he detected an even stronger sense of curiosity than before as well as hope and a note of determination.

'Do either of you want to tell me or ask me anything?' he probed gently.

He sensed that his question had reached its targets and that they were reacting to it in some way but he could not detect any answer. He'd hoped that now the creatures emotions were more positive communication would have been easier but perhaps It hadn't been resisting him before, perhaps It was just hard for It to communicate in the waking world. It seemed to be opening up its emotions to him more but the answers were still not coming. He would just be patient and concentrate harder.

'Anything?' he prodded.

And he waited.

Something was coming, he could sense it building. And when finally he received an answer of sorts he received it in stereo

'Music!'

'Okay I get it' he returned with the mental equivalent of a laugh *'you want music'*

And so bringing himself out of the meditive state he gave them what they wanted.

It was dinner time at the Gateway and the Kitchen rang with lively chatter and laughter. The deliveries had arrived as promised and the new residents had split their day between unpacking, working on their art and talking to the Foundation staff about their properties etc. it had been a good day and everyone was in high spirits.

Earlier Sofia had received a call from Cedric Neale. He told her that Samuel had made some good progress with the Talionis problem and that rather than updating her himself he would e mail her Samuels reports to read.

She found the reports fascinating and her estimation of Samuel rose even higher. This was ground-breaking stuff. After reading the reports a second time and then giving herself time to absorb the information she put in a call to Cedric Neale. She told him how impressed she was with Samuels work and she had a question 'Could she share this information with the Gateway residents.?' Her boss told her that would be fine as someone might have an idea about how to help Samuel further his work. Sofia thanked him and ended the call. Just then Eddie popped his head round the door to let her know that dinner was ready so, although she was dying to tell them about this she decided to wait until after they'd eaten.

Now dinner was over and they were all in the lounge so it was time to spread the good news. The group were amazed and impressed by the news but Sofia noticed a look pass between Mason and Eddie and she knew what that look was about. As the new Dreambringers began a lively discussion about what they had just heard Sofia went over to the silent pair of friends.

'I know what you're thinking' she said addressing them both 'you're finding Samuels sympathetic attitude towards the creature a little unnerving right?'

It was Eddie who answered her.

'Yeah that things dangerous but he seems to think it's the victim here.'

'I understand where you're coming from and you have a point to some extent, but Samuel sees it differently.'

'That thing hurt our friends' this from Mason 'and one of them is dead because of it.'

'That is painfully true and believe me Samuel is well aware of that, but I believe that he feels that the Foundations neglect of this creature is partly to blame for what happened here. He thinks a new approach is needed and it's what he's been working towards for a long time. Continuing to keep the creature locked up is not a good enough solution, he wants to understand It so that a better solution can be found. Now if he approached this with the anger and sadness you are feeling the creature would sense this and would remain as uncooperative as it has been for all these years. By going into this with an open, friendly manor Samuel hopes to win the creatures trust and it looks like it's working. You do understand this?'

'Yes, yes I get it but it's hard you know' said Mason

'I do, and I sympathise, you know I do, but I also think that Samuels attitude to the creature is exactly what's needed.'

'I'm sorry'

'There's no need to apologise Mason, you and your friends have been through a lot. You're feelings are important and I'm here to support you in any way I can, but I'm also behind what Samuel is attempting to do and so I hope you're okay with that.'

'I am, I just had a wobble, I'll be fine.'

'Good, and what about you Eddie?'

'Yeah, I get it too, don't worry, we just need to get our heads around it, but I'm good.'

It was then that Sofia realised that the others had stopped talking and were listening in. they were all looking at Mason and Eddie with concern and sympathy.

'I think we need a big hug-a-thon' said Clea. She then proceeded to start them off with a big hug each for Mason and Eddie. Soon they were all joining in, even Geth (although somewhat awkwardly).

'It's going to be fine, I can feel it' said Clea and everyone, including Clea hoped that it was her Seer talent talking and not just her positive attitude.

Samuel had played for hours with only a couple of comfort breaks but there was method to his madness; he wanted to tire himself so that he was ready to sleep at a normal time. He wanted his next meeting with Talionis in the Dream Realm to take place when it was at its peak. He felt that the presence of the Gateway Dreambringers and as many dreamers as possible would give his own Dreambringer talents a boost that could only help him with Talionis.

'That's enough for today' he said to Talionis 'But I'll see you soon in the Dream Realm.'

Before heading for bed and sleep Samuel spoke to Dorothea, he had a favour to ask her.

'I assume that being a custodian you are still able to enter the Dream Realm as your Dreambringer self if you wish?' he asked

'I am yes'

'Then would you join me in the Dream Realm tonight?'

'Of course I will, but why?'

'I think you can help me with Talionis'

'In what way?'

And so he told her about Xiu Bo and the work he had been doing with the Dark Souls and how more than one Dreambringer working together could be the key to helping them. That although Talionis was different to the other Dark Souls the same approach may work.

'But what exactly would I have to do?' asked Dorothea

'Not much to start with at least, I just need you to be nearby giving me extra dream energy. I don't want you to try to interact with Talionis, I don't think It would react well to that, I just need the extra boost your presence will give me.'

'So I just stay nearby and send you as much dream energy as I can?'

'Yes, exactly. Just concentrate on me, not Talionis, I don't want It to feel ganged up on, It doesn't fully trust me yet so It's not gonna take kindly to someone else wading in. I need you to be near enough to help me but inconspicuous enough so that Talionis doesn't feel threatened.'

'Sounds simple enough'

'And if Talionis becomes aware of you and reacts badly I need you to back off immediately'

'I understand'

'So you'll do it?'

'Of course it will.'

'Thanks Dorothea'

And so now it was time for them to sleep before joining up in the Dream Realm.

The two Custodians found each other easily within the dream landscape and set off in search of Talionis. Along the way they encountered the Gateway Dreambringers. At the first meeting, which was with the Seer of Dreams, Samuel began to communicate an explanation for their presence but was told there was no need, the Dreambringers had been fully briefed on Samuel's work. And so after that the meetings were brief introductions. It was a bit unusual for these first meetings to be between their dream selves but the whole situation was unusual so they all took it in their stride. Samuel was pleased to meet the new Dreambringers but was glad when the introductions were over and he could concentrate of finding Talionis.

This time he came across the strange Dark Soul much quicker than previously. Was this because of the previous visits or had Talionis been looking for him too? Either way he was grateful for the short search.

He approached Talionis alone, Dorothea staying at a distance as arranged. But he was aware of the energy she was sending his way and he was grateful.

He began the communication with a simple greeting.

'Hello Talionis.'
'Hello music man.' the response was gratifyingly quick.
'You can continue to call me music man if you wish but my name is Samuel.'
'Hello Samuel.'
'Which one of you is this?'
'The same as before.'
'Will I get to speak to the Eternal too?'
'Maybe.'
'How are you feeling?'
'Different.'
'In what way?'
'I cannot explain.'
'Are you feeling differently towards me?'
'Yes.'
'How so?'
'I want you to know things.'
'Are you saying that you are willing to open up to me so that I can help you?'
'Yes.'
'Thank you Talionis.'
Samuel felt a thrill of excitement, this was going well.
'I would like to show you what I have suffered?'
'And I would like to receive this information.'
'Are you ready?'
Samuel was more than ready, he felt strong knowing that his own Dreambringer skills were being boosted with Dorothea's help and he was excited to really commune with the creature for the first time. Talionis was opening Itself up to be read as normal dreamers did and so Samuel would finally learn how to help It.
'I'm ready.'
And so the link was made and Samuel was free to explore what Talionis needed from its dreams.

Samuel was shown everything and learnt much more than he expected. What he learnt filled in the blanks on the creatures creation and its life since. He was witness to the conviction and strength of the human as he attempted to merge his soul with his beloved Eternal Dreamer. He was shown the fear and disappointment that this attempt elicited in the Eternal and the effort it used to try to dissuade the delusional human. He learnt that when things went wrong the humans pride was wounded and his reaction to failure was not shame or regret, but anger and that this anger was not directed at himself but at others who did not deserve it. He was witness to the despair produced by the realisation that the creature could not dream and to the damage this caused to both the human soul and the Eternal spirit. He saw the Eternal defeated and retreating and the human soul warped by its negative emotions.

Amongst all that was opened up before him Samuel learnt one thing of particular importance. Soon after their merging a separation had been attempted. The Eternal begged the human to let go of his anger and other negative feeling and release It. It cajoled and soothed the human as best it could until he was calmer and agreed to give the separation a try. The Eternal attempted to break free of its physical prison and was partially successful. But something felt wrong, it did not feel whole, a part of it still remained within the human.

As the Eternal began to withdraw the human momentarily felt elated but then realised that his soul was trying to leave his body as if it was tethered to the soul spirit of the Eternal as it withdrew, and his body began to weaken. The human realised that with his soul pulled free of his body that body would die and then what would become of him?.

'My intent was always to have you within me' the human told the Eternal *'I want us to live together in this body for eternity. If you leave I will die and I cannot have that.'*

'We may live for eternity like this, but what life would that be if we cannot dream' argued the Eternal

'We will find a way' the human insisted his arrogance back *'you will not leave me.'*

When the Eternal tried to fight back the human grew angry and so It retreated, defeated for now, It hoped to try another way.

And then finally Samuel was shown how he himself affected that creature; how his music brought hope to the Eternal and fed it giving it the strength to have some influence over its human. Then with the help of the Eternal how his music calmed the human a little and how him finding and acknowledging It in the Dream Realm had led to the trust it was showing him today in the hopes he could bring the hope he was promising.

The creature's souls had been laid bare and now Samuel must use what he had learnt to bring it a healing dream.

At first he had thought that a dream of being free and separate and human again would be what was needed but now with all the new information he decided on a different kind of dream.

The question was could he succeed in bringing the creature this dream? With a normal dreamer they already had that dream in their soul ready to take form and it was the Dreambringers task to enhance the part of that dream that would benefit the dreamer the most. With the Dark Souls their damaged souls supressed their ability to dream. Talionis was a Dark Soul but with an Eternal Dreamer trapped within. The key must be the Eternal. Yes Samuel thought, he must attempt to form a link with the Eternal Dreamer first and then together they could help the damaged human soul to dream.

He communicated this idea to Talionis. The Eternal was more than willing to help with this plan but as expected the human soul was conflicted. It had let go enough to open up to Samuel but letting the Eternal and Samuel link up felt like a further loss of control that made It vulnerable. But ultimately this seemed like Its only chance to dream so what could It do but agree.

So It let go its hold upon the Eternal just enough to allow Samuel to make a link. The weakened state of the Eternal was evident to Samuel but the link was made all the same. Both Samuel and the Eternal knew what sort of dream they needed to bring but could they bring it to such a damaged soul? Samuel could feel the extra strength being sent to him by Dorothea and hoped it would be enough. Samuel made himself what Talionis needed him to be that was easy enough, but now he needed to bring the Dark Soul into the Dream Realm so its wish to dream could be fulfilled.

He fought through the dark layers of anger and hate looking for a glimmer of hope. He could sense the Eternal was using its own hope in order to reach that of the human. Together they cajoled the light out of the dark. Then, when a dim glow was unveiled they pounced upon it using their own positivity to help it grow. They concentrated all their power and finally, if all too briefly, they pulled the darkness into the light.

For a few minutes Talionis stepped into the Dream Realm and dreamt that he was the being he'd always wanted to be, the perfect combination of human and Eternal, together as one forever. Samuel was there to greet him and give him the acceptance and love he so needed.

But the effort the dream took was exhausting and so it was soon over. And so, after a precious few minutes Talionis was pulled back into the fringes the human and Eternal souls again locked out of the Dream Realm.

The effort had drained Samuel but he noted with satisfaction that the dark mass that represented Talionis appeared a little lighter and the lighter mass within was brighter and larger. He tried to get a read on the creature's emotions but his previous efforts had sapped his energy too much and he was having trouble connecting with the Dark Soul. He sent a question although unsure he'd have the strength to read an answer. But he got one.

'Thank you.'

He was unsure if this came from the human soul, the Eternal or both, but it was enough. And now it was time to go. He left the Dream Realm for his own dreams happy in the knowledge that he had helped Talionis at last.

The Gateway Dreambringers were in the art room but not much art was getting done they were too busy discussing their night in the Dream Realm, or more specifically right now they were talking about someone they had encountered there, Samuel Raven.

'Oh my word but that man is impressive looking' said Clea 'I know we were seeing him as his perfected dream self but he must still be pretty impressive in the flesh.'

'He certainly is good looking' agreed Mary

'I can't really comment on how good looking the guy is but he's certainly an impressive figure. I wonder how tall he is I mean he's a giant in the Dream Realm' this from Max.

'I'd say he's about six foot five' the unexpected answer coming from Sofia as she entered the room.

'I'm sorry to interrupt' she continued 'but I was passing and I heard you talking about Samuel and I'm being a bit nosy I'm afraid. I take it from what I just heard that you saw him in the Dream Realm last night?'

'We sure did' said Clea 'he introduced himself to us all.'

'He had a woman with him too' added Geth.

'Really? It must have been Dorothea the other Custodian.'

'Yes that's it, her name was Dorothea and she was pretty impressive in her own way too' said Clea.

'He must have asked her to help him with Talionis' Sofia said thinking out loud 'Did they tell you that was the reason she was there?'

'Yes they were there to help that Talionis thing' answered Geth.

'Do you know what happened?' Sofia asked the group.

They all looked at each other questioningly waiting for someone to put into words what they had all experienced. Predictably it was Clea who spoke.

'It's hard to explain, I don't think any of us witnessed what Samuel and Dorothea did' the others shook their heads in agreement and so she continued 'we were all busy with our own work, but we were all very aware of the two other Dreambringers and at one point we all sensed an intense concentration of energy taking place. We don't really know what happened though, we were just talking amongst ourselves to find out if anyone knew anything.'

'Hopefully that energy you felt was a sign of success. I'm sure I'll hear from the Foundation soon, or even Samuel himself.'

'And you'll tell us what happened?' asked Aaron

'Yes of course I will.'

'We were wondering if there was anything we could have done to help' said Mary.

'I'm sure he would have asked if he thought you could help' said Sofia

'Maybe we're too inexperienced to be any help' commented Max.

'Or maybe he just didn't think to ask' suggested Aaron.

'Perhaps we should have volunteered to help' said Mary.

'Well it's too late now' Geth pointed out.

'I know that' Mary blushed 'but we could volunteer now, let Samuel know that we want to help if we can.'

'Can we do that?' Aaron asked Sofia 'can we contact Samuel and offer our help?'

Sofia considered her answer before giving it. On the one hand the thought of speaking to Samuel right now was appealing, but on the other hand she didn't want to overstep the mark either with him or the Foundation.

'I think we should wait a bit' she reluctantly answered 'we need to find out how things went last night first. Samuel is bound to put in a report to the Foundation and they will most likely let me know what happened too.'

'But aren't you desperate to know what happened?' asked Clea 'we all are.'

'Of course I am but I feel we should give Samuel time to make his report to the Foundation first. It's not my place to go wading in before then. So how about we wait until after lunch and then if I haven't heard anything I'll call the Foundation and see if I can find anything out.'

'Okay, we'll stay here until then' said Clea 'put our trip to the Factory off until this afternoon.'

'That's fine, hopefully we'll hear something soon.'

Samuel had started the day in a positive mood but as he'd made notes and prepared his report he'd began to feel a little deflated. The revelations that Talionis had opened up to him had been astounding. He'd known the story of the Soul Stealer better than anyone but seeing it from the perspective of the creature Itself had been priceless. He understood Talionis fuller now and this could only help him. A significant breakthrough had been made and he was rightfully proud of what he'd achieved but as he thought things through, he realised that he and Dorothea had put everything they had into it and the reward had been satisfying but very brief.

Where did they go from here?

They had brought Talionis a dream, but it had taken all their energy for just a few minutes. How could they hope to achieve more? Maybe another music session would help strengthen and heal Talionis enough to yield better results, but how much better could they be?

He had discussed things with Dorothea and they had concluded that they needed help. It was obvious where that help could come from but Samuel had reservations. It had taken him a while to gain Talionis' trust and he was afraid that bringing others in would make the creature suspicious and uncooperative. He'd gotten away with Dorothea's help because he was pretty sure Talionis had be unaware of her discreet assistance. But with several others involved it would be harder to hide that help.

Should he be upfront and risk Talionis refusing to accept the extra help, or should he just go ahead and risk Talionis reacting badly? He thought it through for a while and then made his decision. First he would establish if the help he required was possible and then he would ask Talionis if It would accept that help. Springing the others upon Talionis could cause serious damage to the trust he had built whereas if he asked the creature permission at least if It said no the trust would still be there and an alternative solution could be sought. A group effort could bring quicker results but if a slower, gentler approach was needed then that is the route he'd have to take.

And so Samuel sent his report marking it high priority and stating in his e mail a need to discuss something urgently with Cedric Neale. He was hoping for a quick reply so that he had time to get a long music session in because whatever way it went the music could only help the outcome.

He thankfully didn't have long to wait. Within the hour Cedric Neale was on the phone. The Foundation leader was of course very pleased with the progress that had been made and astounded at the information he had learnt from the creature. It was obvious to Cedric Neale that more help was needed and so he listened as Samuel outlined his plan to move things forward. He confirmed what the man had already guessed that the help needed could only come from the new Dreambringers at the Gateway but stressed that he only intended to use their help if Talionis agreed. Eager though the Foundation boss was to have this situation sorted he saw the wisdom in Samuels caution and agreed to let him continue as he thought best.

'I'll leave it totally in your hands' he said 'all I ask is that you keep me updated. I will pass your latest report on to Sofia and I suggest you call her yourself to discuss your idea. I'm sure that she and the Dreambringers will agree so unless I hear otherwise I will assume that things are going ahead for tonight and I will await your report in the morning.'

'Thank you for your support and trust'

'You are most welcome; you have earnt it. I wish you luck and bid you goodbye for now'

'Goodbye sir.'

Sofia was part way through a second read of Samuels report when the phone rang.

'Hello Sofia, speaking'

'Hi its Samuel'

'Hi, just the person I wanted to speak to. I've just read your report. It's pretty impressive stuff.'

'Thanks and I'm glad you've had the chance to read it because there's something I need to discuss with you.'

'There was something I needed to speak to you about too and judging from the e mail Cedric Neale sent with your report I have a feeling we both have the same topic in mind but you go first.'

'I have news' said Sofia as she entered the art room. Everyone immediately stopped what they were doing to listen.

'I've spoken to Samuel and it turns out that not only does he welcome your offer of help but he actually had the same idea and was going to ask you for it anyway.

'So when is this going to happen?' asked Clea.

'I'm pretty sure he'll want to go ahead tonight but what he wants to do is speak to you all together to make the arrangements. He's going to be phoning back in a few minutes so if you could all come into the office so we can put the call on speaker phone when it comes.'

They had all just arranged themselves around the office desk when the call came through. Greetings were made and then Samuel began to speak. He gave them a brief history of his work with Talionis outlining the points he had made in his reports. He then gave them a more detailed account of the partially successful attempt he and Dorothea had made at bringing the creature dreams. Now that the listeners had all the information he went on to the main purpose of the call.

'As I have explained even using our combined strength Dorothea and I only managed to bring Talionis a very brief dream. Although I feel even this short dream was beneficial to the creature it's obvious that a longer dream could achieve even more benefits. Therefore, I am asking for your help. I understand that you were willing to offer this help yourselves, so I am taking that as agreement so now I just need to outline my plans.

First, I want to state that this attempt to help Talionis will only take place if It agrees. I have built up trust with the creature and I don't want to jeopardise that. I also understand that you have important work of your own to do every night and I don't wish to take you away from that for too long. Therefore this is what I propose. When you enter the Dream Realm tonight you will start off as usual whilst I find Talionis and see how It feels about you helping. If It agrees I will call you all to me. Once we are all together along with your Eternals we will concentrate all our Dreambringer energy onto Talionis and hopefully bring It a longer, healing dream. Are there any questions?'

'Are the Eternals onboard with this plan?' asked Max.

'To be honest I've assumed that if you want to help they will too, but you make a good point. You should check with them as soon as we finish here and come back to me. I doubt very much they'll refuse but its only right to ask'

'Okay we'll do that but I think you're probably right' agreed Max.

'How long will it take?' asked Mary 'We all want to help this Talionis but not at the expense of other dreamers, our duty is to them first after all.'

'I can't really say how long it will take, but we will only make one attempt, I don't intend to monopolise you for the whole night, I understand you have other work to do.'

'Will this be an ongoing thing?' added Aaron 'will we need to keep doing this every night?'

'I can't answer that fully right now, a lot depends on how things go tonight and what affect it has on the creature. I may well need your help again but we can make better plans after tonight.'

'Okay, fair enough.'

'Anymore questions?'

No one had any so the call was wrapped up after a little more discussion about checking with the Eternals. It was decided that the Dreambringers would go to the Factory straight away to consult with them. Whilst the group were away Sofia, Mason and Eddie went to the lounge to chat. The two men had been very quiet during the group call and Sofia wanted to make sure they were okay.

'How are you feeling about all this? She asked them.

'I'm okay with it' answered Eddie 'I'm just glad I haven't got to deal with the creature direct cos I'm not sure how I'd feel then, but I understand why this needs to be done.'

'I'm fine too' said Mason 'like Eddie I wouldn't want to deal with It myself but I would like to help in my own way if I can and so I have a suggestion to make.'

'Okay, go ahead' prompted Sofia.

'I want to see if I can still do Dreambringer work in the Dream Realm. I know my link to the Eternal has been severed but not for long so maybe I can still do it. I don't have the Dreambringer talent that Samuel and Dorothea have but I think I'm pretty strong, I called the new Dreambringers here almost singlehanded so that says a lot right?'

'Sure, I think it's worth a try, but what exactly is it you want to do to help?'

'If I can still bring dreams even at a low level I thought that I could make up a little for the short fall whilst the Dreambringers are helping Samuel by doing the normal Dreambringer task. I know that it won't be a big difference but it will be something.'

'I thinks it's a great idea and I'm sure any help you can give will be appreciated. When we call Samuel to hopefully confirm the Eternals agreement we can let him know that you'll be helping in your own way if you can.'

'Yeah, good thanks.'

When the group returned from the Factory with the expected good news they were pleased to hear of Masons offer. The call to Samuel was made and then they settled in for a relaxed evening before the plan was to be put into action.

The inhabitants of the Gateway and the cottage all went to bed at a prearranged time so they would all be in the Dream Realm together.

Mason went to bed feeling both excited and nervous. The chance to return to Dreambringing is what excited him but the possibility of failure was making him nervous. He felt that his presence in the Dream Realm was strong, and he put this down to the fact that even though his link to his Eternal had been severed he still remained physically close to it. Usually when a Dreambringers time was over they moved away soon after the ceremony and so the distance contributed to the weakening of their Dreambringer talent.

Those who went on to certain roles within the Foundation however through training and ability maintained a strong presence within the Dream Realm and Mason figured there was no reason he couldn't do the same. There was however always the possibility of failure and he wasn't sure how he'd cope if he failed, but it was a risk he had to take.

Shortly after entering the Dream Realm Mason met Max who had been watching out for him and the two of them set off along with Max's Eternal to find some dreamers in need of their help.

When the first dreamer was located Mason made his first attempt. It felt a little strange at first without the connection to the Eternal to help but Max and the Eternal were nearby to lend support if needed. Mason was pleased when he found that his talent was still strong enough to help the dreaming soul. He was a little unsure how much the proximity of Max and the Eternal had helped and he wasn't sure if things would go so well when they turned their attention to helping Samuel, but it was a positive start. And so whilst they waited for the go ahead (or not) from Samuel Mason spent time helping Max with as many dreamers as he could. If he failed to carry this on without them nearby at least he would have helped up until them.

Samuel found Talionis a lot quicker than he had on previous nights, he wasn't sure if this was down to luck, practice or the fact that Talionis was more responsive. It was probably a combination of all three but whatever the reason he was glad of it.

After establishing that Talionis was feeling receptive Samuel probed the creature to gauge Its mood. He was pleased to find that the anger felt by the human side of the creature was very much reduced, in fact he didn't really read anger anymore, it was more like severe frustration with a touch of resentment. Self-pity was still evident too, but he also detected a touch of hope which was encouraging.

From the Eternal Within he sensed stronger evidence of hope and also gratefulness. When greeting Talionis he'd received replies from both sides of the creature which again was encouraging. Now he communicated a question to gain more insight.

'How are you feeling?'

'Glad to see you' replied the Eternal Within.

The human side replied with a question.

'Are you going to bring me a dream?'

'I'm going to try. I'm confident I can bring you another brief dream as I did last night but I have a proposal for you.'

'What sort of proposal?' this from the human side.

'I think that with help I can bring you a longer and more fulfilling dream' Samuel paused here to gauge the creature initial reaction. He sensed interest and hope from the Eternal Within and from the human side there was also interest but in this case it was tinged with suspicion.

'Help from where?' the human side enquired.

'From the group of Dreambringers in this area.'

'But they hate me' this tinged with alarm.

'Nobody hates you.'

'But I hurt them.'

'These aren't the same Dreambringers, they're the new group.'

'What good would they be then?'

'What do you mean?'

'They're too new and inexperienced, how can they help?'

'I believe they can.'

'Why would they help, they know what I have done?'

'They will help because like me they understand that in order to prevent you hurting anyone else they must help you, and there's no need for you to be afraid, they would not hurt you and even if they wanted to you know that no one can hurt you in the Dream Realm.'

Samuel received a sense of turmoil then like he had in the beginning when the human and Eternal Within were fighting for control. The Eternal Within was trying to convince the human to trust in the Dreambringers. Samuel awaited the outcome patiently.

'We welcome their help' the answer when it came was from the Eternal Within, it had gained control now and that was good. Samuel felt that with the Eternal in the stronger position it would be easier to connect and bring the creature a dream.

'Thank you, I will call the others here now, it will take a little while until they are all here as they are working their magic elsewhere, but we will begin as soon as we can.'

Samuel sent out the message that Talionis was agreeable to his plan and then he waited. It wasn't too long before all five of the Dreambringers and their Eternals arrived along with Dorothea who would again help. By an unspoken understanding they stayed a small distance from the Dark Soul so as not to intimidate it. Once they were all present Samuel spoke to Talionis.

'Everyone is here, may we begin?'

'Yes please do' again it was the Eternal who answered but Samuel detected no resistance from the human side and so he conveyed to the Dreambringers that it was time to begin.

The group moved a little closer and formed a circle around the Dark Soul. Then together they directed all their Dreambringer energy toward the creature. With the combined efforts of the five Dreambringers and their Eternals plus Samuel and Dorothea the energy created was so immense it was visible in the air like heat waves converging on the Dark Soul and being absorbed by it.

Instructed by Samuel the group concentrated on bringing the dream that Talionis needed. They all felt it when the breakthrough was made, and their many souls connected with the two souls trapped within the dark mass.

And Talionis dreamt.

The dream was strong and healing and once established needed less help from the Dreambringers. On Samuel's instruction one by one each Dreambringer reduced their efforts slowly and then withdrew. They had work to do elsewhere and Samuel didn't want to keep them from it longer than was necessary. When the last of the Dreambringers had withdrawn Samuel and Dorothea remained and together they worked to maintain the dream for as long as possible.

Once Max was released he sought out Mason to see how he was doing and to tell him they had succeeded. He discovered Mason had been doing well, working solidly to bring dreams to those who needed them. There was no real need to tell him of their success though, he had sensed it. The concentration of energy had been evident Mason describing it as a glow on the horizon visible throughout the Dream Realm.

For the rest of the night the Dreambringers brought dreams to many whilst Samuel and Dorothea maintained the dreams of the Dark Soul and all benefitted.

As the time to leave approached Samuel and Dorothea gradually reduced the energy directed at Talionis until finally gently breaking the link. As they withdrew, they were gratified to see that Dark Soul was no longer an accurate description of the creatures Dream Realm manifestation. The mass before them was no longer black and dense, and although not quite the white misty human form of the normal dreamers the swirling mass was much lighter both in colour and density and the darting lights within shone brighter. The emotions that Samuel now sensed from the creature were also much lighter. Hope was now the strongest emotion and he even detected a tinge of joy.

'We must go now' he communicated *'but we will return and I will visit you in the waking world soon.'*

'Thank you!' the message was strong as it came from both souls together.

'You're welcome.'

It couldn't have gone better and Samuel was elated.

Samuel dressed quickly and hurried downstairs. A shower and some breakfast could wait, there was something he really wanted to do first. He was eager to find out how the dream the Dreambringers had helped bring to Talionis had affected the creature in the waking world. He was hoping that the healing dream would mean communication would be easier now in both realms. He also felt that he needed to ascertain the dreams full effect before he could update his notes and then put together a report to the Foundation.

When he entered the creatures cell he found Talionis laying on the bed. He experienced a tinge of disappointment for a second until he perceived a slight movement. For the first time since its capture Talionis was moving significantly whilst Samuel watched. It sat up slowly and then at the same slow pace swung its legs around so that It sat on the bed facing Samuel. It opened its eyes, the strange misty light from them beaming towards Samuel and then with its left hand it made a small jerky movement that he took as a greeting.

'Good morning' he said in return 'how are you feeling today?'

Of course, the creature did not reply in words but it nodded its head in the affirmative. This was definite progress and Samuel was thrilled. He sat down on the now familiar chair and fell smoothly into the practiced meditative state. Before he had a chance to probe the creatures emotions or ask it a question he received a strong message

'Hello Samuel music man.'

'Hello, Talionis', he sent back.

'We dreamt' another clear message.

'Yes you did, and I hope it was beneficial.'

'It was.'

'And how do you feel now?'

'Like this' and the creature sent him a wave of its emotions. Samuel interpreted them as gratitude, relief and joy. He still noted tinges of the old, darker emotions but he couldn't have hoped for more and he made his own feelings of relief and joy known to the creature.

'Will we have music now?' the creature enquired.

'Soon, I have a few things I must do now, but I will be back shortly with my instruments.'

He sensed a note of impatience from the creature which was a little disquieting so he continued *'I am only human and I need sustenance, I also need to make plans for tonight so that you can dream again, but I promise I will be back very soon and I will give you hours of music.'*

'We accept this' replied the creature thankfully placated.

Samuel left the creatures cell feeling mostly happy and upbeat but there was one little seed of worry. Was the creature becoming a little demanding? He would have to remain wary of this possibility but apart from that things looked very promising. The creature could definitely communicate better now and Samuel put this down to its barriers having come down. It now fully trusted Samuel and that along with the healing dreams of the last two nights had calmed It and reduced Its immense anger to the point that it was no longer hindering Its communication skills. Things could only improve with more music and dreams.

It was still early, and he found the kitchen empty, but he thought he heard Dorothea moving around upstairs so he put some coffee and toast on. And sure enough Dorothea walked in just as he was buttering the toast.

'Good Morning' she said brightly.

'Good Morning, help yourself to toast' he said placing a plate full on the table 'and there's coffee in the pot.'

'Thank you.'

Dorothea poured herself a coffee and joined him at the table.

'How long have you been up?' she asked reaching for a slice of toast.

'Not that long, but it's been eventful' he answered and then proceeded to update her on his Talionis news.

'That's splendid news' she said when he'd finished 'so what happens now?'

'Now I get my thoughts and findings in order and type up a report. The report will include my proposal on how to move forward and if you don't mind I'll explain it all to you later when its finished.'

'Of course, that's fine with me'

And so Samuel set to work.

After making notes for his own research he typed up his report. The report outlined everything that had happened since his last one and included his own thoughts and conclusions on how things had gone. At the end of the report he stated the proposal he'd mentioned to Dorothea. This is what it said:

Every time Talionis dreams Its Dark Soul will be lightened which will make it easier each night to bring It the next dream. This will mean that moving forward less Dreambringer energy will be required and so the number of Dreambringers and the time they are needed for will gradually decrease. Therefore, I propose that a new Foundation protocol be put into place. This would take the form of a timetable outlining a structured decrease in manpower and hours until finally I myself will be the only Dreambringer required.

I believe the Talionis problem to be an important one but understand that It's needs should not be put before that of other dreamers. This protocol will mean that the Dreambringers will be able to assist me but their time with Talionis will be pared down to the minimum required leaving them as much time as possible for their usual duties. If you give me the go ahead, I will work out a more detailed timetable but to give you an idea what I mean the basis timetable would be as follows:

Night 1 – All Dreambringers will be required but for a slightly shorter time.
Nights 2&3 – Again All Dreambringers required but for a shorter time each night.
Nights 4-8 – One less Dreambringer will be required each night but with the time required remaining at the same level as night 3 each time.
Nights 9&10 – Myself and Dorothea only will be required.
Nights 11 onwards – I will proceed alone until the task is completed.

The trajectory of improvement is only my estimate based on the achievements made so far and my observations on their effects, therefore small changes may need to be made as we go. This is not an exact science, but I am confident this is the way to go.

228

Something else I can't predict is what exactly the end result of this will be or how long it will take. But I know that my goal is to give Talionis as good a quality of life as possible, which I feel will in turn neutralise completely the danger It poses. What status It will then hold within the Foundation I cannot say but I look forward to finding this out. I welcome any questions or suggestions you may have and hope that you have enough confidence in me to agree to this proposal.

Samuel read through the document again before e mailing it to Cedric Neale. He then went upstairs for a shower hoping for a quick reply.

When he came back down there was no reply. He was feeling fidgety wanting to get back to Talionis as quickly as possible but he wanted a reply first. So he sat in the kitchen chatting with Dorothea whilst he waited.

After forty long minutes the reply finally arrived and this is what it said.

I would firstly like to praise you for the success you achieved last night (rest assured I will also be sending praise to the others involved) however you are the engine of this ground-breaking experiment and deserve the most plaudits.

A few other members and I have reviewed your reports and believe your observations and the conclusions you have made to be sound. As you have stated it is hard to say where this is all leading but we trust this will become clear as things progress. We have faith in you Samuel and therefore I am giving you the go ahead to put your protocol in place.

I have forwarded your report to Sofia, and I suggest you call her to talk it through. And so I will leave things in your capable hands. Please keep me informed of your progress and good luck to you.

Samuel returned an e mail thanking Cedric Neale for his support and then he made the call to Sofia. She had read his report and proposal and so knew the basics so they talked through the plan in more detail. They then planned to speak every morning at the same time as depending how things had gone the night before slight changes to the protocol may be needed.

As Sofia was explaining the protocol to the Gateway residents Samuel was updating Dorothea, then it was finally time for him to head out to see Talionis.

CHAPTER 23

NEW PROTOCOL

It was the morning after night three of the new protocol and Samuel was writing up his notes. And this is what he wrote:

For a third night running things have gone to plan and the results have been very promising.
After the Dreambringers left us Dorothea and I helped Talionis maintain a dream for slightly longer than before. Communication with the creature is still improving and Its appearance in the Dream Realm is moving even closer to the norm.
I am sensing definite feelings of joy from the creature and Its level of anger is dropping accordingly. When I am communicating with the human side of Talionis I am still sensing feelings of frustration and self-pity but they are less strong especially directly after the dream which is understandable. There is still a strong note of arrogance within the human side however which comes through in our communications and still makes it a little resistant to me. It's nothing I can really convey in words or specifics but it is definitely present. The human side also has a tendency to be demanding. It started with the insistence on my playing It music for longer periods of time (which I have never minded) but now I feel it creeping into our communications in the Dream Realm. It is a little disconcerting, but I will try to keep it in check without angering it.
From the Eternal Within I am sensing only gratitude and hope. I have also noted that It is at all times working to placate the more negative feelings of the human side as best it can. I feel that the work we are doing is calming the human side and strengthening the Eternal Within. I am hoping the trend will continue with each dream we bring the creature and that eventually all the negative emotions of the creature will become negligible.
I am still not sure what the end goal is here. I believe in time we will reach the stage where the creature's presence in the Dream Realm can be termed normal and it will be able to receive dreams in the usual way, but what of its physical world presence? Whilst being able to dream will make Its existence far more bearable its physical limits will still be in evidence. I have hopes that once its negative emotions have been all but eradicated it will cease to be a danger to anyone but the question is how exactly will it fit in to the waking world? It will always be a curiosity and I fear a problem. I can only continue with the protocol and hope an end game becomes clear.

Sofia had just finished reading Samuels report on Night eight of the protocol. Things were still improving night by night for Talionis and they were now at the stage where the last of the Dreambringers had finished their stint helping Samuel and Dorothea. From that night on Samuel and Dorothea would work alone.

As had been Samuel's plan the creature had gained enough strength from its previous dreams to need less and less help each night to receive another one. Its dream self was almost as near to normal as it was ever going to get. It no longer dwelled in the outskirts but roamed within the dream landscape as others did. This had caused a little concern to begin with, but Samuel assured everyone that Talionis could not do harm to anyone within the Dream Realm even if It wanted to.

Samuel was still also continuing his daytime sessions which he reported were still having the desired effect of making the creatures daytime hours more bearable. Sofia marvelled at the man's stamina but wondered how it would end. Samuel couldn't spend his days playing music to the creature indefinitely.

Samuel openly admitted in his report that he still didn't know where it was all going himself but he seemed confident that he was doing the right thing and that answers would come. Sofia and everyone else in the Foundation could only trust that this was the case.

Sofia shut down her laptop and headed for the kitchen where the others were having breakfast. She would give them all a brief update and then they had something else important to deal with.

Later today a Foundation car was coming to pick Eddie up and take him to an induction centre for the start of his Dreamwisher training. Or to be more exact to start with he was being taken to be tested to see if he was suitable for Dreamwisher training. If he passed the Foundation's tests he would start training immediately.

Training usually took several weeks so he would be away from the Gateway for a while. As had been planned Mason would remain at the Gateway to do Eddies duties whilst he was away after that Mason's future was unclear.

Sofia was a little worried for the man, he had been through a lot, and she wasn't sure how the next few weeks would be for him. He had seemed happy the last few days as he'd been able to use his Dreambringer skills whilst helping out during the initial stages of the Talionis protocol, but now strictly speaking he wouldn't be needed as the Dreambringers would be back to full strength. She doubted anyone would protest if he wanted to continue to help and after all he could temporarily fill the role that Eddie would be taking up once his training was done, but it could still be hard on him especially now his friend was leaving for several weeks.

Everyone was going to miss Eddie, but it would hit Mason hard she was sure. She'd just have to make sure that everyone rallied round him which she was sure they'd do without prompting. There was one little part of Eddies leaving that would make things a little easier for the two men though. The Foundation had decided that it was time to arrange Mahesh's funeral. They planned for it to take place just before Eddie started his Dreamwisher training (assuming he passed the test). Mason would obviously be attending so would leave the Gateway for the day and night returning the next morning. Gina and Blake would also attend and it was hoped that Claude would too although he was still a maybe at this point. If he didn't attend Mason and Eddie would be able to visit him after the funeral. Either way Sofia felt the two men would be pleased. And so she entered the noisy kitchen to update the rowdy group.

Samuel had been working alone to bring Talionis dreams for eight days now and if he was honest he would admit that it was getting a bit monotonous. It was routine now and the good he was doing seemed to have plateaued.

The question of where was this all going was now more pertinent than ever, but an answer still hadn't presented itself. The night before however Samuel had noticed one small difference in the creatures emotions and it had piqued his interest. It had been hard to interpret, and he hadn't been able to make any sense of it in the time he had before being drawn from the Dream Realm. After writing up what was becoming a very samey report however he had come to a decision. Today during his music session with Talionis he would not only try to find out what this new emotion was, he would also ask the creature Itself where It wanted this all to lead.

It was a bit of a risk because if Talionis demanded something of him that wasn't possible it could undo the good work they had all done. From what Samuel had learnt of the human sides nature if It thought he wasn't doing all he could to help It the creatures anger and hatred could resurface. Nevertheless he'd decided it was a risk he'd have to take.

Mason was alone in the kitchen having a moment to himself before joining Max, Mary and Aaron in the art room.

Geth and Clea were at the Factory and Sofia was in the office getting the days update from Samuel. Mason wondered briefly if today's news would be the same as it had been for days, but then his mind wandered back to other things.

He'd spoken to Eddie the night before. Eddie's Dreamwisher training was going well, and he sounded tired but happy. Neither of them had really had any news to impart so they'd rehashed an old conversation about how well Mahesh's funeral had gone and how good it had been to see Claude, Gina and Blake.

Claude had decided to come to the funeral and although things between him and Gina had been a little strained it had been good to all be together again. It had been comforting to hear how well they'd all been doing too but it had put Mason in a strange mood as it had got him thinking about his own future.

They'd settled into a comfortable routine after Eddie left and Mason was happy enough, but what next? Eddie had a job and a new role to come back to, but Mason would be leaving, but to go where and to do what? It had been established that his Dreambringer talent was strong enough for him to help dreamers without being linked to a specific Eternal Dreamer but where could he go with that? A Custodian role really wasn't on the cards for many reasons and the only option he could think of as a possibility was becoming a trainer. He would work with either new Dreambringer recruits or train up Dreamwishers. He'd had a taste of it when he'd brought the new Gateway Dreambringers together and been with them for their induction. He'd done what no other Dreambringer had done by bringing them all together without the help of his own Dreambringer group and he'd done it well. He'd also managed to bring his damaged friends together in order to perform the Bonding Ceremony so he had some good skills to pass on, but was teaching his thing, would he be good at it and would he enjoy it? He had a lot of thinking to do.

His thoughts were interrupted now though as Sofia entered the kitchen to pass on Samuels update. Samuel hadn't passed on his plan to ask Talionis what It wanted therefore as expected the news was pretty much the same as it had been for several days now. So with nothing much to discuss Mason and Sofia headed for the art room to join the others.

Samuel had been playing his guitar for just over two hours when he decided it was time to put his question to Talionis.

'Okay' he said out load 'I think it's time for a chat'

This wasn't an unusual thing to say, in fact this was the norm now. He would play a while then take a little time to communicate with Talionis to gauge how It was feeling. Samuel no longer had to concentrate to read the creatures emotions, they were so much easier to read now that the creatures barriers were down. The healing influence of the dreams also meant that Talionis found it much easier to communicate in the waking world. They had proper mind conversations now with both the human side and the Eternal Within taking equal part.

Samuel began the communication as he always did.

'Hi Talionis, how are you today?'

He received '*Good*' in return from both with an added '*thank you*' from the Eternal and the emotions he sensed backed that up. The creature was calm and content if not exactly happy. There was no sign of hatred and just a hint of frustration and self-pity. There was the touch of exhilaration that Samuel had learnt came from the creatures enjoyment of his music. And (mainly from the Eternal Within) there was hope. He didn't want to go straight in with the big question so Samuel started with

'How do you think things are going?'

The Eternal Within was the first to answer with

'I think things are going well' and again it added '*thank you.*'

The human sides answer was a little more analytical

'We are dreaming, which is good, it has made us better, but we are still not what we want to be, yet I do not know now what it is that we want to be. The anger gave us purpose, we wanted revenge and we wanted to be the powerful creature we set out to be, not the weak, imprisoned

232

creature we have been all these years. But now the anger has gone we no longer know what we are.'

'Are you sorry that the anger has gone?' Samuel was a little worried what the creatures answer would be but he asked anyway.

'No, we are not sorry, the anger gave us purpose but we were miserable. Now we are more at peace but we are still weak which is not what we want to be.'

'We are happier but still unfulfilled' added the Eternal Within *'we can dream now but we are still trapped within this shell unable to function as we should. This body cannot make music or art therefore the souls within it, our souls, cannot feed each other and bring dreams to others, we are not what we should be, we are not complete.'*

'Are you saying you want to bring others dreams again?' asked Samuel 'because I'm not sure that will be possible.'

Samuel realised that he now didn't need to ask the big question, they'd come around to it in a different, less confrontational way which was good. The creature was being honest and direct but without the hint of the aggression he'd feared.

'We understand it will never be possible in the conventional way' agreed the Eternal Within *'but we are unique and hope that uniqueness can be of help in some way.'*

'We need to atone for the terrible things we did' this from the human side *'We were bitter from our failure and we took it out on those who did not deserve it and so we were punished. That punishment on top of the lack of dreams warped us and we became an angry, vengeful creature who inflicted terrible pain upon others. But that anger is gone now and we just want to be what we aimed to be at the start, a powerful force for good.'*

'Help us be what we should be' added the Eternal Within.

And so Samuel had his answer to what Talionis wanted from this. The question now was how this could be achieved.

'I understand now what you want' he told the creature 'but I am at a loss as to how to make that come about. I do intend however to try my best to come up with a solution. I will consult with others and of course with you and hopefully together we will come up with a solution.'

'Thank you, that is all we can ask' the Eternal Within replied.

'Shall we get back to the music for now' suggested Samuel and the creature readily agreed.

When Samuel left the creature several hours later he was in good spirits. Although he still didn't have a solution he felt that progress had been made. At least the report he'd make the next morning would be more interesting than it had been for a while. He believed that the danger the creature had posed all these years was truly neutralised and that was a major achievement in itself.

Now they just had to find a way to make Talionis' life fulfilling and if they could do that in a way that would also mean the creature could help others then they would really achieve something amazing.

The next morning when Sofia read Samuels report she also felt the possibility of something amazing coming of it all. But she was no closer to working out how exactly to achieve it than anyone else. She only hoped that someone would work it out and she had a feeling that someone would be Samuel. When he rang her later she would tell him that.

It was now three days since the revelation that Talionis wanted to become a force for good within the Dreambringers world, but despite all those in the know having wracked their brains no one had come up with an idea on how to make it happen.

Talionis' presence in the Dream Realm was becoming ever stronger and the creature still loved the music sessions with Samuel.

During their daily communications Samuel sensed that the negative emotions of the creature were now negligible and so with this encouraging news surely a solution was near.

Then during the latest mind conversation with Talionis one of the creature's thoughts caught Samuel's attention. The human side made a casual reference to wishing it could dance to Samuels music. There was no elaboration as to why this wasn't possible because they all knew it was down to the restrictions of the physical body of the creature. But this little wish planted the seed of an idea within Samuel.

After the music session he went back to the cottage and read through all the information he had on the creation of Talionis. He then looked back at some of the notes he'd made after some earlier music sessions. Now the idea was growing.

He did not put this germ of an idea in his report, nor did he discuss it with Dorothea, he just left it to grow in his mind. Then, during their next music session without putting it into words he let the idea run through his mind and waited to see if the creature would pick up on it.

Sensing that It had plucked the idea from his mind Samuel did not try to elaborate on it, he just left if for the creature to absorb and ruminate on. He still had some thinking to do himself, his idea had risks to it and he would need to assess whether he was willing to take that risk himself. He also wanted to wait and see how Talionis would interpret his idea and if It would be willing to take on the risk involved to Itself.

On his next visit they assessed the idea together, weighing the risks and making sure they were all agreed. They did this again the next day, and the next. They had to be sure this plan was right for them all. And still Samuel kept it from anyone else. How could he explain this to anyone anyway? What would he do if the Somnium Foundation told him no? This was between himself and Talionis now.

Mary and Aaron awoke in each other's arms as they did every morning. Their dreams had been particularly strong and energising and they were buzzing with new ideas. Mary had the beginnings of a new poem in her mind. It belonged with the Dreambringer poems that she had written after the dreams of her fellow Dreambringers and this one was about Samuel. It wasn't quite there yet; the words were still forming but she had a feeling it would be her best yet. She would put work on her novel on hold until she had this poem finished.

Aaron had a new face to paint. He was going to paint Samuel as he'd seen him in the Dream Realm like he had his Dreambringer friends, but he had a really crazy idea for the background that included a depiction of the Dream Realm manifestation of Talionis. This portrait would be a departure from the norm and he was excited by it.

Max awoke with a manic zeal that he hadn't felt in a long while. He too had Samuel as inspiration for a new piece of sculpture. He felt that like his Jekyll and Hyde sculptures this piece of work would have a strange twist to it and although he didn't really know exactly where the piece would take him the need to start immediately was very strong.

Geth woke with an urge he hadn't felt for a few weeks, the urge to tattoo. He had enjoyed the different medium of the Chinese dragon paintings but his true love was returning. He'd never met Samuel in person but now found he was desperate to tattoo him. He didn't know when or even if he would actually get to tattoo the man but he could at least work on the design idea he had awoken with. It was unusual and intricate and he couldn't wait to start on it.

Clea awoke with a great design idea but she awoke with something more than that. She had a phrase in her head, one that she didn't really understand but that she knew was important. And so dressing quickly she went in search of the others. She found them all in the art room buzzing with new ideas. The air was electric with the artistic energy that was building and into this charged atmosphere she released the words of a seer.

'Something new is coming.'

Dorothea could sense the art energy being produced at the Gateway even from a distance. Something big was about to happen and it was obvious that it involved Samuel and Talionis.

When Samuel joined her in the kitchen, she did not ask him questions and he told her nothing. Instead, he thanked her for her help and headed off to Talionis' cell. It wasn't Dorothea's place to interfere, so she simply set about enhancing the charged artistic atmosphere with her own talents.

When Samuel entered the room he found Talionis standing ready. Their plans, as far as they went had been made, now it was time to discover if this could work.

The first step was a release. As the human side let go its hold on the Eternal Dreamer Within it began.

The foggy light streaming from the creatures open eyes and mouth intensified and then all its exposed skin began to glow. A white aura formed around its human frame and then a ghostly human shape emerged fully from within and stood before it bringing the light with it.

The human body staggered back a few steps and slumped onto the bed its mouth and eyes now closed, its skin dull and from its chest and head there emanated a few wisps of white fog.

These wisps grew to smoky cords which snaked out and merged into the swirling white form of the released Eternal. Bright white lights within the Eternals form pulsed as it started to pull away from the human form a little which tightened the cords binding them together. The Eternal was pulling the cords into itself and for a short time there was resistance, then with a visible jerk the human body released the object that the smoke like cords emanated from. It was a ball of glowing light much like the Eternals form only smaller and denser. The connecting cords pulled the mass towards the Eternal until finally it was pulled within it where it settled in the centre of the ghostly human form. The human body on the bed slumped further the life gone from it.

The Eternal Dreamer could never be purely that anymore, could never be totally free, its link to its human soul was too strong. The humans soul was now within the Eternal, forever together but now without the constraints of the damaged human body. This entity could have a full Dream Realm life now, with the physical restraints gone it was free to dream fully and even to help others dream. The Eternal Dreamer part of this entity would be content with this state, but the human side could not be completely happy, the human side wanted to experience the physical world too, it did not want to give up the chance to be an artist again. And so another step in its transformation needed to be made. It was time to take the final risk.

From the Eternals form, and from the human soul within it tendrils of smoky light began to extend outward reaching towards Samuel. As they tentatively touched his skin Samuel took a deep breath before opening himself up to them.

The entity moved closer to him as the tendrils moved deeper inside him. It was an unnerving but not unpleasant feeling and Samuel did not put up any resistance. He felt a tingling all over as the white light was drawn within him.

He welcomed the two souls that now entered his body ready to inhabit it along with his own and all three souls let go of the last of their fear along with all the other negative emotions they held.

These souls were not going to fight for control of this strong human body, they would work as one; and together the three souls within this powerful body would become something new, merging to become a new breed of Dreambringer, a force for good, capable of bringing new heights of inspiration and dreams to all.

Epilogue

Do you sometimes dream of people that you do not know?
Their faces unrecognised, but you know their soul.
Some are communicators, and you talk, strange words.
Others are lovers who's touch in for you alone.
Are your dreams of them vivid but then the memory of them fades, released like mist after you wake.
Something of them stays with you though.
It's always there, giving comfort and strength, a memory forever, buried deep until you need it, without really knowing it is so.
I dream of them all the time. I remember them all, deep in my soul. I worship their words and cherish their touch. They live with me, and as I dream I know who they are.
Before I tell you, do you know?
Seek and find them as you dream and for a short while you will remember and understand my words.

Were they there?
Then you know.
They are Dreambringers, forming your dreams.
Welcome them, love them, let them heal your soul.

Printed in Great Britain
by Amazon

18975534R00139